FIVE DEAD MEN

A Novel
By David Alexander

Triumvirate

Publications
New York ● London ● Sydney

FIVE DEAD MEN

A Triumvirate Publications International thriller novel. Published by arrangement with the author.

For more about David Alexander: www.davidalexanderbooks.com.

ISBN-13: 979-8-8926976-3-7

Triumvirate Publications International
2001 Madison Avenue
New York NY 10035

DAVID ALEXANDER

Excerpts from Co-Co-Caleevio
A Mafia Novel
By David Alexander

Dominick "Dee" de Venise's textile warehouse has been in the family for generations, but he'll have to torch it for the insurance money. De Venise has no other choice. The Mezzatesta family is into him for boo-koo bucks and if he doesn't pay off, he's history.

The only other option de Venise has is to stage a big-money heist planned by his crooked lawyer friend Arnie, but he's already turned down that particular deal. Arnie's plan was too risky, and besides, de Venise knew Arnie long enough and well enough not to trust him. De Venise doesn't trust anyone to torch the business either. Wanting it done right, he plans to do it himself, then set up an ironclad alibi.

Everything goes like clockwork until the insurance company refuses to pay off on de Venise's policy, leaving him with no business to run and no money to buy off his wise guy creditors.

With no more cards to play at this point, de Venise agrees to do the heist for Arnie. If nothing else, it will get him out of the country, and if de Venise is really lucky and really smart, there's even an outside chance of him scoring the bucks he needs to get him straight with the mob and put him back in action. Just like when he was a kid, the name of the game is Co-Co-Caleevio – single, double, triple. Catch the ball to win.

FIVE DEAD MEN

The only difference now is that if de Venise winds up out, this time he could also wind up dead.

DAVID ALEXANDER

Crime Does Pay
Co-Co-Caleevio pulls the trigger with a bang!

Co-Co-Caleevio is a crime novel that begins and ends on the mean streets of Gravesend, the toughest neighborhood of New York City's toughest borough and the heart of notorious West Brooklyn. It's a place where organized crime still rules and where wise guys have to think fast, hit hard or get whacked. In between, the novel crosses international boundaries and time zones with the speed of sound as West Brooklyn's most accomplished safe and loft burglar takes on a European job in order to pay back the markers held on him by boss of bosses Tony the Pug. This is a caper novel to end all caper novels, a non-stop pager-turner from start to finish, and one of Author David Alexander's boldest books ever.

■

"Where's the statuette? I've made a rather thorough ransack job of both cabins, but can't find anything. I'm assuming its inside the corpse you and the lady are transporting."

"It's not there. I have it in one of the drawers. I'll show --"

"Don't move. Tell the truth or I'll cause considerable pain."

"All right, I should have known better. Yes, the *Bambina* is inside the corpse in the casket we're taking back to New York."

"What happens then?"

"The funeral parlor gets it, opens up the stiff and takes it out."

"I see. How do I believe you?"

5

"If I tell you will you let us live?"

"That depends on whether you're honest with me or not. But if you don't give me what I need, I promise I will cause you and your whore pain. Her first, as you watch."

"No, okay. Yeah, I got the proof," de Venise said. "No problem."

"Where is it?"

"My phone. It's in my pocket. Cut the cable tie, and I'll get it."

"Tell me where it is."

"Okay. You win. The phone's in my back pants pocket. The right one."

"This better not explode in my face."

"It won't. I can do it for you."

"Shut up. I'm warning you."

He flipped it on and thumbed to the photo folder. He scanned the MRI they'd done of the Greek's remains to show the morticians at Bassamontagna where the statue was. The passenger in the white suit nodded.

"You didn't lie. That's good. I'll make it easy for you. After you die, I'll rape the bitch and make it look like you killed each other on drugs. One shot. You won't feel it."

"Wait, lemme smoke some grass. I got some joints rolled in a Baci tin."

"You get nothing."

"I can pay for it."

"How?"

"The cross around my neck. It's solid gold. I been wearing it all my life. It's worth a lot. You can have it."

The assassin reached for the crucifix. He fingered it, seeing it was pure gold, the real thing. With a tug he yanked it off the chain.

--excerpted from unrevised Co-Co-Caleevio chapter.

DAVID ALEXANDER

■

Today Brooklyn, tomorrow the world ... David Alexander has the names of two conquering heroes and Co-Co-Caleevio is world-class ... a thriller with style, guts and endless quantities of Brooklyn *chutzpah* applied as thickly as mozzerella cheese on a Brooklyn pizza. Alexander is an author who is going places. Hopefully one of them is not jail, as some of the criminal capers described in the novel read almost like he was present at the scene of the crime taking notes.

■

When he came in, hands free, the assassin was flopping on the bed, trying to get up. Blood pumped from his neck. He was still alive.

"You dumb prick."

The torso was still partially intact.

"You can see me right? You can understand, right?"

The killer's eyes registered that he did.

"You listen up. I was crying for Mario, who gave this to me. Now I'm sending you to wipe his fuckin' ass in heaven."

De Venise took off his sports coat then took off his shirt and pants. He stood naked with the gun in his right hand.

"I can wash your fuckin' blood off, and the powder grains will usually come off too. I'll give it three washes. They usually get the shit off your clothes anyway."

De Venise wrapped the butt of the assassin's silenced gun around his hand. He didn't have much longer. The eyes of the Infessura were rolling up in his head from shock. De Venise hoped he could still understand him.

"I hope you choke, you cocksucker," de Venise said, as he shoved the silenced muzzle into the killer's mouth as hard as he could, and jerked the trigger once with the killer's stubby forefinger. There wasn't much noise as the head

7

jerked and the pillow was suddenly stained with glop from the brains that shot out the back end of his skull.

--excerpted from unrevised Co-Co-Caleevio chapter.

∎

Could he also face a murder rap -- as a cop or JFK guard or customs officer was killed in the course of the robbery? It wasn't Dee's fault -- he never carried a gun -- but as an accessory to murder commited during a robbery he could get the hot shot.

There's this cop after him. For years already. He's like a stone in his fucking shoe, this cop. The cop hates him because he's half-Sicilian. He's some kind of fuckin' nut job.

The DA is is in league with the cops. The DA is on a vendetta against corruption with a holy zeal not seen since the Gotti trials. He's going after everybody.

Dee is smarter and more tech savvy than he appears at first glance.

The Boost is an old crony from even before the Aer Lingus heist days.

So there's a progression from the 1st safe and loft job in Red Hook (and from those that preceded it in back story) to the III-V job, and then it connects up with the *tombarolo's* "grave robbing" of ancient tombs. (Cracking safes is like cracking tombs in a way.)

Arnie may use his knowledge of Dee's involvement with the Aer Lingus heist as a lever to force his compliance with the III-V job -- and the rest that follows after the heist is eighty-sixed.

--excerpted from unrevised Co-Co-Caleevio author's notes.

∎

Authors don't come any better than David Alexander, and his tough-as-nails global thriller Co-Co-Caleevio represents his taking the fine art of mayhem to an exciting new level of accomplishment. The depth of insight into the world of the Mafia, black intelligence ops, tomb raiding *tombaroli*, historical arcana, exotic military technologies and the inner mainsprings of political intrigue -- to name but a few of this book's points of focus -- seems at times close to envisaging actual   events.

FIVE DEAD MEN

DAVID ALEXANDER

"When Allah made the Sudan, he laughed."
-- Local proverb

"History is a bloodbath."
-- William James

FIVE DEAD MEN

Introduction

In the North African desert, during the closing years of the nineteenth century, a warrior chieftain appeared from out of the sands themselves, claiming to be the incarnation of the Prophet.

He called himself the Mahdi, and he pledged to sweep the Infidel English colonizers of the Sudan and their Egyptian allies from the land, to scourge the land by fire, blood and steel until not a single interloper was left among the living.

At the head of his minions, called *Ansari* or believers by the Mahdi but Dervishes and "Turks" -- a name for all outsiders -- by the British, the Mahdi rode, wielding his trademark, a jewel-encrusted sword whose origins lay in the time of the Crusades.

At first, the Mahdi was dismissed as a mere madman. But as the Bedouin tribesmen of sub-Saharan Africa rallied to his standard, taking up the sword against the hated Infidel in a Holy War of *Madiyyah*, the Mahdi's forces swept across North Africa in a blood-tide of death and destruction that left nothing but ashes and rubble strewn in its wake.

The British and the Egyptians (the latter who, to this day, maintain interests in the Sudan) built and then manned forts such as mighty Omdurman against the incursion of the Mahdi, but were unable to turn the tide on their own.

As the situation worsened, and before the crisis had passed the point of no return, a military expedition comprised of British regular forces was launched against the warrior chieftain's band in a desperate bid to defeat him. But it too failed to succeed. All but a few of the soldiers were exterminated in the desert wastes of Kordofan, and in its aftermath the Mahdi grew even stronger and far bolder than he had ever been before.

The Sudan's defenders realized that unless drastic measures were taken, and the Mahdi stopped, before long the war would be certainly lost and the entire region of sub-Saharan Africa plunged into an era of barbarism and bloodshed the likes of which had never before been seen.

While the last outposts of once great colonial power manned their forts along the Nile and in the desert vastness further inland, counting the days and weeks until they too would be destroyed by the Mahdi's ferocious hordes of nomadic warriors, foreign mercenaries were sought out in a last-ditch effort to turn the tide of battle in the war against the Mahdi.

The center of mercenary activity was Zanzibar, a small island republic that lay off the East African coast, ruled by its Sultan who was the Mahdi's sworn enemy -- for the Sultan himself held an ancestral claim on the lands of the Sudan.

In the days during which this story occurred, Zanzibar was a place where anything went and any pleasure or vice could be bought by whomever carried enough gold in his purse with which to meet the seller's price. From its slave markets to its hashish dens, Zanzibar had long since earned a reputation for being a hotbed of every form of corruption, vice and sinful pursuit known to man. At the same time it was also a place to which an adventurer might come in order to make both his fortune and write his name forever on the bloodstained pages of history.

At the height of the Mahdi's reign of terror, the desert warlord overstepped himself by kidnapping one of the most beautiful denizens of the Sultan's royal seraglio, an Englishwoman who was the descendent of titled nobility.

The Sultan could not permit such a brazen act of aggression to go unavenged. The Mahdi had taken his favorite wife of all his many other wives and concubines, and he knew that he had to get her back or forfeit his right to rule.

But how? From the renowned military leader, bold adventurer and former Governor of the Sudan, "Chinese Charlie" Gordon, and his colleagues in Whitehall, London, came the solution. It would be based upon the same principles by which Gordon had established the band of cut-throat mercenaries some years before that had come to be called Baker's Forty Thieves by friend and foe alike. Only now they would solicit the aid of one of the most notorious pirates of the day, the American privateer known as Snakeskin Blake.

History states that the Mahdi was never defeated on the battlefield, but instead vanished from the Sudan one day, years later, almost as mysteriously as he had originally first appeared.

This is because history has never recorded the true reason for the Mahdi's sudden demise. As the story chronicled in the pages of this book will reveal, the Mahdi's defeat was brought about by the secret war waged against him by Snakeskin Blake and his band of mercenary heroes

DAVID ALEXANDER

whose exploits made them known throughout the windswept desert reaches of North Africa as the Brothers of the Gun.

FIVE DEAD MEN

Prologue
1. The Sultan's Favorite Wife

The blue blood of English aristocracy flowed in the veins of Angelica Fairchild, bequeathed by a mistress of King George III, whose marriage to Samuel Henderson Fairchild did nothing to prevent the regal siring of a bastard offspring, nor hinder the family's sudden affluence that spurred a move to a country estate at Somerset.

But in the year 1721 the once prosperous family had lost every last shilling it possessed when the frenzy of investment in the South Sea Company -- enjoying a monopoly in English trade with Spanish colonies in America and the Pacific, that had seized hold of England -- led to the bursting of what soon came to be known as the South Sea Bubble.

Millions of pounds of worthless stock in the company, which Parliament had consented to redeem at merely a small fraction of its face value, had forced the Fairchilds to sell Longtree House, their estate manor, and retire to more humble lodgings in the then downtrodden West End of London where they took up lives of genteel poverty.

The elder Fairchild's descent into opium addiction as a member of the notorious Hellfire Club, further reduced the family's fortunes, while the death of her mother left Angelica

16

as the only surviving member of the once noble clan capable of employment. And so, by the time she had reached the age of twenty-two, Angelica had already been living by her wits and her not inconsiderable charms for several years.

At the invitation of relatives in America, the bonnie Angelica had set sail to New York where fresh prospects as an actress on Broadway were said to await her. As it turned out, these prospects involved servicing the denizens of Tin Pan Alley as little more than a common prostitute. But Angelica's noble bearing, charming British accent and ability to fake orgasms with clients from Tammany Hall so won her the esteem of several of New York's leading citizens, that she was able to squirrel away a sizeable nest egg and spend less time on her back.

However, a small contretemps involving the police forced Angelica's rapid departure from her adopted city, and she headed west to California. There, in San Francisco's notorious tenderloin between the wharves and town center known as the Barbary Coast, Angelica found work as a saloon dance hall girl and re-established herself as one of the city's most sought after ladies of the evening.

There too, she had met an American privateer named Timothy Blake whose appellation "Snakeskin" was received along with the half-moon scar that bisected his left cheek. Somewhat resembling a rearing cobra (the effect enhanced by a small tattoo of a serpent's fanged mouth at its top), the scar turned a bright red when he was angry. He was also partial to flaunting a single rattler-skin glove on his left hand – the hand, he had boasted, that was the fastest draw on either of the two guns he'd always carried.

Blake was unlike any other man she had known, a mystery she could not unravel. He was a privateer and a rogue, and worse besides, but he was a man, she felt, quite like no other man alive. Despite the voice of caution, Angelica had become enamored of Snakeskin, perhaps too much so.

As much to fly from the temptation of surrendering herself body and soul to Snakeskin Blake as her long-held determination to marry into old European money and thus restore the Fairchild family fortune, she had left the United States for France following the fall of Napoleon III and had been entertained by the new men of the Third Republic, whose lusts equaled or excelled those of the places she had left.

It was in Paris that she had met a German whose role, (as indelicate as it was for him to phrase it one night when he was in his cups), was to act as royal procurer to a very wealthy Sultan of a very small island kingdom called Zanziber, which lay a few miles off the coast of East Africa. According to the German, this particular Sultan was always in the market for new additions to his royal *haram*.

Informed that the Sultan had looked favorably on the German's recommendations of her charms and accomplishments in the bedroom, Angelica was invited to journey to Zanzibar and become part of the Sultan's *haram*.

It was explained to Angelica by the German that this did not make her a mere whore, a calling in life which Angelica was eager to leave behind. On the contrary, the sexual conventions of the Orient were considerably different than Occidental mores. Quite apart from sullying her virtue, the royal potentate's personal pimp assured her, it was considered a great honor to serve in the Sultan's bedchamber, catering to his kingly hungers.

Besides that, Angelica would enjoy full conjugal rights, including a dowry of a million pounds, and be treated in every regard as a Queen.

DAVID ALEXANDER

Angelica accepted the German procurer's offer both as being consistent with her ambitions and with her determination to never again see Snakeskin Blake, who had sent her letters importuning her return to San Francisco. And so it was that Angelica Fairchild set sail for Zanzibar the following day on a packet steamer bound for the Ivory Coast.

The arduous sea voyage required a fortnight to complete, but was leavened by the attentions Angelica enjoyed from the vessel's staff, all of whom had fallen head-over-heels in love (or at least in lust) with their beautiful passenger. To relieve the boredom, as well as to profit handsomely from the tedious passage, she dallied with quite a few of them, including the ship's captain, who paid her liberally in Spanish pieces of eight, a currency regarded more favorably than even dollars or pounds sterling. Otherwise the trip was uneventful, marred neither by storms nor especially rough seas, and within the predicted time, Angelica reached her destination.

Her contempt for the squalid port of Zanzibar was offset by the gaudy splendor of the Sultan's palace. Unlike the sun-dried mud which composed most of the other structures on the island, the palace of its ruler was a sumptuous edifice of stone blocks, boasting cool green gardens, broad promenades and limpid gazing pools that reflected the blue sky in their placid waters. But the Sultan himself was a coarse little man whose offensive presence would have offended her even more if not for the vastness of the puny potentate's wealth.

Fortunately, the Sultan was an easy mate to please, tiring quickly and losing interest once his immediate needs had been fulfilled by Angelica's practiced ministrations in the bedchamber. Servicing the ruler of Zanzibar consumed only a few hours of her week, leaving her completely free to entertain herself during the rest of the time quite as she pleased.

This arrangement entailed certain pitfalls of its own, however. Used to the fast pace of life in Manhattan's heady swirl or San Francisco's Barbary Coast, to say nothing of the heavy action of Paris, Angelica soon grew bored with the humdrum pace of life in tiny Zanzibar.

Confined to the royal seraglio and in the company of empty-headed local girls who told coarse jokes regarding sex with donkeys, camels, horses and even dogs, she longed to experience the more bracing amusements that only cultured society could afford.

As the months passed, Angelica had begun to bribe her keepers and arrange to steal from the harem and walk the town unattended by the Sultan's eunuch guardians. She had been warned that there was very real danger in this practice.

The hordes of Muhammed Ahmed, who styled himself Mahdi of the *Ansari*, were everywhere on the attack. His spies lurked in practically every corner of town and his long reach extended from his Sudanese power centers in the vast desert realm of the Sahel to beyond the Horn of Africa, and to Zanzibar as well.

Angelica took the warning seriously. In the weeks and months since the appearance of the Mahdi from the desert wastes of the Sudan, his power had been growing with a rapidity which both amazed and alarmed the Egyptian Khedivate and British custodians of the region.

The might of the Mahdi now challenged the power of Great Britain herself, whose far-flung outposts along the Nile river were threatened by this *Mahdiyah,* or holy crusade.

Here in Zanzibar, the Mahdi's calls to the faithful to rise up and take violent action had inflamed the local populace as it had inflamed the Bedouin tribes of the windswept, sand-locked mainland who were their brethren. Angelica's flowing blonde tresses marked her as an Infidel, and that alone might be enough to get her into serious trouble if she did not take care.

Still, Angelica could not at the same time remain in the dull confines of the Sultan's harem and keep her sanity intact. And so, this week, as she had done at other times, the Sultan's favorite stole secretly from the palace confines and took to the Kasbah and the souks and bazaars of Zanzibar.

Draping the black veil of the market women called the *niqab* about her pretty face, she walked the narrow streets of the town as a common village woman might stroll, cloaked from the sinful eyes of men by the *niqab* and the *burka* and kept under the protection of the all-watchful Allah. The many piquant smells from food vendors assaulted her, the sun warmed her face, the sounds of the marketplace surrounded and enlivened her. For a few hours she would remain at large and then steal back to the hated confines of the royal seraglio, there to await the inevitable call to her new husband's bedchamber.

She was not aware that henchmen of the Mahdi, known as Dervishes, had been secretly watching her every movement as they followed her through the city's winding alleys. No event of any consequence in Zanzibar escaped the far-seeing, kohl-rimmed eyes of the anointed one, and the Mahdi had learned of the arrival of the fair Englishwoman the moment she had stepped onto the quay.

Though kept secret from the Sultan and the eunuch guards of the royal *haram*, the surreptitious comings and goings of the palace favorite had been well noted by the Mahdi's spies. Thus the lord of the Sahel and the enemy of Infidels and their hirelings had instructed his Dervish minions that the blonde woman should be captured at all costs and be brought forthwith into his exalted presence.

The moment of abduction arrived as the unsuspecting victim fingered a fetching filigree necklace of Crusader silver encrusted with Frankish gems, for the waves of soldiery unleashed upon the region by the medieval and Renaissance papacy and kings alike -- soldiery that was more the scum of the earth than the noble heroes such as they portrayed themselves -- soon filled their pockets and packs with plundered loot, which in turn fell into the hands of the Turks who slaughtered their would-be liberators and proselytizers in turn and sold the stolen wealth to the sharp-eyed men who stroked their unkempt beards in the souks.

"Come, my fragrant child," said the proprietor, eyes gleaming darkly as he studied his customer. "Venture within the cool of my humble tent, and I shall show you treasures such as those blue eyes have never before beheld and shall surely never see again."

Angelica balked, but the merchant was insistent as he gently led her beyond the tables heaped with glitter and into the darkness behind the door to the interior of one of the stone buildings that lined the street.

"It is cool within, is it not?" asked the merchant, still taking her by the crook of the arm. "Is it not more pleasant than the heat of the bazaar, my fragrant child?"

At this point Angelica saw that the merchant was in fact leading her not to view the plundered treasures of the Knights Templar, but to a foul-looking bed on which a monkey dressed in a small djellaba capered and jibbered with bestial glee.

The merchant's hand tightened on her arm while the other thrust her forward to the bed and hurled her down to it. The merchant fell atop her and pinned her arms beneath his knees as he raised his robes to expose his penis. The monkey mimicked its master.

"Cease thy struggles, fragrant one," he said as he shoved it in her face, "for surely it is Allah's will that you take this mighty rod upon thy lips and its heated nectar upon they thirsty tongue."

"You take your bloody pig's hands off me!" she screamed, but her words were stifled by the foul smelling penis that the shopkeeper rammed between her lips.

Now two things happened almost simultaneously. The first was Angelica's biting hard upon the tip of the penis and eliciting a scream of excruciating pain from the merchant. The second was the sudden presence of several robed men who threw him to the filthy rug by the bed to writhe with blood fountaining from his decapitated organ and whose foul breath she smelled as they roughly yanked her from the bed and shoved a filthy cloth into her bloodied mouth.

Though Angelica struggled like a tiger and cursed like a stevedore, it was all to no avail whatever. Now bound as she had been gagged, she was thrown in the back of an ox cart piled with malodorous dung.

The cart was wheeled from the bazaar without a single soul being any the wiser by her captors. It bumped along the cobble-paved streets to the quay of Zanzibar where a large, lateen-sailed felucca freighted with cargo was berthed. There, its contents were loaded onboard with practiced speed. The vessel soon left port, its destination the continental mainland of Africa.

Within a matter of days, Angelica Fairchild would be facing the Mahdi himself and be charged with fulfilling the reputedly perverse whims of the ruler of the Sudan in his own   *haram.*

FIVE DEAD MEN

DAVID ALEXANDER

2. The Prize is Taken

His Most High and Exalted Excellency, the Sultan of Zanzibar, who had been named Majid Bin Said at birth, sat placidly amid rising clouds of orange-blossom scented steam, his rotund belly bared and resembling in shape and color nothing so much as an enormous acorn that had somehow grown human limbs. His ministers, as naked as their ruler and sweating just as profusely, faced him inside the billowy confines of the Turkish Bath attached to the royal palace.

The Sultan had asked them to inform him immediately of their findings, regardless of where he might happen to be located at the moment at which their announcement might come.

Since having found himself afflicted with a run of the gout not long before, his court physicians had advised the potentate of Zanzibar to take the baths each and every day. The Sultan spent hours amid the clouds of steam attended by court musicians playing the native zither called the *chanoon*, accompanied by flute, mandolin and tambourine.

"She is nowhere to be found, then?" he asked his chief adviser, Jowary Dari.

FIVE DEAD MEN

"Nowhere, Your Majesty, I am sorry to inform you," Jowary replied, wiping perspiration from his round, dark moon of a face.

The Sultan motioned to one of the bath attendants who refreshed his face with a cool white cloth. After a moment, he went on.

"And you are certain that this apparent abduction is the handiwork of the Mahdi's agents?"

"Again, we are certain, Excellency," Jowary replied. "As certain as we know that a winged steed once carried the Prophet to Mecca, and that the pale face of the moon, when virgins gather to bathe their --"

"-- Yes, yes, quite, quite," the Sultan interrupted to cut short the oaths and embellishments of his windy vizier with a wave of his be-ringed hand.

"What do we know so far," he quickly went on, hoping to put Jowary on a new tack.

"Jahno himself was in charge of the interrogation of one of the luckless fools we've captured, Excellency," the vizier continued, indicating the large man standing beside him, who, unlike the others, did not seem to be much bothered by the stifling heat and humidity in the room.

The Gurkha warrior was one of the Sultan's permanent retainers, a gift from the Sultan's patron and friend, the English adventurer Charles Gordon, which had been made with the full consent of the English monarch Queen Victoria herself.

"And you may rest assured that Jahno's work was, ah, most thorough, my great and exalted Sultan."

Indeed it had been, of that the Sultan entertained no doubts whatever. The Gurkha had anticipated that the scum of the bazaar detained for questioning by the Sultan's men would crack immediately. Instead, it had required hours for

26

the rogue's tongue to finally be loosened -- and ultimately pulled from its roots in his throat by a pair of iron tongs held over live coals until they had begun to glow red hot.

Only after the nails had been ripped from each of his fingers, only after the dreaded *shebba* -- torture on the rack -- had been mercilessly applied and the joints of his limbs torn from their sockets, had the felon confessed that he had been one of a number of the Mahdi's Dervishes charged with watching for the Englishwoman for weeks and keeping note of the schedule of the Sultan's Infidel wife.

"I trust that Jahno's work brought forth its usual good results," the Sultan replied, stroking his gray-stippled beard and directing a brief and suitably condescending smile at the Gurkha.

Jahno's only reaction was a brief grunt of what was probably assent.

"What of the other fanatics who were party to this abduction of the Englishwoman? Have they been taken into custody yet, brawny one?"

"Your Majesty's retainers are combing Zanzibar at this very moment, sire, following information provided by the captured Dervish," the Vizier replied, answering for the stolid Gurkha.

"However, your Majesty must certainly be aware that the remainder of the Mahdist gang must surely have fled across the straits by this time and reached the protection offered by the mainland and fled from there into the burning reaches of Kordofan and the Sahel. I am afraid there will not be much luck in capturing them now."

The Sultan selected one of the sweet meats offered on a chased silver tray held up to him by one of his retainers. He reflected as he munched the honeyed walnuts, one of his favorite snacks, clouds of fragrant steam continuing to billow around his majestic personage and wafting the fragrance of orange blossoms into his flaring nostrils.

"There is no question about it," he said as he munched his treat. "We must get the Englishwoman back at all costs. The two nipples on her breasts are alone worth a kingdom."

"But your Majesty --" the Vizier began before he was cut off by a curt wave of the Sultan's hand.

"My mind is quite fixed, Jowary," he intoned in a voice that left no question of his intent. "There is no other recourse. Were it one of the local women, then I would permit the Mahdi to keep his ill-won prize -- and give him my blessings to boot.

"Indeed, were this only an issue of a woman at all, regardless of how sweet her breasts or tempting her loins, then I might feel constrained to allow the abduction to pass unavenged as a mere hostage to fortune.

"However it is more than that alone, you see," the Sultan went on after chewing and swallowing another of the delicacies that he was so fond of.

"By this action the Mahdi has made a political statement as well as carried out a kidnapping. Because Angelica is a British national as well as one of my royal wives, he has flung the gauntlet of challenge into the teeth of both Whitehall and Paris as well. This is a bold declaration of his growing power -- and our growing impotence to effectively meet and deal with it."

The Sultan fell silent, his eyes meeting Jowary's weasel stare through curtains of rising orange-blossomy mist. The Sultan's councilor held his gaze and did not look away despite his desire to leave the bath at once.

"Sire, what you say is true of course," Jowary replied. "But, in the words of the Prophet, he who dares --"

"-- The Mahdi is cunning," the Sultan went on, almost to himself, his dark eyes leaving Jowary's as he stroked his pointed black beard which had lately become stippled with gray under the growing stress of affairs of state.

"By this stratagem the fanatic undoubtedly hopes to goad the British and their Egyptian allies into prematurely committing themselves to a battle they cannot hope to win. If he is successful, then it reasonably follows that Zanzibar will be consumed along with them."

"I had not meant to incur your Excellency's displeasure," the Vizier chimed in when the Sultan had again fallen silent. "Merely to state a point. In any event, the issue is moot. I have just this morning received a telegraph wire from Pasha Charles Gordon. Does your divine Majesty wish me to read it?"

"Go on," the Sultan said, his sudden interest clear in the sharpness of his voice.

The Sultan listened intently as Jowary read the tersely worded telegraph message which had just arrived. It was from that one and the same "Chinese Charlie" Gordon, British mercenary and adventurer, who had become world renowned as the hero of the Taiping Rebellion in China and lately Governor of the Sudan, and it was in answer to an urgent appeal for assistance from the Sultan to his friend of the previous day.

Gordon was the one Frank -- by which term the local populace meant English, Europeans and Americans combined -- that the Sultan trusted implicitly, and he had every faith in the Britisher's judgment. The telegraph cable from Pasha Gordon concerned a man whom the Pasha highly recommended as being the perfect individual to conduct a rescue of the Englishwoman. The Sultan gestured to his tedious vizier and soon held the cable in his heavily perspiring hand.

My Most Esteemed Friend, Your Royal Highness,

I have had the pleasure of receiving your request this morning. In answer to your question I am well and hope to return to the Sudan as soon as I am fully rested.

Now to your second question: there is but a single man whom I feel up to the task you suggest. His name is Snakeskin Blake, his nationality is American, and his talents are beyond my humble abilities to adequately describe in a paragraph or two. Find him, and I assure you your problems will be immediately nearer to solution.

I remain ever ...

Your Humble Servant,

Sir Charles G. Gordon, K.B.E., O.B.E., M.B.E.

"This man mentioned by Pasha Gordon," the Sultan reckoned out loud, handing the now wilted letter back to Jowary, "where can he be found?"

"Your unflawed and pristine Majesty, we do not presently know the whereabouts of Sahib Snakeskin Blake," the Vizier replied. "But if he can be found, Supreme One -- and do not doubt that we shall find him even were it to mean spanning the globe with an eagle's far-seeing eyes -- we shall bring him before you."

"Then make it so," replied the Sultan, dismissing his advisors with yet another flick of his paunchy fingers, which he decided to lick in the absence of treats on his platter.

Then he waved for the chased silver tray of sweetmeats to be brought to him again.

Selecting a tasty morsel, he munched contemplatively while the gray mists surrounded his portly perspiring form and the mingled scents of wild honey, myrrh, jasmine and orange blossoms filled his sweat-dripping nose.

FIVE DEAD MEN

3. Buccaneers of the Spanish Main

Brilliant streaks of aquamarine, strange flashes
of dull purple and brilliant rays of scintillating
gold lit up the churning, dull-gray waters of
the Spanish Main, a region of ocean, shoreline
and islands situated between the east coast of Florida and the
north coasts of Colombia and Venezuela below the Lesser
Antilles with the Caribbean and Gulf coasts lying in
between.

This name was first given to it by the Spanish plunderers
who'd prized it as a route to gather and move the pillaged
gold, silver, precious gems, the hides and furs of rare native
beasts, and other valuables of the conquered civilizations of
the New World, as well as a transshipment point from which
the booty of Spain's colonies in the Orient could be shipped
back to the overflowing royal treasuries in old Madrid.

Later on, long after the old Spanish hegemony had been
forever lost when Nelson won at the Battle of Trafalgar, the
coastlines and waters of the region became favorite haunts
for cut-throats and buccaneers to lie in wait for merchant
vessels flying European flags, whose holds full of rich

plunder would fetch high prices in the black markets and crowded kasbahs of exotic ports of call.

Such was now the case as a new day dawned in the spring of the year 1883.

■

The pirate raider was a two-masted warship, her hull sheathed in nearly five-inch-thick iron belt armor amidships, tapering to half the thickness at prow and bow. The jacketing of iron, intended mainly to gird the vessel -- whose name was Courageous -- for battle against ships of the line also served double duty against the predations of the foot-long wood-eating teredo worm and sundry other similar pests abounding in warm tropical waters in these southern latitudes.

The Courageous had been built as a blockade runner, fleet -- her 1500 horsepower, four-boiler steam engine made for a top speed of almost 15 knots -- and difficult to see until another vessel was abeam of her, thanks to her low draft which displaced less than 1200 long tons yet allowed her to slide through the water quiet as a whisper.

And she was deadly too.

Amidships, behind the prow and before the bow, were positioned twin pillbox turrets, each one clad in armor of five inch thickness, and each one of them containing powerful main guns.

Inside the forward turret were mounted twin Armstrong guns -- 254 millimeter cannons capable of fire that was both rapid and accurate at long range -- and one of the newest compressed air powered Gatlings firing belt-fed .44 caliber ammunition.

The aft turret contained a single Armstrong -- a 40 pounder with a smaller bore, firing 120 millimeter rounds, but was also outfitted with a 12 pound cannon and a second

Gatling machinegun, this one gas-driven. A third Gatling was the sole armament of a smaller iron turret positioned atop the aft brigantine mast, while a fourth and final Gatling, also gas-driven, could be fitted to mounts amidships at port and starboard, as the need might arise.

These same mounts could also accommodate Cosgrove rockets with explosive warheads which could be used at longer ranges than the ship's guns.

And if neither guns nor rockets failed to do their bloody work well enough (or if circumstances favored it) the Courageous was also outfitted with an iron armored ram bow that could stave in the timbers of an enemy vessel and send her straight to the bottom.

She had been wrighted in England by the Lairds, whose boatyard had supplied both Confederate and Union with ironclads and blockade runners during the turmoil of the Civil War. Decades earlier, the same boatyard had built the special ship that President Tom Jefferson had ordered constructed to serve as a decoy in the war against the pirates of the Barbary Coast who had been preying on American shipping in the waters of the Indian Ocean. Disguised as an unarmed merchant ship, she would bare her guns behind concealed panels to port and starboard as the pirates got within range and blast them out of the waters.

So too was the Courageous equipped, but she also had the new Gatling guns bolted to her decks and launchers for Cosgrove rockets positions on her masts in addition to the cannons above and below as well as heavier armaments than Jefferson's warship carried.

Ably manned by a crew of twenty rough though capable seamen, the Courageous was more than a match for any ship that sailed the seas, and the fact that she was equipped with condensing apparatus capable of extracting fresh drinking water from the sea, meant that the Courageous needed few stops at bases and could prowl the seas independent of land for long periods of time.

And while the Courageous was herself a pirate vessel, she was an American privateer, and like her predecessor she too sailed with the secret blessings of the current administration of President Chester Arthur.

She too had a mission, which was to throw a spanner into the well-laid plans of first, the Spanish and French to gain new footholds in the southern reaches of the Americas, and second, the Ukase in Moscow to do the same in the colder reaches of the north. For this purpose the Monroe Doctrine -- officially American, tacitly British as well -- had been promulgated against further attempts to colonize the Americas by the powers of Europe.

While British and American ships of the line policed the open seas, other actions against foreign interlopers would remain secret and never be made known. Such actions included those for which Snakeskin Blake and his Anglo-American crew of larcenous cutthroats were paid in the pillaged buccaneer's booty that they were able to recover from the ships they sent plunging straight down to the muddy bottom.

■

On this particular morning, the Courageous lay at anchor leeward of the reefs guarding the approaches to Two Rocks Island, a rough and broken wind-scoured rock in the ocean that did not appear on any navigational maps, and was thus as much stranger to the seas upon which it lay as it was a welcome and much sought out refuge for freebooters who plied the Spanish Main between the Caribbean Coast and the Gulf of Mexico.

FIVE DEAD MEN

Centrally positioned in the Caribbean midway between Port Au Prince in Haiti and Cartagena on the northwest coast of Colombia, Two Rocks Island was a sharp sliver of stone cast off the skeleton bones of the Greater Antilles which lay scattered across the Caribbean's uppermost reaches in a messy jumble that was the bane of merchantmen and sworn friend of pirates.

As far as islands went, Two Rocks Island was far too small to provide permanent habitation for man or decent foraging for any beasts other than the wild cats and goats that had been left there by the crews of passing vessels over the years to either breed or die out.

But the pirate's lair, replete with rocky coves for safe anchorage and sea caves that led far inland, and were thus perfect spots to stash away plundered loot or hide from British men-o-war was large enough to completely hide the Courageous from the view of any other ships approaching the island on a north-by-northwest course heading. And in the thick salt fog that now hung low over the surface of the sea like a briny blanket, the Courageous was doubly shrouded from detection by her unwary prey.

■

All hands were already awake and a lookout manned the crow's nest high on the foc'sle, the sailor's sharp eyes scanning the far horizon for signs of the expected prize of the day. The object of the lookout's search was a Spanish merchant vessel. The name of the ship was Alonso de Palensia, and highly reliable reports bought dear in the seaside scum lairs of old Kingston town in nearby Jamaica indicated that she had put out to sea from the port of Malaga some two days before. Following a northwesterly course that would carry her across the waters of the Mediterranean Sea, around the Cape of Good hope, and then into the Atlantic, the Alonso de Palensia was bound for New Orleans.

The merchant ship's hold bulged with casks of Portuguese wine from Oporto, crates of Caribbean tobacco, heavy sea chests full of African Ivory plus sugar, coffee and other valuable trading commodities. But there were also two chests of finely smelted Libyan gold secreted onboard, and even a single chest of such a prize was worth more than all the other cargo onboard the Alonso de Palensia combined.

■

In the captain's quarters of the anchored pirate raider, Snakeskin Blake stood bent over his nautical charts.

Snakeskin was a medium tall man, and well-muscled rather than too slender of build. His face was hard and angular, marked by a cruel mouth as quick to show anger as to break into a broad grin at a good and merry jest.

His hard gray eyes were fixed with a seasoned mariner's calm precision on the chart as he stroked the cobra-shaped scar on his left cheek. From his lips jutted a burning cheroot, tipped with an inch of smoking gray ash and redolent of the rich Napoleon brandy into which he had let it steep before drying and lighting it.

Snakeskin was checking for last minute questions that might arise, making certain that the taking of the Alonso de Palensia would proceed as smoothly as clockwork.

That the merchant vessel was carrying the three mahogany chests of pure Libyan gold, Snakeskin took as an article of faith. He had received the information separately from the Spanish brigantine's charted course through an agent in Tripoli who, if not completely trustworthy, was nevertheless smart enough to understand that the money Snakeskin had paid for the information meant that he would pay with his life if the information turned out not to be genuine or if a trap was in the making.

Snakeskin heard a sudden rapping on the shipmaster's cabin door and straightened to his full height of five feet, nine inches. Although he was not as tall as some, his shoulders were broad as the length of an axe from the top of its head to the tip of its handle and his mastery of the skills of Chinese Boxing, learned while serving with Chinese Charlie during the Teipei Rebellion, insured that few men could stand up to him in a fight and that those foolish enough to try would likely as not come out second best.

"Come in," Snakeskin said in a voice as rough as sandpaper.

"Begging your pardon, cap'n," the man who entered replied.

Big Little Jopling wore a leather vest over a striped sailor's blouse. His right eye was patched and a badly healed puckered scar ran down the left side of his face. He was Snakeskin's first mate, and another Taipei veteran who had served with Charlie Gordon's motley assortment of British and American mercenaries.

"But you wanted me to report when the Alonso de Palensia was sighted."

"Show me," Snakeskin said, indicating the navigational chart spread out on the table.

Jopling crossed the cabin and bent over the chart. Placing one thick finger down on the lines describing shipping lanes, he indicated the position of the Alonso de Palensia and said, "She's *here*, Cap'n, thirty degrees north, fifty west. Just about where we expected her to lie. Nary a mile off course, cap'n. I figure she'll be within hailing distance in fifteen minutes."

DAVID ALEXANDER

"Excellent," Snakeskin pronounced, rolling up the map and stowing it away in one of the polished teak cabinets on the cabin walls. "Tell those scurvy dogs I pay good money to man this ship to proceed to their stations. There's a bottle of unwatered Haitian rum for every stinking cur among 'em if we pull this off -- make sure they know it.

"Aye, cap'n," Jopling acknowledged, his smile at the contemplated pleasures of action and rum-guzzling revealing gapped and broken wolf's teeth in a sinister mouth. "I'll tell the men."

"I'll meet you topside in a few minutes."

Jopling gave his assent and rushed out into the companionway, closing the cabin door behind him. Snakeskin went to his drawer and took out a matched set of .44 caliber LeMat revolvers.

Each of the white ivory handled LeMats (he'd had the handgrips specially retooled by a Singaporean gunsmith to replace the original checkered walnut grips) were equipped with an outsized cylinder capable of firing nine shots in rapid succession and a centerpiece, smooth bore barrel, that was made for firing grapeshot like a rifle.

The formidable weapon had been devised in New Orleans by the Confederacy's leading gunsmith, and it was in the port of New Orleans that Snakeskin had obtained the matched pistol set of the last remaining .44 editions, which took standard cartridges, in a game of Five Card Stud that had ended with the gun's former owner on the floor with an unfired derringer in his hand and a hole in his belly, courtesy of the smoking Colt under Snakeskin's end of the poker table.

Snapping open the wheels of both weapons, the captain of the Courageous checked to see that rounds filled each of the nine slots in their rifled cylinders, as he smelled the odor of oil rising from the well-cared-for firearms. The inspection was performed more out of habit than necessity as Snakeskin always kept his prized guns cleaned and loaded.

Then, jamming both LeMats into the broad and well worn belt of engraved Moroccan leather that encircled his trim waist, Snakeskin followed Jopling's path from the cabin, feeling the blood pound in his ears as every nerve came alive with anticipation.

And now, like the Courageous' first mate, the captain of the privateer grinned too, savoring what was about to come next.

4. All Hands on Deck

Faintly, beyond the creaking of the ship's timbers and the steady cadence of waves lapping at the stony outcroppings of Two Rocks island, Snakeskin heard the Spanish merchantman in the distance as she plied the calm waters off the southern shores of Curacao midway between the Windwards on the underbelly of the Caribees and the shoal-infested coastal waters that lay hard off Baranquilla on the South American mainland.

Snakeskin knew she'd follow a straight course for Jamaica, where she'd turn to complete the last leg of the voyage to the Mexican port of Valparaiso. That course would have her pass within no more than a league or two of Two Rocks Island.

The sun had just risen as though reluctant to light the world and reveal the flagrant sins of mortal men to the eternal vigils of heaven. It was now little more than a faint yellow blotch on the color-streaked horizon. The dense fog insured that twilight still held sway and would for at least awhile longer.

FIVE DEAD MEN

The sailors aboard the Alonso de Palensia would be on guard for an attempt to take the vessel by the cutthroat buccaneers which plied these waters so often traversed by richly laden treasure ships of the Spanish navy. By now the word of the valuable cargo that the merchant was carrying in her hold would have become an open secret. A prize as rich as it would make the Alonso de Palensia an attractive target to pirate vessels.

The crew of the Alonso de Palensia would be especially watchful, Snakeskin knew. And even through the dense fog, the eyes of an experienced lookout could discern the telltale silhouette of a ship against the faintly lit horizon as well as a hen could recognize her brood of chicks. If the Courageous were spotted in time, offensive measures could be taken by the Spanish merchantmen's crew that would not be pleasant - - her cannon were modern breech-loaders manned by experienced gunnery crews. Far better to catch the prize all unwary and take her fast, quitting the area with booty before any alarms she might have raised could bring other, and more dangerous vessels, into the area.

While the Courageous was well armed with its revolving gun turrets and Cosgrove rockets and its crew carried rifles and revolvers in their belts, Snakeskin wanted to avoid any needless confrontation or bloodshed.

The tactics that had allowed him to survive in his treacherous business called for stealth, speed and surprise to catch the enemy unawares, seize the initiative and make off with the prize.

The last thing Snakeskin wanted or needed was a bloody fight at sea, if he could at all avoid one.

In pursuit of this objective, the Courageous had hoisted its mooring anchor slowly and quietly, its cable, capstans and hawse pipe all well greased to avoid making unnecessary sounds and to prevent any fouling of the cable as the great black flukes of old Admiralty iron broke free of the bottom and a ton of dead weight dangling from its cast metal crown began rising slowly off the floor of the ocean.

Blake's buccaneers were forbidden to smoke or to speak as well, and although they looked seedy, they were all professional thieves to the last man. More than that, they were more loyal to Snakeskin than to any other living soul, willing to follow him straight into the gaping jaws of hell itself if he asked them. Every mate onboard the Courageous knew the reason for their captain's orders and would follow them to the letter.

Snakeskin now pricked up his ears, straining to interpret the meaning of every one of the faint sounds coming through the blanket of swirling mists. He knew that he was hearing the sounds of the approaching merchant ship, and that it was only a matter of minutes until the vessel broke through the mists and bore down upon them.

And then Snakeskin saw the prow of the Spanish treasure ship break through the dense gray fog bank. Jopling had also seen the Alonso de Palensia suddenly loom within range and was watching Snakeskin intently for the signal to heave to from the anchorage just around the leeward side of Two Rocks island. Snakeskin raised his hand just before delivering the signal and then brought it sharply down.

Jopling made circular motions of his own hand to the helmsman who immediately issued the order to apply main power to the ship's engines. There would now be no escaping the sounds made by these operations. No matter how silent the crew remained, the sounds would be audible to any listeners onboard the oncoming merchant vessel, echoing across the sea in the fog.

FIVE DEAD MEN

Snakeskin felt the Courageous lurch as her twin screws churned under the combined force of half of her eight boilers and she swung out into the tide. Within a matter of seconds the pirate vessel had slid past the small, rocky island. Seconds later the lookout in the crow's nest high above the foredeck of the hapless Alonso de Palensia spotted the telltale black silhouette moving like a wraith through the gray shreds of curling sea mist.

He instantly raised the Very pistol loaded with the red flare cartridge that signaled imminent attack by privateers and pulled back the trigger. The flare burned like a red star of ill omen above the ship, illuminating the ocean for at least a league all around in its fitful, sizzling glare, and sent the crew of the Alonso de Palensia into violent motion as sailors ran for their battle stations.

The cry of alarm too had roused the captain of the merchant ship to sudden wakefulness as he jumped from the bed, ignoring the imprecations of the East Indian whore who'd warmed him as he slept. Hastily throwing on his black breeches and bright red waistcoat, jamming his loaded revolver into his belt holster and putting his three-cornered and cockaded hat on his closely shaven head, the treasure ship's captain gained the deck and shouted for general quarters to be sounded.

Standing on the afterdeck, the ship's yeoman began to ring the alarm bell to call all hands to action in a frenzy of warning. Seconds later, hands from stem to stern aboard the Courageous were in position to take the Spanish prize.

"First mate -- hoist the ship's battle ensigns. Fly the Jolly Roger!"

"Aye, Cap'n Snakeskin," shouted Jopling in reply, as he went at his appointed task with black-hearted relish.

Her stacks blowing dense plumes of brown-black smoke as her engines made all eight boilers work to earn the coal that fed their furnaces, the Courageous shot from its cove in the lee of Two Rocks island and hurtled toward its prize.

Now Jopling ordered that the privateer's ensign be raised aloft, and the sailor up high on the masts unfurled the great banner of yellow Chinese silk bearing the emblem of a great sea serpent coiled about a whale and preparing to devour its prize with the motto "To the Victors Belong the Spoils" surrounding the bold depiction.

Taking up his binoculars, Snakeskin trained the twin lenses on the Spanish merchantman now looming closer in the distance and glassed her over. He could now see men rushing about confusedly on the Alonso de Palensia's decks.

Swinging up the glass, he could see other crewmembers hurrying to change the vessel's main sail's cant so that she could tack to starboard in order to try and evade the trap into which she had stumbled. The ship appeared as though preparing to turn and make a run for it, having applied reverse torque to her screws. As it did, the Alonso de Palensia faltered before heeling hard about in the direction from which she'd come, and she began to cut a wake in the choppy sea.

"Damn! She's trying to make a break for it," Snakeskin shouted to Jopling, letting the binoculars drop on their leather strap about his neck. "Alert bow and stern turret gunners. Have them fire warning salvos across her starboard bows."

"Aye-aye, Cap'n Snakeskin," Jopling replied, and relayed the order to the crew of cannoneers posted at battle stations throughout the Courageous.

A few moments later, fulminating clouds of cordite smoke rolled and billowed across the Courageous' heaving decks and every plank vibrated as the sound of the automatic cannon fire echoed through the dense fog.

Hoisting up his glasses again, Snakeskin could see multiple stitch lines of glowing green phosphorescent tracer fire belched from the flaming muzzles of the turret guns arc across the bows of the merchant ship's deck.

"She's not changing course, Cap'n," Jopling commented after a few heartbeats had passed. "She'll try to run for it. Maybe lose us in the Windwards and then make for Jamaica."

"Not a bad guess," Snakeskin wagered. "Same as mine in fact."

It was apparent that the Alonso de Palensia had chosen to run from the attacking vessel rather than stand to for boarding by the pirate crew.

"Orders, Cap'n Snakeskin?

"Hard to starboard! We'll cross her bows and punch a few holes in her stern close to her ordnance stores. If we get too close to hitting the magazine it may change the captain's mind."

"Aye-aye, Skipper," Jopling replied, relaying Snakeskin's orders to the helm of the Courageous and to her gun crews in the turrets fore and aft as well as the artillery near the stern.

Snakeskin felt the Courageous heel sharply about as the pirate vessel gave chase to her desperately fleeing quarry. The merchant vessel was fast, but she was no match for the far fleeter blockade runner. Within minutes the Courageous was standing hard across her bows as Snakeskin had ordered, cutting off her single avenue of escape toward the Spanish port of Jamaica.

"Is the cannon gun crew ready?" Snakeskin asked at a shout.

"Ready as a groom with the bride's nighties off, Capn'," Jopling replied, affirming this with a glance at the crewmen to starboard who again stood ready to pull the chains that would ignite the big powder charges to send the .30 millimeter shells arcing across the open water.

Minutes before, under the direction of their skippers, they had strained on the ropes to haul the guns back from the side of the ship where they were secured by heavy tackle and mounted on wheeled recoil carriages. The cannoneers had then loaded the heavy deck guns, rammed the powder charges down the rifled gun barrels to the far end, followed in turn by the heavy artillery shells with their high explosive warheads.

"Order them to fire," was the command Snakeskin next issued as the Courageous' pilot succeeded in putting her starboard bow abeam of the merchantman.

In a second, the big deck guns roared, making the Courageous' deck planks shudder and the air echo with deafening reports. The rounds fired at the Alonso de Palensia from the muzzles of the artillery pieces were jacketed with pellets of pig iron held together within the shell casing in a waxy matrix. This shrapnel, as it was called, would fragment on impact or on fuzed proximity to a target. Well, not quite fragment -- that was too tame a word. For in an age of largely black powder weaponry, rounds might hit with a savage fury that tore limbs from torsos as the rule, not the exception.

Yet while the shrapnel-filled artillery shells could be far deadlier to the crew of the merchant ship than the cannonballs of previous naval engagements (while still capable of tearing the limbs clean off any luckless soul in harm's way), such rounds would still present less chance of sending the merchant ship to the bottom -- an outcome that Snakeskin did not desire.

Snakeskin watched the cannon shot find its targets amidships of the now badly mauled merchant vessel. A sudden explosion at the stern of the stricken craft told him that its ordnance magazine had been struck dead center.

Within a matter of seconds the entire aft section of the Spanish treasure ship was engulfed in flames and awash with dense billowing black smoke. She was riding lower in the water too, indicating that the sea was flooding into breaches ripped in the Alonso de Palensia's ironclad hull by the Courageous' accurate cannonades.

Snakeskin Blake was close enough to hear the screams of crewmen unnerved by the assault and beginning to panic as they'd seen fellow sailors struck by the maiming, limb-tearing, bone-shattering shrapnel. Snakeskin ordered the Gatling-armed turret crews to fire tracer bursts at the masts and shatter them as the Spanish merchantman slowed and her wake flattened behind her.

Finally the Alonso de Palensia stopped dead and Snakeskin knew the Courageous and her crew had won both the contest and the prize that belonged to the victors. The merchantman's captain did not have any fight left in him. To his credit he was wise enough to know that he was beaten and behaved accordingly.

Soon Snakeskin saw the white flag of surrender hoisted high up on the main mizzen boom. The prize was finally his! A great cheer rose up from the Courageous. Blake's buccaneers had won.

Those of the crew who were still alive and whose wounds did not prevent them from feeling it, knew the anticipation of being within reach of valuable booty. The merchantman would have ample provisions and plentiful food, ale and barrel stacked upon barrel of good, stout Portuguese wine and dark Jamaican rum as well, and soon they would be enjoying the plunder of their defeated enemy.

"Bring her hard to," Snakeskin instructed Jopling from his perch on the flying bridge of the Courageous. "And have the men make ready to board our hard-earned prize. We've got her -- and the treasure in her hold."

"Aye, that we do, Cap'n Snakeskin," Jopling replied with a broad smile, and relayed Snakeskin's orders to the Courageous' cheering crew, every man among them eager for grand plunder and bars of Libyan gold.

5. An Unforeseen Development

The Courageous closed with the Alonso de Palensia amid the scudding sheets of heavy fog that continued swirling close under the guns of the raider vessel's crew.

At Snakeskin's shouted command, boarding planks were extended across the narrow gap of open water separating the hulls of the two adjacent vessels. Cheering and swearing, brandishing their weapons in an exultation of victory, the Courageous' crew spilled onto the decks of the merchant ship through the cloud of burning timber that enveloped her, shouting like madmen eager to plunder the captive merchant vessel and savor the spoils of victory to their fullest. Snakeskin followed in their train, his gray eyes sober in contrast as he surveyed the unfolding situation.

"Tu gringo *cabron*, thou bloody bastard," the Spanish captain cursed at him in the stilted manner by which the Spanish nobility still spoke, even now in the late 19th century.

He was a portly man with a fat, florid face, his broad, pugnacious nose shot through with the veins characteristic of the veteran drinker of rum. "Thou hast killed fifteen of my best men."

FIVE DEAD MEN

"You shouldn't have run, captain," Snakeskin answered him coolly, taking his eyes off the ruddy face of the Alonso de Palensia's captain to make sure that his men were herding the captive crew of the English ship into corners where they could be well guarded before going after the booty onboard. "We fired warning shots across your bow."

"This is outrageous!" shouted the master of the captured ship, his face turning livid. "These are international waters, I remind thee, sir. Repercussions will be most severe! I dare say that thou shalt hang by the neck for this crime on the high seas."

"And I remind you, *sir,* that I have your ship in tow and your crew under my guns. You are my prisoner. No more threats or calling me 'asshole' in front of my crew, some of whom understand that word in Spanish, if you please, or I shall have you clapped in irons. Now direct my man Jopling to the gold you carry."

"*Ir directamente al infierno, hijo de puta!*" the captain snarled with hatred, and he made a sudden, brisk downward motion with his right arm. Snakeskin knew he was going for a derringer concealed beneath the lacework of his foppishly frilled cuffs.

The pirate master moved quickly, his hand grasping for one of the heavy-weighted belaying pins ensconced in a niche on the captive vessel's gunwales. Having anticipated the Spanish skipper's actions, he brought up the five-pound iron cudgel just as the small, single-shot handgun appeared in the captain's hand, then slammed it down hard on the captain's wrist, his blow rewarded by the crisp snap of crunching cartilage.

The Alonso de Palensia's master shrieked as he dropped the pistol, his hand now a shattered mess pouring forth blood onto the deck of the stricken Spanish merchant ship.

Following through, Snakeskin brought the belaying pin upward in a sharp, accurate motion, landing a heavy blow to the side of the captain's head.

The skipper's eyes crossed and he sagged to the deck with a grunt like a slaughtered pig, blood trickling from the large gash that had opened along the side of his head.

"Sleep well, captain," Snakeskin wished the unconscious man, slipping the bloodied pin back into its sconce. "Get the Slaughterer to bind his head and put him in one of the longboats with a bottle of rum within easy reach."

Soon much of the rest of the Spanish crew would be put over the side in the merchantman's longboats. Those who could not find room -- and there would be many, as there were always too few emergency boats available -- would have to fight mates now turned enemies or risk being chewed up by the man-eaters that infested these subtropical waters.

But over the side they would go, to the last man of them. The Alonso de Palensia was to suffer the fate of all captured treasure vessels -- set ablaze and sent to the bottom.

"Aye-aye, Cap'n Snakeskin," said the second mate, an unshaven, one-toothed eye-patched rogue called Sunny Jim, who went to rouse the ship's surgeon from his bottle and his wonted place in the shadowed dark of the hold.

Just then Snakeskin saw Jopling's massive head and broad shoulders appear in the swung-open hatch amidships that laddered down to the depths of the Spanish ship's hold. In his hands he carried a bar of dully gleaming metal. Behind Jopling, several other crewman groaned and grunted as they struggled to carry two sea chests fashioned out of coarse-planed black ebony wood.

"Here they are, Cap'n!" Jopling cried excitedly, handing Snakeskin the dull cast ingot of Libyan gold as the men laid the sea chests down in front of Snakeskin. "These must be them, all right. They're the only ones down in the hold what look like the one's we've been after."

"We'll soon find out," Snakeskin concurred, drawing the two LeMat pistols from his belt. Quickly taking aim, he fired one shot from each single-fire gun barrel straight into the steel locks that secured the heavy weight hasps of the treasure chests. The custom load heavy caliber bullets snapped both their locks amid acrid wisps of gunsmoke.

Crouching down, Snakeskin pulled the shattered locks from the iron hasps, then flipped back the lids of the wooden coffers. Heaped within them were neatly stacked ingots of pure, solid gold from the Barbary Coast treasure rooms of old Tripoli.

Snakeskin reached down and picked one of them up, almost unable to lift the heavy metal bar. Like all the rest of the gold ingots, it bore the imperial seal of the Royal Libyan treasury; an imprint of a lion rampant with the inscription in Arabic script which read "Power Shall Rule" incised into the top of the ingot of pure grade yellow metal.

"Looks like we've hit pay dirt," Snakeskin said with a smile as he laid the ingot back into the coffer atop the pile of thirty bars just like it and then re-closed the heavy lid of adzed ebony. "Get these beauties onboard the Courageous and put them under heavy guard."

"Yes sir, Cap'n, sir," Jopling replied with roguish glee.

Soon the crewmen were negotiating the boarding planks, which creaked and groaned under the added weight of the precious burden they carried.

"What about the rum and Port?"

"Break open the barrels, Jopling, and let the men bathe in it if they like," Snakeskin ordered, adding as a caution, "but not until after we sail."

DAVID ALEXANDER

While the bloodied master of the Alonso de Palensia lay groaning at Snakeskin's boot-shod feet, he could see that his crew was making fast work of the remainder of the contents of the prize vessel's plundered hold.

Casks and packing crates were being pulled from the Alonso de Palensia's plundered cargo hold and carried by cursing, groaning, sweating and laughing crewmen across the boarding planks onto the decks of the hawser-lashed Courageous bobbing in the swells alongside the merchantman.

Blake's mercenaries knew their work, and knew it well. Before the twin destructive forces of the flames that were consuming her deck timbers and the sea that rushed into her hold sent the Spanish merchantman to the bottom, the Courageous' crew would have brought ample provisions aboard to last them for many months at sea.

■

Within a matter of minutes, the transfer of the bulk of the Alonso de Palensia's treasure and other cargo had been fully completed. Lightened now by thousands of pounds, the Alonso de Palensia's hull showed five inches above the waterline while the Courageous now rode lower on the waves, her own cargo deck filled with the pillaged booty which the merchant vessel had been carrying in the depths of her hold.

Back onboard the Courageous, Snakeskin issued instructions for the boarding planks to be taken back aboard the pirate vessel. Apart from this, there would be no further indignities visited by Snakeskin's crew on the men of the Alonso de Palensia.

Other privateers might not have been content with anything less than burning the Alonso de Palensia and sending her to the bottom, but Snakeskin was not of that kind. He considered himself a businessman, if a ruthless breed of businessman. He took what he needed and did not destroy the rest unless circumstances pressed him to do so. Fortunately for the crew of the Alonso, the rich plunder taken from the ship's hold was incentive enough for the master of the Courageous to stay his hand.

"Cast off -- Helmsman, take her away," Snakeskin shouted.

The orders were "aye'd" and within a matter of minutes the Courageous slowly began to put open sea between it and the stricken Spanish vessel.

A light tropical squall had begun to move in, adding to the speed with which Snakeskin's ship could disappear into the gloom, a gift of nature for which Snakeskin was grateful.

It was as the Courageous was moving abeam of the Alonso de Palensia that the lookout posted high on the crow's nest spotted a sight in his telescope view field that made his breath catch in his lungs.

Not believing his eyes, he lingered on the sighting for a long while. But what he had seen was no mirage. It was as real as he was, he knew, and it frightened him to the pit of his stomach.

There on the horizon the lookout saw a squadron of ships.

From their bulking silhouettes, it was clear to the lookout that they could only represent but one particular type of British battleship.

"Three ships on the horizon!" he shouted down from his lofty perch. "Heading north-by-east."

Then he raised his Very pistol skyward and fired its single red phosphorescent flare.

Snakeskin heard the shouted cry and whipped his binoculars up to his eyes. Turning the knurled knob with his thumb to increase their magnification, he swept the glasses in the direction indicated by the lookout's warning shot. To his amazement, he confirmed the sighting of three ships of the line which he also took to be British battleships.

A thrill of shock raced along Snakeskin's nerves as he recognized the silhouette of the first ship in the British battle line.

It was the Campendown, damn if he wasn't sure of it. If so -- and by George it had to be -- then they were in serious trouble.

He'd seen the carnage the Campendown had wrought in the waters off Shanghai the previous summer during the British armed suppression of yet another of the colony's ongoing rebellions. The vessel's main guns were huge cannons mounted in swiveling pillbox turrets fore and aft -- two guns to each turret, and both turrets were massively armored with new welded steel plate.

So they had been cozened after all! Well, he might have known, and he probably should have seen it coming -- they had been used as a pawn by the British Admiralty to take the treasure from the Spanish. Now, the dirty work done and the blame taken for the theft by Snakeskin's crew of freebooters, the Royal Navy aimed to turn the game around and take the king's ransom in Libyan plunder away from them and declare yet another brilliant victory over piracy on the high sees.

Well, perfidious Albion and lack of honor among thieves be damned -- Snakeskin pledged that there would someday be a payment exacted from the treacherous Arab whelp in Tripoli who had sold him the information, and a dear one at that, but this would have to come later. Those double-screwed, turbine powered, oil burning British warships were each as fast as the Courageous was, and they were crewed by the cream of Her Majesty's Royal Navy.

FIVE DEAD MEN

More than even that, the men-'o-war carried some of the best armament on the seven seas. The most formidable of these were her main battery guns, two of each positioned fore and aft, and both guns formidable three-inchers capable of rapidly hurling the Royal Navy's standard two-pounder shrapnel shells packed with high explosive Lyddite to strike targets at great distances with supremely good accuracy. Such cannons, Snakeskin well knew, had better than one third more the range of his own deck artillery. Three British warships combined stacked the odds heavily against the Courageous and her crew.

"They've spotted us, Skipper!" Jopling warned.

That this was the case was evident from the movements of the still distant vessels who appeared as dim silhouettes on the far horizon. The HMS Campendown and her two sister vessels were mirroring the course heading of the Courageous. And now a squall had come up with the characteristic suddenness of storms in this part of the Caribbean between the Windward Islands and the northern coastline of Venezuela.

Snakeskin threw on a slicker and buttoned it up against the worsening squall. The fog was thicker now than it had been at daybreak. A cold, driving rain was also falling over the sea, pattering down on the vessel's deck. It was just possible that Snakeskin could outrun the hostile crown warships.

Making rapid mental calculations, Snakeskin fixed his mind upon a hasty plan. Using the bad turn of the weather to his advantage, he would attempt to outmaneuver the oncoming British juggernauts. Unable to track him well enough through the enveloping fog, they would not dare risk using their cannon for fear of hitting one another with their fusillades.

Snakeskin would employ a series of evasive faints to south and west. All the while his real destination would lie north and eastward, in the many coves of the islands which made up the Antilles chain only a few hundred miles distant from the Courageous' present position on the now choppy waters of the Caribbean. If he could succeed in gaining enough distance from the British war vessels, he might lose them after the weather broke.

If they did not suspect his true destination, then Snakeskin might yet slip them completely. A narrow chance indeed, but the best and perhaps the only one that they stood at the moment.

FIVE DEAD MEN

6. Take It Or Leave It, Sir

Again, Snakeskin issued orders which called for all hands to refrain from speaking and smoking and to exercise care in moving about unnecessarily on the ship's decks. The promised dispensing of the dark wine of Oporto and the dark island rum of Port Au Prince would have to be put off as well, and Snakeskin was thankful that he had not permitted his crew to get blind, stinking drunk just yet, in which case his cause would certainly have already been as good as irrevocably lost.

In the dense fog, sound would be the means by which the Courageous' position could be betrayed to the ship's pursuers by the sea hunters. Even the slightest whisper or cough could carry for many miles from deck to deck under fog conditions on the open seas, on the currents of warm, humid air which transmitted sounds with uncanny efficiency.

As the helmsman steered the Courageous by compass, first tacking north for some twenty leagues, then steering suddenly hard to the west, Snakeskin listened carefully.

As his ears filtered the sounds made by the sea and those produced by the ship as its prow cleaved the waters, he was alert for any sign that might indicate the presence of the Campendown and the two other British ships of the line.

Snakeskin heard nothing, though.

The minutes became hours. In time the Courageous followed a course that would take her west of the Windwards toward safe anchorage in the island ports east of Barcelona and south of Barbados, such as St. Vincent and Tobago, that lie above Trinidad.

In the harbors of such places, and in secret coves and dockside warrens known to desperate and often hunted men such as he himself, Snakeskin could count on the help of men reliable enough when sufficient gold doubloons crossed their eager palms.

The sudden squall had already died down, the rain having completely ceased its steady falling now. The fog was lifting too as the rays of the returning tropical sun began to grow strong enough to begin to burn it off.

Soon the fog was gone completely and they traversed the ocean beneath a clear blue sky. From his high perch, the lookout scanned the horizon. There was no sign of any ships. They had lost them!

Within a matter of time the skeletal finger bones running north to south in a shallow arc above the Spanish coast were sighted from the port bow. The island chain marked the place where the Caribbean began to turn into the colder reaches of the broad Atlantic.

Snakeskin ordered that the Courageous make for the archipelago at full speed. He did not feel safe until the pirate vessel had swung into the Grenadines in the southern reaches of the Windwards, and then again around the leeward side of St. Vincent and was hidden within the protection of a wave-swept limestone cove a little east of the buccaneer's haven of Kingstown, the island's capital, main port of call, and site of a certain tavern whose keeper could be trusted, up to a point, and once his payment terms were met.

FIVE DEAD MEN

■

That night, the men celebrated. Feral goats that ran wild over the crags of the island had been caught and campfires had been lit. The promised rum and Portuguese wine from the Alonso de Palensia's casks now flowed plentifully, salted pork and biscuit and great wheels of cheese were eaten with the hunger of men accustomed to meager rations as the raider's crew played on musical instruments and caroused drunkenly on the beach of the deserted island.

But unlike his crew Snakeskin was in a sanguine mood. The brush with the Royal Navy's ships of the line had left him shaken. An odd sensation of foreboding had taken hold of him, and it was one that he could not seem to shake off, try as he might.

It was a feeling that his rational mind could not explain, but that his instincts felt with a deep and powerful intensity. Something was amiss. Why had not the men-'o-war followed them? Their escape, even with the explanation of luck in their favor, had been far too easy a thing which could as little be attributable to skill as to fortune.

Suddenly the sharp-eyed sailor whom Snakeskin had posted as lookout on the first watch of the night sounded a warning.

"Lights on the sea!" his cry split the cold night air. "I make them as two ships proceeding directly toward us from north northwest!"

Indeed, there were lights on the sea, coldly aglow in the black distance.

"They've stopped dead, Cap'n," was the next report, made within minutes of the first sighting, nor did the situation alter in the least as the minutes became the better part of an hour. And then the lights began to flash from far out at sea. They flashed rhythmically in a cadence recognizable as International Morse Code.

It was the Campendown, signaling its intention to conduct a parley.

They had not escaped their pursuers after all. Snakeskin ordered an acknowledgment and acceptance to be flashed back to Her Majesty's warships in return.

■

The captain of the Courageous stood on the small island's wind-whipped strip of crescent beach watching the longboats being rowed ashore by uniformed seamen.

In the double circle of his binocular field of view, beneath the silver light of a full moon, he saw the bright red coats and the three-cornered cockaded hats of the British ratings who manned the oars. Perched at the head of the boat was a dour-faced periwigged officer who sat stiffly and whose eyes appeared to stare fixedly on the beach ahead of him.

Swinging the spyglasses to the left, Snakeskin now swept his gaze across the three British warships that were anchored at sea some distance from the island's beach line. He could see that their cannon had been turned and aimed toward the island, a deliberate gesture no doubt intended to intimidate with an overwhelming show of potential might.

Under the circumstances, the threat was clear enough. There was no chance of escape, not even time to weigh anchor, Snakeskin knew. The Royal Navy had them under their guns, trapped like cornered bilge rats.

Nevertheless, something was odd. The Morse code had not spelled out an order to surrender. Instead it had indicated an offer to parley on the part of the captain of the HMS Campendown. What sort of gambit were they playing and what aims did they intend to pursue?

FIVE DEAD MEN

Snakeskin feared a trap but saw little choice but to let the British play out their hand.

In the meantime, his crew of privateers had taken up defensive positions amid the craggy landscape of the island. Through the sights of their breech-loading Remington rifles, they could hit any point on the beach with sustained and generally accurate small arms fire. Any hostile act on the part of members of the landing party would result in their being instantly cut down to a man.

Snakeskin was under no illusions that this would have any lasting effect on the ultimate fate of his crew, however. With their three inch barrage guns, the men-'o-war lying offshore could pepper the beach with grapeshot, spreading terrible carnage. Snakeskin's men would not stand a chance, do whatever they might.

The Courageous was anchored offshore and could turn her own formidable panoply of turreted cannonry and Gatling machineguns on the three ships of the line, but she was outnumbered as well as outgunned, and Snakeskin had no illusions that she would not be sunk in the end by a cannonade across her side.

Still he waited and watched. For the present, it was all that Snakeskin could do.

The British marines pulled the longboats out of the sea, beached them on the sands, and came ashore. Under the watchful eyes of Snakeskin's men, their leader walked toward him.

The epaulettes on his shoulders bore the insignia of a commodore. He did not smile as he approached.

"Am I in the presence of the American privateer Mr. Timothy 'Snakeskin' Blake?" he asked.

Snakeskin nodded.

"Then I shall be brief," he went on dourly. "I am Commodore Ishmael Marks. Her Majesty the Queen has issued instructions that you be informed that your services are required in a somewhat delicate affair of state -- with, I might add, the approval, if tacit, of your own government and its Department of the Navy. If you consent, certain concessions are possible for you ... And your, well, your rather foul-looking cutthroat crew."

"Spell it out, if you please," Snakeskin replied.

"Is there somewhere we can talk privately, sir?" Commodore Marks asked.

Snakeskin indicated the mouth of a small limestone cavern which overlooked the beachhead. The periwigged naval officer nodded his assent and he and the Royal Marine walked toward it, while Snakeskin's men covered every step with their Remingtons.

"Now say your piece," Snakeskin told the officer who had come ashore.

Commodore Marks sat down on a rock and fanned himself with his hat.

"Been a damnable hot day, hasn't it?" he began, before relating to Snakeskin the entire story of the Sultan's problems with his British mistress -- her kidnapping from the souk of Stone Town as well as the potentially serious political repercussions of the Mahdi's brazen act of terrorism -- and what was expected of Snakeskin, should he agree to the terms of ... if not surrender then, as Marks put it, perhaps more accurately ... a pact of mutual assistance.

"I want more than a royal pardon from you British," Snakeskin said at the end. "The United States will have to agree to the same. We've played a double game too long. Officially, we're still rogues, and subject to summary trial and death by hanging in any dozen ports of call."

FIVE DEAD MEN

"We have assurances to that effect from your Secretary of the Navy, Mr. William Chandler," the Royal Marine replied. "It's all in these documents I've brought with me."

He produced them from a leather dispatch case that hung from his waist.

Snakeskin took the dispatch case and carefully but quickly read through the documents. They seemed genuine enough, each of the papers bearing official seals and signed by the pens of high-ranking members of both respective governments.

"Possibly we might do business," Snakeskin said.

"Possibly, sir? Only 'possibly.' I remind you of everything I have said before. You shall have your pardon in full."

"And the booty we took from the Spanish merchantman ... what of it?"

"That we will have to, um, confiscate. I am sorry to say."

Snakeskin looked down at the papers, then he produced a lucifer and struck its phosphor head against the sole of his boot.

"Even knowing that you will surely be annihilated, sir? Even then?" asked Commodore Marks, somewhat astonished by Snakeskin's rashness.

Snakeskin merely held his stare.

"Very well then, the plunder too," he said. "You drive a hard bargain, Mr. Blake."

The Royal Marine stood up and made to leave. He turned and looked reflectively at Snakeskin for a long moment.

"Yet somehow I hadn't thought that you would have agreed quite so readily to the terms that were presented," he said. "Even with the full might of our guns trained upon you and even with two treasure chests of Libyan gold in your thieving hands."

Snakeskin smiled in response.

"In other circumstances," he said with a smile, "you would have been right."

"Oh, and why not now?"

"Let's say I have my reasons," was Snakeskin's reply, a moment before he turned away and, hands clasped behind his back, paced away from the beach and into the shadows, leaving Commodore Marks to carry his signed contract to the longboats beached beyond the creaming night surf.

BOOK TWO

GUNS
AGAINST
KHARTOUM

7. Brothers of the Gun

The passage of the buccaneer ship Courageous to the East African coast had progressed uneventfully. Both the caprices of nature and the violent stratagems and machinations of man seemed to have conspired to speed the Courageous' journey around the turbulent coastal seas of the Cape of Good Hope and into the more tranquil waters of the Atlantic which lay beyond that antipodal terra incognita that seasoned mariners often called "land's end."

As it turned out to be, the crossing of the African cape was favorable. The prevailing winds were unexpectedly fair and the seas were unusually becalmed for the season. And -- whether or not this was due to the acceptance by Snakeskin of the British emissary's terms -- there were no warships sighted while en route to the Courageous' destination.

In the space of a fortnight, the shores of Zanzibar were sighted, lying hard off the Courageous's port bows. Through the magnifying lenses of military binoculars trained on the coast could now be seen the glimmer of white-washed adobe structures crowding the bluffs and palisades above the shore and date palm trees growing above the sparkling volcanic beaches of the main island.

FIVE DEAD MEN

For Zanzibar was in fact an archipelago, a group of islands lying north of the dry coast of Dar es Salaam in the upper latitudes of the Indian Ocean. The archipelago was dominated by two large islands, Unguja -- the largest of the two -- and Pemba, in whose mountainous jungles grew the rare trees that since time immemorial had made sailors call them the Spice Islands. It was on the shores of Unguja, whose name in Arabic meant "Coast of Blacks," that Zanzibar City was founded, and made its name synonymous with that of the island on which it stood.

A city had been on Zanzibar for a thousand years. It stood there when the ancient Persians had made it their trading port between Africa and the Middle East, just as the Portuguese traders who had come long after them had done. Zanzibar's early sultans were black-skinned Africans, and its structures little more than fragile huts.

In 1832 Said Bin Sultan, who held title to the ancient throne of Zanzibar, moved his retinue from Muscat to Unguja. He soon died, and his two sons quarreled over rights of succession, but the British, within whose sprawling African empire Zanzibar lay, upheld the rights of Majid Bin Said as Sultan, and it was to Majid that Snakeskin Blake and his pirates had been summoned to lend their aid.

The brothers' quarrel had not been over nothing, but over much. The throne of the Sultan of Zanzibar bequeathed upon its potentate a host of perquisites. His ancestral dominions in East Africa ranged from the coast across the straits, known anciently as the realms of Zanj and which included Mombasa, Dar es Salaam, and the sprawling skein of desert caravan routes extending into the African interior for many hundreds, and perhaps even thousands, of miles, such as the route leading to Kindu on the Congo River, and from

Mozambique to old Kipini in what long afterward became Kenya.

Here were lands abounding in ivory, in trade of camels, in cloves, nutmeg and other spices, and lastly, in the traffic of slaves, which passed through Zanzibar's main port, called Malindi.

Eager to make landfall after months spent at sea, and eager to sample the many delights which the narrow, twisting streets behind Malindi port were justly famous throughout the world for having in abundance, the crew of the Courageous crowded the gunwales as the helmsman steered the privateer raider into the harbor through the shoals of niggerheads marked on his map.

It was a harbor filled with a varied assortment of vessels large and small, of every shape and size conceivable, from humble native skiffs to square-riggers of American merchant vessels.

Beyond Malindi harbor lay the quayside. It too teemed with activity as shopkeepers set up their stalls in the relative coolness of the sun-drenched morning. Beyond the quay there stood row upon row, tier upon tier, of whitewashed buildings of baked clay linked by narrow cobbled alleys that meandered between them without any apparent plan.

Zanzibar was a free town, a haven for men of all political persuasions and countries of origin, and the seaport of Malindi teemed with opportunities for sailors far from their homes to lose themselves in the heady exhilarations of flesh, and rum, and opium and the drugs called majoon and kief that were supplied in the dens, where some men entered but from which others never emerged again into the light of day.

Here too were found Dervishes who followed the path of the *Hashishim* -- the ancient order of assassins trained to kill silently with poison, knife, dart and gun which had sprung up in the days of the Crusaders. Though Dervishes of Zanzibar were secretive and their gathering places little known, their eyes and ears were everywhere, and what they saw and heard would surely be known by the Mahdi within a very short time, or to an overlord of the Sahel almost equally powerful - - the notorious Arab slave trader and pillager Tippu Tib, a name which all men who were truly among the wise were careful to speak only in whispers.

Snakeskin knew that the Sultan of Zanzibar, though a devout Muslim, tolerated commerce of all kinds and turned a blind eye to the indulgence in drink and fornication by the Infidels and Franks who ventured onto his sub-equatorial domain.

In addition to this, Zanzibar's location was far enough removed from the far-reaching jurisdiction of the British on the African mainland to escape the watchful eye of the Queen's administrators who, in their own ways, were as strict in their condemnation of certain practices beloved of oceangoing thieves, cutthroats and worse as they were to any loyal follower of the Prophet.

The net result of this happy conjunction of events was that anything whatever could be had for a price in Zanzibar, and any vice which was not for sale on the small island was a vice not yet practiced on the face of the earth.

With a well-armed skeleton crew chosen by lot left onboard the Courageous to guard her from the curious and the thieving, the bulk of the raider's deck hands noisily debarked the ship. Eager to tread solid ground after a long time spent negotiating rolling deck planks, the crew quickly spread out through the quay, as Arab beggars clothed from head to foot in tattered *jibbas* descended upon them, merchants hawked their wares, prostitutes bared breasts pierced with tawny rings of gold through the ends of long, black nipples, and fortune tellers offered to peer into their futures for a few mere pieces of copper.

"Behold, thou of broad shoulders, and smell the moist promise wafting from Alanna's warm thighs."

Snakeskin was inspecting some gaudy colored trinkets in a street seller's wares-crowded stall. Idly he cast glances at a snake charmer coaxing the head of a king cobra from a wicker basket to the exotic strains of a native bassoon.

"This perfume guards the wild honey of Alanna's she-ness," she went on, "but it will part its wings before the might of thy staff, oh bold one."

Snakeskin smiled at the girl, whose face was veiled but whose breasts hung bared from the filmy gauze of her costume. He fingered the golden ring dangling from one hard nipple.

"You may cost more than I can spend."

"For thee, oh bold adventurer, Alanna will give pleasures of heaven for next to nothing."

She guided his hand to the cleft between her thighs.

"Touch the place of sweetness, giant one," she said, her breath in his ear. "See how I am intact. I will climax as one with you."

Snakeskin was surprised that her clitoris was truly intact. Female circumcision was a universal practice in these Muslim lands, and it was rare for a street prostitute to have avoided the slash of the knife intended to steal lifelong pleasure from women of the Sahel so they would better serve the men who were their masters from birth and produce an ever-increasing family from their numbed loins.

It was then that he felt the cold pressure of the knife that Alanna held in the hand that had caressed the nape of his neck as she drew close with parted lips.

FIVE DEAD MEN

"Closer, bold one. Thou shall know -- "

Before Alanna spoke the word "death" and the knife could sever his jugular with the swiftness of a striking cobra, Snakeskin grabbed the girl's hand and twisted the wrist hard. As the bones snapped he saw the flash of the long, sharp knife of the Hashishim fall to the dusty earth.

The snake charmer reached into his basket and grasped the cobra by the throat. He advanced on Snakeskin holding the spitting angered serpent whose fangs dripped clear poison and pushed the snake's yawning mouth at Snakeskin. The old man, certainly another Dervish allied with the Hashishim, smiled malevolently, baring broken teeth blackened from a lifetime of chewing the potent stimulant herb *khatt*, and muttering a strange ululating cry that sounded like, "Alleeyammuu, malleeyammu, mallleeeyammmu, alleeyammmuu!"

As Snakeskin grabbed a large, potbellied clay jug by the handle and swung it savagely at the snake charmer -- caving in the front of his face and sending him crashing into the jug-seller's stall with a scream as the cobra sunk its fangs into his groin -- the American felt the wind made by a thrown dagger as it whistled past his ear.

The dagger struck one of the pillars in the bazaar used to hold up tents and its razor tip bit hard into the soft stucco facing. Scant inches from Snakeskin's head, the assassin's knife buzzed like an angry hornet, its hilt wagging back and forth like the clucking tongue of a mocking devil.

He saw now that a group of native cutthroats were facing him. Snakeskin recognized these men as Dervishes; they were either the fanatical followers of the Sudanese warlord calling himself the Mahdi, or the Expected One of Koranic prophesy, or of Tippu Tib. Either way that added up to their being Hashishim, and dangerous men skilled in the arts of dealing death.

Each of the Dervishes brandished long knives with curved blades called *janbiyas* that they'd drawn from their belts. They wore the brightly patched robes called *jibbas*, a motley whose patterns marked them out as followers of Tippu Tib. Moreover, they were mostly black-skinned Sudanese, known to be most prevalent among the followers of Tippu Tib.

Yet at the same time Snakeskin noticed the black leather pouches depending on leather thongs from the necks of several of the Dervishes. Those pouches, he knew, marked the killers as Mahdists, for they contained small books of the Mahdi's teachings that had been printed in Cairo and were revered by the Mahdi's followers. Following each morning's prayers the Dervishes kissed their amulets and studied their master's teachings. Then they sharpened their knives and began the chewing of *khatt* to sharpen their appetite and wet their lust for bloodshed.

The largest of Snakeskin's assailants, a tall Sudanese in a wine-colored *jibba* and a black turban whose cloth tassels were tied to conceal the lower half of his long face, now took a step forward.

The killer's lips moved beneath the black cloth as he kissed the small black talisman containing the Mahdi's wisdom. Then, tucking his treasured amulet back into the folds of his *jibba*, the assassin approached his intended victim with open menace, a cruel smile obvious beneath the concealing cloth.

The janbiya clutched in his hand swung back and forth, its wickedly honed cutting edge describing a glittering, deadly arc. Through a broad grin, teeth stained black from chewing the intoxicant known as *khatt* shone dully and malevolently.

Snakeskin sidestepped the quick, deadly knife swing as he took a fighting stance learned in Peking, one belonging to an unarmed combat discipline called Wu-Shu by its practitioners in China but elsewhere known as Kung-Fu. Snakeskin's outstretched right hand formed one of the eight-trigram palm boxing figures, a claw-like bending of fingers. Within seconds, Snakeskin had ripped into the face of his assailant who was struck before he knew what had happened.

The Dervish shrieked an Arabic oath and his knife fell from nerveless fingers into the dirt at his feet, as his momentum sent him catapulting into the cart of the merchant behind Snakeskin. Pots and pans clattered and earthenware jugs and dishes crashed to the ground as the merchant's cart behind Snakeskin overturned, spilling its many wares all over the fallen Dervish's prostrate body.

The Hashishim backing up the first assassin moved in tandem, neither of them wanting to risk taking on the foreigner who had bested his attacker with such speed and apparent ease.

The boldest among these now swung a long, curved scimitar called *muhaddab* by the Arabs, *talwar* by Indians and *kilij* by Turks. The type of saber was favored for its light weight and thin-edged blade which could be honed to razor sharpness. It was a weapon made for slashing and cutting, and in skilled hands the *muhaddab* could easily slice off an arm at the shoulder, a hand at the wrist or sever the head from the base of the neck with a single stroke. Indeed, an ancient tale held that a warrior had once slain a tiger with a single blow of such a sword as that which Snakeskin now faced.

Shouting curses, the Dervish armed with the saber strode forward, while a somewhat less bold comrade stood off to one side, brandishing a long-handled Sudanese hunting spear with a bronze cutting edge, feinting jabs and shouting curses at the Frank while keeping a safe distance.

Snakeskin picked up a wooden barrel beside him just as the more dangerous Hashishim who wielded the *muhaddab*, whirled, pivoted on one leg, and swung the weapon at throat level in a decapitation strike.

Instead of lopping off Snakeskin's head, the scimitar's blade bit into the wood of the barrel, shattering it, and catching in its staves, to become covered in the thick, fragrant honey of wild African bees it contained. As a brief tug of war ensued between Snakeskin and the Hashishim, who desperately tried to free the honey-dipped blade while getting covered himself in the viscous fluid that gushed from the cask, the more timid spear-wielding Dervish made a sloppy rush with the spear.

Snakeskin used the power of his arms and the momentum of the saber-armed Dervish to propel the swordsman into the path of the spear at the moment it was thrust forward again by the timid Dervish. His eyes widening in sudden agonizing pain as the spear's blade was thrust deep into his kidneys to emerge from a bleeding red hole in his lower abdomen, the swordsman lost his balance and sagged on buckling knees, covered in bee honey and arterial blood.

Snakeskin used the instants of indecision while the timid Dervish pulled his bloody and now broken spear from the back of his comrade's torso to bash the barrel and its dregs of honey hard into the top of his turbaned head. The impact produced a satisfying carrot-snap of breaking neck cartilage. Snakeskin finished the timid Dervish with a boot to the gonads, the steel-sheathed toe tip catching the assassin squarely in the midsection, sending him crashing to the ground, his groin crushed.

A final Dervish armed with a dagger lunged at Snakeskin with a wild scream of rage and hatred escaping his lips. The lunge was undisciplined and easily parried, and Snakeskin caught the outstretched arm of the knife-wielder with a simple movement of his own arms. Once the arm was scissor-gripped between Snakeskin's forearms, pressure broke it with a sharp snap.

The Dervish's arm swung limply as a side kick sent Snakeskin's final attacker thudding head-first into another merchant's cart. The rest of the group of Hashishim feinted with their weapons, but they were faint-hearted runts who had hung back from the fight, and their halfhearted tactics meant nothing. A moment or two passed as they looked sheepishly at one another and backed off, turning and running at the sound of police whistles.

By now Jopling and the rest of the crew had been alerted by the commotion. From all corners of the bazaar they came running, having drawn their Colt repeating pistols. Brandishing the guns, the Courageous' hands rushed up to Snakeskin's defense, shoving their way through the thick crowd clustered about the scene of the fight. Jopling was among the first of the crewmen to reach the Courageous' master.

"Thank God you're all right, Cap'n," Jopling said to Snakeskin. He looked around him at the three Dervishes who had fallen in the attack. "Who do you think they are?"

"Assassins," Snakeskin replied right away. "Sent by their reputed Mahdi, no doubt, and possibly by way of the warlord Tippu Tib. Both have a legion of spies and cut-throats in Zanzibar, and elsewhere too."

"Madhi?" Jopling asked. "What in blazes is that?"

"Simply put, it's trouble," was Snakeskin's curt reply, "especially if it's us they have an interest in. But you'll know all you need concerning the Mahdi soon enough, I can guarantee that."

Just then, another pair of newcomers broke through the jammed mob marketplace crowd which was now seized by a wild commotion. These men were wearing the tan uniforms of the Sultan's royal police force. The crowd was now angry. Shopkeepers whose wares had been destroyed and stalls overturned were throwing stones at the Infidels who they believed to have started the trouble. Market women joined in too, and as stones began to strike native Zanzibarians, the melee began to turn ugly.

The police, a mix of black Sudanese and Arabs, had been trained by the British controlled Khedive of Egypt's military in brutal tactics of crowd control that had been developed during over two hundred years of the British Raj in India and transplanted to North Africa and the Middle East. The Sultan's police were not only well-trained, they were also well-armed, with Gatling guns and repeating rifles.

Their initial tactic was to cow the crowd by lashing out with cudgels of hard ebony called *curbashes* by the native population, smashing at heads with the butts of their Enfield rifles, and using fists and kicks when all else failed. Fortunately for the crowd, the beating they suffered, savage as it was, was sufficient to push them to the fringes of the marketplace and send them scattering. Had they not done so, the police would have quickly switched from gun butts to gun barrels, and hundreds could have fallen bloodied to bursts from the Gatling machineguns that were already being trundled into position.

With the bazaar now cleared, the new arrivals inspected the scene, quickly assessing what had taken place. Members of the now considerably thinned crowd were talking to them in Arabic and a mixture of other tongues, all of them gesturing and pointing at Snakeskin, Jopling and the other crewmen in the area.

"It appears that you have met with some difficulties," one of the policemen, a Sudanese with ritually scarified cheeks, said to Snakeskin in British-accented English. "You know these men, perhaps?" He meant the bodies of the Hashishim lying bloodied at their feet.

"I've never cast eyes on any of them before," Snakeskin replied.

"I see," the constable told him, raising an eyebrow. "They are scum that Tippu Tib has sent."

He gestured to a subordinate who stooped and lifted a corner of the saber-armed Hashishi's bloody *jibba*, exposing a tattoo or tong sign prominently visible on the upper calf.

"Tippu Tib's men are tattooed just as this one is. The rest of them too."

"Thank you, constable," Snakeskin said. "You've arrived just in time. That crowd was in an extremely ugly mood."

"In any case, *siddi*, you'll have to come with me in order to answer some questions."

"I don't think so," Snakeskin replied. "I have an appointment with the Sultan."

"Really."

The police constable lifted an eyebrow.

"Take a look at this."

Snakeskin removed the *firman*, an official document detailing his mission to the Sultan, from his dispatch case and showed it to the constable. The constable's expression instantly changed from one of arrogant condescension to a look of complete servility in a matter of seconds.

"I am sorry to have troubled you, *siddi*," the policeman replied, now giving true emphasis to the local term of supreme respect he had applied with mere professional courtesy before. "I will personally escort you to the palace of his most revered Excellency."

With a toadying bow, the constable and his men ushered Snakeskin from the marketplace as the crowd sullenly watched and muttered darkly.

8. His Excellency Greets His Guests

His royal Excellency Majid bin Said, Sultan of Zanzibar, reclined his ample bulk on a throne of incredible splendor. It had been fashioned of solid gold applied densely to a wrought iron frame by the famed Parisian house of Cartier at its headquarters on the Rue de la Paix, a firm rapidly becoming a legend even among the renowned jewelers of France.

Its creators had, however, been sworn to secrecy (and well paid to keep their silence), as the amount of smelted gold into which the iron frame of the throne had been dipped to coat it had been sufficient to bankrupt the treasury of France and would have raised an international scandal had the truth come out. Beyond even this, there was the fact that its two golden arms and four golden legs were encrusted with emeralds, rubies and an assortment of other precious gemstones to boot.

Just behind the dais, which supported the throne, a large mural covered the rear wall of the chamber. It depicted scenes from the holy Koran, many of which graphically illuminated scenes foretelling the pleasures that believers would enjoy in Paradise at the hands of beautiful houris who plied them with sweet wine and luscious fruits dipped in honey as they enjoyed their eternal reward for adhering to the faith of his ancestors.

FIVE DEAD MEN

The Sultan's raiment was every bit as splendid as the decorations which adorned his royal throne room. He wore a robe of silk brocade which flowed down to his feet -- feet which were shod in sandals of rich gold brocade with curling upturned tips adorned with little iron bells at the toes that jingled whenever he moved his pudgy feet.

Rings adorned each of his fingers, flashing and glittering beneath the pale but even light cast by gas lamps projecting from the walls. The turban that was wrapped in artfully mantled folds around the skullcap on his head was woven of gleaming yellow silk, the silk windings fastened together just above the forehead with one of the largest star sapphires that Snakeskin (or any living man, for that matter) had ever beheld.

"So you are the American whom the famous Pasha Gordon has sent to assist me in my time of need?" the Sultan declaimed to his guest in flawless English -- a language learned in childhood from English tutors sent from Egypt by Lord Charles Canning, Queen's Viceroy and Governor General of India, and of immense power and prestige amongst the British Empire's colonial possessions in the region.

"If the situation outlined is in fact as stated, then, yes, I think I can be of some assistance to your Excellency," Snakeskin replied.

"Reports that have come to me indicate that you displayed a great deal of courage and martial prowess against the accursed sons of dogs who attacked you in the marketplace," the Sultan went on. "I am frankly amazed that you dispatched a brace of Tippu Tib's strapping rogues wielding knives and swords with such apparent ease -- rogues intoxicated by hashish, no doubt."

"It wouldn't happen to have been some sort of test, by any chance, would it?" Snakeskin asked, now suspicious. Had it been Tippu Tib, or the Mahdi for that matter, or an attack orchestrated by the Sultan himself?

"I can assure you that your assailants were not sent by myself," the Sultan returned with an ease that somehow had a suspect ring to it. "Undoubtedly they were the Mahdi's agents, dispatched by that dog of a robber Tippu Tib. I am afraid I must inform you that you may now consider yourself officially marked for assassination by the Sudanese fanatic and Tippu's *Hashishim*."

"That I would consider an occupational hazard, all things considered," Snakeskin replied. "Besides, it would not the first time. During my service in China during the Opium Wars there was a five hundred dollar price on my head payable in Portuguese gold pieces of eight. I don't need to add that nobody ever collected a cent of that bounty."

"May Allah in his infinite wisdom and mercy continue to bestow his blessings and protection upon you, Mr. Blake," the Sultan replied with a laugh.

Then he directed a question to the tall Gurkha standing beside them. "Jahno," he said. "What do you make of Mr. Blake's martial skills? Be honest, now."

"If your Majesty will permit me to say so…" the Gurkha replied with a scowl on his dark and moonlike face (which like the moon itself bore craters, scars and other marks resulting from a lifetime of collisions with hurtling and often sharp objects) "…Mr. Blake's success owed as much to luck as it did to skill, to say nothing of the martial deficiencies of his adversaries. Prevailing in a contest against such rabble is one thing…"

Jahno now glared hard at Snakeskin through gleaming black eyes before finishing his reply.

81

FIVE DEAD MEN

"...But against fighters who are truly skilled in the deadly arts, surely it is another matter entirely."

"Well, then, Mr. Blake," the Sultan replied with clear amusement outlined on his doughy features and shining doll's eyes. "It would seem that not everyone here is as impressed with your martial prowess as am I." The Sultan's eyes vanished beneath fleshy brown hoods for a moment, and then he continued, "Might I suggest a contest between yourself and Jahno so that I may judge your skills as a fighter for myself at first hand?"

"You need only name the time and place," Snakeskin agreed without a moment's pause.

"Splendid," answered Majid bin Said, clapping his fleshy hands together in open merriment, the gems flashing green, amber and red on his short, pudgy fingers. "Tomorrow, then. In any case, you are now a guest in my palace. A feast is already being prepared in your honor."

Snakeskin saw the emotionless shark eyes of the Gurkha watching him coldly as he was escorted from the throne room toward his quarters elsewhere in the palace complex. It was impossible to read what was in them, but envy was certainly chief among those on Snakeskin's list.

9. A Sumptuous Feast for Her Majesty's Pirates

On the night of Snakeskin's arrival in Zanzibar, the Sultan arranged a sumptuous celebration. Victuals from every corner of the island and the African mainland lying less than twenty miles across the straits from Stone Town had been sent for to provide the makings of a feast.

Sturgeon pulled from the coastal waters of East Africa and still smelling of sea brine, dates and pomegranates swollen huge and swimming in the finest honey in the realm, as well as the strong dark wine distilled from elderberries known to Zanzibarians as Clarissa (who were said to relish its heady powers and rare bouquet so fervently that men had been killed for a single draft of it), had been gathered for the feast, as well as the finest *kief* and hashish to fill the hookahs and pipes of the many guests in attendance at the fete.

As the Sultan's honored guest, Snakeskin had found himself the recipient of a panoply of gifts, which by custom he was as honor-bound to accept with due display of gratitude as his host was obligated by sacred custom to offer his demurrals and his humblest apologies for their poor quality and inferior workmanship.

As he returned from a walk about the ramparts of the Sultan's palace early one morning, Snakeskin discovered a new set of clothes hanging in the closet of his rooms.

There were a number of the long, flowing caftans. The *jibbas* were ornately patched with cunningly woven embroidery, the dyed cloth interlaced with gleaming threads of spun gold. A stout pair of leather boots and a wide belt with an iron buckle went with the *jibbas*, as well as several fezzes.

Snakeskin also found the makings of ornate turbans: embroidered skullcaps about which an assortment of ornamentally patterned scarves could be wound and pinned together with jewel-encrusted clasps to make the traditional headdresses.

But by far the most beautiful gift of all was the one Snakeskin found lying on his bed. The boxes of artfully inlaid sandalwood, each one larger than the other nested within, opened to reveal the objects that would complete Snakeskin's sartorial transformation.

And nestled within a scabbard of black leather that still smelled of the cobbler's oils there was a newly forged *muhaddab*, its curved blade of tempered steel etched with flowing Arabic script offering blessings to the sword's owner and curses upon his enemies destined to fall before its vicious sharpness.

Lifting the sword by its hilt, Snakeskin held up the weapon and watched the sunlight glinting off the blade as he turned it this way and that, feeling the weight and balance of the edged weapon.

Laying the sword aside for the moment, he next opened the smaller box. Within this one there was a fine specimen of the curved dagger called the *janbiya* which was worn by all adult males as a symbol of masculinity. With pride, Snakeskin slid it back into its sheath and went to put on the *jibba*.

■

"My dear Snakeskin, dressed as you are you look more like a Sultan than I myself," the Sultan remarked that evening.

As his guest of honor, Snakeskin was seated at the Sultan's right hand as they reclined on sheepskins heaped upon Persian rugs scattered across a marble floor tessellated with bits of stone and many-colored glass that stretched across the vast dining hall of the palace.

Behind them, ranked row upon row in token of the places they occupied in the palace pecking order, were the other court retainers, followed by their servants, slaves and concubines. None in the central portion of the large room, except for the servants who bustled around carrying delicacies on trays of chased silver, and the dancing girls who would come later to entertain the celebrants in the privacy of their rooms, were women.

But this was Zanzibar and customs were considerably different than those that prevailed at the court of Muscat, Oman where Majid bin Said's forebears had ruled. Women squatted on the periphery. Attired in gauzy harem costumes which revealed their breasts, their arms and fingers adorned with trinkets, their noses, ears and nipples pierced by rings cunningly wrought by skilled jewelers, the gates of their vaginas guarded by large, gleaming pearls, their lissome bodies perfumed and their black hair quaffed to perfection, the women of the palace squatted in comfort, puffing on the hubble-bubble pipes laced with *kief* and chattering amongst themselves about which of the men they would later choose to share their quarters for the night.

The festivities soon commenced, and Snakeskin joined the Sultan in puffing on the hookah, an art he had mastered in China years before where such smoking contrivances were also commonplace, though found in somewhat different form. Here the water-cooled hubble-bubble pipe was commonly called the Sheesha, and its fragrant tobacco mixture customarily laced with the intoxicating resin of the hemp plant known locally as *kief* or *majoon.*

Snakeskin found the Sultan to be both an amiable and knowledgeable host, and despite the differences of culture, geography and religion that set them apart, he soon found himself to harbor a genuine affection and regard for the hereditary ruler of Zanzibar. There were bonds of kinship, impossible to understand, intangible, yet bonds nonetheless, that transcended personal history and the whims of culture. In Majid bin Said, Snakeskin knew he had found a brother spirit.

Others in the room, however, were not of the same opinion regarding Snakeskin. In their hating eyes he represented the eternal foe.

The Mahdi's reach was long, stretching across the vast African deserts of the Sudan, and even into the palace of the Sultan itself on his island hundreds of miles away. Even as Snakeskin enjoyed the fragrant, kief-laced smoke of the water pipe with the Sultan, and traded opinions on the charms of some of the women at the feast, other eyes full of cold malice were trained directly upon him.

"Allah is merciful," the man with the rodent's face stage-whispered to the Occidental gentleman whose leonine features set him apart from the swarthier, darker peoples indigenous to the region.

"The Great One delivers the Infidel into our hands. A drip of poison in his wine cup --" he made a dismissive gesture with one hand, "-- and the foul, leprous dog troubles us no more."

"I should think not, Hassan," the foreigner answered, his clipped accent marking him as a Britisher, its cadence indicating formative years spent at the Royal Military Academy at Sandhurst and an hereditary membership amidst the ranks of the British upper classes.

"It would be best to postpone our mutual enemy's demise until a later time I should think."

"But why not, siddi?" asked Hassan, disappointment and distrust clear in the tone of his voice. "Has not the great Mahdi, blessed be his name, charged us with killing this befouled, urine-dripping dog of an Infidel at the first available opportunity? Let us do it now and be gone from this accursed house of sin and vile corruption. See you the women here? They are surely accursed as whores."

"You are forgetting, Hassan," the Britisher dryly remarked, "that it was *I* and not *you* whom the Mahdi entrusted with the specifics of carrying out our assignment. You, then, are nought but my bootlicking slave and my craven footstool and you live only to carry out my will. Challenge my authority again and I shall cut off your dog's penis and toss it into a box filled with hungry locusts and cockroaches to sport with as they like."

"Yes, effendi," Hassan replied, now thoroughly cowed by the blue-eyed foreigner's words which he knew from past observations were not mere bluff, "I will do as you ask. But surely we will strike soon, will we not, siddi?"

"All in the fullness of time, my good fellow," replied the Britisher, whose Christian name was Sir Montague Strawplait, but who, on his secret conversion to the Mahdist cause, had adopted the name Ghazawan el Safiy-Allah al Madiya (which roughly translated to the grandiloquent, "Allah's Chosen One, Companion of the Prophet and Warrior of the Mahdiya"). "All in the fullness of time. Of that, my dear Hassan, you may firmly rest assured."

Strawplait smiled as he accepted a delicate morsel from the perfumed fingers of a palace concubine named Aroush, which meant "Angel of Paradise."

Although he thought her face was more like a dog's than an angel's, her mouth was large and her lips full and ripe. He marked her down for later, when, tightly clutching her long black hair, he would repeatedly mash Aroush's mouth against the hard pole of flesh that had begun jutting from his robes at the sight of her ample bosoms thinly veiled beneath nearly transparent purple gossamer.

∎

The great festivities continued apace, and the victuals went burning hot from the serving trays of well-wrought silver chased by artisans with inscriptions from the Koran in flowing script into the expanding bellies of the celebrants, while the pungent odors of hashish and fragrant *kief* quickly began to fill the air with great gray-brown clouds. Soon the dancing girls in revealing *bedlah* costumes fringed with jingling Arab coins came out to entertain the Sultan's guests.

As the first belly dancers began to undulate coquettishly in the shimmying, breast-heaving, hip-tossing *Raqs Sharqi* style to the music of drums and snake charmers' flutes played by the Sultan's personal musicians -- the same ones who regularly entertained him in a private chamber of his Turkish bathhouse -- the Sultan extolled the many talents and accomplishments of the dancers.

"All of these fetching creatures, upon whom all-merciful Allah in his great and infinite wisdom has bestowed an astonishing bounty of earthly beauty and heavenly grace, are my wives," the Sultan announced with pride to Snakeskin Blake who sat beside him.

"Informed of your visit, they have been practicing for this night for many weeks. See how beautifully and gracefully these women cavort. Verily, my good Snakeskin, they are like the houris of Paradise come down to earth to sweeten the hearts of living men and give them a foretaste of even greater delights that await them in *Behesht Zahra*, which is what we call our heavenly paradise."

"You must be a happy man," Snakeskin replied, his eyes fixed on one of the dancers in particular as the scantily attired women whirled about the floor, cymbals clacking tinnily in their fingers, firm breasts and rounded buttocks gyrating to the hypnotic beat of the music.

"Especially if that lovely creature in the center, there is one of your harem girls."

"Ah, I see you are a man of discriminating tastes," the Sultan replied to Snakeskin with a laugh that made his ample belly jiggle like pudding as he noted the woman that Snakeskin had picked out.

"Her name is Alika, which simply means 'love' in Arabic. She is new to my *haram*. There is much fire in that one, my good Snakeskin. And she is an able learner, well schooled by my eunuch Achmed in bringing delight to her master."

"Yes, I well believe you," Snakeskin replied, watching Alika launch her lissome body into the voluptuous undulating movements of her shimmying dance while flexing and relaxing her abdominal muscles and thrusting out her breasts.

"Watch her swaying breasts," advised the Sultan, "for she is a master of the art of moving them about for us to relish with our gaze. See how nimbly she tosses them up and down and from side to side? It is, as we call it, like the movements which one experiences in riding a camel."

"One with two humps, I take it," Snakeskin quipped.

"Yes, precisely," said the Sultan. "Two humps. And the rider astride them, ravishing each moment of the journey until he finally comes to his destination. I see we think alike. Perhaps you will ride the camel tonight, my friend, and come to the same destination which I have reached many times. I, as your friend and host, can arrange this."

"I like to drive my camels hard," Snakeskin said.

"The harder the better, for the she-beast likes it best that way."

Snakeskin and the Sultan continued to watch enthralled as the large pink jewel set in Alika's navel sparkled in the lamp light while her nubile hips swayed to and fro to the hypnotically driving music. Her long, lustrous blue-black hair tossed this way and that as she tantalized the Sultan's guests with sensual movements of hips, breasts and shoulders, her tawny-brown face barely concealed behind a translucent silken veil of spun gold thread.

After a few moments, Alika's large, doe's eyes met Snakeskin's and she smiled coyly at the American. Dancing close to him, brushing lightly against him with hips and breasts, she clicked her small finger-cymbals in his face and then just as quickly whirled away amid a swirling flurry of colorful silken scarves, leaving a perfumed scent trail behind her.

"I think Alika has taken to you," the Sultan told Snakeskin with a broad smile. "This is good."

"Yes," replied Snakeskin. "If you'll forgive the pun, I can confidently say that 'I like her' already."

"Ah -- cleverly put," the Sultan answered, and good-naturedly slapped Snakeskin's knee. "Clever indeed, my friend."

Majid bin Said had made up his mind then and there that he would give this precious treasure to him to do with what he pleased, as befitted an honored guest in his joyful house.

"Tonight, or perhaps tomorrow night after I have personally prepared her for you, you shall be the one to spur my two-humped mount until she cries out in heat and bucks beneath you while seized by the throes of lustful joy."

DAVID ALEXANDER

BOOK THREE

THE QUEST BEGINS

10. A Walk Through Stone Town

The following day, Snakeskin dressed himself in one of the ornately embroidered native *jibbas* provided him by the Sultan, donned a turban of striped Shantung silk, armed himself with the pommels of both scimitar and knife arranged to make them fashionably jut up from the belt at his waist, and went out for a stroll around the palace grounds.

With his face burned by the sun and his beard allowed to grow out, Snakeskin looked more like an Arab than many another Zanzibarian, albeit taller and broader in the shoulders. While he took pleasure in displaying the ornate cutlery bestowed upon him by his doting host, the robes also concealed his prized LeMats, worn discreetly in chest holsters cross-strapped beneath their billowing expanse.

On his walk he heard the muezzin's bell tolling from a high minaret which overlooked the spacious courtyard, its strident clanging announcing the call of the faithful to assemble for the morning prayer in the purlieus of the palace mosque.

Eager to find a vantage point high enough to permit him to survey the island, the sea, and the mainland that loomed across the straits, Snakeskin decided to ascend to the top of the bell tower as soon as the tolling ceased and the faithful had assembled to give their thanks and send their praises to Allah.

He found the minaret unguarded as he had expected. Inside, a spiral staircase of steel ascended up through the cool dimness to a patch of light that marked the belfry many feet overhead. Mounting the stairs, Snakeskin began his climb. Some time later, after completing the tortuous ascent to the summit, Snakeskin's efforts were rewarded by a view of breathtaking magnificence.

All of Zanziber's Stone Town now lay spread before him, like a woman awaiting her lover, surrounded on three sides by the enveloping ocean whose calm surface looked for all the world like a plate of burnished steel gleaming in the sub-equatorial sun. To the east, the flaming disc of the just risen sun glowed like an enormous Chinese gong made of highly polished brass.

Beneath it, calm blue seas stretched away to distant horizons that seemed an eternity removed from the earth and its manifold cares. Snakeskin felt reduced to a mere speck by the hugeness of the world around him, but he felt a glorious speck for all of that, his heart gladdened by the exquisite beauty of what he beheld, as the land smell of Africa filled his nostrils with spicy pungency and the sea wind whipped his hair from his head and sent it flying in a coal-black spray.

Snakeskin now turned his gaze to the west, squinting hard to stare across the straits, where the African mainland lay beyond a rocky headland. Snakeskin lingered on the undulations of the brooding continental landmass that were the mountains which rose like humps of sleeping rhinoceri just behind the coastal plain.

His thoughts now turned to the mission that lay ahead. It would be one that would require fighting shy of heavy odds. Under any other circumstances Snakeskin would have dismissed it as too reckless. Even as matters stood, and his heart's desire awaiting him at the end, he knew it was folly to pursue it. No woman was worth such unholy risks, even considering the king's ransom that he would earn, in advance, paid in gold Spanish reales from the Sultan's treasury.

Those pieces of eight would be of no value to a man struck dead by a Dervish spear or the knife of one of Tippu Tib's Hashishim. Nor did Snakeskin especially relish double-crossing the Sultan, whom he had grown to love as a friend. Double-cross him, he would, though, in the end. Snakeskin knew that much. Once he possessed both the woman and the fortune in gold, Snakeskin would not soon let either of them go.

Snakeskin's reverie was broken with sharp suddenness by the sound of someone calling to him from the courtyard below. Looking down, Snakeskin saw one of the Sultan's retainers gesticulating at him.

Although he could not make out a single word the robed man was shouting at him, his gestures seemed to indicate that he wanted Snakeskin to come straight down. Motioning back to indicate that he was leaving the tower, Snakeskin descended the staircase.

"Siddi, forgive my intrusion," the retainer, a black Sudanese dressed in a striped white *jibba*, said with a polite bow, "but his highness the Sultan has been searching frantically for you."

"Frantically? Why?" asked Snakeskin.

"Sidi, there is grave news, I fear," the man answered him.

"News concerning the accursed dog who calls himself Mahdi. This paper which I hold may explain the nature of the concern."

DAVID ALEXANDER

Snakeskin quickly read the cable from the Khedive of Egypt that he had just been handed. According to the report cited there, the Mahdi had just captured one of the principal Egyptian forts on the western bank of the lower Nile, killing most of its inhabitants in an orgy of wanton slaughter, then subjecting the fort to plunder.

"It is bad news, yes?" asked the Sultan's retainer.

"Yes," Snakeskin answered somberly, the glory he had felt only minutes before now forgotten as a sudden blackness consumed his thoughts, "damned bad."

■

Later that day, Snakeskin received another message. This one was a reminder of his prior pledge to participate in an exhibition fighting match between himself and Jahno, the Sultan's bodyguard.

A grassy section of the royal gardens was cordoned off with a rectangle of white paint as the two combatants squared off at opposite corners of the ring. The entire royal court had assembled to witness the contest, including the crew of the Courageous which had been abetting their enthusiasm with liberal doses of dark ale, red rum and the local Clarissa wine.

The agreed-upon rules of the exhibition called for three falls, with whoever succeeded in besting his opponent twice declared winner of the match, which was entirely freestyle, and where anything went. The Sultan would act as referee.

Jahno moved first, springing like a cat, and advancing much more quickly than a man of his size and girth might be expected to do, faster in fact than Snakeskin had anticipated. The first of the three falls went to the Gurkha who threw Snakeskin with a *koshti*-style hold, characteristic of Persian wrestling.

FIVE DEAD MEN

Snakeskin soon took his opponent's measure, though, and won the next two falls, his speed and martial arts techniques succeeding where Jahno's strength could not alone prevail.

The Sultan was impressed with Snakeskin's performance, so much so that he conferred the honorific title of "Pasha" upon the American freebooter and mercenary. This carried with it special powers and privileges.

A sumptuous dwelling in choice Zanzibarian real estate also came with the privilege. A villa in Stone Town overlooking the harbor with a view across the narrow strip of Indian Ocean separating the isle of Unguja from the East African mainland, and with the minarets and spires of Dar es Salem, southward along the coast, glittering by day and twinkling by night, was provided Snakeskin for as long as he lived by royal decree.

Upon entering his new abode, Snakeskin found to his extreme pleasure that Majid bin Said had bestowed yet another precious gift upon him. Alika, the beautiful concubine who he had watched dance the previous night, was also his for the taking.

In the center of the shaded portico that formed the center of the villa and cooled the heat of the day there was a pool of inlaid mosaic tiles. He found her awaiting him in the pool, her smoothly sculpted, tawny brown arms stretched to either side of her head along the curved edge of the basin, her cantaloupe breasts and plump black nipples dappled with beads of cool water.

"Come to me," she called. "Shed your robes. I would taste of you."

Snakeskin unbelted his *jibba* and permitted the robes to slide to the tiled floor at the edge of the pool while Alika's large, dark eyes watched him admiringly.

"You are big," she sighed. "I am pleased. I would not have liked it so much if you were not."

Snakeskin stepped into the pool and straddled her. Stretching out one hand she cupped his genitals while with the other she caressed the bulbous crown of his stiffened tool.

"I will delight you, yet you must hold your milk within," she purred. "Can you do this?"

Now she parted her full, gleaming lips to show Snakeskin her tongue. Its tip was cleft and pierced with two beads of polished steel. She drew his love machine close to her lips and began to stroke its shaft with her surgically altered tongue.

Snakeskin felt a shudder of keen pleasure course through his body as she began to suck his turgid member, playing the twin steel balls across the swollen underside of its glans until he was driven almost mad with the urge to ejaculate. She tortured him with her mouth, driving him to the brink of explosion until he could finally hold back no longer.

She released him suddenly.

"Now take me fully," she told him. "Drive deep into my cave of honey. Show me that you are a man."

Stepping back, Snakeskin reached down and grasped her beneath the crook of her knees, simultaneously pushing her shoulders back against the tiles that rimmed the basin and propping her legs at the sides of his thighs.

She gasped in pain as the tiles bit into her shoulders, but Snakeskin was a bull in heat, and as he looked down he beheld a sight that inflamed him even more, for the vulva that guarded the red folds of a woman's heat had been removed, to expose the secret places within.

And in the midst of the water-beaded blossom, more steel balls like those that tipped her tongue had been implanted around the entrance to her passage to paradise, guardians of the seven gates of delight intended to drive any man mad with strange ambrosial thrills.

Small wonder, thought Snakeskin, that Alika was prized by the Sultan. The surgical cutting of women in this part of the globe to increase their pleasure value was well known. Though Snakeskin had never before encountered such a thing, it was rumored that the removal of the labia intensified the experience of sexual pleasure beyond normal bounds.

Snakeskin's strong hands grasped her beneath her knees as he drove his shaft deep into her with a single powerful stroke that penetrated to the heart of the concubine. Again and again he thrust into her, while she gasped and moaned as she climaxed in a mixture of pleasure and pain, her cries echoing off the tiles of the portico.

"Now, fill me with thy hot spouting, oh bold one," she cried out. "*Now*. Spurt powerfully within, I beg of thee!"

Snakeskin drew back and thrust inside Alika once again, feeling the insane shudder of release as his mind exploded and tears of exquisite pleasure rained from Alika's eyes. He thrust in again, spurting, and again, to erupt finally in the tightness and wetness of the girl before withdrawing.

She clung to him now, weeping against his chest, and he kissed her hair, and then bent down to thrust between her lips and mingle his tongue with hers. Then he picked her up as easily as a doll and carried her from the water and took her upon the tiles, again and again, until he was fully sated and her kohl-rimmed eyes were raw with tears.

"Now I am thine, Pasha Snakeskin Blake," she said when the tears had finally stopped.

11. A Farewell to Zanzibar

More than a week's time had elapsed since Snakeskin's arrival on Zanzibar island.

In the days that had passed since Snakeskin and his crew had made landfall at Stone Town, the Sultan had not seen much of his American house guest. His Excellency's servants reported that the American had sequestered himself in his new dwelling with the new wife that Majid bin Said had bestowed upon him. They also reported that Snakeskin was hard at work constructing an infernal machine of some sort.

While the royal palace was abuzz with rumors, the Sultan himself was filled with growing curiosity. What was his guest up to, he wondered? He determined to find out as soon as he could, and since Snakeskin had not seen fit to tell him personally, the Sultan decided that he would go directly to his guest to inquire.

Alika bid the Sultan enter with a bow as Majid bin Said and a suitably regal retinue appeared at Snakeskin's villa.

FIVE DEAD MEN

"Siddi, what brings you to this humble home?" she asked, bowing respectfully and revealing the cups of her ample breasts in the process.

"By Allah's name, woman," the Sultan replied in his polished Eaton accent, "you know perfectly well what I am here to see. Your new husband is up to something other than fucking your horny little ass night and day, and I mean to find out what this prodigy might actually be. Is he here?"

"He is working out back," she answered. "I will announce your arrival."

"Do not trouble yourself, my young jiggler," said the Sultan, cupping Alika's chin and bestowing a sloppy kiss on her bee-stung lips, before moving his ponderous bulk toward the rear of the house, "I shall see him myself."

The sight which greeted the Sultan's eyes was shocking even to one such as himself who had thought to have seen everything. He had never before seen the like of what his guest was busily laboring on. The cigar-shaped cylinder, tapered at both ends, roughly fifty feet in length, stood on wooden supports at the center of the walled garden.

Attending the bizarre contraption, some wielding an assortment of tools, others at work at a bellows where rivets were being heated at the forge, were members of the Courageous' crew. An assortment of scrap iron, tools, wood, braces for making molds, kegs of nails and screws, and what appeared to be several large wooden packing crates -- one of which was being pried open at that instant with a crowbar by three men -- were scattered about helter-skelter fashion. At one end of the walled enclosure two large black cast iron kettles from which rose a stinking black pall were being stirred by heavily perspiring laborers with neckerchiefs tied around their faces to protect them against inhaling the fumes.

The Sultan heard clanging sounds coming from within. In a moment or two, Snakeskin's head appeared through a hatch set in the top of the massive cylinder, making many of the Sultan's retinue jump backward in fright.

"What is this?" asked the Sultan, recovering his wits. "I have never seen anything like it."

"It's called a 'David,'" Snakeskin agreed. "You've no doubt heard the Biblical story of how David bested Goliath with a stone cast from a slingshot?"

"Yes, of course."

"David, here, does something similar."

"I'm afraid I don't follow you, Pasha Snakeskin."

"The David is a kind of semi-submersible originally developed during our American Civil War," Snakeskin began.

"So it is a type of submarine," the Sultan interjected.

"Not quite. You've probably heard of the Hunley, which ran fully submerged, but had too many problems. Unlike the Hunley the Davids could be safely operated and built at considerably less cost using nailed wood slats covered with layers of pitch."

"Which is what those noxious black clouds are all about, I gather."

"Yes, your Excellency," Snakeskin replied.

He went on concerning how the Davids functioned, leading the Sultan around the garden while his retinue automatically followed their leader like wind-up toys.

The crates, he explained, contained the main components for each of three Davids that Snakeskin was in the process of building. The first was a steam boiler and stack which burned anthracite coal sufficient to power a single double-bladed propeller at the vessel's rear. The Davids' second main component was steel ballast tanks, one for each boat, which would be hand-pumped by a single crewman. When enough water was drawn into the tank, the David submerged to up to eighty percent of its profile with only the boiler stack jutting from its stern.

As such, and especially by night, the David could approach targets, such as casemated ships at sea or in harbor, or creep up near beaches for close reconnaissance or covert landings. Since the anthracite coal burned by its boiler was nearly smokeless, there would be little to give away a David to enemy eyes.

"Marvelous!" the Sultan exclaimed, clapping his hands in glee. "I would call these contrivances exemplars of stealth."

"Stealth," Snakeskin replied. "I like that word. Yes, the David does embody stealth, doesn't it?"

"Since I have coined the word, these will now be called 'stealth ships,'" said the Sultan. "Much easier to pronounce than 'semi-submersibles' I dare say."

"Absolutely, your Excellency."

The first Davids had been built by the Confederacy as torpedo boats, Snakeskin went on, about twenty of them had been made. They had originally been equipped with an explosive gunpowder mine weighing over one hundred pounds positioned at the end of a metal spar projecting from the David's bow. The charge would be backed into a ship or other target, then detonated. The David would finally back away and break for friendly lines.

That was how the New Ironsides, a Union ironclad, had been sunk in Charleston Harbor back in 1863. Even with the boiler dead from a dousing of seawater, the David's crew had been able to abandon ship. The single casualty suffered in the raid had resulted from rifle fire, not drowning.

"The three Davids I'm making won't have torpedoes, though," explained Snakeskin. "I intend to use them to conduct reconnaissance and land unseen on certain islands. They can permit men to steal up upon an island undetected, for a David's approach cannot be seen from the land. We'll be armed, of course, but only with rifles and pistols. We'll carry dynamite but only for specific demolition purposes."

"Have you thought to give names to our, ah, new stealth ships?" asked the Sultan.

"This one here is called Alexander. I intend to name the second one Caesar, and the third ... " Snakeskin suddenly had a flash of inspiration, for instead of saying 'Hannibal' as he had originally intended, he turned to the Sultan and said with a smile -- "the third, of course, will be called Majid, after the worthiest general of all."

"You flatter me, Pasha Snakeskin Blake," said the Sultan. "But now I shall leave you to complete your work on these wonderful stealth machines of yours."

With that, the Sultan and his retinue departed and Snakeskin disappeared back inside the pitch covered wooden cigar whereupon the sound of hammering commenced once again.

■

The sheltered cove on the seaward side of Unguja Island that Snakeskin had selected to test the Davids was one that he believed to be as secure as possible from the prying eyes of the Mahdi's watchers.

The cove was in an uninhabited place and visibility on the landward side was limited to the cliffs directly above it, which were under guard by Snakeskin's men. The side facing the Indian Ocean was also guarded by rock outcroppings that rose from the bay and could not be seen from passing ships. The limpid water was fairly deep, minimizing the danger of a sudden sea surge smashing the Davids against any submerged rocks.

Shortly after daybreak, pulled by the moon, the third quarter neap tide had risen to its highest point of the month. Snakeskin pushed the cigar-shaped stealth ship into the water and entered it through one of the two hatches in its top, dogging down the iron cover to create a watertight seal.

Blowing the ballast tanks, he submerged the Alexander until only the tip of its six-foot boiler stack projected from the surface. The Sultan and his retinue watched in awe, convinced that once he had disappeared beneath the surface of the water, Snakeskin would not be seen by living men again -- of this they were completely certain.

Yet to the amazement of the superstitious Zanzibarians, the craft bobbed up to the surface like a huge cork several feet away from the point where it had submerged.

Snakeskin promptly stuck his head out of the two watertight hatches at its top and waved to the spectators. Then he re-closed the hatch and filled the Alexander's ballast tank to its maximum, submerging until virtually nothing but the smokeless stack projected above the waterline.

Using the foot-operated paddles, Snakeskin used the handheld lever which worked the rudder of the David to point it toward the shore, with the propeller easily powering the lightweight craft. The incredibly clear Indian Ocean water was almost completely free of turbidity and so Snakeskin had little trouble seeing when he had reached land. Thereupon Snakeskin bilged out the Alexander's ballast tank to restore the David's watertight hull to full neutral buoyancy and completely resurface again.

"I have witnessed a miracle!" exclaimed the Sultan as the David came bobbing back to the surface only a foot or two from the edge of the pier. "My dear Snakeskin Blake, I truly believed that I would never cast these two eyes upon you ever again."

"You should not have feared," replied Snakeskin, his mind already working on the numerous details he would have to attend to before the pocket sub would be ready for the mission he had in mind. These included poorly riveted joinings which had leaked sea water during the trial, and the rudder control, which was not as responsive to the touch as he would have liked it to be. All in all, however, the test of the first David had gone off with nary a hitch.

But Snakeskin had another matter he needed to discuss with the Sultan, one that concerned his intended use for the Davids when the appropriate time came.

He told the Sultan that he would soon be ready to undertake the mission for which he had been commissioned by Chinese Charlie Gordon, who had summoned him to Zanzibar on Her Britannic Majesty's behalf. The operation that had been planned to rescue Majid bin Said's most cherished *haram* concubine from the grasp of the Mahdi in the Dervish leader's stronghold in the Sahel, as well as to free a kidnapped British subject and thus show the world that England would not stand for such behavior, was getting close to the launch point.

But first, Snakeskin explained, he must gain the invaluable help of certain gifted and capable men. Their individual skills would be of extreme value in the rescue mission and in fact critical to its ultimate success.

"How long will it take you to gather these men?" the Sultan asked Snakeskin.

Snakeskin told him that it would be a matter of weeks, at the earliest, before he could bring the assembled rescue team back to Zanzibar to begin final training.

"Can anyone else besides yourself bring them here?" the Sultan asked, "in order to save time?"

"No," Snakeskin responded. "Only I can gather them together. Such men as they are will trust no emissary. They will go only with me -- if I am lucky."

"Then go with my blessings and the protection of Allah," the Sultan replied. "And tell these men that I shall reward each of them handsomely should they come to the aid of my beloved concubine.

"But come back at your earliest possible moment. Every day that passes makes the Mahdi more dangerous and the chances of rescuing the most precious jewel of my *haram* -- she of pliant breasts, cunning tongue and caressing thighs -- less than even the day before."

DAVID ALEXANDER

12. Sir Montague Strawplait

Cursing the green-black bottle flies that surrounded both himself and his sweating dromedary in a great buzzing cloud, Sir Montague Strawplait rode hard across the arid wastes of the great northern desert that bordered his master's trackless sandy realm. His destination was the Mahdi's current main encampment in the Sahel -- that strip of parched brown and scrubby vegetation running across the midriff of the desertified Sudan like a fuzzy belt -- and he had been riding without more than a few minutes letup since the break of dawn of that same day.

The mission on which Strawplait had embarked some forty hours previous to that moment had begun when he had stolen by night from the office of the British consul in Zanzibar, after having given orders to his subordinate, fellow secret Mahdist, and co-plotter, Major Giles Faversham-Sidney, to carry on in his absence. Strawplait had then made his way to the quayside of Stone Town under cover of darkness. Shuttling across the straits just as dawn broke by a boat piloted by his manservant Hassan, Strawplait was to seek council from the man whom the Englishman acknowledged as the true and supreme incarnation of the eternal and all-wise Prophet of Islam.

Though Strawplait had been ordered by the Mahdi to execute Snakeskin Blake, he had since devised a scheme which he felt would bring even greater glory to the Mahdist cause. Indecision had staid Strawplait's hand following the initial attempt by Tippu Tib's henchmen to quickly kill him in the marketplace. As the Madhi did not tolerate failure, and Strawplait saw that killing Snakeskin Blake would not be an easy matter, he decided on a different course. His plan would call for Snakeskin's life to be spared, at least temporarily.

Being a prudent man, Strawplait dared trust no other emissary to seek the Mahdi's council but himself alone. And so he had set out to make the arduous journey on the back of a trotter camel single-handedly and completely unaided across some of the most treacherous arid terrain to be found anywhere in the world. Strawplait was already on the second leg of his journey, having stopped to rest only when darkness fell, and he could no longer tell the way for certain.

He had mounted his camel again at first light. By the morning of the third day, Strawplait had reached the heart of the Sudan where he crossed from sand desert into the less harsh aridity of the Sahel.

The great hump of fat that had swelled on the back of his dromedary on reaching the African coast had by now been reduced to only a small protrusion after the arduous and waterless trek across the desert, and his mount's hoofs were swollen from the endless trodding that the beast of burden had been forced to endure in carrying its burden for many long miles.

Nevertheless, Strawplait now sighted the Mahdist encampment straight ahead across a level plain and some miles distant. Already outriders mounted on camel and

Arabian stallions of the *Ansari* had noticed his arrival and were riding forth out of the *zariba* of dense thorn bushes which encircled the remote Dervish stronghold.

Strawplait pointed his Enfield rifle at the sky and fired off a series of shots in a sign of joyous greeting as he neared the Dervishes. The Dervishes and Fuzzy Wuzzies of Tippu Tib spilled sleepily from tents and sweating from forges and languidly from woven reed mats in the cool of the shade where they had lain with the young recruits turned into *mahmoonim* due to their weakness amidst the ranks of real men and true believers, and Strawplait was pleased to notice that an emir of the Mahdist camp named Muntarb el Hashemi was present, riding his mount at the head of the group. Hashemi was a man known to him and would see to it that his path to the Mahdi would be cleared of dangerous encumbrances.

"So, Ghazawan el Safiy-Allah al Madiya," said Muntarb el Hashemi, "you have returned to us after a long departure."

"As Allah has willed it, as it has pleased his Prophet, so I have indeed returned into the embracing nearness of the Blessed One who is Mahdi," agreed Strawplait, replacing his rifle in its saddle holster, and then taking up the small leather pouch dangling from a thong around his neck and bestowing kisses upon the amulet.

"And I have a matter of gravest urgency to discuss with our great leader, blessed be the sweetness of his name."

Hashemi turned toward one of the men astride a horse and shouted, "Go and say to our Mahdi, blessings upon him, that Ghazawan el Safiy-Allah al Madiya has returned unto our encampment," he commanded the Dervish horseman.

The man acknowledged the order from Hashemi and rode off amid a cloud of ochre desert dust that rose in the air and billowed like strange smoke.

FIVE DEAD MEN

To Strawplait, Hashemi said, "let us ride together, my brother. I am anxious to hear all that you can tell me of the Infidel -- accursed be his gonads -- and the evil designs that grow from his wickedness."

Within half the space of an hour, Strawplait and Muntarb el Hashemi had ridden to an encampment in whose midst stood a spacious tent whose walls of finely woven fabric billowed in the hot desert winds. This was the tent of the Mahdi.

Approaching its entrance, Hashemi announced the arrival of the Frank (for all Europeans were called this, whatever their actual nationality) and called for a servant to come and wash the dust from their feet, as befitted those who attended on the Most High.

A black Sudanese robed in pure white, both his arms and both his cheeks ritually scarified, appeared carrying a large pitcher of brass that slopped with clear well water. The servant abased himself before the two newcomers and at a nod from Hashemi to indicate that the Frank would have the honor of going first, Strawplait slipped off his dirty sandals and sat upon a low chair of polished ebony. The servant poured water over Strawplait's feet, while chanting verses from the Mahdi's songs of praise to Allah, wiped them dry with a cloth, then carefully fitted on a fresh pair of sandals.

Once Hashemi's feet had been laved in the same way, the two travelers entered the Mahdi's private tent, where the Dervish leader already informed of the Englishman's arrival, was waiting for him.

As was his custom, the Mahdi sat on a sheepskin, fragrant with the special perfume he was wont to wear and known as the "Scent of the Mahdi" throughout the Sahel and the desert regions beyond. Upon seeing Strawplait enter, the

Mahdi held out his large, gaunt hand, the fingers of which were covered with a panoply of glittering rings.

"My Mahdi, my Blessed Prophet, my Beloved Leader and Glittering Star of Destiny," Strawplait sniveled, bowing low and kissing the Mahdi's hand with lavish surrender, his lips lingering on the gaunt fingers of the Chosen One as though from their well-manicured and painted tips was exhaled the breath of life itself.

"To behold the light that shines from your precious face once again is to receive blessings a thousand fold from the mouth of Allah."

"It pleases me too that you have come to grace my tent. Peace be unto thou, Ghazawan el Safiy-Allah al Madiya," replied the Mahdi in perfect English, learned as a boy who was educated in the manner of all highborn sons of prestigious members of the Khedive's government service.

"I have been told that your presence here concerns urgent news. Does this mean that you have brought me the head of the Infidel cur hired by the Sultan to defile our sacred cause?"

"No, Most High Excellency," Strawplait sniveled. "But I have an idea that I have the greatest expectations will please your will even more."

Strawplait almost jumped as the Mahdi raised a plucked eyebrow above one flawlessly kohl-rimmed eye and touched the jeweled knuckle of his hand to the tip of his chin.

"Do I hear you speak, oh Ghazawan el Safiy-Allah al Madiya, that you have chosen to defy my will?" The Mahdi stroked his jaw with the glittering emerald beyond the knuckle. "Is this what you have ridden long miles to tell me?"

"No, Excellency. Absolutely not, Oh Glorious One."

FIVE DEAD MEN

Strawplait had begun to whine and whimper as he fought a shudder of fear that threatened to make him sag at the knees and fall groveling and vomiting to the enthroned figure's perfumed sandaled feet.

"If your highness will only permit me to tell you of these plans, you may understand why I have not brought the head of this miserable Infidel to you as I am aware that your have instructed me."

"Speak your words, then, Ghazawan el Safiy-Allah al Madiya," ordered the Mahdi. "I shall listen to what you have to say and decide on the course to take."

"Yes, Divine Excellency. Thank you, Oh Radiant Star of Mecca and Guiding Beacon of the Holy."

What was left unspoken, but understood by all, was that if Strawplait's words garnered the Mahdi's slightest displeasure, they then might likely be the last words that he would ever live to utter.

13. Assassins by Night

"For he's a jolly good fellow! For he's a jolly good fellow ... For he's a jolly good fellow... " sang the assembled hands of the Courageous. The crewmen were seated at a table at one of Zanzibar's more prominent hashish dens, the House of Abdul Chewy, so called because his mouth was constantly masticating either freshly picked *khatt* or resinous *kief* still muskily fragrant from the hempen sap from which it had been distilled and dried.

"...That nobody can deny," they continued, keeping time by pummeling the tabletop with their bunched fists, the pommels of their knives and the butts of their pistols.

Though liquor was putatively banned according to observance of the letter of Islamic law, and the smoking of kief and hashish were substituted in its stead, the proper bribe to the proper parties could usually be counted on to make the authorities turn a blind eye to tippling, at least by Infidels who knew no better.

In this case, the baksheesh had been duly paid to the innkeeper by Snakeskin, and the men of the Courageous were permitted to drink all of the dark rum they wanted by Abdul Chewy.

Since the proprietor saw to it that the patrons at his establishment had plenty of hashish to smoke as well, the celebration quickly assumed auspicious dimensions.

Unlike whiskey, few evils were associated with consorting with women or even *mahmoonim* in this part of the world, and the same payment that had brought forth the innkeeper's hospitality had insured that a bevy of Zanzibar's most accomplished courtesans would be on hand as well -- concubines boasting the absence of labia majora and augmentation of the clitoris with studs of steel and small clusters of pearls -- enough to whet the appetite of any true seafarer.

Those who had not chosen to sample the peerless charms of the ladies of pleasure in the trysting rooms upstairs, joined in a drinking contest in the public rooms that Abdul kept below. Snakeskin was among these latter who toasted one another until hardly a man could stand upright any longer.

In the small hours of the morning, Snakeskin was returning home with first mate Jopling in tow. Jopling was far too drunk to be trusted to return to the Courageous under his own steam, and Snakeskin had decided to put his trusted friend up for the night at the villa that the Sultan had given him.

However, Snakeskin was only a little more sober than his friend was, and as the two men weaved their way precariously through the narrow streets of the town on rum-rubbery legs, unsure of the direction in which they walked, hostile eyes watched their steps from the concealment of shadows.

When the Dervishes who had followed Snakeskin and Jopling from the House of Abdul Chewy realized that they were walking into a cul de sac, they drew their long knives. Snakeskin reacted to the sound of the Dervishes and drew up the broad sword scabbarded at his belt by its pommel.

He lashed out and severed the arm of one of the Mahdists who was lunging at him with a wickedly sharp and ably wielded *janbiya*. Jopling promptly pulled his single-action Colt, cocked back its hammer, and fired a shot point-blank into the belly of one of two Dervish assassins who had fallen on him.

Despite his brain having soaked up more than its share of rum, Jopling's aim remained accurate -- especially at close range. Jopling aimed, cocked and fired a second shot. As the assailant fell with a cry of pain brought on by the bullets that had smashed through his rib cage and burst his heart, Jopling smashed a heavy ham hock fist into the bearded face of the Dervish left standing, shattering his nose and bloodying his head.

The rest of the Dervishes lacked the stomach to fight. They ran off into the night, disappearing into the darkness and the meandering streets as effortlessly as they had appeared. Snakeskin and Jopling were now sobering up quickly as adrenaline coursed through their bloodstreams and began to chase away the stupor of the alcohol they had drunk. They remained on guard the rest of the way, but the Dervishes never returned for an encore.

FIVE DEAD MEN

14. Islands of Salvation

The infamous rock awash in the south Atlantic some nine miles off the eastern coast of French Guiana known as Ile du Diable -- Devil's Island -- was the final stop for political prisoners considered too dangerous to the security the French republic to be permitted to live unfettered on her native soil. The island was one of three that together made up the Îles du Salut -- the Islands of Salvation.

Each of the three was devoted to a different class of prisoners. On the Île Royale, largest of these and hard off the mainland, were kept the worst and most hardened offenders. The Île Saint-Joseph was where even the worst of the worst were kept in solitary confinement and subjected to the whims of sadistic prison gendarmes. The isle of the Devil, however, was solely devoted to jailing political prisoners, men whose thoughts themselves were deemed to present a severe threat to the government of France. Established by French Emperor Napoleon III in 1852 as a leper colony, the conversion of Devil's Island to a prison had been practically simultaneous with the events that had sent Snakeskin Blake on his mission to Zanzibar.

DAVID ALEXANDER

The island was aptly named. It was not hard to believe that the devil himself had fashioned the place from the same ground plan as that of hell. Viewed from the sea, and in clear weather especially, the palm-covered and rock-fringed isle, resting on calm blue-green ocean waters, with gentle ocean combers breaking almost playfully into white spray against its chocolate-brown shores, appears completely innocuous, even idyllic.

But venture inland from the narrow boulder beach, and the terrain quickly becomes a treacherous quagmire of steaming mangrove jungle in which disease-infested insects, and a dozen varieties of poisonous snakes, abound.

On Devil's Island there was little solid ground underfoot and those hapless souls attempting to venture from the marshy interior to the rock-bound coast would have to make their way through swamps teeming with voracious alligators and bogs of quicksand that could suck a man into their depths within a matter of seconds and then suffocate the life out of him in a final wet caress.

Ringed by a barrier of treacherous submerged rocks, with patches of underwater quicksand in the shallows off its rocky shores, the island was in itself a fortress created by nature's caprice to be a scourge to seafarers, more than a few of whom had been dashed to pieces against her shoals when storms tossed sailing vessels into the treacherous waters surrounding her headlands.

Situated miles from the east-west transatlantic shipping lanes that made landfall at the port of Georgetown and never strayed into unsafe waters, and served by a packet ship that arrived twice a year bearing medicines, relief troops and food, the island lay in waters infested with sharks that were as perpetually ravenous as any of their voracious brethren elsewhere in the waters off the vast Atlantic coastline of South America.

The only safe route to the Ile du Diable was via a six hundred foot-wide sea channel stretching between it and Île Royale, beyond its southwestern tip and closest of the Salvation isles to the Guyanese coast. Small wonder, then, that the majority of the more than eighty thousand prisoners sent to Devil's Island never made it back alive.

Those few prisoners who in the past had been brave or foolhardy enough to attempt escape from the less remote arms of the French Guyanese prison system soon found to their everlasting chagrin that even the most hellish tortures inflicted on them by their brutal prison masters were as nothing compared with those tribulations which nature held in store just beyond the confinement of the island's palm-fringed and deceptively inviting shores.

■

Fallicon La Crosse had been a prisoner on Devil's Island for three long, suffering-filled years. On the day of his sentencing, virtually all of France rose up in angry protests, for La Crosse was a man loved by the people, nobility and commoners alike.

Once crowds of angry men and women had lined the Boulevard Haussmann to shout their support of La Crosse in defiance of the gendarmerie as the heavily guarded and shackled prisoner was driven through the 14th Arrondissement from Santé Prison to an embarkation point on the Seine to begin his far journey into final exile.

Now, years after commencing his term of hard penal servitude, La Crosse was a forgotten man, shunted out of the limelight by other names and other causes that had eclipsed his own in the public imagination.

DAVID ALEXANDER

He had originally been sentenced for his involvement in a plot in 1877 to unseat the half-mad cousin of Napoleon who ruled France in a deranged imitation of the Bonaparte era, but the changing fortunes of post-Bourbon France had placed La Crosse on the losing side soon thereafter. As a warning to others, the highest court of France awarded La Crosse the ultimate sentence of life imprisonment on Devil's Island.

Doomed by his countrymen to spend the rest of his days rotting in the jungle hell to which he had been consigned, La Crosse had long since given up all hope of escaping Devil's Island while yet breathing. Over time he had resigned himself to a slow decay in the steaming jungle hell and burial in the common grave that was the fate of practically all inmates imprisoned on the hated rock.

To amuse himself, and to keep from going insane, La Crosse had taken up the practice of constructing windmills out of odd scraps of wood. This was a strange pastime, because La Crosse, who had never been to the Netherlands, had never before seen an actual windmill in his entire life.

Nevertheless, one day La Crosse had found himself putting together these random bits of scrap wood without conscious plan or deliberate intent. The result -- to his complete and astonished surprise -- was a windmill.

He had at this point been making them for something like a year since his first success and selling them to the prison gendarmes, bringing in enough money to purchase cigarettes and other necessities.

His once blond hair had long since turned gray, and in the course of a beating by a sadistic and drunken guard, one of his eyes had been damaged and had eventually flickered out entirely, leaving him with a disquieting mien in which one eye gleamed with an almost golden hue, while the other was as dark and dead as a spent lump of burnt coal.

And by now also the once garrulous Frenchman -- whose speeches and fiery rhetoric had at one time electrified listeners in the cafes and on the street corners of Paris -- rarely spoke. What for? Speaking accomplished nothing, and life had long ago degenerated into a mere slow, continuous, counting of the passing days in anticipation of that final and inevitable moment when a liberating death claimed him forever.

Now, as night fell -- another night in a long procession of nights -- the Frenchman sat in the isolation of his dank stone prison hut, making a windmill by the flickering light of an oil burning hurricane lamp. Slumped against the sweating stone wall, he heard the jungle come alive with the hooting of birds and the gibbering of arboreal monkeys.

And as Fallicon La Crosse worked on his windmill, thinking of the week's supply of Brazilian coffee it would suffice to buy him, he did not realize that his deliverance from his living death was almost at hand.

15. The Courageous

Her main stack billowing as her newly coaled twin boilers powered her screws, the Courageous plowed her way through the balmy reaches of the lower Indian Ocean on a compass course that was to swing it like a stone cast from a sling around Cape Town where the ship would be caught by the Benguela Current that would more than double its speed as it hurled the vessel northward.

With any luck and if the deep water current, hard-driven by southeasterly trade winds at this time of year, held up to expectations, it would be a little under two days sailing from Cape Point in Africa to their ultimate destination -- landfall at the mouth of the Amazon just above Belem on the Brazilian coast.

Some other matters deliberately slowed the journey somewhat. One of these was the opportunity to catch a bounty of fish that the upwelling of the Benguela made too good a thing to pass up. Off the towering bluffs of Coatinha Beach on the rock-bound coast of Benguela, Portuguese Angola, for which the current was named, mariners could simply cast forth their nets and haul in an abundance of fresh game fish that would make for a feast for a hungry crew.

Of more pressing interest was the necessity to make a final test and conduct final training on some of the special gear carried by the Courageous on its special mission. Chief among this equipment were the three Davids that had been carefully constructed back in Stone Town. Here, in the trackless reaches of the widest part of the Atlantic, Snakeskin's crew could count on being safe from all prying human eyes.

While the majority of the ship's crew feasted on the bounty of fish drawn from the Benguela, six hand-picked men in addition to Snakeskin and first mate Jopling trained on Alexander and Caesar, while Majid (like its lackadaisical namesake) stayed lashed to the deck of the Courageous to serve as a spare. The trials slowed the advance by half a day, but the delay, which enabled small unnoticed leaks to be sealed with pitch and the tightening of all fittings and joints including boiler mounts, was well worth the trouble.

Snakeskin now felt completely capable of using the small stealthy boats as a means to carry out the mission's dangerous objective.

Soon the combined force of the Benguela and running the ship's engines at full speed, brought the Courageous to landfall at Belem, by nightfall of the second day out from Cape Point. The crew was supplied with rum from ship's stores but all but Snakeskin and Jopling were forbidden to disembark for shore. There would be no carousing in the saloons that fringed the unlit, narrow streets behind the docks of Belem tonight.

Before sunrise the Courageous would set sail again for its final destination a short distance along the continental coastline. But amid the scum of Belem was an old mariner and former French official who had something that Snakeskin Blake was willing to pay for in Spanish pieces of eight.

■

Rested and prepared for action, Snakeskin Blake conned the coast of French Guiana through the twin eyepieces of upraised binoculars. The magnified images that merged into a monocular view in the framed circle that floated before him showed a group of three islands jumbled like the bones of a smashed finger and overgrown to their stony fringes by acres of dense stands of coconut palms.

The Islands of Salvation lay dead ahead, and the easternmost, Devil's Island, was to become the scene of the prison break that the French government had done its best to make impossible.

The broad channel that linked Devil's Island with Royal Island was connected by an ingenious cable car system that rested on pylons propped securely on sunken concrete casements at the bottom of the shallow waters. Prisoners, official visitors, guards returning from or going to shore leave, and all supplies not prohibitively bulky or heavy, came ashore by cable car and not by ship.

The channel would ordinarily provide the speediest and least dangerous route onto the island, but since it was the only recognized safe corridor to it, this was out of the question. The channel was constantly guarded and the cable cars continuously shuttling back and forth across the blue water straits between the two prison islands. But there was an alternate corridor into Devil's Island -- if only by boat because no man could swim it and survive -- that was known to one man only, and that man had sold the secret to Snakeskin Blake in old Belem town for a king's ransom in gold.

FIVE DEAD MEN

On the morning after making landfall at Belem, the Courageous found itself anchored on the windward side of a small island a few miles off the Brazilian coastline where the town of Amapá guards the five mouths of the mighty Amazon at the small coastal port of Cunani. From tiny Cunani it's less than two miles to the windward, South Atlantic, side of the lowest-lying of the three Salvation Islands, Saint Joseph, from which point less than a mile remains to reach the lower tip of Devil's Island.

The windward sides of these two outer islands in the Salvation group, islands facing the broad reaches of the Atlantic, were not well guarded and far from the main shipping lanes that used the Benguela to maximize speed and minimize costs, thus virtually invisible from the sea. But they compensated for these security drawbacks by being guarded by shoals of ancient coral and submerged rocks that had gained the well-earned fear of sailors for ripping open the bowels of ships hapless enough to pass above them.

One man did not fear the windward approach to Devil's Island, however. Embittered, cast off from his beloved Paris, in the same purge that had seen his compatriots who had opposed the mad Emperor sent to rot on a rock on the sea far from home, an exile in Belem among the scum of three continents, that man no longer had a name.

But he possessed one thing: a chart showing a safe approach to Devil's Island across some of the most treacherous and unsparing waters on the face of the earth. And he possessed one thing more: a burning desire to free Fallicon La Crosse from his prison. The man's name was Gaston La Crosse, and he was the elder brother of the prisoner that Snakeskin Blake had come to free today.

DAVID ALEXANDER

He had freed Gaston with Spanish gold the night before. Soon he would free the younger man with bullets and dynamite, or whatever else it might take.

■

The first of the two operational Davids splashed against the surface of the sea and bobbed like a cork riding lengthwise atop the wave crests. Then the winches aboard the Courageous were raised for the second David, which was in turn lowered into the water. The three crewmen of each boat then clambered down ropes along the sides of the Courageous and were helped inside by each of two sailors positioned at the combination boiler stack and conning tower at the bow of each David. The engineers of each vessel then lit the boilers while the drivers busied themselves with last-minute checks of the dual throttle that controlled the single-blade propeller at the stern and the bilging of the ballast tanks.

As the boilers built up heads of steam Snakeskin and second mate Jack O'Dreams climbed to the top of each David and got behind the conning towers. Equipped with binoculars they would play the role of navigators to lead the Davids safely ashore. Within minutes the boilers had completely fired up and a nearly invisible plume of effluent rose up the stack.

Snakeskin now signaled to the driver with a pre-arranged three raps on the hull to commence bilging in the ballast. Soon the tanks of each David, also powered by a turbine fed by the steam boiler, began to fill and the vessels grew less buoyant until most of their hulls had vanished below the level of the black waters.

The coating of black pitch covering the cigar-shaped hulls as well as a shallow draft that placed most of the vessels below the waterline all contributed to making the

FIVE DEAD MEN

Davids nearly invisible on this moonless night. Like Snakeskin, Jack O'Dreams riding lookout on the Caesar was also garbed from head to foot in black clothing with his face daubed with black boiler ash.

Now, taking up his binoculars, Snakeskin focused in on their destination. The southern tip of Devil's Island, shaped like the point of a chisel -- lay dead ahead, no more than a mile distant from the sparsely patrolled Atlantic waters windward of the Salvations at which the Courageous was anchored. Snakeskin took the first of his planned compass bearings. They were on course for the safe channel plotted on the nautical map that had been furnished him by the elder La Crosse brother.

Snakeskin closed the compass and let it drop at the end of the leather thong around his neck, then raised the dark lantern lashed by a strap to his belt to open and close the shutter twice to inform the other David behind the Alexander that the first course check held true.

As they proceeded closer to the rocky beachhead fringing Devil's Island, the powerful offshore currents began to be felt, tugging at the craft. Thanks to their steam turbine powered propellers, however, the Davids successfully resisted the vicious eddying of the currents in a way that the earlier Hunley submersibles, powered by peddling an inverse-ratio reduction gear operated screw, could not have withstood.

Another check of compass bearings and map, and a visual sighting showed Snakeskin that the Davids had passed the midpoint of their journey and were in sight of their destination. The narrow inlet between rocky outcrops was looming larger with each passing minute. The inlet was blocked from direct landward view by an upsweep of palm-fringed high ground. Waves foamed a phosphorescent white against the rockbound sides of the narrow channel, but the waters in between were vacant and black, further confirmation that the inlet was free of dangerous submerged obstacles.

Snakeskin now turned the dark lantern toward the following Caesar and flashed a signal to halt, then both navigators pulled on black lines attached to small bells inside the hulls that signaled the helmsmen and boilermen, in this case to throttle back on the propeller turbine and bring the Davids to a stop at a point where the currents were at their least treacherous. The reason for this halt was soon apparent as the sounds of engines began to echo in the night.

A small patrol boat rounded the chisel-point of the island's shore-facing tip showing running lights at bow and stern. The French patrol was a regular night patrol that went part-way around the island, then doubling back in order to avoid the most treacherous of the off-shore currents. As the Davids drifted slowly toward shore on the night tide, the patrol boat passed between them and the island's windward shores, then began swinging back toward the other end of the isle in the direction of Île Royale.

A snatch of conversation from the deck echoed across the waters and then suddenly a searchlight beacon lanced out amidships from its port side, moving back and forth across the ocean. The cone of the beacon described a wide arc whose sweep brought it close to the Davids drifting in on the tide, but the stealthy, pitch-black vessels remained hidden from the view of the French gendarmes aboard.

In a few minutes, the searchlight was extinguished and the patrol boat chugged onward toward the northeast end of the island, to disappear entirely around the projecting headlands leaving silence in its wake. That was just as well - - in the spill of light from the sides of the beacon, Snakeskin could see the twin deck-mounted Maxim guns on the patrol craft, either of which could cut the unarmed Davids in half.

Once the French patrol was totally gone from sight, Snakeskin pulled on the signal line and the helmsman opened the throttle again to power the stealthy vessel toward the safe channel. The progress of the two semi-submersibles was aided considerably by the ocean currents, which flowed toward Devil's Island and carried them shoreward on the island's windward side.

Another yank on the black cord as the mouth of the rock-ribbed inlet came into close proximity and the helmsman bilged out the ballast tank by one-half of its capacity to raise the hull bottom well clear of any hidden obstructions at the channel bottom not shown on the chart. At the same time, he throttled back to slow the screws to a virtual stop and allow the Alexander to ride the in-sweep of the sea tides as noiselessly as possible into the safe passage while Snakeskin and Jake O'Dreams, behind the boiler stacks, conned the beachhead and the rising land beyond.

Detecting no French patrols in the immediate vicinity as the first David drifted abreast of the stony black fringe of tropical beach, Snakeskin signaled both helmsman and boilerman to prepare for landing.

As the David slowed to almost a full stop, Snakeskin jumped off into the shallows (which the map indicated were free of quicksand). Gripping hold of one of the black iron davits set along the hull, he manhandled the David ashore and beached it, while the second David abreast of the Alexander did the same.

In minutes the two craft lay alongside one another with ballast water gushing from the bilge holes at their port and starboard sides. All six men, each of them now armed with pistols at the belt and short-barreled Enfield repeating rifles strapped across their chests or hung from their shoulders, had by this time emerged from the Davids. Dressed entirely in black, their faces (as well as the heads of those with light colored hair) were all blacked with soot.

A two-man guard would remain to watch the beached Davids while the rest of the party tramped inland to perform their part of the mission, equipped with special gear and supplies they had pulled from the Davids. The guard detail had instructions to wait one hour, destroy one of the Davids with a delay-timed charge of dynamite, and return to the Courageous in the surviving stealth boat should Blake not return. Attempts to hide the vessels were not made as the black craft were naturally camouflaged against the black stones of the shoreline fringes and the night was devoid of all but starlight. As the guard detail hunkered behind rocks a few feet from the Davids, the shore party used broken palm leaves to brush the sand behind them until all traces of their footprints had been erased.

Snakeskin consulted his wristwatch, its radium dial glowing faintly in the almost total darkness. Sunrise was still hours distant and the start of full daylight hours beyond. Snakeskin signaled the team to take a five minute rest break in order to gather strength for what would almost certainly be a grueling ordeal. They would need every bit of physical stamina for the rigorous trials that lay ahead as they attempted to break into Devil's Island, rescue La Crosse and break out once again.

When they were rested and had drunk some of the water they had brought along, Snakeskin and the rest of the shore party slung their packs over their shoulders, ported their rifles and followed map and magnetic compass through the jungle.

FIVE DEAD MEN

The dense foliage proved treacherous, as did the ground underfoot, whose verdant covering of tropical grass and jungle vines formed a thin mat across the rocky ground beneath. Nature had endowed Devil's Island with quicksand pits, poisonous snakes and every imaginable sort of entrapment, they were well aware.

Because of their overwhelming need to remain unseen, and to make certain that they did not wind up falling victim to the island's numerous pitfalls, progress into the interior was deliberately slow. Though the night sky was still deep black, the stars had begun to set and a faint dusting of light limned the far horizon when they reached the perimeter of the prison reservation.

Taking care to shield the lenses of his field glasses so that the lights of the prison encampment would not glint off of them and give their position away to the French gendarmes of the penal colony, Snakeskin carefully scanned the area.

A night guard detail of several French sentries was walking the perimeter, attired in their characteristic blue uniforms and peaked caps and carrying rifles. Snakeskin continued to scan the area, making notes on his map, taking his time to construct a workable plan that would not only enable them to break La Crosse out, but to survive the escape as well.

16. The Prisoner's Secret Charger

It was still night, but the darkness brought no relief from the stifling humidity of the tropical island hell.

Snakeskin thought to himself that the island was aptly named. If the devil lived anywhere on earth, then certainly this island was perfectly suited to provide him every comfort that hell had to offer.

Moving silently through the darkness and keeping to the path marked in red ink on Snakeskin's terrain map -- a path that had been compiled from the accounts of those few men who had succeeded in reaching at least part of the way to freedom and which was known to skirt the greatest of the island's many obstacles -- they succeeded in reaching the perimeter of the French prison camp well before the break of day.

The fence was made of barbed concertina wire strung between stakes hammered into the ground. Snakeskin and his company were encouraged to find that the fence was not well patrolled. Apparently, the French jailers had little concern about prisoners attempting to break out, trusting in the fact that the jungle itself was a far more effective barrier to successful flight than any artificial impediment that could be devised by the hand of man.

A few snips with a pair of stout cutting shears and Snakeskin had severed a section of fence, exposing a space wide enough for himself and his team to make their way through into the compound beyond. They moved a few feet inside when Snakeskin suddenly held out his hand, upraised in an unmistakable sign of warning. He had heard a sound and quickly saw the origin of the disturbance.

A French sentry had detected movement. He was now striding in their direction, and although he had not yet seen them, the gendarme's curiosity had been aroused. The raiding party froze where they crouched in the dense undergrowth and saw the sentry kneel down in order to inspect the cut-out section of perimeter fence. Then he rose to his feet and turned in alarm, and they realized that if they did not kill him quickly before he could sound an alert then all would be lost.

Snakeskin stole silently behind the sentry. He placed an arm around his throat and covered his mouth with his hand. The sentry squirmed in his grasp. Snakeskin was forced to use the dagger that he had drawn from its sheath and which he now clutched in his other hand.

Plunging it between the spars of his adversary's ribs, the point of the dagger found the gendarme's heart and burst it. Blood poured into his chest cavity and spurted from his nose and mouth. Within seconds, he had gone limp. Snakeskin let the dead man sink to the floor. He wiped the blade and his hands on the gendarme's mud-stained uniform before he and Jopling dragged the corpse into the brush.

Motioning to the others, Snakeskin proceeded into the compound. Not far ahead of them rows of small, square-sided prison huts in four columns could be made out in the gloaming. The huts were constructed using the large black and gray rocks common on Devil's Island for walls and sawed palm trunks, tarred to keep out the worst of the heavy rains that frequently fell on the island, for roofs. Under the lightening heavens of false dawn, Snakeskin began searching out the Frenchman's prison hut. Conspicuously lacking were windows and bars, as there was little need of either on an island hell from which escape was deemed impossible.

"La Crosse!" he hissed.

Inside, the sleeping Frenchman was roused from nightmarish dreams. He was being chased by insects with long fangs that wanted to suck all his blood from his veins. They called out his name in hissing voices like snakes from a pit, while serpents' tongues flicked from their mouths.

Then the ghouls changed shape and became men, and La Crosse grew mortified, for the men were the cut-throats Dumas and Garnier, and they were chasing him down in the jungle with machetes poised to hack him to pieces so they could steal his "charger" -- the small metal canister containing money and valuables which inmates of Devil's Island carried wedged inside their rectums, deemed the only safe hiding places available.

"La Crosse!"

The Frenchman now came awake with a fitful start. He was certain, after a moment or two of disbelief, that a living voice had indeed spoken his name and not some apparition out of a feverish dream. After a moment La Crosse eventually thought that he even recognized the whispered voice, but this only made him grow more perplexed. What he had heard was an impossibility -- Snakeskin Blake.

Then he heard his name called again, and La Crosse realized that he had not been imagining things, that the unimaginable was indeed taking place -- that friends had come to free him from his island hell.

And as he muttered a prayer of thanks, for the first time in years, a smile creased the Frenchman's face.

Yes, it was Snakeskin Blake's voice that he had heard! There could be no doubt about it. He stood up quickly and went to the crude hole bored at the top of the rotting wooden door to his prison cell.

"Over here!" he whispered hoarsely.

Snakeskin and his two men crossed quickly to the cell from which the Frenchman's voice had been heard to call out an answer. Snakeskin pushed aside the bolt securing the door slowly and carefully, so as not to make any but the slightest of sounds in the night, and he peered inside.

The face had aged a great deal since Snakeskin had last seen the Frenchman, and one of the eyes was dead. In China, the Frenchman had been the Armor Artificer of soldier-saint Chinese Charlie's forces at Taiping. La Crosse had once been as handsome as he was as skilled at his craft of building weapons.

Snakeskin's heart sank at the sight of the changes that time and hardship had worked on his old comrade in arms. He hoped that La Crosse still had what it took in the field of combat or they had come a long way, and risked a great deal, for nothing.

"Can you walk, Frenchie?" Snakeskin asked the prisoner.

"Oui, *mon ami*," La Crosse answered in a hoarse whisper and moved his gaunt, bare legs. The rattling of heavy chains told Snakeskin that they were shackled to his bed.

"Once these are removed, I can at least try. "But walk to where precisely? This island, in case you have not yet heard, is quite inescapable."

"Why did they chain you?" asked Snakeskin, who was already at work examining the lock which secured the shackles by a heavy hasp. It was a standard mortise cylinder, invented only a few years before in 1823. Snakeskin was prepared to pick it quickly and silently with burglar tools.

"Ah. Good question," replied La Crosse. "I have an equally good answer. Tonight, *mon ami* Snakeskin, was the night I was to die. You see, two of my fellow prisoners bribed a corrupt gendarme to have me shackled as you found me tonight. All the better for the cut-throats Dumas and Garnier to kill me for my charger."

"The ... I see, the little goodie bag up your ass."

"Yes, and this means that Dumas and Garnier may be along any minute, so you had better deal with these chains fast. What good it will do I can't imagine, as there's no way off Devil's Island."

"You're forgetting that I found a way to get onto this pestilential hellhole, Frenchman," Snakeskin replied. "And I have every intention of getting off it again, with your worthless ass -- and even the little treasure inside its no doubt stinking brown depths -- in tow."

Snakeskin had already taken a snake pick and tension wrench from the leather case which he had slid from his pocket. He now inserted the pick into the keyway of the lock cylinder.

Next he placed the tension wrench inside the keyway. Probing carefully, working by touch, he gently raked the cylinders of the keyway, feeling them line up within a matter of seconds with a sharp metallic click.

When the rake pick had done its work and the cylinders were neatly and precisely lined up, Snakeskin twisted the tension wrench with a sharp motion of his wrist. The lock snapped open in a second.

"What the hell are those?" Snakeskin asked, seeing the many constructions that filled the small, stifling cell.

"Those, *mon cher*, are my windmills," the Frenchman replied. "I have made them to pass the time. I have become quite good at the craft."

"You'll have to leave them," Snakeskin said. "There's only enough room for you, I'm afraid."

"A pity, but I can always make others," La Crosse replied sadly. "Still, I don't grasp how you intend to get me off this island. Have you pairs of angel's wings, perhaps, so that we can fly away like birds?"

"Something even better, Frenchie," Snakeskin answered, smiling a graveyard grin.

"Let's get going."

17. An Escape Bid

Even while night still draped the jungle-covered interior of Devil's Island, the heat was growing oppressive, and the moisture-saturated tropical air adhered to the flesh like a sticky membrane, making the clothes on their backs cling uncomfortably to their skin. And then with a shock, came the cries of French gendarmes from the interior.

"Dumas and Garnier were no doubt disappointed," said Snakeskin to La Crosse.

"Yes, the rogues must have called for the *cochon* Falour, their bribed guard, when they found me missing." He added. "They'll use bloodhounds. Is there still any hope of escape?"

"Just keep moving," snapped Snakeskin, hacking through the underbrush with a machete.

Navigating to the landing site where the two Davids were beached in front of the safe channel, Snakeskin stopped for a moment to get a compass bearing against his map. There were only mere minutes left to reach the beach before the two men he'd posted to guard the Davids carried out their orders to blow one and launch the other.

FIVE DEAD MEN

Snakeskin needed to cancel the order and would have to chance sending up a blue flare. The guard detail would see the emergency signal and wait an additional ten minutes, but the French gendarmes would then be able to better pinpoint their location as well.

Cocking the Very pistol Snakeskin launched the flare and pushed his raiders -- with the almost crippled La Crosse propped up between two Courageous shipmates -- toward the island's rocky beach strip. Yet the sudden clamor raised by their pursuers -- sounds betokening their gaining on them with unexpected speed -- forced him to order a detour from their intended escape route.

A foul-smelling swamp, overhung by the branches of densely clustered mangroves, now lay directly across their line of march.

Fearing the perils posed by alligators and quicksand bogs the party could nevertheless afford to waste no time in attempting to circumnavigate the swamp.

Their only way back to the beach was to cross the swamp, despite the perils that it held for them, as the gendarmes were now right behind them, their hounds sending up a maddening braying as they tracked on the scent of the escaped prisoner and those who had orchestrated his break.

"Damn! They've found us out!" Snakeskin cursed as he struggled to wade through the bog, mud sucking at his boots.

Suddenly the Frenchman cried out, uttering an oath in gutter French. Snakeskin turned and saw the reason for La Crosse's shouted cry. A large snake with a mottled head was rearing up from a branch preparing to lunge at the Frenchmen. It looked like a krait, a species of highly venomous serpents indigenous to the area, and its poison would bring a swift death.

In his confusion, La Crosse had taken a step backward. The misstep proved to pose more of a danger than the snake had.

In a moment or two it became apparent that the Frenchman had stumbled right into one of the many quicksand pools that laced the island. He began sinking quickly, and his thrashing motions to swim through the quagmire to safety only pulled him deeper into its grasp.

"Don't struggle!" Snakeskin told him. "You'll only make it worse. The motions of your body will drag you under."

Snakeskin used his knife to quickly sever a branch from one of the mangroves that grew at the water's edge and tossed it to the Frenchman.

He grasped at the makeshift tow line but missed. Snakeskin tried to cast the branch toward him once again. The Frenchman caught hold on the third toss.

"Hold on tight!" Snakeskin warned his struggling comrade. He pulled with all his might, using his legs to position himself against the soggy mud of the bank, giving little more purchase than the quicksand pool itself.

Finally the Frenchman came free, his striped prisoner's gown and trousers encrusted with foul smelling mud. Snakeskin helped La Crosse to rise to his feet. He shoved him forward and the group pushed on.

■

Behind them, bloodhounds were sniffing the ground and baying excitedly as they chased the fugitives' scent. Their trainers held a piece of filthy rag that had been taken from the Frenchman's cell in front of the hounds' noses.

They caught La Crosse's scent and were let off their leashes. The dogs bounded into the jungle after the escapee and whoever it was that had helped free him from his cell.

FIVE DEAD MEN

"There were at least ten of them, I tell you!" Dumas –
who, like his partner in crime Garnier, claimed to have had
witnessed the escape -- was saying.

"He had help. A small army. We would have been killed
had we tried to come between such desperate men and their
plan."

"Impossible!" the guard shot back, not believing the
ragged prisoner whom he held by his collar, almost
strangling the mass of skin and bones. "No living soul can
get on or off the island. I tell you --"

"Sir, please come here," one of the French gendarmes
interjected with a wave of his hand for emphasis.

The guardsman dropped the human cadaver whom he
had been interrogating (for such had the once burly denizen
of the more seamy quarters of Paris become in captivity) and
hastened over to where the guard was stationed. Glancing
down he saw the corpse of another prison gendarme lying
sprawled limply on the muddy ground.

The pool of congealed blood spreading from his torso
left no doubt in the captain's mind that he had been killed
some time before.

"Murderous scum!" the captain yelled, gritting his teeth.
"Whoever first gets those dogs will receive a month's pay as
bonus."

Maybe the wretch was correct after all, thought the
captain of French gendarmes. Maybe La Crosse did have
help after all, however impossible that might seem. When
they caught up with the prisoner's fleeing rescuers, the
captain would personally make certain they confessed every
detail. Torture would loosen their tongues ... and then pull
them out by the roots.

■

The escaped prisoner who was the object of the captain's wrath could barely move his legs by this point and now lagged behind, carried by two Courageous crewmen, as the raiding party fled through the jungle. The racket made by the baying of the bloodhounds as they tore after their fleeing quarry was a constant reminder that capture or death was close at their heels.

Anticipating that the bid to break La Crosse out of jail might result in the gendarmes loosing their hounds on them, Snakeskin had come prepared.

Stopping briefly, Snakeskin took from his pocket a bag containing a compound that he'd had specially made up in Zanzibar.

The mixture of cayenne pepper, tamarind, sage and other spices would confound the sensitive noses of the hounds and render their sense of smell temporarily useless. Shaking the mixture onto the ground, Snakeskin moved on and quickly rejoined the other men who had struggled on ahead.

While Snakeskin's gambit worked, it was only half effective. The hounds, though confused, were still on their scent. The progress of the escapees was further slackened by the need to double back in their steps and break to the side, then wade across streams, brackish pools and sodden ground.

Nevertheless, the stands of coconut palm and jungle undergrowth eventually began to thin out and Snakeskin, La Crosse, Jopling and the rest of the raiding party – aided by the markings on the map -- emerged onto the beachhead on the other side of the island. The blackness of night had given way to the dusk of twilight and far off on the distant horizon the first glow of the rising tropical sun signaled that dawn was only a short while away.

Telling the Frenchman to keep himself hidden in the concealment of the undergrowth at the edge of the beach where the jungle ended, Snakeskin cautiously reconnoitered the rock-strewn coastal strip.

The beach appeared deserted. The tide had come up, almost to the edge of the places on the boulder-littered scree where the two Davids had been beached on landing. Motioning to first mate Jopling to help the lamed Frenchman from cover, Snakeskin slowly approached the two semi-submersible boats.

As he drew near the two-man guard detail sprang from the concealment of the down slope of the beach and ran toward them.

"We saw the flare just as we were about to cast off," said one of the men. "We saved the bundle of dynamite with its timer in case you might want it."

"I might at that," Snakeskin told them and confirmed that the steam boilers were lit and the Davids ready to be pushed from the beach into the ebbing tide and out to sea.

And now the Frenchman grasped the means by which Snakeskin had succeeded in getting onto Devil's Island.

"Now I understand!" he cried delightedly. "An ingenious stratagem. But I don't think I can do it, Snakeskin."

"Now's the wrong time to say that, La Crosse," Snakeskin countered with a scowl.

"I'm serious, *mon ami*," he told him sincerely. "You see, I am an incurable claustrophobic."

"You've spent the last four years in a tiny stone cell that would have given even a monk pause," Snakeskin retorted angrily. "How in the name of heaven can you call yourself a claustrophobic?"

"A cell is one thing," La Crosse answered. "But this ... this *mechant damne*, it is quite another sort."

"Just the same, La Crosse, you're coming off this island one of two ways," Snakeskin angrily advised his stubborn charge. "Either with us or in a casket. Those gendarmes back there are out for nothing less than blood chit. Don't forget that we were forced to kill one of them in the course of fetching you."

Ultimately realizing that he had no choice, and that Snakeskin was perfectly capable of forcing him bodily into the Alexander, the Frenchman joined Snakeskin and Jake O'Dreams in pushing the pocket submarine toward the waterline where the sea lapped at the island's stony shore.

O'Dreams was climbing into the Caesar's hatchway when he suddenly went limp and fell with a splash into the water. A dark mist of blood spread through the lapping waves. A bullet from one of the gendarmes' guns had struck him clean through the heart.

"There's nothing for him," Snakeskin commented, pushing the Frenchman inside. "Keep your head down and do exactly what I tell you."

Grabbing hold of the bow runnels Snakeskin used legs and arms to push the David into the sea, ebb tide making his job harder. A few feet away, Jopling was similarly occupied, while inside the Alexander and Caesar the steersmen and boilermen were hard at their tasks. French rifle bullets were now sparking against the pocket submersible's hull spars and boiler stack as they went ricocheting off the rubble-strewn scree.

Wading in the shallows with his boots in the muddy bottom talus as rifle fire continued to rain down on the escaping rescue party, Snakeskin suddenly sank down to his knees in pebble-strewn muck. Quicksand, he suddenly realized. It only took another second for the pit to suck him down to the waist, but by now the Alexander's boiler was at full steam and its churning screws were backing the stealth craft from the beach into the channel.

FIVE DEAD MEN

The tug of the quicksand pit was unbelievably strong and for a moment Snakeskin felt as if his fingers would be pulled from the iron runnels they gripped for dear life, but the force of the boat easily overmatched the downward pull of muddy death. As Snakeskin's boots were freed from the quicksand he scrambled up top where the boilerman was waiting to haul him up. His gesture nearly cost him his life as a bullet creased his cheek and temporarily knocked him out. Snakeskin pulled the unconscious sailor into the vessel which was backing out of the channel at full speed. Shouting to the steersman to push the throttle hard, Snakeskin crawled back up top to conn the shore as the vessel continued backing out of the channel.

The Devil's Island gendarmerie had turned out in full complement. As officers shouted orders, they had advanced to the edge of the beach fringe and were firing their rifles pell-mell.

Snakeskin noted, however, that the bullets were landing farther and farther away as the Davids moved out of range. But through his binoculars he also clearly saw French troops struggling to pull two medium range cannons down the slope of the heights beyond the beach and set them up.

At the same time, Snakeskin knew that the patrol boat that the raiding party had seen pass in the moonless night was certain to put in an appearance. He was sure its crew had already been telegraphed with orders. Snakeskin unshipped the Very pistol from its belt holster and fired a red star shell to warn the Courageous that the Davids were returning under fire. A glance over his shoulder and a thumbs-up signal from Jopling, who like himself was conning the boiler stack to reconnoiter, told Snakeskin that both boats were making good time to the rendezvous point with the Courageous.

DAVID ALEXANDER

As the patrol vessel came into view a few hundred yards out beyond the channel's mouth, the Courageous also spotted her and made to stop her with its deck guns. The pirate ship's ensigns flew, the banner of yellow Chinese silk bearing the emblem of a great sea serpent coiled about a whale and preparing to devour its prize with the motto "To the Victors Belong the Spoils" surrounding the bold depiction, waved atop the converted blockade runner as the Courageous' first cannon volleys boomed out across the open water. The shells landed close, throwing up huge gouts of white spray and rocking the Davids so hard that had not Snakeskin and Jopling made sure to hug the conning stacks they might have been thrown overboard into the water.

In moments a second artillery salvo followed on the heels of the initial volley. The shells hit closer as the gunners began to get the windage of the French boat and tape it with their guns, but the Davids had turned now and were speeding beyond the range of their own artillery.

The shore cannonry had been set up too late to do the French garrison any good either. With both Davids now turned toward the windward side of the island with the sea to their fronts, and the welcome sight of the Courageous drawing nearer by the minute, Snakeskin knew they would make it back to the ship alive.

Except ... where had the French patrol boat gone? It hadn't been sunk and he could no longer see it. The thought that something was amiss and he couldn't put his finger on exactly what that something might be made Snakeskin's blood run cold.

18. Double or Nothing

Bilging out water as fast as possible, the Davids broke the surface a few feet off the port bows of the Courageous and bobbed like corks in the chop and swell.

FIVE DEAD MEN

Jopling's second mate His Highness was waiting at the gunnels. His Colt pistol was kept trained on the hatch of the first David to arrive as the hatch opened and a head pushed up. So were the cocked rifles ported by the other crewmembers as the iron cover was raised up fully and then slammed back against the deck of the boat with a resounding clang.

To His Highness's great relief, he saw at once that it was Snakeskin who poked his head up out of the open hatchway a few moments later.

"Looks like some men are missing, skipper," he observed.

"Two didn't make it," Snakeskin told him. "But we at least have the Frenchman. Hoist up the Davids and make for the sea immediately. And put shooters in the amidships and mast turrets. We'll need 'em."

"Aye, aye, cap'n. Right away."

"And order the lookouts to keep watching the leeward side of the island for French gunboats -- or bigger."

His Highness's weathered mariner's face clouded over and the puckered star carved on his jowl by a dockside whore on a night long ago stood out like a welt.

"Bigger? That means trouble."

"Let's hope a gunboat's all we'll face. Get to it."

"Aye, cap'n Snakeskin," His Highness replied and began buttonholing crewmen and shouting orders to the rest.

"You heard the skipper!" hollered His Highness through cupped hands to the ship's winch crew. "Hoist up them Davids and prepare to sail full steam right away!"

"Aye, sir!" was the shouted reply as the crews sprang into action amid the clatter of chains and the creaking of thick-braided Indian hemp straining against wooden blocks and tackles.

But now the Caesar was bobbing even further away as the disturbed waters pushed it to and fro. Because the semi-submersible had moved before Snakeskin had had a chance to dog the hatch behind him, seawater was now spilling inside the hull.

"Forget trying to haul her in," Snakeskin shouted to His Highness, as he heard the sudden unmistakable reports of deck guns. "She's as good as sunk already. Bring us aboard instead, and be quick about it!"

"Right, Cap'n!"

Turning his head, Blake now saw the French patrol boat round the northeastern bend of the island as it had done the previous night, but now instead of hugging the beach line on shore patrol, the boat was tearing out to sea from the sheltered cove in which it had taken refuge from the bigger guns of the Courageous.

And then Snakeskin saw that just behind the French gunboat was a larger ship, a French frigate by her looks. Suddenly there was a flash from the starboard deck and a shell whistled overhead.

Almost simultaneously the lookout stationed high in the crow's nest shouted a warning.

"Ahoy! Frigate to starboard. Frigate to starboard!" He noted the French tricolor high on its foremast. "She's a French ship, cap'n!"

The frigate had come around the leeward side of Devil's Island. The big black guns on her main deck began cranking out cannon fire the instant that the French crew caught sight of the Courageous. The frigate's crew was intent on sinking her, and with both two-to-one odds and frigates against a glorified blockade runner like the Courageous, they were more than confident that they could do so in a trice.

FIVE DEAD MEN

Once again, the big twenty-two inch guns on her main deck boomed threateningly, hurling artillery ordnance across the ocean amid belching clouds of cordite smoke.

Stretching out his hands, Snakeskin tried to catch the swinging end of the hawser line that moved precariously as the ship heeled in the roiling waters. Despite the salt spray that splashed his face and blinded his eyes, he managed to grasp hold of the line after a few unsuccessful tries.

Pulling himself up, he reached for the Frenchman's outstretched hand. La Crosse struggled to reach it but lost his footing and went tumbling into the water.

He fell into the drink as his kicking heels sent the cigar-shaped submersible rotating on its side, and seawater now poured into its open hatchway in a great inrush. The interior of the David filled quickly and the stealth boat began sinking to the bottom of the channel as La Crosse floundered in the cold ocean chop and swell.

"I cannot swim," he shouted. "*Mon dieu*! I will drown!"

The Frenchman was flopping around as more volleys struck the water. Spray foamed and splashed everywhere. Snakeskin leapt from his perch on the swinging boom. He managed to grab hold of the floundering Frenchman just as he was about to go down for the final time.

Reaching up, Snakeskin caught a firm grasp of the end of the hawser line. The booming cannon fire from the French frigate was coming faster now, each shot placed with greater and greater accuracy by its deck artillery crew.

Jopling, now back in command of the ship's crewmen, was shouting from his position on the gunwales of the vessel. The hawser crew was cranking furiously to raise the gaffe. Still more cannon fire from the frigate's deck pounded the churning waters at the same time as the twin Maxims on the deck of the French gunboat came within range and bullets stitched the waters. White foaming spray was everywhere, tossed skyward in immense geysers that blinded the eyes and drenched sailors to the skin.

The surface of the sea had come alive as though devils below were sporting and frolicking at the carnage taking place above them. A thousand fountains were sending jets of violently spurting white water as high as fifty feet in the air as artillery and bullets smacked into the sea.

With the Frenchman now in tow, Snakeskin was being hoisted up to the deck of the raider. Many hands combined to help him and La Crosse up onto the Courageous's deck.

But now the turret gunners had the French patrol boat in their sights and in range of their madly chattering Gatlings. Its boilers a'steam, its prow cleaving a long, foaming white V as it skated across the waters and turned hard to bring its port side Maxim into firing range, the gunboat unleashed a sustained burst of blowback-driven automatic fire amidships of the Courageous while the frigate -- still far to its leeward -- continued to shell the pirates' blockade runner.

Green and white tracers crisscrossed from gunboat to cruiser as the turretmen leaned on the triggers of the twin Gatlings and the big welded plates of the squat amidships turret were pocked repeatedly by bullet hits. To and fro, back and forth turned the moveable pillbox mounted on deck, having become sheathed in a dark pall of acrid gunsmoke through which the rapid twinkles and gouts of yellow flame bespoke the destructive fury of the Courageous' armament, while at the same time the single Gatling mounted midway up the stern mast also ratcheted out its blazing fury.

Now aware that its impudence in chasing down the pirate vessel had brought it seriously in harm's way, the French gunboat heeled about and tried to flee, throwing bursts of Maxim fire to cover its maneuver. The patrol boat never survived to complete the turn as the combined Gatling salvos from the pivoting, swinging plate steel turret amidships and the crow's nest turret converged on its flanks and pierced its ammunition magazine, igniting an explosion that sent men flying overboard in cascades of pyrotechnics amid sprays of white water.

Another salvo from the turret ship finished her off, stitching across her deck and practically chopping the gunboat in half. Its boiler exploded and the vessel broke apart and disintegrated in a billowing fireball. Rising smoke and wreckage that fell smacking to the surface and lay burning on the waters was soon all that was left of the gunboat.

The frigate was now making full speed toward the Courageous, and its deck artillery was aiming truer as its prow cleaved the waters. The frigate was fleet and its maneuvering showed a grasp of naval tactics on the part of its commander -- the French ship was jockeying to get into the T formation to gain the tactical position of superiority from which to deal a blow to the Courageous -- but there was no comparison between the agility of the two vessels.

The American ironclad, built from a high-speed casemated hull as a fast Civil War blockade runner, then augmented with extra boilers and twin props, was by far the fleeter of the two. And although the riveted plate steel from which the French vessel was made could withstand bullet strikes, the Gatlings would still be lethal when brought in close and sustained fire from the three machineguns poured into the enemy ship's sides and stitched across her decks.

Besides, the crew of the Courageous had perfected an array of lethal tactics against larger vessels. Now, while the turret gunners reloaded and let the barrels of the Gatlings cool down, while they wiped the sweat and soot from their hot faces and rested hands that had gripped hard on triggers and ammo belts, rocketeers prepared their Cosgroves for immediate offensive deployment against the frigate which was still in hot pursuit and trying to lay fire on the Courageous' flanks to break her hull in two and sink her.

This was not to be, however, as the frigate was now in range of the rockets which were sent arcing up and away on trajectories that rained their high explosive warheads down across the French ship's decks. The series of flashes and booms threw up clouds of smoke that further obscured the aim of the gun crew and officers onboard, and like the gunboat before it, the frigate now tried to flee.

As it turned, the rocketeers saw the big, flattened cylinder of welded plate steel begin to swing menacingly and the twin Gatling barrels that jutted from its firing slits start cranking out streams of phosphorescent tracer fire. The mast turret gunner did likewise, the high Gatling angled downward and pouring out continuous automatic bursts in tandem with the turret amidships of the Courageous.

The swiftly maneuvering pirate vessel easily outpaced the fleeing frigate and its combined gunfire stitched across its starboard flank and its decks from stem to stern, chewing apart wood and steel and bursting the bodies of living men to send them to their deaths amid showers of blood and gore. Through the pall of smoke that wreathed the deck of the frigate, crewmen aboard the Courageous saw men cut down like stalks of corn in a field, saw the dark shapes, already shadows and specters, topple over the gunnels and splash to the water and drown.

Still the guns of the Courageous inflicted their carnage on the already crippled French ship which had stopped dead in the water as its screws were broken by bullet strikes that struck the French frigate just aft of its starboard bows, smashing the ship's rudder to flinders, while more Gatling and cannon fire went crashing into the ship's deck amidships.

All of a sudden there was a terrific explosion. A scorching ball of yellow flame blossomed from the side of the stricken vessel and blazing tongues of orange and red went licking and scorching up toward the skies. Now French sailors were jumping off the side of the ship, plunging headlong into patches of fire that floated on the sea.

"By God, we hit her magazine! Right up the bitch's ass!" Snakeskin shouted out elatedly as another set of explosions were heard suddenly to rend the air, and yet more fires broke out at the stern of the burning vessel. Within seconds, the ship had keeled over onto its port side as water rushed in through the huge breach torn in its hull, burning like a torch on the ocean and sending a plume of dense black smoke heaving and tumbling in the wind.

Then the frigate broke apart and began to sink in the keel-up position. Amidst the ocean swell the dark figures of several survivors were seen treading water and gesturing toward the Courageous.

Then suddenly, before Snakeskin could give orders to pick them up, there were the cracks of repeated rifle shots. One by one, the bobbing heads sprouted bloody gashes and sank beneath the waters. Snakeskin reflexively wrenched his head half around to see the gaunt figure holding the Enfield and smoking a cigarette.

"Three less *cochons*, *mon ami*," declared Fallicon La Crosse, now dressed in borrowed dry clothes, standing shakily on his shackle-damaged feet in oversized boots.

"That's how I see it."

Snakeskin smiled grimly but did not respond with a nod.

"Captivity has done nothing to spoil your aim, Frenchie," he told him and took the rifle from his hands.

On the shores of Devil's Island, the French garrison had lost visual contact with the Courageous. The officer in charge now ordered the two cannons brought back up the mountainside from the rock beach, and his perspiring subordinates cursed as they struggled to obey the command under the harsh glare of the hot tropical sun.

Sweaty work, but these dogs were born to it, thought the officer, who cast a glance over his shoulder to confirm that his orders were being obeyed before mounting the rise himself. When he returned to the command post of the gendarmerie there would be a rush telegram to Paris, by way of the mainland of French Guiana, that he had already begun to compose in his mind.

BOOK FOUR

STAND BACK

DAVID ALEXANDER

19. Slay the Mahdi

Amid the Chinese of the Orient, the port of Macao was unique in the fact that it had managed to retain a distinctive Portuguese character throughout the course of two hundred years and seven major political upheavals whose aim was to cast out the hated colonial masters of the island republic.

Portuguese traders had founded a colony on the small island -- which lay off the southeastern coast of China opposite Hong Kong on the South China Sea -- in the Sixteenth Century. Macao had been deeded to their descendents of the Portuguese House of Braganza thereafter by the Chinese who continued to police their own while Europeans in the colony remained exempt from local justice that applied only to the despised coolies over which they lorded.

Throughout the period of the Taiping Rebellion, Macao had been used as a conveniently located staging area and launch point for British and French troops sent to fight the rebels who operated on the Chinese mainland and whose numbers grew with popular support for the ouster of colonial occupiers.

The self-styled Taiping Kingdom of Heaven had been led by one Hong Xiuquan, who announced that he had learned, by way of numerous visions, that he was the younger brother of Jesus Christ. Like his elder sibling, Hong loosened his hair and refused to wear the queue that was the hated emblem of the coolie. His followers, quickly becoming known as "longhairs," did the same.

At least in terms of his ultimate demise, this was not entirely untrue, for Hong ended up secretly poisoned by traitors in the midst of his heavenly army, and in dying a slow, lingering and extremely painful death, paved the way for the rebellion being crushed by French and British troops fighting alongside Chinese loyalists.

These latter, for whose ultimate success they were named "The Ever Victorious Army" were trained (and sometimes led) by Sir Charles George Gordon, then holding the rank of Major-General in the British Army, having just previously served with valor in the Crimea. The result was defeat for the rebellion and victory for the Qing Dynasty, which by then had become a mere puppet of Anglo-French colonialism in the region.

It was against the Longhairs that Snakeskin had been hired as a mercenary by Sir Charles, whose success in the endeavor had earned him the cognomen that had attached itself to him ever since -- Chinese Charlie. Gordon had found Snakeskin a soldier and sailor after his own heart, for the American soldier of fortune shared his lust for adventure, his thirst for action, and his excitement for the application of novel tactics against dangerous foes.

DAVID ALEXANDER

In the course of their relationship the two men -- similar in build and features as well as in their youthful years -- had begun to view one another as brothers in spirit as well as in arms. The bonds between American freebooter Snakeskin Blake and professional soldier Chinese Gordon were strong enough to withstand the passage of years and the distances of miles, and they included a mutual sense of disillusionment and cynicism even in victory, for both Chinese Charlie and Snakeskin Blake had come to admire the ends for which their enemies had fought, even as they had bent their wills to crush them into the dust of defeat.

The Longhairs' reforms had included the rights of women (who often fought alongside men in the rebellion's bloody battles) and the relief of the oppression of those Chinese who lived in poverty while the Qing Emperor and his government officials enjoyed wealth and privileges that included the power of life and death over mere coolies. While their side had won, while their thirst for adventure remained unchanged, the nature of victory itself had made cynics of both men. It had been those bonds that had led to Gordon's personal recommendation to Lord Canning -- who as Great Britain's Viceroy and Governor-General of all India, was also administrator of the region which included Zanzibar -- to push for the American's hiring to the service of Sultan Majid bin Said against the Mahdi's kidnapping of his English-born wife.

But there were other friendships that had alike been forged in the fight against the Longhairs and in the disillusionment with the colonial powers in the aftermath of the Taiping Rebellion. There were some of Snakeskin Blake's compatriots from that foreign war who had stayed on here, and Snakeskin knew they were still to be found living in Macao. This was fortunate, as he would need their

157

assistance in locating the next individual on his recruitment list for his brotherhood of fighters.

The name of this particular brother in arms was Chow Bang Chow, and in Snakeskin's opinion Chow Bang Chow was one of the greatest Wu-Shu masters in all of China. The term embraced fighting skills such as Qiqong and Chinese Boxing as well as individual fighting styles within the disciplines. It was Chinese Boxing, also known as Kung-Fu or "the way of masterful accomplishment" that the fighter practiced with a skill above all others. Proficient in multiple styles and with edged weapons, sticks, and the strange two-headed club that the Longhairs had called "nunchaku," as well as with the throwing stars they had called "shuriken," Chow Bang Chow was a master at this martial art who feared no weapon turned against him. His mind, the former Longhair had claimed, was his greatest weapon.

Snakeskin's first encounter with Chow Bang Chow had been while soldiering for Chinese Charlie against Hong's forces in rebel-held Nanking. Millions had already joined the Longhair cause against the Manchu-led Qing Emperor, and the revolutionaries in an uprising that would wind up claiming twenty million lives, by some estimates. The uprising had caught fire among the long misruled populace of Shanghai. Occupied by foreigners and divided into zones of occupation, the people were ripe for rebellion.

The flashpoint had been a coup staged by Longhairs that had resulted in the takeover of one of the Manchu's palatial imperial compounds in old Shanghai. It was here that a combined Imperial and European force on the one hand, and irregular Chinese trained by Chinese Charlie, on the other, were poised to strike back. Within a matter of hours, angry crowds had set numerous houses in the city afire, and soon all of Shanghai was engulfed in an immense conflagration with smoke from the fires casting a pall over the sea.

The native population might have in itself not caused the major debacle that ensued, but the heads of the rebellion had brought in thugs from outside the city to bolster their ranks against what Hong's spies had predicted would be massive opposition. Many of these thugs were simply Highbinders and Hong Men that had been drawn to Shanghai from haunts as far apart as the seedy tenderloins of San Francisco's Barbary Coast, Hong Kong's Kowloon district and the squats of Singapore, by the Manchus' promise of Spanish doubloons and carte blanche for plunder and rapine.

Swollen with these newcomers, and egged on to violence by paid agents of the criminal societies -- the tongs or triads -- the mob marched on the British, French and Portuguese trading compounds as well as Manchu residencies in Shanghai, overwhelming some, laying siege to others. Other mobs of the amok citizenry rampaged about the city, pillaging, raping and looting as they vented their rage on anyone and anything that stood in their path, then began putting to the torch anything that could be made to catch fire and burn.

At the same time, forces loyal to the Manchu Emperor had been equally bolstered by Highbinder gangs that were if anything a far worse lot than any of those recruited by Hong, for most of them were little better than the scum of the seven seas paid in Spanish pieces of eight, then given rifles and a mandate to kill. Gordon had sanctioned this army of rabble because he had needed raw numbers. It was an army which, though putatively British, was nevertheless made up of a large percentage of Americans and other foreign mercenaries lured to China by adventure, gold, hopes of a glorious death in battle or a mixture of all of these.

FIVE DEAD MEN

Through tortuously twisting, often unbelievably narrow streets that meandered into sudden blind alleys formed by the walls of ramshackle buildings, Snakeskin had led a contingent of troops, their mission to destroy a band of especially brazen looters who had already been responsible for the deaths of several of their comrades in arms.

It was around a sudden turn in the labyrinthine lane that Snakeskin witnessed a sight that he would never forget. At once he recognized the leaders of the gang of Highbinders that it was his assignment to exterminate. But the Chinese were themselves preoccupied with a lone man -- a fighter whom they appeared to have surrounded, with the obvious intent to do him serious bodily harm.

The cause of the confrontation seemed clear, for to one side of the standoff were two women, one of middle years, the other a girl in her twenties. Both women were practically naked, clothed only in the rags that were the remnants of their clothes. Their bare breasts bore the bloody marks of violation, and they wept as they huddled within the embrace of an old Chinese in fine robes who tried to comfort them. The elder Chinese too had been injured, apparently in a fight to protect the women who it was equally apparent, were his wife and daughter. His cap was off, his gray queue cut in half and his face bloodied.

Snakeskin held out his hand in a sign for his mixed force of American and British soldiers armed with repeating Enfield rifles to halt as he watched the events unfold. All stood riveted as one of the Chinamen in the gang of thugs raised a pistol and made to fire at the man the group had cornered, but to Snakeskin's amazement, the intended victim simply dodged each of the pistol shots. Snakeskin watched as the lithe Chinaman continued to perform the miraculous feat of dodging bullets from a dead-aimed pistol, even going so far as catching them with his hands with what looked to Snakeskin like effortless ease.

But the feat which the Chinamen next performed was even more amazing to Snakeskin Blake. When the thug's Colt pistol had finally run dry, and its hammer had struck down on a cylinder slot containing only a spent bullet casing, two iron martial arts throwing stars flew from the martial artist's hands. Snakeskin could not detect even the faintest blur of motion as the shuriken sliced through the air at incredible speeds.

The deadly multiple pointed martial arts throwing stars became immediately embedded in the heads and throats of the Highbinders who had been intent on the plunder of the Shanghai merchant. However, for the would-be rapists and murderers of the two women, the martial artist reserved a somewhat different punishment, for these Highbinder thugs were first castrated with shuriken strikes to their genitals, and only then dispatched with a second throw of ninja stars to the throat and head.

The other members of the Highbinder band were quickly put away with a lightning series of kicks and punches -- many of these delivered in the course of incredible leaps into space that were almost like flight -- that sent the lucky survivors of the conflict toppling like so many nine pins to the cobbled street. Before Snakeskin or his soldiery knew what happened, the Chinese Boxer (for such they assumed he was) had disappeared into one of the neighborhood's narrow alleys, almost as though he had never existed at all.

Determined to seek this ghost fighter and learn his motives, Snakeskin used his network of contacts to trace his identity. Ultimately he was able to meet Chow Bang Chow, whose invitation to study the ancient fighting arts of Wu-Shu was eagerly accepted. Snakeskin learned secrets from Chow

Bang Chow that no foreigner had ever known and they became fast friends.

Over the course of the years that had since passed from Snakeskin's China days, he had learned that Chow Bang Chow had fallen in with rebels hostile to the Empress Dowager Tz'u-Hsi and had been forced to go into hiding, as there was now a high price on his head.

Snakeskin had heard nothing about Chow Bang Chow's whereabouts for more than a year, though the American was certain that Chow Bang Chow was still alive, somewhere in the vastness of China.

But alive or not, the martial artist would certainly be an intensively hunted man, for the fighter had incurred the wrath of the Dowager many times since the days of the Longhair uprising and Empress Tz'u-Hsi, though beginning to grow old, still retained a grip on power, an unbending will, and a thirst for vengeance against her foes as strong as it was in her youth, when she had risen to prominence to become first concubine of the Manchu potentate Xianfeng.

Perhaps even worse, the master of the martial arts had also incurred the wrath and deadly retribution of the Highbinders, whose collective memory was long, and whose bloody hand reached into the four corners of the earth.

Snakeskin was also certain that if anyone were to know Chow Bang Chow's whereabouts, it would be Van Bronck.

The portly Dutchman lived in the Portuguese trading colony in Macao. His business was in running American and English guns and trafficking in Chinese opium, with a bit of white slavery on the side when commerce grew slow. And Van Bronck, Snakeskin well knew, was a man who never lost track of anybody who had ever crossed his path, be that person living or dead, or anywhere in between.

DAVID ALEXANDER

20. In the Shadow of the Phalanx

Walking the narrow, twisting streets of the old section of Macao in the vicinity of Senado Square, Snakeskin Blake reflected on how the old trading colony had changed since he'd last made port. The once bustling streets, thronged with human traffic through which rickshaws borne by coolies threaded, filled with the pungent smells of cooking food and the discordant sounds of a busy population, were now virtually deserted. At their sides, buildings that had once been well kept now showed all the signs of severe neglect, while some were in partial ruins.

Snakeskin was glad of three things -- the clear blue sky overhead, the fresh morning breeze from the harbor where the Courageous was anchored, and the comforting touch of the LeMat revolvers holstered snugly on left thigh and right, from which a quick and practiced hand could draw and fire either or both of the weapons if danger threatened.

The seedy look of Macao marked a city that had been bypassed by the trading routes of nations since the British Crown had won Hong Kong from China and the deep water port of Victoria Harbor was opened to the large European merchant shipping that could not put in at the port of Macao. Once the ships full of goods had taken their business elsewhere, Macao had begun a slide into decline, and not even its being declared a free port by its Portuguese masters had been able to do anything to stop the downward slump.

As was inevitable once the processes of decay had set in anywhere, the city had consequently seen an influx of human vermin inversely proportionate to the outflow of business. As the ships docked elsewhere, as the *godowns* on the wharves of Macao's crescent harbor were abandoned and left to decay, traffickers in other commodities began to arrive.

Today, Macao's largest export item was human beings, for Macao had become the region's main transit point in the trade in coolie laborers from southern China. Kidnapped from the provinces, they were taken to makeshift prisons, sold on the auctioneer's block and then packed into vessels to be shipped off to Cuba, Peru and other South American ports to spend the rest of their lives slaving in banana plantations or toiling in the airless depths of Spanish gold mines.

Intent on not losing his way, Snakeskin was aware that hostile eyes had undoubtedly been watching his every step since his arrival ashore. His lone presence here was for a purpose. Snakeskin's quarry was shy and once found might decline to talk to anyone but him.

The house for which Snakeskin was searching stood amidst the dark confines of a narrow street called the Magdalene. He had been forced to ask directions of passersby several times, but ultimately he succeeded in finding the address for which he'd searched.

The Dutchman's shop was not an easy one to spot, and deliberately so, because the Dutchman valued his privacy as highly as a miser coveted his hoard of gold. The place was little more than a window and a doorway on an alley that dead-ended in a crumbling brick wall that was the rear of the courtyard of a decaying Portuguese church.

At first Snakeskin thought that the Dutchman was not at home. But then the door was finally opened after a short wait and he found himself looking into the familiar pudgy face he recalled from years gone by.

It took only a moment before the Dutchman's eyes went wide with recognition.

"Snakeskin!" he cried, astonished. "What on earth are you doing here, my lad?"

"Looking for a certain drunken, overweight and completely worthless Dutchman, that's what."

"Well, you've come to the right place," Van Bronck said as he clapped Snakeskin on the shoulder. He ushered Snakeskin into the tumbledown building whose interior was dark inside and musty smelling, and its floor covered with rubble and debris.

The shouts in Macanese, and the clatter of footsteps from the street outside receded into the background as the Dutchman lit an oil lamp against the gloom that hung heavy within the confines of the little ramshackle shop.

Pulling open a door, the lantern's light illuminated a flight of narrow steps leading down into the basement. Van Bronck gestured for Snakeskin to follow him down into the shadowy area below and the lamplight moved shakily as the fat man clutched the banister and descended with hesitant steps. In the gloomy basement Snakeskin saw a humble table and chair of plain hewn wood which stood amid assorted wood-slat packing crates and iron-hooped barrels.

Van Bronck took a second turn onto another staircase made of cut and crudely dressed stone slabs. Instantly

FIVE DEAD MEN

Snakeskin smelled the dankness of naked rock walls and saw a tiny stream of ground water that slowly trickled down their length to stain the floor. The stairs ended in a cavernous space beyond, that might have been a storage room.

Here, too, there was a table and a few chairs clustered around it. Dimly, by the flickering torchlight, Snakeskin could make out racks filled with numerous weapons and other military equipment that lined the walls of the ancient rock.

Placing the oil lamp in the center of the table, Van Bronck ensconced his well-padded form in one of the chairs which seemed too small to support his great bulk. Snakeskin followed suit.

"It's actually a rather funny thing that you've come around just now, Snakeskin," the Dutchman said, lighting up a pipe made entirely from the soft mineral known as meerschaum -- so called because sometimes found floating on the sea and known to the French as *écume de mer* -- whose bowl was carved into the likeness of a large-breasted mermaid, and then tamping down the Cavendish nestled within its chamber.

Snakeskin watched him strike the phosphorus head of a wooden match and suck the flame down from the flaring match head into the bowl of the pipe until the aromatic mixture caught. With the bit clamped between his teeth and blowing fragrant smoke through his nose and mouth, the Dutchman flung aside the match and regarded his visitor searchingly, awaiting an answer.

"Why do you say that?" Snakeskin asked, instantly on his guard.

"Oh, there are certain rumors adrift in the wind," the Dutchman replied coyly.

DAVID ALEXANDER

"Cut the bullshit, Van Bronck," Snakeskin retorted. "You know something. And now, before I go on, I want to know what you know."

The Dutchman leaned forward and sucked contemplatively on his pipe awhile as he regarded his American guest with a blank stare designed to conceal a multitude of sins. Snakeskin could see the gears turning behind his eyes as his mind worked, however. He knew the Dutchman from long ago, and was wise to most of his recondite ways.

"The Phalanx," he replied after a while, coming to a decision, smoke escaping from the corners of his mouth. "They're onto you, Snakeskin."

Snakeskin was silent as he digested the import of what the Dutchman had just revealed to him.

The Phalanx, he knew, had its dark roots in the *Union Corse*, the Corsican criminal organization that had originally been established to oppose the rule by the French and Italian governments which had alternately dominated the island republic for over a hundred years. Some claimed that it went back even further -- much further -- back to the days of the Holy Roman Empire where it had begun as a secret brotherhood called the Héiron du Val d'Or, or the Brotherhood of the Valley of Gold.

While the exact meaning of the name has been debated, there was no doubt as to the Brotherhood's stock in trade. Plainly put, this was murder and theft. Most believed that the Brotherhood, which was thought to have been created by the Knights Templar in the Holy Land, was simply another name for the followers of the Shaykh al Hashishim -- the Assassins -- which was but another creation of the industrious temple knights.

FIVE DEAD MEN

The Phalanx, or Phalange -- literally "knuckle," as if the striking point of a fist -- was simply the ancient brotherhood of killers doing its dirty business under a new name. During the early part of the eighteenth century the Phalanx had divested itself of the political underpinnings of its parent organization to become a purely criminal enterprise.

It was an organization, which, though practicing every form of robbery, extortion and theft specialized in the clandestine arts of assassination. Though of French-Italian origin, the Phalange owed no allegiance to any single nationality, group or creed.

Its reach was global and its aims were purely mercenary. Snakeskin knew well that the Phalanx was a power to be feared and respected, as well as to be stayed away from if at all possible -- and the further away the better.

It had at its command some of the most formidable killers in the entire world. Like the legendary hydra of myth, the Phalanx sported a thousand deadly arms, any one of which, once severed, was quickly regenerated to strike a fresh blow at its victims, wherever they might run, wherever they might attempt to hide.

"How do you know about the Phalanx?" Snakeskin asked after a pause.

"You might say that a man in my line of work tends to pick things up every now and then," Van Bronck replied cryptically, puffing away on the meerschaum with seeming contentment.

"There have been whispers of something very big going on. Your name was mentioned in connection with this specific endeavor. If you've run afoul of *Le Phalange du Le Heiron du Val d'Or* -- that organization which is called the Phalanx in English -- my dear Snakeskin, then I am afraid you have gotten yourself in shit very deep indeed."

"Maybe so, but --"

Snakeskin suddenly stopped in mid-sentence. He froze in position, his eyes questing this way and that.

"What is it?" asked the Dutchman, alarm apparent in his voice, though he knew enough to keep it at a barely audible whisper.

"Quiet!" Snakeskin hissed.

He had already bolted up out of his seat, the big, double-barrel LeMat revolver filling his hand with its hammer cocked and the safety catch disengaged.

The noise that Snakeskin had heard had originated from the top of the stairs that straggled down to the basement. Snakeskin stood up and mounted them quickly, but saw nothing on the ground floor of the building above. Still, he was certain that it had not been his imagination playing tricks on him. Someone or something had produced that sound.

"Does anyone else live here with you?" he asked the Dutchmen when he returned, still gripping the pistol, whose hammer remained cocked, with his finger on the trigger.

"No one," Van Bronck answered with a dismissive shake of his curly gray head. "Perhaps you heard my cat, Esmeralda. Easy, Snakeskin. Let's not chase phantoms."

Snakeskin put away his pistol in the leather holster at his belt. The news about the Phalanx's involvement to the contrary, there was urgent business to which he needed to attend in Macao.

"I want two things from you, Dutchman," he began, "the first concerns the whereabouts of our mutual friend Chow Bang Chow."

"And the second?"

"First tell me about Chow Bang Chow," Snakeskin countered. "Do you know where he is?"

169

FIVE DEAD MEN

"As a matter of fact, yes, I do," the Dutchman replied, nodding his head confidently. "At least in general terms, I do. He is currently in hiding in a section of the mainland in the environs of Yunan Province."

"That's in the north, isn't it?" Snakeskin ventured.

"Quite right," Van Bronck affirmed, nodding his assent. "I think he can be reached but it may take some time and perhaps not inconsiderable effort."

"That's a commodity I'm in short supply of."

"It will also cost not inconsiderable money, I'm afraid."

"I knew you'd get to that point."

"Well, I shall try my best," Van Bronck promised. "Now to the second matter you had on your mind? What was that, my good Snakeskin?"

"Weapons components and gunsmith equipment," Snakeskin replied to the fat man. "I have a detailed list of everything that's needed."

Snakeskin removed the neatly folded sheet of paper that he had been carrying in his pocket. He unfolded the foolscap and laid it flat on top of the table.

On the list, the Frenchman had itemized everything that would be necessary for his production of certain small arms of his own individual design. Having had plenty of time on his hands during his confinement and little to fill it with, the Frenchman had dreamed up some unique refinements on proven and field-tested firearms equipment.

"Yes, I think these items could be procured, Snakeskin," the Dutchman replied after quickly scanning the paper. "I have most of the stuff in stock right here, in fact. It'll cost you, though. These items aren't cheap."

"I'll pay whatever you want," Snakeskin told the portly man seated across him.

He reached into his pocket and produced a wad of bills, watching the Dutchman's eyes light up as he saw the thickness of the sheaf of money. Snakeskin peeled off several hundred dollars in American greenbacks and slid them across the table toward Van Bronck.

"I expect that will do for a down payment."

"Quite nicely," the Dutchman acknowledged quickly, pocketing the money he had just counted.

"I can promise delivery of the merchandise next week, as well as some news of Mr. Chow Bang Chow."

"Make it in forty-eight hours," Snakeskin insisted.

"I'll see what can be arranged," the Dutchman replied deadpan.

Still experiencing the uneasy sensation that he was being followed, and that the eyes of unseen watchers were on his back, Snakeskin left the Dutchman's place. Snakeskin's eyes saw no sign of pursuers, but his mind told him otherwise. Although he took the standard precautions as he departed the Dutchman's haunts on Magdalene Street, Snakeskin suspected that he would need to be doubly on guard from this point onward.

And he would have to now include in his plans the fact that the Phalanx had suddenly entered the picture.

FIVE DEAD MEN

21. Some Unwanted Visitors

The waterfront hostelry in which Snakeskin's rooms were located stood above a tavern frequented by the dockside scum and slags of the Macao waterfront. Snakeskin found La Crosse seated comfortably at the long bar of the smoke-filled saloon nursing a glass of pale hock and crushing a cigarette into an ashtray piled with dead butts.

"How did it go?" asked the Frenchman as he exhaled smoke.

"I paid off Van Bronck in dollars, meaning he'll keep his word or else. There's some possible trouble, though."

Snakeskin told him what the Dutchman had said concerning the Phalanx.

Trudging up several flights of stairs, after making their way through the noisy, smoke-filled bar in which a burlesque floorshow was in progress, they found that the place had been thoroughly ransacked.

One of the ransackers had not quite made his exit yet, however. Snakeskin hurled La Crosse to the plank floor just as a fusillade of gunfire from the window pocked the cheap blue fleur de lis wallpaper covering the slat wall behind the Frenchman and showered the unvarnished plank floor with chips of plaster and wood.

"Stay down," Snakeskin shouted, quickly unholstering his LeMat pistol, "I'm going after the bastard. He might be persuaded to talk."

Snakeskin climbed out of the window and gingerly placed his boot sole atop the narrow masonry ledge that ran below it. For a fleeting instant, highlighted against the ramshackle rooftops that cut haphazardly across the deepening blue sky, he glimpsed a moving figure dressed in black from head to foot.

Leaning out the window, Snakeskin raised the LeMat, cocked its hammer, flipped the fire select stud on its spur, aimed the gun with its underbarrel propped atop his crooked left arm, and squeezed back on the trigger. The combination shotgun-revolver cracked as a salvo of steel buckshot exited the LeMat's lower sixteen-gauge smoothbore barrel amid a streaming flare of yellow flame and the figure darted clean out of sight, while the report of Snakeskin's hand cannon echoed like thunder in the alley below.

Had this not been Macao, but London or New York instead, the sudden crack of gunfire would have sent police rushing to the scene. But this was indeed Macao, scum hole of the South China Sea, and nothing at all came of it except the drunken laugh of a whore who leaned out the window with her large white breasts shining like pale moons in the night before being pulled back inside by two hairy pairs of arms.

Snakeskin hesitated only for a minute, straining to detect any hint of movement in the dark but nevertheless unable to see a thing. He didn't know if he had hit his man, but he didn't think that he had succeeded in doing so.

FIVE DEAD MEN

Skittering across the shaggy broken line of jaggedly canted rooftops below, Snakeskin looked down into a narrow back alley paved with stone cobbles tamped crudely and unevenly into the dirt. Its floor was strewn with foul-smelling trash and heaps of human and canine excrement, and it was lit dimly by a flickering gas lantern hung from the side of a building near its mouth which gave onto the avenue to which it ran parallel.

Suddenly there was a resounding crash. Something went streaking off below that caused Snakeskin to point his gun at a cat racing for the alley's mouth. Snakeskin let out the breath that had caught in his throat and jumped down onto the cobblestones. Though he saw no sign of human presence, Snakeskin could not shake the feeling that he was not alone.

A loud crashing noise, as of crates suddenly overturned, and the sight of a running figure glimpsed as a blur of motion out the corner of his eye made Snakeskin jerk his head to one side. There he was -- the same figure, clad in black from head to foot, who had nimbly jumped from the window of the saloon only a matter of minutes before after firing at La Crosse.

Snakeskin gave chase but he swerved hard around just before reaching the top of the alley. Already suspecting what was about to happen, Snakeskin hastily ducked to one side as a gout of flame lit up the walls to either side of him and a heavy caliber bullet augured into the brickwork of the wall beside him, spewing sharp chips of masonry that cut into his face and drew blood from a dozen places.

By the time Snakeskin had jumped into the alley and pointed his weapon, the black-clad assassin had already gained the mouth of the alley and had jumped aboard a horse-drawn carriage that had been waiting outside. In the space of a heartbeat, the galloping of hoofs was heard and the assassin was spirited away into the night.

"What happened, *mon ami*?" asked the Frenchman as Snakeskin returned to the room long minutes later, after re-entering the saloon and climbing the stairs again. "I heard more shooting."

"That was our uninvited visitor," he explained, detailing what had just occurred in the alley below. "He was either a bad shot or liked aiming at the wall."

Snakeskin then told La Crosse what had happened next and how the black-clad figure had made good his escape moments afterward.

"I would say it is time to clear out, *mon ami*."

"I agree."

They immediately grabbed their gear and left by way of the window. The Dutchman had suggested safer accommodations should the Phalanx show its hand, which it had appeared to have just done. Snakeskin had memorized the directions to the safe house which proved to be accurate as well as circuitous -- on arrival they realized that the Dutchman had sent them on a zigzagging route designed to smoke out hidden watchers.

The address was an old Portuguese villa standing behind a stone wall and entered via a heavy gate of wrought iron fleur de lis. Two Nubians with skin the color of ebony escorted them inside the villa. The owner of the house was a fat woman who called herself Pilar.

"I understand that you have come recommended by the Dutchman," she said to the newcomers. "But you two I think are special trouble. Your stay will cost you extra."

"I expected to hear that," Snakeskin replied, and peeled off several more US banknotes.

"Thank you," the fat woman said, and tucked them away in her ample bosom. "Follow me. I will show you to your accommodations."

The rooms were small but nevertheless they appeared to be well tended. The view from the single window overlooked a walled courtyard in which there grew a few twisted dwarf olive trees. Over their leafy tops could be seen the mountains that rose to the northwest, beyond the panhandle of the Macao Peninsula.

Snakeskin saw two more Nubians patrolling directly outside the window. All of these tall African mercenaries were armed with the newest magazine-equipped rifles capable of repeating fire. Apparently Pilar was as security-conscious as she was stout, and that was a good thing in Snakeskin's eyes.

"For extra money I can procure for you number one opium or number one woman if you like -- beautiful black woman with big breasts, cunt lips -- *feesh* (she made a kind of blowing noise, accompanied by a slicing hand motion) -- no have. You eat such pussy like sticky red fruit, then fuck it all night," Pilar added, pantomiming intercourse with her stout hips. "You let Pilar know."

"We'll do that," Snakeskin said as he shut the door and locked it behind the portly mistress of the safe house.

A two-handed game of cards was interrupted by Pilar's servant wench informing Snakeskin and La Crosse that dinner was served in the dining room, and that Pilar would like them to join her. They found Pilar already seated with a wine glass in one hand. She gestured for Snakeskin to take the seat nearest her.

"I hope you will enjoy the company of Wanda as your dinner companion," she said to La Crosse, as the Nubian serving wench, who had changed into a scanty outfit of lace and taffeta which revealed her every physical endowment, seated herself beside the Frenchman.

As they feasted on pheasant and bouillabaisse by gas light, Pilar spoke about how she had come here with her father. He had been a Portuguese missionary, intent on saving souls who had wound up running afoul of the Phalanx, which entertained other ideas concerning the trafficking in coolies. On the day after Pilar's father had been gunned down by the Phalanx, she was kidnapped by the Brotherhood and sold to a house of prostitution. There, she discovered that she liked her work and the riches it brought her.

Returning to Macao, she found that rents had gotten cheap since Victoria had become the main port of call on the South China Sea and had bought the former villa of a wealthy Portuguese merchant who had since fallen on hard times. Business had prospered and Pilar now owned another house of prostitution across the straits in Kowloon. Both villas had been turned into virtual fortresses, patrolled by Pilar's private army and safe from even the assassins of the Phalanx.

As Pilar told her story, she plied Snakeskin with wine and her fingers danced on his crotch, while the Nubian wench Wanda treated La Crosse with similar attentions. Before dinner was over, Snakeskin found himself thinking that Pilar was quite a handful of woman.

■

Snakeskin was startled awake by a sound in the night.

Sitting bolt upright he looked around quickly, but saw nothing in the darkness. Pilar, who had warmed his bed before he had fallen asleep, was gone. Snakeskin groped for the LeMat that he'd stashed beneath his pillow, felt the reassuring roundness of its grip in his hand. Cocking back its trigger, Snakeskin listened intently, but heard nothing except the ordinary night sounds blown in by the wind through the open window sash.

Then a shape passed across the light cast by the moon which had risen over Macao while he'd slept. Snakeskin was up from the bed in a second, stark naked but for the LeMat clutched tightly in his fist, hammer cocked and a bullet chambered in its upper barrel, while the smoothbore barrel beneath was ready to discharge another buckshot load.

He barely missed being struck by a brace of three expertly thrown Wu-Shu throwing stars which, instead of slicing through his head as had been intended, embedded their sharp spiked metal teeth deeply into the wall beside him instead.

Snakeskin raised the LeMat's barrel up toward where he thought he'd seen an almost invisible figure clothed in black who used the shadows for cover. But something struck him sharply on the back of the head before he was able to reach the spot. The revolver went clattering out of sight somewhere in the shadows of the room.

Before the ninja warrior could strike him again, Snakeskin lashed out with all his might. His open-handed blow connected with soft cartilaginous tissue. The ninja shuddered under the impact of the edged hand strike. Not intending to give his attacker a moment to recover his wits, Snakeskin followed through with a punishing side kick to the ninja's lower body, feeling cartilage snap as the blow landed hard against the rib cage.

Now he was finally able to discern the black silhouettes of other ninja warriors in the darkness of the room. Two of the masked assailants came at him with the gracefulness and deadliness of predatory cats. One of the attackers was swinging around the weapon known as nunchaku, consisting of two wooden cudgels secured by a narrow length of steel chain links.

With a whipping motion of his hand, the Ninja twirled one of the cudgels around in an overhand swing aimed at the crown of Snakeskin's head, but its whistling tip missed connecting with Snakeskin by a hairsbreadth. Snakeskin was already countering the weapon assault with a snap kick delivered from a vaulting leap that caught the assassin on his chin, crushing his cheekbones and septum and making gouts of blood spew and gush from the caved-in face.

The last remaining ninja tried to finalize the attack with other shuriken throws, but Snakeskin had already found his pistol where it had fallen to the floor. Squeezing the weapon's trigger, Snakeskin fired the .42 caliber handgun, striking the black-clad figure squarely in the gut.

Spurting blood from the gaping bullet wound, the Ninja was violently propelled backward and went crashing through the window amid the clatter of shattering glass. Striking the iron bars beyond it, he slid down into a sitting position, covered with a scattering of glass shards from the broken window.

Snakeskin now heard a shriek coming from the room beyond.

With gun in hand, he lurched out the door. The shriek came again, even louder than before. It originated from the Frenchman's room. Snakeskin tried the door but found to his dismay that it was locked.

Raising the pistol, Snakeskin shot off the lock and bolted into the room. He was just in time to see another black-clad ninja raising his knife to strike a naked whore.

The Frenchman was in bed, a small gun in his hand, trying to draw a bead on the Ninja but unable to because his line of sight was distracted by the frantically struggling odalisque who, unlike Pilar, had remained in the Frenchman's bed, and had been caught straddling his hips. La Crosse now found himself in the unenviable position of having to aim his gun spoiled by Wanda's large breasts holding his face in their soft confinements.

Snakeskin grabbed the knife hand and wrestled the Ninja to the ground before the ninja could thrust the tip of the blade between Wanda's bare chocolate brown shoulders. The lithe masked figure proved skilled in floor fighting and was up like a cat. Two throwing stars held between bunched knuckles of both hands caught the gleam of gas light.

An instant before they were thrown there was a crack and a hole spewing blood appeared in the center of the Ninja's head. The pistol in the Frenchman's hand was smoking: thanks to Snakeskin, he had finally been able to throw off the whore whose breasts were flopping into his eyes and get his target centered in his gun sights.

Now Pilar's armed Nubian bodyguards had come rushing in and patrons from other rooms in Pilar's bordello-fortress stumbled out into the hall, many of them with naked or half-dressed women in tow.

Snakeskin suddenly realized that the Dutchman too might be in danger. Pilar assured him that the Dutchman would be all right, but Snakeskin reminded her that she'd said the same thing about the villa's safety against the Phalanx. Snakeskin wanted to see for himself.

Making their way cautiously through the serpentine alleys and back streets of Macao, in the gathering light of dawn, with Pilar's armed Nubian retainers flanking them every step of the way, Snakeskin and the Frenchman finally reached the seedy quarter in which Van Bronck's ramshackle shop was located. Its front door was ajar and they filed cautiously inside, fearing the worst.

"Van Bronck!" Snakeskin called out in the emptiness of the deserted ground floor.

There was no answer.

Snakeskin and the Frenchman searched the house. Still there was no sign of the Dutchman. Going downstairs to the basement, they found that the place was in complete disarray. It had been ransacked thoroughly.

They returned to Pilar's place. To their surprise they found the Dutchman there waiting for them with Wanda nakedly perched astride his ample paunch.

"I anticipated trouble," he told them, his chins dancing as he peeked out from between her oversized breasts, chuckled and kissed her protuberant brown nipples.

"I must admit that I was getting a trifle worried about you two. Fortunately Wanda here helped to keep my excitement in check somewhat."

22. New Word on an Old Friend

"I have just received word concerning our old friend and comrade Chow Bang Chow," declared the Dutchman.

"So quickly?"

"The Chinese can be extremely fast, making greased lightning appear a thing pathetically slow by comparison," he continued. "They have methods of relaying information which I fear we Europeans will never quite understand."

"Where is he, then?"

"A Buddhist temple. One said to be called White Turban to be precise," the Dutchman told Snakeskin. "Have you heard of it?"

"No, I haven't," Snakeskin replied, at a loss to recognize the name of the Buddhist cloister.

"Well, it's to be found in some rather rugged hill country lying north of Yunan province," the Dutchman explained. "The place is quite isolated. The monks there are openly mere Buddhist anchorites. Secretly they are devotees of the Iron Fist school of Kung-Fu, a style related to that which is taught at the Shaolin temple. The monks are protecting him. He knows he's being hunted by the Phalanx."

"We'll leave first thing," Snakeskin said, with La Crosse nodding his assent.

"It won't be quite that easy, I dare say," the Dutchman reminded Snakeskin. "You'll need to have some valid appearing papers for identification purposes and a reputable guide. Without those, I'm afraid that the local bandits and soldiery might unpleasantly cut short your stay in China."

"And our peckers too, eh, *mon ami*?"

"Quite so."

"I suppose you know about where I might contract with a guide?" Snakeskin opined.

"For that honor, I would propose my own humble talents," the Dutchman assured him. "I know the mountain country in this part of the mainland and speak the local dialects quite passably. And I have already taken the liberty of preparing papers expertly forged, I hasten to add, for all three of us, as well as the appropriate costumes to help us blend in with the local flora and fauna."

"Costumes?" the Frenchman interjected. "What about these costumes, *mon cher*? Are they really needed?"

"Quite, my Gallic compatriot," the Dutchman replied. "As three Occidentals traveling together, we would be recognized at once. It would be the sort of attention that we would not wish to draw. However, if we were disguised as Chinamen, why then we might just have a Chinaman's chance in hell to pull the bloody caper off."

"One question," Snakeskin began, "just why are you being so damned accommodating?"

"Snakeskin, you astound me with your ingratitude," Van Bronck began, spreading his broad, fat hands in a gesture of feigned surprise.

"Don't give me that bullshit innocence act," Snakeskin cut in. "You'd stab your own mother in the fucking back if there was a nickel of profit to be made. You've got something up your sleeve. Out with it."

"Well, yes. I do admit that there might be a chance of some, oh, small, really insignificant remuneration to me," Van Bronck responded grudgingly.

"You see, Snakeskin, there is a slight possibility of my being able to negotiate for some Ming artifacts kept by the monks of the temple and the property of the abbot, one Vajra Pani. In these trying times they might be persuaded to part with such modest treasures. For a suitable sum, of course. I would then stand to make a tidy though not unreasonable profit."

"Well, I don't believe a single word you've just old me," said Snakeskin, standing up and going over to the window where he stared through the iron bars into the interior courtyard. "But we'll let that pass for the moment. Now I want to know about the merchandise I ordered. What's the situation with those items?"

The Dutchman paused before replying to Snakeskin's question and re-lit his pipe, making a show of getting it going while Snakeskin waited impatiently. He stood watching Van Bronck until aromatic clouds of fragrant Cavendish smoke arose from the meerschaum's bowl before beginning to make his reply.

"Sensing acute danger from the minions of the Phalanx, I took the liberty of putting together the consignment of goods quite on my own," Van Bronck began. "The merchandise is already loaded onboard a steam freighter and waiting on the quayside for instructions to sail. I only require a destination, and the deed is done."

"I wanted the opportunity of looking the stuff over, Dutchman," La Crosse put in angrily. "How do we know you haven't cheated us, you overweight pipe-smoking larcenist!"

"Why I never -- this is astonishing!" Van Bronck cried out in protest. "To doubt my veracity! To impugn my honor! To sully and to tarnish my good name! Dear friends, I fear that you have cut me to the quick! That you should entertain even the slightest suspicion that I should have deceived you -- why, I simply cannot believe it!"

Snakeskin traded glances with the Frenchman and shook his head in grudging resignation.

With the killers sent after them by the Phalanx now part of the picture, they could not afford to attract undue attention. There was nothing to do now except to take the Dutchman at his word -- however little that might be worth.

"All right, Van Bronck," Snakeskin told the Dutch gun runner. "We've no choice now except to trust that you did what you said you did with the merchandise. But if you've crossed us up, I'll personally see to it that you have cause to regret it."

"I can assure you that you'll have no reason for complaint whatever," the Dutchman protested, a little too readily for Snakeskin's liking.

"And now I regret that there is the small matter of the remainder of payment due me in compensation for my services, in addition to incidentals such as freight licenses and the like."

Taking a long pull on his meerschaum, Van Bronck held out his pudgy and grotesquely small hand.

■

The Dutchman having been paid off, and the bill for room and board settled with Pilar, who insisted on what she termed a farewell "*mama binbin*" before she would accept his cash, Snakeskin sent a telegram back to Zanzibar.

His cable message informed the Sultan that Snakeskin and the Frenchman would be returning to the island city

185

within the space of an estimated two weeks' time. It went on to inform the Sultan to expect the imminent arrival of a consignment of armaments and ordnance being shipped to Snakeskin in care of His Excellency by merchant vessel direct from the port of Macao.

These duties having been dispensed with, Snakeskin rejoined the Dutchman and the Frenchman at a safe house that Van Bronck had readied for their use. The safe house contained all the necessary items necessary to prepare them for their journey to the mainland. These items included the forged papers, clothing and disguises that Van Bronck had mentioned earlier, as well as weapons, ammunition and spares sufficient for protection as well as compact enough for concealment, and emergency rations in case local victuals and other provisions were for some reason in short supply.

A ferry from Macao to Shanghai, that wound northward around the Chinese coast, would next serve as their method of negotiating the first leg of their journey into the interior of the Chinese mainland. From there, posing as silk merchants, they would hire the services of a local coachman to take them the remainder of the way to White Turban monastery, high atop the mountain range that stood at their journey's end.

According to Van Bronck, there was a small town located not far from the temple complex at which they hoped to find Chow Bang Chow. It would be from the village that they would debark on their journey's final leg.

The rest of the distance would be traveled on the backs of doughty mountain ponies and on foot, the better to keep inquisitive and potentially hostile eyes from observing their journey too closely and from gleaning their true intentions.

"And now," proposed the Dutchman, who had finished pouring the drink which the denizens of Macao called *Abre*

Coração -- the heart opener -- from a dusty bottle into their three tall drinking glasses, "a toast. To our noble enterprise."

He hoisted his glass of golden Portuguese rum and they downed the potent *aguardente*, sealing an unspoken pact between the Brothers of the Gun.

FIVE DEAD MEN

23. The Amusing Mr. Tar Tallow

The ferry voyage from Macao to the mainland of China passed without incident, although the boat was characteristically crowded with coolies and peasants who turned its three decks into a home away from home, even to the point of lighting cooking fires in braziers for woks they'd brought along and stringing lines to hang their washing on, while it seemed like every third or forth passenger was engaged in smoking a pipe of raw opium to help pass the time.

The Chinese peasantry aboard also clearly demonstrated why China was the most overpopulated country on earth, as virtually every younger woman onboard had at least one infant sucking at the lactating nipple of a bared breast or screaming its little head off as its mother rocked it in her arms.

A few of the passengers busily engaged themselves at the job of bringing more Chinese infants into the world as they fornicated atop crude heaps of rags and stuffs that served as makeshift beds while their fellow journeyers went about their business without so much as batting an eye.

DAVID ALEXANDER

As a result of all of this, the interior of the ferry was filled with a thick, greasy smoke that smelled pungently of wok-fried pork and burning opium and resounded with a bedlam of moans, curses, shouts and loud conversation in several Chinese dialects. Snakeskin, La Crosse and Van Bronck found themselves the sole Westerners aboard the ferry, and were obliged to step over aisles in which sleeping, drugged or fucking bodies lay in various states of torpor, excited movement or total stupefaction. Small wonder that they spent most of their time on the open decks.

Snakeskin and company were also constantly on the lookout for agents of the Phalanx, fearing yet another attempt on their lives. The chaos onboard the ferry was business as usual to the Chinese, but among the many Chinese aboard might well be found ninjas sent by the Highbinder tong in the service of the Phalanx following the Brothers and biding their time to strike to the death. And while it was unlikely that Hashishim in the pay of Tippu Tib would be found in this part of the world, neither could their involvement on behalf of the Mahdi be fully ruled out.

Either because of their careful preparations, good luck, blind chance, or a combination of all three, no imminent threat materialized, and although they could not be completely certain of it, the Brothers did not seem to have been followed from Macao by Phalanx spies.

Snakeskin had taken the opportunity to do some careful thinking about the situation that had developed so far while he walked the decks of the ferry and watched the Chinese mainland drift past in a dreamlike monotony of browns, greens and blues. The entry of the Phalanx into the equation was a seeming wild card, one which no one could have predicted in advance. But, in hindsight at least, the interdiction of the Phalanx was a perfectly logical consequence of the developing situation.

The Mahdi, knowing about the Sultan's plans to send a group of skilled mercenaries into the Sudan to rescue his abducted English mistress, would have been determined to stop the party at all costs.

His own Dervishes, feared as hell's demons to the unlettered and superstitious Bedouin tribes (such as the Bejas tribesmen from whose ranks the Hadendoa clansmen, called "Fuzzy-Wuzzies" by the British, followed the Mahdist cause) upon which they descended like locusts on fields of ripe wheat, nevertheless lacked the subtlety and martial skills to confront the likes of Snakeskin and his compatriots. Beyond this they would stand out easily from the denizens of this part of the world, as much by their language and customs as by their Arab and African faces, and be next to useless as killers away from the Sudanese desert of the Sahel that was their home ground.

The wily Mahdi would therefore certainly opt to use the fortune in plunder that he had amassed to contract outside his own regular forces for the talent necessary to destroy the gathering brotherhood of gunmen sworn to destroy his power, his vast stores of captured loot enabling him to pay whatever bounty was asked for their deaths.

In his Chinaman's robes, Snakeskin now took yet another walk around the upper deck of the ferry, which was lugubriously making its way across the straits toward the mainland on the opposite shore. It had now covered more than two thirds of the distance between Macao and the Chinese headland across the South China sea. Within the space of a half hour the small vessel would make port at Shanghai and the quest for Chow Bang Chow would begin.

DAVID ALEXANDER

Making his way to the prow of the ship, Snakeskin Blake looked at the land lying off the port bows in the near distance. His pulse quickened, and thoughts of the past suddenly filled his mind.

He had left Shanghai some thirteen years before, and had believed he would never return.

China was a place filled with a mixture of memories for Snakeskin, all of them poignant, most of them bitter. His experiences there had been the most vivid of his entire life, but all had ended in disillusionment. He had been younger then, and his service with Chinese Charlie's forces against the Longhair rebels in Taipei had tested his courage and had honed his combat skills to the fullest measure possible, but it had also spelled the end of his innocence and had wiped away his earnest readiness to believe the declarations of politicians, potentates and soldiers without testing them first for the presence of the lies that Snakeskin in Taipei had learned almost always lay at their heart.

Now he was returning, if for only a brief time, to this place of exaltation and suffering, with mixed emotions. Snakeskin thought about Angelica too, and how he had believed that he would never see her again either. Here too, his belief had been wrong, for Snakeskin Blake knew deep within him that his mission to rescue the beautiful and sexually gifted prostitute would succeed, and that in the process he would break the power of the Mahdi and take from him the icon that was both the treasure and the token of his immense power.

It was astonishing to Snakeskin how all of these diverse threads of his life, so long unraveled, were beginning to intertwine again. But to what design and to which place on earth were they being drawn together? The Madhi seemed to be the focal point, the center from which all the strands of the web emanated, and to whom they were all linked. But was he the real center? Or was it something so vastly different from Snakeskin's expectations, and something so darkly wrapped in terror, that he could not at this point even admit to himself that what he so secretly feared truly existed.

■

In Shanghai, Chinese Charlie's three agents went about the first step of arranging their trip into the mountainous interior where White Turban monastery stood high atop the peaks of Yunan province. This first step lay in obtaining a means of transportation and carriage of their gear. The Dutchman, who spoke fluent Mandarin, Cantonese, Yunanese and other Chinese dialects, was elected to obtain the services of an itinerant Chinese merchant who had a horse and cart for hire. One was located without too much difficulty, and Van Bronck, Snakeskin and La Crosse soon set off across the flat, dusty landscape of northeastern China with the merchant at the reins.

As they traveled the rutted roads leading into the interior from the coastal plain, the Dutchman was engaging the cart driver in conversation. Although he spoke and understood Min, the main dialect spoken in Taipei, Snakeskin could not understand the bulk of what was being said in the strange-sounding Gan dialect used by the carter and the Dutchman and asked Van Bronck to explain.

"Chin -- that's our driver's name -- and I were just discussing the perils of traveling in this rather troublesome region," the Dutchman explained a trifle too quickly, Snakeskin thought, as if he had expected to be asked and had the answer ready on his lips.

"What sort of perils?"

"Well, my dear Snakeskin, apart from poisonous snakes, mischievous demonic spirits and the occasional severe earthquake," he replied, "the numerous bandits which infest the entire region represent the greatest peril that a traveler might face in these parts. One of the most notorious of the aforesaid is the group of cutthroats led by a certain bandit named 'Tar Tallow' who is said to operate hereabouts."

"Any chances of us running into this 'Tar Tallow?'" asked the Frenchman, whose Gallic nose appeared almost comically out of place beneath the floppy hat of woven straw of a Chinese peasant, and whose slender frame, gaunt from years of a diet of little better than bread and water on Devil's Island, was completely hidden beneath the long flaxen coat he wore.

"That was in fact the last thing Chin and I were discussing before Snakeskin interrupted our talk," the Dutchman returned somewhat brusquely. "Chin's contention is that the Chinese army has chased Tar Tallow out of these hills. However, I frankly wonder about that. In my opinion it would be best to remain on guard."

The Dutchman lit his well-worn meerschaum and went back to conversing in fluent regional Chinese with the cart driver. Snakeskin tried to follow what was being said, as he didn't trust Van Bronck, but soon stopped trying. This was far too different from Min for him to handle. He couldn't understand more than disconnected snatches of the conversation nor fathom the directions that the Dutchman's easy palaver with the carter was taking. His own command of Chinese was rusty and had not been all that good to begin with.

On top of that, Van Bronck, in using Gan, was speaking one of the numerous local dialects which made translation all the more difficult, if not impossible -- for in China dialects had evolved which were unintelligible even to native speakers of different villages, let alone to people from other regions of the immense and inscrutably ancient country.

Snakeskin resignedly settled into the ride, watching the landscape pass them by as the cart slogged along the dusty mountain road, having made up his mind to be as much on his guard against the Dutchman's treachery as he would be against a surprise attack or ambush by Tar Tallow's robber band.

The endlessly rising terrain continued to remain as monotonous as it had been when they had first mounted the cart to commence their travels. As far in the distance as the eye could see marched a grim procession of ancient wrinkled hills. The taller peaks bit like jagged animal teeth into a blue sky which was clear to the south, but in the north dense with brooding clouds betokening a coming thunderstorm, or even early snow, for in these high latitudes snow fell all year round.

Soon they came to the small hamlet that stood in the shelter of the mountain on whose clouded heights nestled White Turban temple. The old driver Chin stopped his carriage and exchanged some additional words with Van Bronck in parting.

"What did he just say, Dutchman?" asked Snakeskin.

"He says that he is thankful for our patronage," Van Bronck told him and La Crosse. "He thanks his ancestors and the gods of his hearth that he has had the good fortune of serving us and asks if there is anything else we might require of him."

Snakeskin thought for a moment.

"Yes, in fact there is," he remarked. "Ask him to keep his mouth shut. If anyone questions him, he knows nothing. Make sure he understands."

DAVID ALEXANDER

The Dutchman conveyed Snakeskin's instructions to the driver. He gave Chin the additional incentive of a large gratuity in the highly valued gold reales of Macao. The Chinaman bowed low, kowtowing in the custom of the local inhabitants and said something to them all before mounting his cart and driving off with the small fortune in gold he'd just been handed.

"What was that all about?" Snakeskin asked.

"Chin said that not even the most savage tortures could free a single syllable from his lips," the Dutchman replied with a wink that could have meant anything, including precisely the opposite.

■

They next rented donkeys from a member of the local peasantry. Apart from agriculture, the primary business of the villagers seemed to be raising sheep. Next to that, breeding donkeys appeared to run a close second, since the animals were found in abundance virtually everywhere. Another commercial practice among the locals seemed to be the selling of their women folk, at least from the strong sales pitch offered by the peasant found by the Dutchman.

In addition to the donkeys Van Bronck had just procured for the trio, and a fourth for Chow -- if they succeeded in finding him -- the peasant also offered one of his young and very nubile daughters to the newcomers as well, promising that she was an excellent cook and was guaranteed to bear the Dutchman many strong sons with (what Van Bronck translated as) "great turgid white-ghost-shooting dragon-cranes."

When they balked at the offer, he tried a hard-sell approach, dragging the two girls out of the stone hut in which the family apparently lived and making them open their clothing to show them their breasts, cunts and asses

FIVE DEAD MEN

(here again, Van Bronck translated the peasant's Hakka dialect, telling Snakeskin and La Crosse that the Chinaman said that his daughters' cunts would conceive an army of brave warriors and that the milk of their breasts could nourish and give the strength of ten to each member of that same army). This generous offer was declined, however, and the trio set off at once toward the monastery perched high on the mountaintop with just the mules.

The sun was still high in the sky, as it was early afternoon, but it would be setting before long as it was late autumn in the hemisphere and the days were short. The Temple of the White Turban was located at the top of a high bluff that overlooked the valley on which the hamlet was located. The trio made haste to climb higher via an old path that wound its lugubrious way up the mountainside toward the monastery in the distant mists looming above before darkness would force them to halt in peril of losing their way.

As they continued their donkey-borne ascent to the summit, the sun began to slant and the intense yellow rays it had beamed down in the afternoon had started to weaken and cool to somber shades of a more mellow, coppery gold. As twilight approached and the color of the sky began to deepen above the mountaintops they could hear the clanging of a great yet distant bell, its basso peals echoing off the now russet-clad hillsides with a steady, dinning cadence in the chilling air.

"It is the time of the temple's dinner hour," the Dutchman explained as they rode their little donkeys up the meandering mountain path, surefooted as they climbed despite the saddlebags laden with weapons, ammunition and miscellaneous provisions and gear that they bore in addition to their riders.

196

"The great bell of the monastery is sounded when all of the monks come together for a convocation before the abbot of the temple."

"What do they do at this ... convocation, did you say?" Snakeskin asked him as they rode the backs of their stolid but reliable mounts above a dizzying drop down to the jagged rocks below.

"Yes, at the evening summons to the temple court, a convocation of monks as I called it. This is not always, mind you -- but often the monks put on a martial arts display," he replied. "It is said to be quite astonishing, really. Each of them tries to outdo the next practitioner in the prowess which he can demonstrate. If we are lucky, good Snakeskin, we may witness a sight not often seen by Chinese, let alone by Occidentals and other foreigners, especially *gwailos*."

Soon the journey up the steep path that threaded its way up the side of the mountain was nearly over. Having grown steadily larger as they climbed, the temple complex of White Turban monastery now rose on the crest of the high bluffs in all its grandeur.

And by now, as its immense, majestic portals loomed in splendor before them, the setting sun had sunk so low that it was almost eclipsed by the needle edges of the mountain peaks. The trio prodded their tired donkeys onward, eager to reach the summit, and perhaps the comfort of warm beds and hot food, before the imminent fall of night.

FIVE DEAD MEN

24. The Twin Pools

Built atop the mountain summit, White Turban Monastery was founded by Wang Shi, a local chieftain, between 1440 and 1446 during Ming Emperor Yingzong's reign. An array of spacious halls and great galleries made up the temple complex, connected by rectangular courtyards in which incense constantly burned and in which the monks incessantly practiced their Wu-Shu as they had done for centuries.

The halls and connecting galleries all had special uses. There were halls devoted to the practice of yogic meditation, halls for the recitation of prayerful sutras and for fasting, storage halls for weapons of the martial arts and halls in which penance for misdeeds and evil thoughts were to be performed before stern effigies of Buddhist deities who glowered at the penitents with eyes as red as burning coals. There was one hall, and only one, however, that was different from all others both in form and in purpose.

This was the main hall of the temple, a hall larger than all others, whose roof was covered with black and green glazed tiles and whose walls were ornamented with the intricately carved stone blocks called *dougong* which supported the immense vaulted space. The walls of this inner cloister, carved with scenes from the life of Buddha and symbolic of the mysteries of life, enshrined the subtle and inscrutable teachings of the Buddhist Way.

And at the center of the hall stood a statue of the goddess Quan Yin, carved from the wood of the rare *nanmu* tree and sheathed with pure beaten gold, she of a thousand hands and a thousand eyes, she who brings the light of infinite mercy into a dark and troubled world. Against the far wall opposite the statue upon a dais slightly raised above the polished stone floor was a humble prayer mat. This was reserved for the abbot and was his seat alone.

A saffron-robed acolyte with a head shaven close against the skull in the fashion of Buddhist monks opened the main temple doors for the three men who had trekked there from afar. Although the doors weighed several tons they were nevertheless hung in such a manner that they could be opened and closed by a single unaided person. The monk bowed deeply to the newcomers and the three visitors duly and respectfully returned his humble gesture of welcome.

Van Bronck asked in Chinese where the monk by the name of Fo Yen ("No Face") would be found, and indicated that it was important that they speak to him at once.

The acolyte uttered a few syllables in response to the question proffered by the Dutchman, and gestured for the trio to follow him into the first of the temple's many vast and incense-fragrant interior spaces.

As they walked through the halls and galleries of the monastery, Snakeskin took a careful look around him. Giant faces of Buddhist gods glowered down from above. Fashioned from single blocks of quarried stone, some of them looked as benign as Gautama Buddha himself, while others were fearsome, showing the Buddha's wrathful aspects. All were artists' depictions of the many faces of the Bodhisattva, the incarnation of the spirit which the religion's adherents believed permeated the universe as well as every living being that dwelled within its confines.

Soon they passed a temple courtyard where a group of monks dressed in the same plain saffron robes in which the acolyte was garbed were engaged in the practice of the Shaolin-style Wu-Shu fighting techniques taught at the monastery.

It was said that the Shaolin monks had originally developed their individual style of Wu-Shu hundreds of years before as a protection against assault, when China's foreign Mongol rulers had forbidden all native Chinese to go abroad armed by day or night. The martial art was designed to make the hands, the feet and, above all else, the mind of the Wu-Shu practitioner into weapons both formidably dangerous and completely undetectable -- for they did not even exist as weapons until the moment that the need to use them arose.

But as with so many other things Oriental, the practice of the Chinese martial arts had another and subtler side in addition to its more concrete purpose of self-defense and unarmed combat. Concentrating on the movements, or *kata*, of his practice, the monk was able to submerge his identity and forget his ego-self, turning off his thought processes and shifting his mind into another plane of thinking and the experience of individual reality. For the monks of the temple, Wu-Shu was a discipline of religious meditation every bit as much as it was also an effective art of self-defense. Here, in short, the practice of Wu-Shu was a way of life.

Having passed through the outer halls, the trio of newcomers eventually reached the interior chambers of the

200

temple that contained a variety of large pools of clear water that filled basins of white stone. At some of these pools, monks were seen washing clothes, bathing and drawing water. But at one of the pools in the chamber, Snakeskin noticed a monk appearing to be chanting over a large turtle that waded sluggishly in the shallow water and somehow appeared to Snakeskin to be in pain.

"Ask the monk what that one over there is doing," Snakeskin said to the Dutchman, intrigued by the strange sight. There followed a brief exchange of dialect Chinese as the acolyte described what was taking place.

"The pool in question is one consecrated to the care of animals that are sick, in danger, or otherwise having been caught outside of their natural element," Van Bronck explained, translating from the Mandarin as the monk narrated. "Each of the temple's monks are enjoined to care for all creatures found on the earth.

"Why a turtle?" Snakeskin inquired.

"In this case, the monk had found a turtle that was clearly ill. He is attempting to nurse the creature back to health and is saying prayers to that effect. He will remain steadfastly by its side until it either recovers or dies. If it lives, he will feed and care for his reptilian charge until the coming of spring, then release it unharmed to wander the hillsides below these peaks."

The group moved on into another chamber of White Turban monastery's many halls and galleries. This one contained only a single pool. Larger than all the others they had seen in the previous hall, the pool was also shaped differently from the others. It took the form of a perfect circle, divided into two intertwined sections. Van Bronck spoke to the their guide.

FIVE DEAD MEN

"He calls this the pool of yin and yang," he then told Snakeskin and La Crosse. "It is, he says, a pool of destiny."

Unlike the several other pools which they had just passed, this last pool seemed to originate from the flowing waters of a natural thermal spring. Bubbling hot water pushed its way up from magma-fed channels deep below the temple in the bowels of the mountain, its effervescing bubbles rising and bursting as they broke the surface in an endless procession, throwing up clouds of faintly sulfur-tinged steam.

Bowing low, the monk who had led the trio to the spot turned and left without saying another word. A lone figure in the unadorned saffron robes of a temple monk sat in what appeared to be a state of deep meditation at the other end of the pool.

Snakeskin, Van Bronck and the Frenchman stood for a long beat listening to the sound of the bubbles of boiling steam bursting from the surface of the hot-spring pool and watching the silent figure which was apparently sunk into the fathomless depths of the most intense prayer and meditation.

Minutes passed without any of them moving, and then the figure suddenly raised his smoothly shaven head and looked at the visitors through unblinking gray-green eyes. Despite the total absence of hair and the blank expression on his face, Snakeskin recognized the monk immediately.

It was Chow Bang Chow.

Snakeskin walked slowly toward his old friend and extended his hand.

"Chow Bang Chow, it's good to see you. I've –"

"I know why you have come, Snakeskin," Chow Bang Chow interrupted as he stood up and regarded his old friend with a slight smile on his face. "And why you have brought Van Bronck and La Crosse with you.

"It has been many years. You must surely know that I have taken a vow not to leave these sacred temple precincts. If I am caught, the Dowager Empress Shi Tzi will spare no effort to have me hunted down and killed."

"Then ... you're telling me that you won't join us."

"I did not say that," Chow Bang Chow replied with a shake of his head. "You have noticed, perhaps, the multiplicity of forms adorning the many halls through which you have passed to reach this chamber. Gods, demons and other fanciful beings? Sutra cabinets which revolve so that prayers may be sent to the four corners of the compass. Buddha seated upon lotus thrones, with faces both benevolent and wrathful. You have seen all of these as you've progressed from the two great entrance doors, have you not?"

"Yes, we have," Snakeskin replied, recalling the many intricacies of design and architecture that had surrounded them as they'd passed through the pavilions of the temple and then had entered the innermost cloisters of the monastic palace.

"All of them are forms of the single reality of which were are all but a part," Chow Bang Chow explained. "The monks teach that all of us, despite outward appearances, are potential gods. Each of us has the ability to achieve Buddha-nature if we but follow the sacred Way. Yet each individual path toward the Way is entirely different and separate from all others."

"Look here, Chow Bang Chow," the Dutchman put in, stepping up to stand beside Snakeskin with La Crosse close in train. "We haven't got time to exchange religious dogma with you even if you've convinced yourself of its truth. We require your services in an undertaking of some importance and posing not inconsiderable danger and risks. A simple yes or no will suffice."

Chow Bang Chow did not answer Van Bronck. Instead, he began to strip off his robes. Standing before the trio completely naked, the muscles on his shoulders and torso taut as iron bands, he stared transfixed into the pool for many long minutes.

His eyes became focused on the superheated bubbles of natural steam that exploded incessantly from the depths of the thermal hot springs below.

"On entering the monastery, each applicant is given a question to ponder. When he knows the answer to the question, he has then achieved the supreme state of ultimate knowledge that is called enlightenment," Chow Bang Chow began, not taking his eyes off the boiling hot waters that foamed and churned beneath his gaze.

"My question, the one I have been pondering for some years, concerns this very pool. You see, this is one of two spring-fed pools in the monastery. Legend has it that one of them is the spring of immortality. The other, however -- it is the pool of death.

"Bathing or drinking from the one prolongs life, restores health or causes a man to become immortal. From the other, an agonizing demise is the result.

"As I've told you, I was given a question to ponder when I entered the temple for the first time. It was given to me by the abbot who approved my sojourn here and welcomed me as a fellow monk and practitioner of Wu-Shu.

"The question that I was given when I came here was to determine which pool was which. Only today, after years of meditation, I believe that I have found the path to the answer."

Saying this, Chow Bang Chow breathed deeply and lowered his eyes with half-closed lids. Without speaking another word, he dived headlong into the turbulent waters and was lost from view as he disappeared with a great splash into its depths. The newcomers became concerned after a few minutes had passed and Chow Bang Chow had still not arisen from the pool.

Snakeskin was preparing to jump in after him when Chow Bang Chow's head suddenly bobbed up to the surface. Extending an arm he climbed to the edge of the deep natural cistern and hauled himself out of it to sit on the inlaid stones that formed its edge.

"Well -- " the Frenchman asked Chow Bang Chow, a condescending smile on his gaunt face which told of his disdain for such metaphysical wastes of time, "-- which of the pools was it, *mon ami*?"

Chow Bang Chow smiled back enigmatically at the Frenchman, his body red and steaming from the heat of the water.

"That, my friend, is only for me to know. It was my question to ponder and mine alone for which to learn the correct answer."

Chow Bang Chow rose and dried himself with a towel, then donned his saffron monk's robes.

"Now, we will go."

"Just like that?" Snakeskin asked, surprised to hear the Chinaman say that he would leave the monastery after all these years. "Haven't you taken vows or anything?"

"Yes, I have taken vows," he answered with a nod.

"Well, perhaps you would wish to speak with the Abbot, or whatever you call the head man here," offered La Crosse.

"That is not necessary," replied Chow Bang Chow. "I possess no belongings here and there is nothing in this place to hold me. All who stay at the temple may come and go as they choose, even break their vows as they wish, if they believe it right to do so."

Chow Bang Chow put on his robes and took one final look at the pool before turning away from it.

"But in going from this place, I have not broken mine."

■

Leaving the White Turban Monastery, the four travelers now returned to the small hill village nestled at the foot of the mountain from which Snakeskin, Van Bronck and La Crosse had originally set out. There they were able to arrange for the services of another villager who was leaving for Shanghai the following morning. The peasant knew the country and claimed to have friends or relatives among the bandits and could all but guarantee safe passage on the long journey to the coast.

From there the now four-strong Brothers of the Gun hoped to take a ferry to Hong Kong, because from the deep harbor at Victoria they would face few obstacles to booking passage aboard a fast coaster southbound on the South China Sea to the port of Singapore that sufficient Spanish doubloons wouldn't easily fix. The Courageous, already summoned by telegraph to await their arrival, would then speed them westward along the sub-equatorial steamer routes toward Zanzibar -- and damn the crew if it had not sobered up in time, for the saloons and brothels of Singapore were among the most beguilingly insidious dens of iniquities this side of hell itself.

At sun-up, the group rode from the village. The rugged mountain ponies they had hired in place of the donkeys that they had traded at the village trotted along a high pass that led them through a narrow defile while the four men drank locally fermented wine from a goatskin and shared out bread and cheese.

And then, following behind their guide as the villager, on his own mount, vanished around the bend, the four Brothers were suddenly confronted by a band of rough looking men on horseback and armed with rifles. The peasant whom they'd hired as their guide sat on his pony beside the leader of the bandits. Looking behind him, Snakeskin saw that retreat was cut off by more bandits on horseback at their rear.

"It appears that we've been ambushed," announced Van Bronck.

"You have a rare gift for sizing up situations in an instant," Chow Bang Chow told him. Then, to Snakeskin, he said, "Shall we die meekly or take some of them down with us."

"Do nothing," Snakeskin, who had been carefully watching the bandit leader, said. And then Tar Tallow laughed and rode up to them with the villager alongside, and Van Bronck carried on a brief conversation in the local dialect.

"It seems, my friends, that our peasant benefactor was not joking when he declared he had friends among the bandits as he happens to be the younger brother of Tar Tallow himself who has personally come out to greet us and see us safely out of these hills."

The bandit chieftain said something else to Van Bronck and again began to laugh.

"Tar Tallow has advised us that he expects no payment for his services to us because being of help to his brother will earn him great rewards from heaven. He adds that we were lucky to pay his brother well which demonstrates that our hearts are large and we are good men. There are other bandits roaming these hills, according to him, and unlike Tar Tallow himself, they are rogues without honor."

Tar Tallow signaled to his men and reined his horse around and spurred its flanks, and the Brothers shared out their wine to their newfound traveling companions as they rode in safety toward the coast.

25. Another Telegram Arrives

Having returned to Hong Kong, Snakeskin was forced to make final arrangements to find a steamer sailing to Zanzibar as a cable awaited him there with the bad news that the Courageous had developed unforeseen engine trouble and needed repairs. Since the telegram bore the private identification code that he had arranged between himself and First Mate Jopling, Snakeskin knew that the cable was genuine.

Since there was now no telling when the Courageous might leave the port of Singapore, Snakeskin telegraphed back that the ship was to make for Stone Town as soon as possible following completion of repairs and await his return. Meanwhile, he and the three other Brothers of the Gun needed to book passage on a departing steamer as quickly as they were able.

Fortunately they found one that was departing westward, but not immediately. The Malagasee Star would not be leaving port for another three days, however, and for the moment the mercenaries could find no other means of passage.

FIVE DEAD MEN

Snakeskin used this time waiting for passage to Zanzibar to sketch out a general plan for the desert rescue mission. Snakeskin had already mapped out the basic elements of his dominant strategy, as well as the route which the Brothers were to follow to their destination and the supplies which would be required in order to to carry out the plans for their mission.

His strategy called for the exploitation of the abilities of a small force of elite fighting men to the utmost advantage that their specialized skills and small numbers made possible. That such a strategy could work had been proven better than forty years before when just such a special force was sent into the Sudan under the secret orders of President Thomas Jefferson to carry out the rescue of kidnapped Americans. Though today it was the Mahdi who had taken a hostage and not some other group of fanatics, bandits or pirates, the basic principles and strategic challenges remained the same. Snakeskin was certain that the Brothers of the Gun would prove far more than merely equal to the demands of the mission, however great.

Snakeskin was counting on the vastness of the desert to work in their favor, presenting the Mahdi's large, though decentralized forces with the formidable challenge of finding a moving needle amid a gigantic haystack.

The tactics he would use were those that he had learned in his days serving with Gordon in China, where small units culled from the cream of Gordon's royal dragoons had been used in battle in a novel way.

Snakeskin had learned from experience that hitting the enemy, and then disappearing, only to attack again from an entirely new and unexpected direction, was a devastating assault strategy. He would count on it now to help him win the day in his coming efforts to rescue the Sultan's woman from the Mahdi's grasp.

It was also during the slack time spent cooling their heels in Hong Kong as they awaited the westward departure of the Malagassee Star that Snakeskin received a telegram from Stone Town in Zanzibar. The telegram was from the Sultan himself. It read:

M. has struck again. This time seized villages along cataracts of lower Nile. Stop.

Situation becoming increasingly urgent as M. grows steadily stronger and bolder. Rumors that British fort at Omdurman in imminent danger of attack. Stop.

You must return and commence mission very shortly or it is feared chances will diminish to zero. Stop.

His Excellency,

M. B. S.

In reply, Snakeskin composed a telegram of his own in which he informed the Sultan that arrangements were being made to secure shipboard passage and that the group would proceed back to Zanzibar with all deliberate haste.

Having sent off his message by cable, Snakeskin rejoined his compatriots at a noodle shop where they were lunching on the local fare. As they ate, a diminutive Chinaman approached their table. He was attired in a high-collared black silk *changsan* emblazoned with dragon and phoenix embroidery in gold threads and he sported a horseshoe-shaped moustache and a long, braided black pigtail trailing across his shoulders from beneath his matched silk pillbox hat.

The Chinese bore a pasteboard business card in his hand. Bowing low with a practiced kow-tow, he delivered the card to Snakeskin and pointed at the gentleman in the white tropical suit and matching Panama hat seated at an adjacent table and currently sipping a cup of jasmine tea while reading the English-language *Hong Kong Times,* which he perused folded into neat quartos in the manner of cultured Englishmen.

The card identified the sender as one Major Giles Faversham-Sidney of Her Majesty's Royal Fusiliers. On the back of the card, in what was surely the major's own militarily precise handwritten script, was a request that the major join them for a discussion. About what, the card did not say, but Snakeskin took for granted that it concerned their mission.

After Snakeskin, La Crosse, Chow Bang Chow and Van Bronck conferred, it was decided to allow Major Faversham-Sidney to come over to the group's table to converse with the party as he wished.

Faversham-Sidney was a man with blunt features, features which matched his way of speaking, and though he was in mufti at the moment, his military bearing and his brisk and officious manner were that of a man accustomed to wearing a uniform at most other times and of usually having his orders obeyed without the need for further clarification or discussion.

"I represent Her Britannic Majesty's Government," he told them without preamble. "We are most concerned in regard to certain rumors that have been bruited about concerning an impending mission of some consequence in a certain region of Africa."

"Don't know what you're talking about," Snakeskin said.

"Oh, really, Mr. Blake," replied Faversham-Sidney, professing amusement. "Let's not play silly buggers, shan't we? I know perfectly well the full particulars of your plans."

212

"And what would they be, Monsieur Panama Hat?" asked the Frenchman.

"You know as well as I that you have been hired to sneak the Sultan's bloody whore out of the Mahdi's camp."

Realizing he'd allowed himself to get ruffled, Faversham-Sidney composed himself. In a more controlled tone of voice, he added, "Things like that tend to get about rather quickly, you know."

Snakeskin began to interrupt but the major cut him off with a curt and dismissive wave of his hand.

"Let me simply say that Sir Charles Gordon, whom it is known has sanctioned and abetted your efforts, represents but one of several interested factions in Whitehall. At this point in time Her Majesty's Government would prefer it if you would not interfere with the affairs of sovereign states."

"Why not?" Snakeskin replied. "I would think that support for Chinese Charlie would be unanimous. If any people on earth were interested in paying back that religion-intoxicated lunatic out in the desert it would be you Brits."

"As I believe I've just made luminously clear," Major Faversham-Sidney replied in his clipped Eaton accent, "that is a matter of some delicacy, and it is also one that I am not prepared to elaborate on at the present time."

"Well, you can shove your response, major," Snakeskin snapped at the Englishman. "As long as Gordon backs us we'll do as we damned well please."

As they got up to leave Major Faversham-Sidney set down his tea cup and gestured with a flick of his fingers toward the shadowed recesses at the rear of the noodle shop. An almost imperceptible nod from a coolie seated there signaled confirmation of an unspoken command.

After Faversham-Sidney's man had left the noodle shop, the major too rose and went out the door. He was a

213

gentleman, and gentlemen kept power's iron hand ensconced in velvet gloves whenever possible, unsheathing it only when all other attempts to arrive at a solution had failed them. This was one of those times, however, and the major suffered no compunction at sending power forth to nakedly perform its bloody tasks.

The shantytown street meandered between dilapidated wooden houses as it sloped toward Victoria Harbor, which could be seen from its high points, but disappeared, blocked by tenement rows, in the midst of its turnings.

Snakeskin's company became aware by degrees as they walked down to the docks that the street had gone silent except for the clatter of windows slamming and door latches snapping shut. In a place where law was reserved for their masters only, the coolies learned to close their ears and eyes when Hong Kong's criminal triads fought for turf.

The sudden silence spelled trouble and put the group immediately on guard. Then, almost on cue, masked figures in black silk jumped from side alleys and blocked their path, seeming to have appeared from out of the thin air. More of the silent, more of the almost ghostly figures appeared behind the four men and took up blocking positions.

"The Phalanx!" shouted Van Bronck, for he, like his companions, had seen the tong sign of the Highbinders tattooed on the hands of the thugs and noted the telltale black ribbons tied high on their queues that bound them close to the tops of their heads from which their gang's name was derived.

Plainly intent on dealing a killing stroke and wiping out their opposition, the Highbinders attacked frontally and from their rear, and the Brothers instinctively took up back-to-back positions to make their stand using a moving counter-tactic for circular defense.

DAVID ALEXANDER

Pulling his two matched LeMat pistols from their holsters, Snakeskin started shooting. His aim was accurate, and a salvo of bullets bored a series of red punch-holes in the belly of an attacker who raced at him with a snarl on his face wielding a sword with dazzlingly fast movements of his arms.

More bullets caused him to jerk spasmodically and seem to perform a clumsy imitation of a toe-stepping ballet dancer as they ripped up his body. Yet, more dead than alive, the assassin continued coming at Snakeskin, driving the point of the sword into the plank wall of the hovel at Snakeskin's rear before he slumped over, toppled, and fell on his back, his life spent.

As Snakeskin turned to reload the wheel gun, the circle broke and Chow Bang Chow executed a somersault followed by a flying snap-kick to take down three Highbinders who were attacking with spinning nunchaku sticks linked together by short iron chains. Snakeskin noted to his satisfaction that a series of kicks and a flurry of punches dealt effectively with more of the black-clad thugs sent by the Phalanx.

But at that moment, he was forced to turn his attention elsewhere. Van Bronck had sought cover in a doorway vestibule from which he alternately fired and reloaded a Remington six-shooter at Highbinders attacking with swords, spears, throwing stars and other edged weapons, often dispatching the attackers with face and belly shots at point-blank range.

As to La Crosse, Snakeskin saw that the Frenchman, though holding his own, was beset by massed Highbinders. As La Crosse struggled to eject a dud round from his jammed pistol, the circling Highbinder sharks smelled blood. Eight ninja stars whirled through space from between the knuckles of two practiced hands. Metal clunked against the pistol and steel teeth bit into the hand that gripped it, making the fingers go instantly limp. The pistol dropped to the dust and La Crosse saw the Highbinder launch a flying heel kick at his head.

Red slop sprayed from the skull of the Highbinder as a smoothbore round from the underbarrel of Snakeskin's pistol smashed through his teeth and the Highbinder fell to the dust, breaking his legs in his last seconds of life. A flip of the select lever above the LeMat's trigger spur put the hand cannon into pistol mode, and the matched twin pieces in Snakeskin's fists blazed in fury at the ninja-suited Phalanx thugs who'd closed in on the Frenchman to burst them like blood-filled balloons.

And now the Frenchman, aided by the respite that Snakeskin had given him, picked up the pistol in his functional hand, cleared its fouled chamber, managed to reload the cylinder with the gun clutched to his side with his injured hand, and shot down two more sword-wielding assassins who were within an ace of chopping him to pieces.

Snakeskin, now on his third reload, was gunning for ninja with both LeMats spitting flame at left and right, scoring kill after kill, until a straggler with a sword who seemed to leap at him out of thin air swung at his midsection, and Snakeskin blocked the sword swing with one LeMat while simultaneously shoving the muzzle of the other into the Highbinder's chest and pulling the trigger straight on his heart, with the result that the heavy bullet blew the now pulpy red mass out of the exit hole in his back, drenching the wall behind him.

The violent confrontation ended almost as quickly as it had begun, with first La Crosse and then Van Bronck wounded in the struggle. The Dutchman had been stabbed in the shoulder as one of the assassins plunged his sword into his arm before he was able to cut him down with the last two shots in his gun straight to the gut at point blank range.

Now that Highbinder corpses littered the street and the fight was over, the coolies felt safe to again emerge. Window blinds were raised and doors came open as bystanders gathered on the sidelines to view the carnage. Within a matter of minutes the neighborhood came back to life. It was just another day in shantytown.

As to the fallen, they would be thrown in the middle of the street to rot in the sun until Hong Kong's colonial police force got around to cleaning them up.

26. A Stranger Among the *Ansari*

The Malagasee Star made good time on its westward voyage to Zanzibar, while Snakeskin continued to make plans onboard, wishing he were already back in Zanzibar to finalize them. If the Mahdi were indeed again on the move, it surely meant that the Brothers of the Gun might miss their chance entirely, since if all the Sudan fell into his grasp, the Sultan might well decide to abandon all attempts to free his wife and in the end make his peace with the desert fanatic.

There was in fact talk of Great Britain doing precisely that in any case after years of protracted fighting and the expenditure of hundreds of thousands of pounds sterling without showing any permanent strategic gains but suffering many tactical setbacks.

Wouldn't it be better to leave the entire stinking mess to the kaffirs to straighten out for themselves, went the current reasoning in Whitehall. Many in Parliament favored simply withdrawing from the Sudan entirely and substituting a policy of self-government for the Fuzzy-Wuzzies, Dervishes, black Sudanese and other denizens of the arid wastes of sub-

Saharan Africa and the Sahel. Simply emancipate the bloody wogs and leave them to fight it out amongst themselves.

This would translate into control of the Sudan by the Mahdi anyway, once the Egyptian garrisons backed by Britain withdrew from the forts scattered across the desert and left the Empire's outposts in the Sahel and Kordofan. Chinese Gordon, lately dismissed from his governorship of the Sudan, was again being talked of to return to the dark continent and re-assume command as Consul-General in order to stage a coordinated and orderly withdrawal.

And so things stood as the Malagasee Star completed its westward transit of the Indian Ocean and Snakeskin and his brothers in arms reached the port of old Stone Town after an absence of nearly three months since Snakeskin had first departed for the Salvation Islands in French Guiana to break La Crosse out of Devil's Island.

Having debarked the steam freighter a messenger brought word that the Sultan awaited their arrival at the palace and was eager to welcome back Snakeskin and meet his fellows in arms.

Luscious viands and most comfortable rooms, their beds sheeted with the silk of Samarkand, as well as nightly visits by the choicest and zestiest of the Sultan's most skillful concubines, awaited the royal chieftain and lawgiver's honored guests.

Nevertheless, Snakeskin knew that the hourglass had been tipped on end and that the time needed to stage and complete the mission had begun to trickle like sand through the eye of a needle.

■

Several hundred miles away, and virtually simultaneously, another rider had arrived at his destination deep within the trackless interior of the lonely Sahel. The man, dressed in the gaudily patched *jibba* and black cloth turban of a Sudanese native, complete with a curved sword hung at his belt, dismounted his pack camel, helped down by Dervishes armed with repeating rifles of the latest European design, plundered from a recent confrontation with the British interlopers and their comrades, the stooges of the Egyptian Khedive.

A force led by Hicks had left Khartoum to relieve the Mahdists' siege of the desert city of El Obeid, but had been routed and nearly destroyed by the appearance of an army of more than forty thousand *Ansari* rigorously drilled in British tactics and well equipped from the ever-growing stocks of arms and ammunition captured in the course of previous battles against the Infidel occupiers.

The result was that none of those who the *Ansari* called "Franks," save one, was left alive, and plentiful new stockpiles of arms and ammunition were captured from the unbelievers to replenish the caches of military supplies already used up in battle. The lone prisoner was already giving the Mahdi vital information on the strategies and movements of his impious and villainous foes.

The newcomer to the encampment spoke a few words in the dialect called *Sfinaria*, and meaning "sword of fire," a ladino of Spanish and Arabic that was the region's *lingua franca*. The *Ansari* escorted the rider through motley, barbaric ranks that parted to witness his arrival attended by Dervishes in patched *jibbas* loudly blowing the horn that the *Ansari* called the *ombeyah* until their tongues and lips were swollen. Many of those in the encampment had never before seen a "Frank" (as all Europeans were known to black Sudanese and Arabs alike), a misnomer dating back to the expedition led by Napoleon nearly a hundred years earlier, which had captured Egypt for France.

DAVID ALEXANDER

Ahead of him, an enormous and thorn-infested *zariba* had been set up around a mixture of low stone buildings and tents of various sizes and shapes. The nomadic lodge constructed of thorns surrounding a wooden superstructure, was resplendent with a panoply of colorful banners, many of them inscribed with slogans in flowing Arabic script praising the exalted greatness of Allah and the Mahdi who spoke and fought in his hallowed name.

The visitor knew but a little of the local language nor cared a fig for the local customs of the country. He longed for the coolness of the interior of the tent and a long, quenching draft of the tart-sweet Clarissa wine to slake his dry throat, one that had been scorched by the hot wind of the desert and parched by grains of its fine sand that got into the nose and mouth no matter what sort of protection one used against it.

Dervish warriors drawn from black Sudanese and Ethiopian tribes, who were prized for their fierceness in battle as well as their undying loyalty to whoever happened to be their masters, stopped him when he had gotten inside.

These black *Ansari* subjected the rider to a careful search, one which was conducted with a professional thoroughness that the rider had expected of his hosts. Carefully practiced hand movements covered every inch of his body. No concealed weapon would have escaped detection by the searchers. Had one been found, it would have meant his immediate execution, for even the suspicion of harm to the Expected One would bring instantaneous death to the unfortunate interloper whoever he might be, and whatever mission he might have come to this place in pursuit of.

With a gesture, the head Dervish -- a tall, dark Addis Ababan with piercing eyes as black and as shiny as lumps of anthracite coal, wearing a white turban and sporting a flowing, gray-black beard, unkempt in the manner of one to whom earthly matters mean nothing and the love of heaven everything -- gestured to the newcomer.

He would not consent to speak directly to the Infidel Frank, hating all their ignoble kind. Although he knew that this son of a dog had converted to the holy religion, and had also embraced Allah, blessed be his name, he yet did not trust him. But his master had business with the man and he could only obey his leader's commands, for such was the will of God.

Beckoned silently to follow, the visitor went after the tall, commanding Dervish. He was led through a curtain hung with glass beads of many colors and festooned with the charm called the khamsa; the eye within the palm of the hand that wards off evil.

Behind the tinkling beaded curtain there was a large open area, its air filled with the fragrance of incense that burned within ornately filigreed brass censers. At the other end of this spacious interior, seated on a bare reed mat, there was a figure frozen in the deep stillness of meditation.

■

At either side of the seated one, voiceless, sightless Dervishes stood obediently holding long, broad fans made of plucked peacock feathers tied together in gaudy sheaves. At an early age the tongues of these servitors had been ripped out and their eyes extinguished with burning oil so that they could neither see nor speak but only stand and serve the Mahdi who was their ultimate master.

Nearby, there stood Dervishes as tall as the visitor's Nubian escort. All of these wore the long, curved knives with ornately decorated, often bejeweled, pommels called *janbiya* in the woven cloth belts which fastened their cotton robes. They were all armed with the latest revolving pistols and rifles as well, the booty taken from the defeated Franks and placed into the ready hands of the faithful by the will of almighty Allah, whose will they obeyed.

Ordering the visitor to halt some distance from the silent figure seated meditatively on the mat, the Dervish usher walked slowly toward him.

Kneeling down, he prostrated himself in the gesture of a supplicant before his master's humble yet splendid throne, bowing low three times. Only when he had completed this show of humility before the Mahdi did he permit himself to address the man who had as yet not shown even the slightest indication of having been aware of his presence.

At last, the seated figure looked up. His thickly kohl-rimmed eyes had a faraway gaze and they spoke of secrets held captive in their inscrutable brown depths. The strong scent of *Paif el Mahdi* -- the concoction of sandalwood, jasmine and verdigris known as 'Odor of the Mahdi,' which was said to convey the delectable aromas of Paradise itself -- wafted across the room and touched the wizened brown face of the *Ansari* like an invisible hand.

Although the Ethiopian guide from Addis Ababa had killed many foes in battle and feared nothing in this world or in the hereafter, he was instantly filled with an all-consuming terror. Those limpid dark eyes seemed to swallow him up. They were hypnotic, and utterly placid, as though peering through all earthly things into the mysterious ambit of heaven itself. The guide had never beheld anything quite like them, and to him they indicated, above all other earthly signs, that the Mahdi was indeed the Expected One foretold by prophesies of the coming Messiah.

"Inform the unworthy Ghazawan el Safiy-Allah al Mahdiya that he may now be permitted to approach me," the

Mahdi told his retainer, using the name which the European had adopted on the day of his conversion to Islam.

The tall Ethiopian turned and gestured to the Frank, withdrawing as the European visitor came forward. Unlike the Expected One's retainer, the European bowed only slightly as he drew up to where the Mahdi sat. With a slight gesture of his be-ringed fingers, the Mahdi wordlessly invited him to sit before him.

"What fresh news do you now bring?" he asked the Frank, having summoned servants who came bustling up, bearing silver trays for the traveler heaped with pitchers of Clarissa wine and other choice refreshments.

"The Sultan is making preparations since we last met, Excellency," he replied in reasonably good Sfinaria. "The mercenaries that he has hired have returned to the palace. I believe they are now set to begin training."

"How many men are there?" the Mahdi asked softly. "What size is this army that this wretched son of a she-dog dares to assemble against me?"

The visitor sipped his strong Clarissa wine, feeling the cooling liquid bring relief to his parched throat. He wiped at his beaded brow with the sleeve of his travel-stained robe, but the moisture would not stop in the infernal heat of the Sudan that wafted in through the fluttering silk door of the large and spacious tent of striped canvas cloth.

"My poor words apparently do not well convey my message, oh Luminous One," said the visitor, somewhat haltingly. "My reference to mercenaries alluded merely to a handful of men, four or five at the utmost."

"So few?" replied the Mahdi, his eyes peering into the European's searchingly, so that for an instant it appeared that the grave face of the chieftain would break into a smile, and from the Expected One's mouth would emerge peals of laughter.

But this did not happen, and with the Mahdi's customary grave mien, he went on, "What can that fool hope to accomplish with only a handful of unbeliever mercenaries? He must surely have lost his senses as he will soon lose his kingdom -- and, yes, surely even his worthless head."

"These men are highly capable," the visitor explained to the Mahdi. "They are all experts at their respective specialties. You would do well to regard the threat which they pose as seriously as any other you might encounter from the unbelievers who have invaded your realms."

The Mahdi pondered this last remark awhile, stroking his beard, his dark eyes flashing inscrutably in their kohl-rimmed sockets.

"Perhaps," he muttered.

"I wonder if I might see the woman," the visitor asked, and, realizing the abruptness of his request, recoiled in the shock of his own intransigence before the holy one.

"Why is this desired?" the Mahdi asked sharply.

Now the Expected One's eyes had become guarded and there was suspicion and skepticism in his silken voice. All outsiders were suspect and all unbelievers were enemies. Thus, the Mahdi preserved his own life from the snares of the Infidels.

Ghazawan el Safiy-Allah al Mahdiya, though he had professed love of God, was a Frank nonetheless, and would therefore never be completely trusted, however useful his services might be to the holy cause.

"I have reason to believe that the woman may be acquainted with the leader of the mercenaries whom the Sultan has retained in his employ," the visitor explained. "If this is so, then she may have information of some value."

225

FIVE DEAD MEN

"She has not been cooperative," the Mahdi answered with disdain. "She refuses to follow the great Lord Allah's will, may blessings be upon him, and also to abide by the rules of my royal *haram*. I have asked my other wives to speak with her, but she refuses to listen."

"May I speak with this unworthy and truculent she-ass of a woman?" the visitor asked again. "She may speak to me although refusing all others."

"Very well, Ghazawan el Safiy-Allah al Mahdiya," the Mahdi replied, deciding that perhaps one of her own countrymen might indeed persuade the Englishwoman to change her ways before more unpleasant means might have to be employed in order to elicit words of truth from her pretty though surely treacherous mouth.

After the visitor had eaten of the roasted haunch of lamb, dates cooked in wild bee's honey, and other rare and luscious delicacies brought for him with which to refresh himself, Ghazawan el Safiy-Allah al Mahdiya was brought into the tent where the prisoner was kept. Angelica was seated in harem clothes of silk and organza, her belled pantaloons of a gauzy blue, her bodice of white fitting snugly at the midriff to reveal her navel to the delectation of male onlookers, the contours of her rump barely hidden beneath a semi-transparent covering of filmy gossamer. She was looking dourly at Ghazawan el Safiy-Allah al Mahdiya as she saw him enter.

He saw at once that she was stunningly beautiful. The visitor envied any man who could possess her sylphlike body, kiss her plump breasts and caress her lissome white rump, even for the space of a moment.

He hated the Sultan and the Mahdi for laying hands on this perfect creature, but such was the way of the world. To the powerful went all things of beauty, and to the weak only fleeting dreams of possessing them were ever permitted.

"What the hell are *you* doing here?" Angelica asked him.

"I'm trying to help you," Sir Montague Strawplait retorted.

"*Help* me?" she hissed back. "It's *you*, you bloody lying barstid, who got me into this bloody fucking mess to begin with."

"Unfortunately, things got slightly out of control," the Englishman answered her, remembering to remain calm. "You brought it on yourself at any rate. Going out like that showed extremely poor sense. All the Mahdi's men had to do was keep watch on you."

"What do you want, then?" Angelica demanded, glaring at him.

"Do you know a scoundrel named Snakeskin Blake?" he asked.

"Why do you want to know?"

"Because, my dear, a Mr. Snakeskin Blake has recently been retained in the employ of your, ahem, husband the Sultan. His mission is to rescue you, although I don't see how the American, who is actually little more than a common thug, has the slightest chance of pulling off that particular feat despite all the bravery in the wide, sweet world."

"What do you want of me, then, Sir Bloody Strawplait?" she asked. "I haven't seen Blake in years."

"Tell me what you know about this man," the visitor asked the captive Englishwoman. "The Mahdi's forces will surely hack him to pieces. This is of no consequence to me, however our fanatical friend may be angered enough to take it out on your pretty head. I would not like to see that, but there are others whom the Madhi regards more highly than myself who most certainly would enjoy witnessing you being put to the *shebba*."

"Come here and I'll tell you," she said, with a sudden look on her face that the visitor could not resist.

He drew close, his heart beating in anticipation. She lunged back and then she kicked him smack in the testicles. The newcomer howled in anger and abruptly sank to his knees. The harem eunuchs ran in and carried Strawplait off in a spluttering heap.

"You'll pay for that!" the groaning man cursed through tears of pain, rage and humiliation. "You'll pay dearly, damn your pretty eyes!"

27. Wu-shu Practice

"Very good," Chow Bang Chow said to Snakeskin as they practiced the *Chi Sao Lung* discipline, "you are improving, my friend."

Chi Sao Lung literally meant "sticking" and often "sticky hands," and its goal was to enable practitioners to develop the ability to sense the changing energy fields in their opponents' limbs and bodies.

Mastery of this technique would enable a Wu-Shu practitioner to predict the movements of an opponent almost before they were made.

In the discipline of sticky hands, bodily movements were severely constrained. The object here was not to throw one's sparring partner to the mat with kicks or punches, but to nullify his every move a fraction of an instant before it was launched, in effect ending a fight before it had even begun. In practicing *Chi Sao Lung* the hands of Snakeskin and Chow Bang Chow moved with lightning rapidity, each blocking the other's motions.

In the midst of this sparring, Jahno, the Sultan's Gurkha bodyguard, interrupted. The hulking janissary had two messages to commit to Snakeskin's care. One of these concerned himself, and this message was simply to report that the Sultan had given him permission to join Snakeskin's company on its foray into the Sudan where both the Sultan and the Gurkha believed his skills would be of considerable aid.

Jahno's next piece of news was of more immediate importance as well as of keen interest to Snakeskin.

A nest of the Mahdi's spies had been located in Zanzibar, Jahno informed Snakeskin and Chow Bang Chow. The Sultan's police force had planned a raid and within a short space of time, it was to launch it and make arrests. Jahno asked if they would like to come along and watch the Dervishes hidden in the midst of Zanzibar be captured and subjected to a variety of tortures, ones, he hastened to add, that he would personally administer.

"I have a better idea," Snakeskin said to the Gurkha. "Let us take the Mahdists alive, at least some of them. If we can do this, then we rid the Sultan of some troublesome problems and we can also test out some new techniques we've devised at the same time."

Jahno thought about Snakeskin's suggestion for a while.

"I will attempt to convince the Sultan as to the merits of your idea," he replied, "but only under the condition that I be permitted to come along and be present when these 'techniques' are applied against the Dervishes."

"Done," Snakeskin told Jahno with a smile.

■

Elsewhere within the palace, La Crosse has been busying himself with the task of preparing an assortment of highly specialized weapons for the upcoming secret journey into the Sudan and the undoubtedly hazardous bid to rescue the English hostage taken by the Mahdi.

The Frenchman had already constructed the prototypes of a hybrid between pistol and rifle that was capable of repeating fire. These weapons he had dubbed "Automatic Repeater Submachineguns," choosing this name because they were handgun-sized variations of the considerably larger full-sized machineguns developed by Gatling, Maxim and others.

The Frenchman's submachinegun weapons were, in fact, based on the designs of Maxim which had been adopted by the French military. Unlike Gatling's original machinegun, used principally by the Americans, which was driven by hand-cranking the firearm, the Maxim design used an ingenious mechanism that siphoned off part of the gasses of the exploding projectiles to automatically reload and re-fire the weapon without the need for human control. As long as the finger rested on the trigger (and as long as there remained bullets in its magazine) the weapon continued to fire. Conversely, once pressure on the trigger was removed the firing ceased.

La Crosse had first devised these new weapons during the long hours of solitude in his cell on Devil's Island, secretly making diagrammatic sketches on bits of paper and scraps of pasteboard and wood from which he'd fashioned the many windmills that had adorned his stone prison hut.

The French gendarmes had never guessed their true purpose, nor had the other prisoners who had stolen them in the night. When La Crosse had made several diagrams and was satisfied that his windmills contained the complete plans, he consolidated the drawings into a single precise schematic of the finished weapon on small scraps of writing paper. He kept these diagrammatic sketches secreted inside his prisoner's "charger."

FIVE DEAD MEN

Beyond this, though, even if, in the event his charger had been stolen and the diagrams of his inventions had been lost, the Frenchman had committed every detail of their fabrication to memory and could confidently finish them given enough time. The plans for the automatic repeaters had required a significant amount of work to translate them into the finished product, but they seemed to have proven successful. Within a relatively short space of time, La Crosse had assembled enough of the special weapons to train and equip the Brothers of the Gun.

After learning of the plans for the raid on the Mahdist spy ring, Snakeskin popped into La Crosse's workshop and asked him if he could have some weapons ready within twenty-four hours.

"What do you need them for right now?" asked La Crosse, fondling the metal frames of the weapons that lay upon the work table in front of him. "They are like my children. I don't want to see them wasted before they are absolutely ready to be used."

"There is to be a raid on a Dervish spy nest tonight," Snakeskin told him. "I've arranged with the Sultan to permit us to use these new repeater guns of yours in smashing the nest and arresting the Mahdist band."

"Then I suppose it is time for my beauties to make their debut and I must show you how they work," La Crosse offered, and spoke to his creations. "Very well, my pretty ones. You shall taste of first blood tonight."

Then, to Snakeskin, "Let us step outside, *mon ami.*"

Gesturing for Snakeskin to accompany him to the shooting range he had constructed, La Crosse picked up one of the prototypes of the new weapons he had fashioned to meet his radical design concepts.

Snakeskin had never seen anything quite like this new type of gun that La Crosse had devised. It most closely resembled a squat-barreled Enfield rifle, although it was less than half the size of any rifle that Snakeskin had ever seen, largely due to the extensive shortening of the weapon's muzzle.

Its bolt action and ammunition magazine were also of a unique construction, the former being situated well to the center of the receiver, the latter taking the shape of a drum packed with bullets, located immediately in front of the weapon's trigger housing and depending from the underpart of the snub barrel.

"Squeeze the trigger gently and see what happens," La Crosse suggested with a toothy smile, indicating the target at the end of the shooting gallery with a gesture of his hand.

Snakeskin did as the Frenchman ordered him to, and was amazed at the striking results of the test. Instead of the single bullet that he had expected the weapon to have fired (despite his knowing its multiple-round capabilities), a burst of several rounds was instantly ejected from the weapon amid stuttering flashes of hot yellow flame.

A glance at the target in the distance told Snakeskin that he had just fired a salvo of at least four rounds with a single trigger pull. Although none of his shots had apparently been placed very close to the center of the target that La Crosse had set up, the performance of the La Crosse Repeater was truly astonishing.

"On fully automatic fire, the weapon is not very accurate," the Frenchman explained. "However, this factor is relatively unimportant. Using this sort of gun requires a different approach to hitting a target, one in which you don't try to accurately place a single shot, but instead aim toward placing your fire within a general target area."

FIVE DEAD MEN

Snakeskin fired again, using this new technique, sweeping the Repeater's muzzle from side to side as he pulled the trigger. The long burst of automatic fire produced far better results this time around, scoring several hits across the center of the target bulls-eye.

Although Snakeskin was impressed with this new type of weapon, La Crosse also had another surprise in store for him. Returning to his work shop, he took up another of the Repeater prototypes he had produced. This Repeater was different from the others in that it was augmented with a cylinder of perforated metal screwed into the barrel mouth. The perforated cylinder added about three additional inches to the gun's overall length.

"And what might this be?" Snakeskin asked.

"It's something I must confess I've stolen from Maxim as well," La Crosse told him. "This particular invention, however, has never been made public. It seems that its potential for warfare was too much to stomach for the same military men who have adopted the Gatling and Maxim weapons in America, Britain and Europe. Maxim was forced to burn all his plans, but I was able to commit enough to memory to duplicate them -- and to make them even better."

"I understand he tried to make a silent bomb once, but I've never seen one. Has this something to do with it?"

"He did and it does," replied La Crosse. "The attachment fitted to the Automatic Repeater is designed to silence this weapon too. You will note a significant reduction in the noise of the bullet's discharge when burst-firing the weapon, which is considerably reduced by what I've called, bowing to the obvious --"

"-- A silencer, of course," interrupted Snakeskin.

"Yes," La Crosse snapped, a bit peevishly at being deprived of his moment of boastful bravado.

"Try it."

Snakeskin did, and was further amazed by how quiet the weapon proved to be in operation. The bullets produced only a faint series of sputtering sounds as they were discharged from the perforated cylinder that extended from the Repeater's muzzle, and much the only sound made as the multiple-round burst was fired was the clatter of the bolt action as the firing pin was repeatedly struck and shell casings were ejected from the breach.

The Frenchman was to be congratulated. His genius had just advanced the development of small arms much like his compatriot Bertillon's genius had advanced the science of criminology with his anthropometric photographic filing system.

Thanks to the La Crosse Automatic Repeater and its Silencer attachment, death could now be meted out with a gun almost as silently as it could be dispensed with the blade a sharp knife -- and in the Sudan, such power was a blessing.

28. A House of Spies

"Although these weapons have been tested, I consider them prototypes," the Frenchman explained, adding that he was able to complete production of no more than a relative handful of his revolutionary new automatic guns.

"I can't vouch for their operation completely," he added, as they still needed to be further tested.

Though Snakeskin was present, La Crosse spoke for the benefit of Chow Bang Chow, the Gurkha Jahno and the rotund Dutchman Van Bronck, all of whom had not been present when Blake had tested the weapons earlier.

Now, on the eve of the La Crosse Repeaters' first trial against the Mahdists in tonight's upcoming Zanzibar raids, he set about making sure that the inventions he called "his beauties" were used with proper respect, indeed with special reverence for their unique capabilities.

Snakeskin Blake held one of the new weapons that the Frenchman had designed, admiring it once again after initially seeing it in La Crosse's workshop. And again he was impressed by how extremely light in weight and how streamlined it was, far more so than any weapon that he had ever handled, while its killing power was something that he'd witnessed first hand. The Frenchman passed out similar such weapons to the assembled Brothers of the Gun, all of whom inspected the cunningly designed weapons with keen interest.

"What are these cylindrical attachments to the muzzle?" asked Jahno, curiously eying the odd-looking gun.

"They're called 'Silencers,' *mes amis*," the Frenchman replied. "I am also considering the term 'Sound Suppressors.' They have been designed along the lines of secret work done by Maxim, and are intended to muffle the reports of bullets discharged from the muzzle. *Mon ami* Snakeskin has personally witnessed how easily my Silencer can make shooting with this beautiful machinery of noiseless killing."

Each of the submachineguns used in the forthcoming raids on the Mahdists and their Dervish and Hashishim confederates in the Zanzibar underground was equipped with a Silencer extending from the barrel. The long cylinders added to the overall length of each weapon, but the compact weapons were still considerably shorter and lighter than any conventional rifle, even with full drum magazines attached.

Armed in this fashion by La Crosse, and equipped with extra ammunition magazines, the Brothers of the Gun, now including Jahno, filed from the Frenchman's workshop. With La Crosse toting one of his own creations and eager to test his "beauty" in a realistic setting against actual living targets, and Snakeskin in the lead, the group made its way on foot to the assembly point on the outskirts of Stone Town where a large nest of Mahdist spies had been pinpointed by informants working for the Sultan's police force.

Agents of the Zanzibar gendarmerie had for some days been watching a particular dwelling in the vicinity of that section of Stone Town called M'nazi-Moya, which roughly translated as "One Cocoa Tree." The Sultan's constabulary had already quietly surrounded the enclave, having thrown a *cordon sanitaire* around the area in which the house was situated.

Now, as night began to fall and twilight bedecked Stone Town in a blanket of blue velveteen, the police ringing the Mahdist nest remained in place while, under the Sultan's express orders, the Brothers of the Gun tried out their special tactics and new weapons -- the same ones that were to be used in the rescue mission to the Sahel -- against the local spies.

They deployed as follows: Chow Bang Chow climbed to the roof and readied himself to rope down to the top floor window. The Gurkha posted himself at the crudely fashioned rooftop cupola in order to follow the Chinese Wu-Shu master into action and to cover him with his gun. Van Bronck and Snakeskin, with La Crosse at their head, stationed themselves in the narrow, cobblestone street at front and corners to provide covering fire for their teammates as well as to kill any Mahdists attempting to escape without surrendering.

Then it came -- the sound of a canister charge exploding and the flash of a rapidly ascending star shell that burst overhead into a burning red flare that was the signal to move in.

From the rooftop the Chinaman rappelled down and kicked in the window, swinging into a room thick with surprised Mahdists and landing to fire the Repeater, their faces expressing shock and pain in the flashes of bullet bursts that knocked them against the walls and overturned furniture, plates of roasted lamb and hashish-burning hookah pipes.

Close behind came Jahno, kicking in a locked and bolted wooden door and fast-stepping down a flight of stairs to add the fire of his Repeater to Chow Bang Chow's as more of the Mahdists fell and others began to flee the scene of carnage in mortal panic.

From the street, La Crosse commenced firing point blank at the lock on the ground floor door, blowing its latch clean off and kicking hard to knock it half off its hinges, then tossing in a lit flare that burst in white phosphorescence, exposing the robed figures inside, and raking them with crosswise bursts of submachinegun fire.

Snakeskin rushed in behind the Frenchman and fired his own Repeater, leaning on the trigger to instantly stitch two Hashishim across their middles and watching their bodies jerk and the blood jetting out of them in the sizzling light of the flare that had begun to set the house on fire.

And then Van Bronck went storming in with the ungainly shuffle characteristic of the overweight, yet as caught up in the heat of action as the rest of the Brothers, rushing past them into the rooms beyond the main enclosure, his Repeater spitting out bullets and puffs of flame.

And then came the shouts of the gendarmerie on the perimeter line of the *cordon sanitaire*, shouts of men who could not bear to hold themselves back, even at the Sultan's express command, and who rushed the house with guns drawn and blood in their eyes amid the stuttering light and the staccato reports and the screams and shouts of Dervishes dying or surrendering, amid the crackling of flames and the clouds of eye-stinging, throat-choking smoke.

Then the tunnel of perception receded as the heat of action ebbed and time, which had seemed to race forward at breakneck speed, contracted to a perceivable pace as another door, a thick one made of something that might have been

239

oak, went suddenly flying off its hinges under a hard kick from a snakeskin boot, and a Dervish came at Snakeskin brandishing a long scimitar, its curved blade glinting a dull metallic silver as he swung it with a terrible cry of vengeful rage.

A second Dervish now came at Snakeskin from a different direction. He squeezed the trigger of the Frenchman's remarkable hybrid weapon, but the repeating gun jammed as he attempted to fire. Snakeskin cursed as he dodged aside still clutching the Repeater which had apparently been fouled and was now useless.

He was fast enough to barely evade being run through as the Dervish charged him pell-mell, intent to chop off his head with the edge of his sword. Instead, the point of the glittering scimitar bit deeply into the wall and remained fixed there as the Dervish struggled to pull it out. And then Snakeskin lashed out with the butt stock of the jammed weapon and it connected solidly with the jaw of the Mahdist as he struggled to disengage the crescent-shaped Arab cutlass from the wall.

The butt end of the jammed weapon, at least, turned out to be serviceable, even in the absence of its ability to fire. A loud and sickeningly wet sort of crunching snap that marked shattering collarbone and breaking neck cartilage sounded as the wooden stock connected with its intended target. The stunned Mahdist sank heavily to his knees. Gushing blood from his fractured skull the Dervish toppled sideways and lay unmoving with his legs splayed and his arms behind his back.

Elsewhere, Chow Bang Chow and the Frenchman were busying themselves with other Dervishes who had chosen to fight rather than surrender. The Mahdists were fierce in their defiance of death, shouting praise to Allah even as they embarked on their journeys to his mysterious abode, but their mortal flesh, bone and blood proved to be no match for the skilled warriors, their advanced repeating weapons, and the extra bullet magazines brought along by the Brothers of the Gun.

Those Dervishes who survived the surprise attack on the Mahdist stronghold chose to martyr themselves by blade or rifle, or hurl their bodies from rooftop and windows instead of suffering the humiliation of surrender to the unbeliever Infidels whom they despised and ridiculed.

As the Gurkha closed in on a barricaded door at the rear of the second floor he heard the sounds of horrible groaning which came from inside. Shooting out the lock with a burst of automatic fire, he found several Mahdists writhing on the floor in a tangled heap.

As he bent close, he smelled the bitter odor of almonds. It was cyanide, beyond a doubt. Those inside, with enough time to act on a prearranged plan, had elected to kill themselves en masse rather than surrender, believing that they would be reborn in Paradise and preferring death at their own hands to capture by the hated Infidels and the enemies of their beloved Mahdi.

■

The lone surviving Mahdist who had been captured in the raid was brought back to the Sultan's palace. Although badly wounded and missing his left eye, he could count himself fortunate to have survived the raid at all, since the Zanzibar gendarmerie, eager to participate in the killing, slaughtered every living Mahdist in sight, (and even shot some of the dead for good measure) before the blaze that consumed the building sent them rushing helter-skelter outside again.

FIVE DEAD MEN

Deep beneath the rock-bound foundations of the royal palace, Jahno had caused to be constructed a well-outfitted torture chamber within the dank catacombs that extended beneath the palace. The torture chamber could boast of a room with dripping rock walls equipped for the torments of the strappado and the iron maiden, and a furnace for the heating of implements for the pulling out of tongues and eyeballs or to light firebrands for application against the soles of the feet, but its specialty was the regional variation on breaking the human body on the rack known as the *shebba*.

Having been remanded to the tender mercies of the Sultan's royal torturer, the captured Mahdist was now bound to the rack, his wrists secured at one end and his feet at the other.

While Blake watched, the Gurkha twisted the shebba's wheel and the straps at wrists and ankles tightened with the audible creaking of leather thongs subjected to many force pounds of stress. The man on the rack grimaced and groaned, but he still did not utter a single word in answer to the torturer's demands.

Far from being disappointed, the Gurkha seemed to relish the silence with which his recalcitrant subject was repaying his efforts to loosen his tongue. It only meant that he would have the opportunity to inflict yet more pain on his subject who would, as they all did, eventually sing like the fabled nightingale -- before he ultimately died and sailed heavenward to join Allah in celestial glory.

And even as they all did eventually, so too this victim of the shebba groaned and began to talk, pleading for mercy as the words poured out of him to the accompaniment of the snapping sounds from his extremities as the joints of his skeleton were pulled apart and the inexorable tug of the shebba tore him limb from limb.

Though his words might have been expected, they were nevertheless anything but reassuring. The Mahdi, he said, had hundreds, indeed thousands, more just like him, all eagerly awaiting the call to do their master's bidding and ready to forfeit their lives in order to see that it was carried out. The Sultan's hirelings, he warned, even the Sultan himself, were marked for death, and it was only a matter of time until the Expected One's will was made manifest.

Again the Dervish pleaded for mercy, which Jahno decided to grant him by breaking his legs and crushing his skull with a heavy iron rod. But then a shot rang out and the gushing red cleft in the middle of the Dervish's forehead inflicted by the single bullet from the LeMat pistol in Snakeskin Blake's hand released the Mahdist with a mercy greater than the Gurkha's before Jahno could rain his first blow down.

29. At the Sultan's Command

The whitewashed stone building overlooked the broad expanse of the slate-colored Arabian sea, the residence provided Snakeskin Blake "Pasha" by his patron the Sultan. Greeted at the door by his servants, the American freebooter shed his sandals and walked barefoot across the large Persian rug spread across a floor of inlaid tile, relishing the massage of its high knap against the hot soles of his bare feet.

Also inside, and also awaiting his arrival, was Alika, the dancing girl whom the Sultan had given him to ride like a two-humped she-camel at his first arrival on the island kingdom.

Snakeskin's pulse quickened as he was handed a frosted glass of iced Clarissa wine by a servant. He had hoped that Alika would be there to await him on his return to Zanzibar. He recalled with pleasure the lovemaking she had given him during their last encounter, and the smell of her palm-oiled and perfume-scented, almond colored body.

He also knew, as he entered the bedroom where she awaited him, that there would probably be little time before he would have to leave the island again, possibly for the last time and never to return.

"My bold one, I have missed you so," she told Snakeskin, wrapping her arms around him and pressing her lissome hips so close to his groin that he could instantly feel the heat that streamed from her flowing womanhood. "I have ached to press you to me, to take your manhood deep within me."

She released him and went to a divan upon which lay an ornately carved long-stemmed pipe, whose stem was fashioned of ebony and whose bowl was formed from a matching black stone called jet, which Africans knew as "the black jewel."

"I have instructed the servants to prepare a feast, bold one," Alika told Snakeskin as she lit the mixture in the jet bowl and began to nurse at the bit of the pipe. "We two shall first feast on love in the coolness of our bedchamber."

The pipe contained a potent mixture of Chinese opium, Moroccan kief and Libyan hashish.

When the mixture in the bowl was lit, Alika drew the smoke deep into her lungs and held it there while she passed the pipe to Snakeskin Blake, who took it from her and did as she had just done.

"I will dance for you, bold one," she said, as she sat him down on the edge of the large, four-poster bed, and went to the gramophone that stood on four legs at a corner.

The gramophone was another gift of the Sultan. As sounds of reedy snake charmers' flutes, crashing cymbals and rhythmic drums began to fill the air with their hypnotic Eastern cadences, Alika began her shimmying performance. It was to be what the French called *le danse du ventre*, otherwise known by the name of the Dance of Seven Veils.

As he smoked the pipe Alika had given him, Snakeskin began to lose himself in an hallucination of eroticism. Alika's body exercised a mesmeric fascination for him, and he reached out, and pulled the dancing girl toward him, crushing her breasts against his chest while his mouth sought hers. He began kissing her, then moved down toward her ripe, firm globular bosoms. Their taut brown nipples stood erect and hard as cherry stems. He took them into his mouth, and began to suck them, then moved down to her oiled flat belly.

Alika moaned as he reached further down, and opened her legs wide. Snakeskin's pulse thundered in his ears as he lost himself in a dream world, tasting and smelling her musky erotic sweetness.

The fragrance that lay between her parted thighs filled his mind and for a fleeting instant stole away his being. She moaned suddenly and shuddered, pulling his head down and thrusting it against the hot, deep wetness of her vagina.

And then Snakeskin was on top of her, exploding inside her, riding her hard as befit the she-camel the Sultan had given him in her, and as the heat of the day grew and the sun rose overhead, replacing the cool of the Zanzibar morning with the burning flame of the noonday sun, he rolled from her body in a delirium of rapture.

Then Snakeskin Blake began to dream that he had become a Crusader of old. He wielded a heavy sword and sat astride a pure white Arabian stallion, charging into battle against the ranked enemy, the Turks who held Jerusalem, which by treachery had been lost, but which by the sword of kings and their knights would be retaken. His broadsword flashed as it hewed into the mass of Turks who were trying to unhorse him, and then one of the Turks lunged at him with a spear. Snakeskin was unhorsed. He seemed to be falling a very great distance, falling endlessly into a bottomless pit.

And then suddenly he awoke in the darkness of the room. He caught a glint of metal in the darkness and reflexively lunged sideways.

The sharply honed cutting edge of the *janbiya* wielded by the Hashishim-trained killer penetrated the pillow that had lain beneath his head, ripping a gash in it. Snakeskin rolled off the bed, reacting rather than thinking.

The knife gleamed again, following him in the hand of his would-be killer that clutched its hilt. In the semi-darkness of the shuttered bedchamber, he could make out a lithe figure, following him with catlike speed, and the flash of the knife as its long, curved blade was positioned for a death-dealing strike.

Still drugged and semi-delirious, Snakeskin stumbled as the knife-wielding assassin lashed at his midriff with an expert's practiced movement, meaning to disembowel him at a single stroke that would open his abdomen and send his entrails steaming to the tiles of the bedroom floor.

More by blind luck than skill, he evaded the death strike with a sideward lurch of his body, suffering a deep slash wound to his hip and lower right forearm in the process, but managing to block the next strike on the follow-through and close with his assailant. Now locked with the killer, Snakeskin pushed the assassin down on the bed, and as his vision cleared, lay face-to-face atop the thrashing body beneath him.

It was Alika.

She fought and scratched at him in a blind fury, her face contorted and bloodied. He squeezed hard on her wrist and heard the *janbiya* fall from her grasp to clatter against the tiles. Holding her immobilized beneath him with the strength of his limbs and the weight of his body, he felt the hot spittle that flew from her lips strike the eyes that she had only lately kissed in the torrid heat of passion.

"What's going on?" he asked, astonished.

"I hate you as I hate all unbelievers who shun the word of the Prophet Mohammed Ahmed, blessed be his name," she shouted back, the utter scorn she felt evident in her eyes which blazed with unconcealed fury.

"Long live the Mahdi! Long live the Expected One! Death to the foes of the Mahdiyah! Death to the Infidel and all his wretched kind!"

Then, suddenly Alika broke free and -- picking up the dagger with a single, effortless sweep of her lithe dancer's body -- rushed toward the door. Snakeskin caught up with her just as she plunged the steel blade of the jewel-hilted assassin's knife deep into her own heart and twisted the pommel back and forth to work it deeper and make the hot blood gush out in pulsating jets.

As a spray of dark arterial blood spurted all over the damasked Ottoman broadloom that covered the tile floor Alika slumped down to the carpet, flexing her wrists to hasten the out-rush, cursing her lover as she died and entreating heaven to lengthen her beloved Mahdi's life even as her own spilled out of her open veins in a hot, black torrent that stained the veils of silk upon which she fell.

DAVID ALEXANDER

BOOK FIVE

SWORD OF THE MAHDI

FIVE DEAD MEN

30. The Nile Felucca

"A sad thing it is truly about Alika," remarked the Sultan as he walked in the cool of his garden.

"She was a fine she-camel and a mount worthy of a thousand pleasurable rides across the hot sands of lust. Alas, the reach of the Mahdists is truly long. But, still, you are quite fortunate to be alive, Snakeskin Blake Pasha. Allah be praised."

The Sultan of Zanzibar and Snakeskin walked side by side within a whimsical maze of topiary fashioned from hedgerows in the manner of a garden of an English manor house. Jahno, the Gurkha, followed behind them at a discreet distance, with picked warriors posted here and there, armed and watchful.

The Sultan had obtained the services of the most famous of Britain's renowned topiary artists to decorate his own gardens after those he had admired during his stay in London and sojourns in the Kentish countryside years before.

The verdant labyrinth boasted foliage sculpted into the shapes of camels and elephants and hippopotami, of sailing ships and sea monsters drawn from the annals of myth, of soldiers and maidens and sultans and prophets.

Yet, whatever the artfully conceived foliage might have meant to His Excellency, in Snakeskin's mind the labyrinth of the garden stood out as a symbol for the tangled maze of intrigue and deception into which he had been plunged willy-nilly since his arrival in Zanzibar at the behest of his friend Chinese Gordon.

No secret appeared to be safe from the Mahdi's many ears -- at any rate, not for very long. And his reach did indeed extend exceedingly far. From his stronghold in the Sahel, the Mahdi had stretched out his hand from the teeming marketplace of Zanzibar a thousand miles across the wide expanse of the Indian Ocean to the dockside tenderloin of Portuguese Macao to strike at his enemies.

Since their whereabouts were all too well known to their enemies, remaining in Zanzibar was pointless and, as was becoming more apparent daily, exceedingly dangerous. It was now held as an article of faith that the Mahdi had spies and assassins stationed everywhere in the Sultan's island realm and that the protection of the Sultan was of little value.

The truth of the matter was that so long as Snakeskin Blake and the Brothers of the Gun remained in Zanzibar, they could not count themselves safe. The Mahdist assassins would strike again, that was a certainty. Their presence in Stone Town, even given the protection of the Sultan, would only lead to further attempts on their lives. Sooner or later, one of those attempts was bound to succeed. If that happened, then all their efforts and planning thus far would have been in vain.

Because of this, Snakeskin decided that the group would leave Zanzibar as quickly as possible. While he would have preferred more time to train his group for the mission, they were as ready to go now as they would ever be, and in mobility they would find their greatest protection. Blake's raiders would now have to go on the offensive. They would have to take the fight into the center of the Mahdi's power.

"I wish, by the Prophet, that I could be going with you," the Sultan added as he and Snakeskin strolled through the verdant maze of transplanted English topiary.

"Such sublime adventure! Such supreme challenge! What I would not give to be a younger man."

"Your Majesty will be better off here, where his subjects can benefit from his munificent rule and the love which Allah bestows upon his exalted personage," Jahno advised the Sultan, adding, "just as our friend Van Bronck has played his part in China and has returned home to Macao."

"Yes, certainly correct," the Sultan gravely responded, bowing to the inevitable with his customary aplomb. "And so, good luck," he said to Snakeskin.

"And may the wind be your brother."

The American thought about his friend's remark.

"What do you mean?" asked Snakeskin, puzzled at the Sultan's parting words.

"It is an old Arab proverb," he explained, quoting: "He who has the wind as his brother may pass without notice even into the tents of his enemies."

Snakeskin drew his matched LeMat pistols with their custom rattlesnake grips.

"I think I prefer these deadly vipers of mine to the wind," he declared. "They enable me to kill my enemies, whereas the wind promises at most to help me steal into their midst."

"Well put, my friend," said the Sultan. "Perhaps our proverbs are a bit out of step with the these fast-changing times."

Still, Snakeskin thought he had heard just what he had needed to provide him with a final missing element.

The team he had assembled had its mission, its weapons and other supplies, and its training too. What it lacked was a name, one that would bind it together as a cohesive unit and furnish it with an identity that it could wear with pride through the vicissitudes of battle and fate. He had wanted to coin a name that was as effective as that of Baker's Forty Thieves, the mercenary unit formed by Chinese Charlie years before that had struck a chord in the minds of all who'd heard it.

Now, Snakeskin Blake thought that he had finally found what he'd sought. Thanks to the Sultan of Zanzibar, Snakeskin knew what he would call his team.

He would not call his raiders the Brothers of the Wind. Instead he would call them the Brothers of the Gun.

■

The group was attired in native garb, but only outwardly. Long, flowing *jibbas* which were colorfully patched in the native North African style concealed the western attire that was worn underneath by Snakeskin and La Crosse. Jahno and Chow Bang Chow accepted their Sudanese outfits complacently, the former because he had worn such garb frequently during his service as head of the Sultan's armed retinue, the latter because the transition from the monk's robes he had worn for the last two years to those he'd now donned was an inconsequential change.

Snakeskin's plan called for spiriting his team of desert raiders out of the palace and then onto the wharves at Shangani Point, which lay at the tree-fringed harbor-side of the island, without their being noticed by any of the Mahdi's many local spies. It could be taken as an article of faith that Dervishes, possibly aided by Highbinders, would have already staked out the palace and would be watching for any indication that Snakeskin's party had made a bid to escape from Zanzibar. Whether the presence of the *Ansari* could be detected or not, the need to evade these unseen watchmen was a vital necessity.

The method which Snakeskin hit upon to accomplish the group's breakout was concealment in a cart full of foul-smelling refuse. The cart always set off from the palace entrance at its usual early hour, one which would not arouse a great deal of suspicion. Blake, La Crosse, Jahno and Chow Bang Chow would make use of it to hide themselves in before it left the palace precincts. The cart was easily large enough for the job and was pulled through the streets by two oxen who trudged sullenly under the whip of the royal trash collector on their journey to the dumps near the harbor where the garbage would later be burned.

Just as Snakeskin had surmised, Dervish watchers had been posted in the narrow, filthy streets which surrounded the palace environs. The Mahdists standing lookout did indeed see the refuse cart leave the palace on one of its regular trips to dispose of the Sultan's royal waste, but they, like everyone else in the vicinity, paid this event scant notice. They were not looking for dumpsters full of trash but for armed mercenaries setting out on a journey filled with peril.

Unnoticed in the gloom, the refuse cart proceeded on its clattering way along Stone Town's winding, narrow streets until it finally reached a square-sided dwelling which abutted the Zanzibar docks. Pulling back on the reins to bring his tethered bullocks to a stop, the driver of the cart looked cautiously about. When the royal trash collector had assured himself that there were no watchers present in the neighborhood, he pulled back the canvas tarp that covered the foul-smelling burden he hauled.

"Hamid sees no one, effendis," he whispered into the darkness beneath the canvas.

The royal trash collector did not bother to hold his nose, as he had long since grown used to the odors which rose from the bed of the cart.

"You're certain?" asked a gruff voice from within.

"Hamid's nose may be dulled by years of smelling these terrible fumes, effendi, but his eyes are as sharp as those of the desert hawk. Be assured that you are unseen by your enemies."

Snakeskin and the rest of the raiders now jumped from the conveyance, as wary lest the Sultan's trusted man turn out to have led them into a trap as they were eager to leave its malodorous confines.

With Snakeskin in the lead and the Gurkha bringing up the rear, they moved quickly into the halfway house that they had established through Jahno's agents in preparation for their secret departure from Zanzibar under cover of night.

There, in the house by the dockside, the Brothers waited until it had become safe to commence the final leg of their journey.

As Snakeskin and his men passed the early morning at the halfway house, another group, disguised as Snakeskin and the rest of his mercenary band, left the Sultan's palace with considerable fanfare. This was a diversionary move to throw whoever might be watching off the scent.

The diversionary tactic had worked to perfection. The Mahdists, having allowed the royal rubbish cart to pass them by unnoticed, now followed the decoys through the narrow streets of the sultanate. Word quickly spread by means of a highly effective network of *Ansari* couriers and an ambush site was picked out on the fly, one from which escape would be impossible.

FIVE DEAD MEN

A band of Mahdists sworn to avenge the deaths of their fellow Dervishes assembled at a point where the narrow street down which the assembled Franks swaggered toward the dockside gave onto a small stone-flagged square with a well in its center. The well was always attended by women with pails of water and screaming urchins clutching at their burkas, but the Dervishes had chased them away like black geese, and now the square was silent, surrounded by stone houses with shut-up windows.

As the Franks swaggered into the square of the well, shouting and carousing among themselves, the ambush was staged. It had not occurred to the Dervishes that Franks did not swear in street Arabic, nor go about unshaven as did the foreigners and unbelievers. All they saw were the guns and the dull olive hues of the Frankish mercenaries' clothing. This was enough to bring them down upon the group as wolves upon the fold.

As the decoys flung themselves down and crawled to the well head for cover and a place to return rifle fire against the bullets that had suddenly greeted them as they'd crossed the pocket square, the Mahdists swarmed across the stone-flagged pavements, intent on finishing their grisly work. Then a makeshift bomb made of a bottle filled with petrol and lit with a rag fuse was flung at them, exploding into flames as it struck the well head and setting fire to the hated Franks. More petrol bombs followed and soon the human torches flailed wildly, screaming and howling as the Mahdists jumped on them, eager to take their lives.

Some of the Dervishes emptied their rifles into the flame-wreathed bodies of their hapless victims in a frenzy of mindless slaughter. Other members of the decoy party were hacked to pieces with curved Mameluke swords, *janbiya-*

daggers and stabbed with the short spears called *assegai* as they thrashed on the ground, hideously burnt.

To cap off their gruesome work, the Mahdists then cut off the heads of all the victims of their ambush. These they quickly wrapped in bloodied rags and then scurried like rats into the shadowed alleys feeding off the pavements of the square of the well which their gruesome handiwork now defiled with gore. As they ran, drunk with victory, they screamed hymns of praise to their leader, blessing the Mahdi's name for having again shown them the path to victory over their hated foe, the Infidel Frank.

The severed heads of their fallen foes would serve as proof of their victims' identities. The Mahdi would insist on seeing them to be certain that his words had been heeded and that his infallible and supreme will had been obeyed.

■

Many hours later, Snakeskin and his party set off on a native *felucca*, a sail-driven boat made from Nile rushes used for hauling produce and native manufactures to and from the African mainland. The night was moonless and the waters of the twenty mile-wide straits that separated the continental land mass of Africa from the tiny island off its eastern coast were tranquil and mirror-like as Snakeskin's raiders departed.

Soon, helped along by a quickening breeze, fragrant with the smell of the brush and desert of sub-Saharan Africa that blew vigorously from east to west, they made landfall on the African coastline opposite the island.

The Sultan's mercenaries emerged from the felucca wearing their square-patched *jibbas* whose large hoods were pulled down low over their faces, concealing them from view. However, all members of the raiding party had been tanned by the hot sub-equatorial sun, and all had allowed their beards to grow in thickly during their stay in Zanzibar.

FIVE DEAD MEN

They would appear only as "Franks" to those who chanced to regard them with a more than casual degree of scrutiny. Anyone giving the group merely a passing glance would be convinced that they were native Sudanese, or if not that, then Arab, or perhaps even Indian merchants from Bombay or New Delhi, trading in ivory, hides, gum-copal, pepper or even slaves, a not uncommon sight in these parts.

Now that the Brothers had made landfall, it was time to arrange for transportation along the next leg of their journey inland. If the Sultan's agents had done their work accordingly, a reception committee of friendly partisans from among the Kababish -- one of the native tribes which led a nomadic existence in the vast desert behind the coast -- and who were willing to render assistance to the party, would await their arrival. Just in case of treachery, Blake ordered all hands to man their silenced repeat-firing weapons while Jahno flashed the prearranged recognition signal.

Crouching, the Gurkha lit a match in the darkness. It flared and was extinguished. Nothing happened for a second or two, but then, from a short distance away in the pitch blackness, a small answering flare briefly glowed in response. Snakeskin permitted himself to relax as the prearranged recognition codes were exchanged and accepted.

Soon, the sound of footsteps muffled by the sand below and the winds above was heard to approach. The Kababish materialized from the darkness like ghosts. Their ancient tribe had sworn loyalty to the Sultan of Zanzibar a century before, and they continued to remain hostile to the Mahdist cause. They had come bringing freshly fed and watered packhorses, dried figs, yoghurt, and the carcasses of freshly slaughtered goats to roast on campfires along the way.

The mercenaries loaded their saddlebags onto the backs of the Kababish horses that they had just been provided with and placed more supplies onto the camels that had also been brought by the tribesmen.

With Jahno now in the lead because of his knowledge of the terrain across which they were to travel, Snakeskin following behind, the Frenchman in the middle and Chow Bang Chow bringing up the rear, the four mercenaries rode through the night, with many more miles still remaining before they were to come in sight of their destination.

FIVE DEAD MEN

31. A Desert Mirage

Alert for danger, the Brothers of the Gun pushed on through the night with only brief stops to rest and to water their exhausted beasts of burden.

A bleak, cold dawn found the travelers approaching the border regions of the Sudan. These comprised a vast area whose boundaries shifted with the political winds, and which encompassed the greater portion of Eastern Africa.

Keeping to a near northwesterly route that would bring them directly into the heart of the Mahdi's territory, the Brothers traveled into the interior over well-trodden caravan tracks. These roads across the desert, explained Jahno, had been used by itinerant merchants over the course of thousands of years. They were already ancient in the time of the Egyptian Pharaohs. Jahno believed that they would outlast the colonial powers that even now struggled to retain their hold on Egypt and the Sudan.

Dressed in their native costumes of dull white *jibbas*, with colored squares of cloth sewn into them in Mahdist fashion as a token of virtuous poverty, and wearing turbans to match, Snakeskin's raiders would attract only minimal attention. Their greatest risk of discovery would probably not come from Dervishes but instead lie in crossing the path of desert robbers. They had been warned by the Kabbabish tribesmen who'd aided them that bands of these brigands infested the area.

In the event they did chance to meet up with a robber band, the mercenary brothers would have to kill its members quickly and bury the bodies before any discovery of the carnage was made by a roving band of *Ansari* or other tribes who did not share the hostility to the theocratic rule of warrior-priest Mohammed Ahmed Ibn el-Sayyid Abdullah. Reports of armed conflict on the desert, if related by living witnesses, would not escape the all-hearing ears and all-seeing eyes of the ever-present and -- if accounts of released captives were correct -- ever-smiling Mahdi.

The raiders continued moving through the early part of the day as the air temperature soared, passing the hundred degree mark within a matter of minutes. It had now become a fairly easy matter to fry an egg simply by breaking the shell and dropping the yolk onto any convenient rock, leaving the sun's fiercely radiant heat to do the rest.

Pointing ahead of them toward a tiny black dot on the sandy plain across which they rode, Jahno indicated that a tribal village would be in their path. This village too held tribesmen allied with the Kabbabish who were unfriendly to the Mahdist cause and whose *mudir* or leader was an outspoken critic of Mohammed Ahmed and the sheikhs who served his messianic revolt yet oppressed the villagers of the land. In this village the travelers would acquire some food and water for themselves, and also fresh water and fodder for their beasts of burden.

As it turned out, the village was a dusty affair. It was comprised mainly of a few ramshackle tents and *zaribas* which were made out of the thorny brush and scrubby bantam trees that comprised the greater percentage of vegetation indigenous to the arid region. Natives with wizened faces silently and distrustfully regarded the group that entered its environs, their coal-black eyes betraying no more than did the rocks or the sands, and giving the inhabitants the strange appearance of beings just as ancient.

At the largest of the huts belonging to the tribal chieftain, the raiders exchanged Spanish gold for tribal food, water and other necessities in order to replenish their supplies.

The Gurkha spoke the native dialect fluently, which proved to be an immense help. Jahno conversed easily with the village chieftain who was explaining to him that the village had lately grown concerned about the Dervishes.

Emboldened by recent territorial gains of the Mahdists, Dervish raiding parties had become commonplace even here on the remote fringes of the Sudan. Their hordes swept in, flying the green flags emblazoned with words of wrath from the holy book of Islam, with those in the vanguard wearing helmets of bronze and coats of chain mail that had come from the piled up spoils of centuries since the Crusades had first brought the knights who'd worn them in battle to die on the sands of this parched landscape.

When the Dervishes overran a village, they plundered, raped and slaughtered without mercy, always setting some living tribesmen aside from the others. Often, when the pillage was over, they encamped to hold jousting tournaments with any weapons available, ranging from rifles to spears. Their minds deranged by hashish and kief smoked in hookahs they carried with them, the Dervishes now used those captives they'd set aside on their earlier rampage as human targets. When this second slaughter was over, the

Mahdists left the village a burned-out place of desolation that would never again be inhabited by living men.

But they often left one thing behind. Nailed to a charred upright beam that had once supported a village house, or a library whose ancient parchments might have borne the writings of lost, ancestral tribes, overlooking the charred corpses of that dwelling's former inhabitants, the Mahdists nailed a proclamation:

> *Let all show penitence before God, and abandon all evil and forbidden habits, such as the degrading acts of the flesh, the use of wine and tobacco, lying, bearing false witness, disobedience to parents, brigandage, the non-restitution of goods to others, the clapping of hands, dancing, improper signs with the eyes, tears and lamentations at the house of one's friends, slanderous language, calumny, and the company of strange women. Clothe your women in a decent manner, and let them be careful not to speak to unknown persons lest they lose their virtue. All those who do not heed these principles disobey Allah and His Prophet, and they shall be punished in accordance with the Mahdi's law.*

Not staying very long, the group moved off again before the day grew too hot and they could no longer take advantage of the relative coolness of the morning hours in which to travel. Before long, the desert sun had risen to its blazing zenith in the sky and the temperature of the air was as hot as that of an oven.

FIVE DEAD MEN

Snakeskin's plan was to find a spot in which to make camp. The Brothers then would rest and move with the fall of night, taking advantage of both the security from hostile eyes and the coolness which the enveloping darkness offered the journeyers. The borderlands of the Sudan were fast giving way to the interior, where the Madhi's rule was unchallenged, and in which the danger they faced correspondingly increased with every mile that they traversed.

In the Sudan, the Mahdi's word was law. His forces of loyal *Ansari* were everywhere, and their swords were as thirsty for blood as they were keen of edge. If caught, the Brothers could expect harsh treatment and certain execution at the hands of the Dervishes. Consulting their map of the area, Snakeskin and his men decided to make for a dry wadi lying about five miles distant.

It was just after they began their trek across the sands toward the wadi, that Chow Bang Chow, acting as lookout, noticed a mounted figure on the back of a horse some distance away.

"There," said the Chinamen, stretching his hand out and pointing at the far horizon.

Snakeskin took his binoculars out from beneath the native robes he wore and scanned the horizon, but through their lenses he could only see a vague, shadowy silhouette, far off in the distance and distorted by shimmering waves of heat rising from the desert sands and the blinding reflection of the sunlight that glared from every rock and every tree and every speck of dust in the vast ocean of emptiness surrounding them.

While there did indeed seem to be something there, precisely what it was -- or if it were even a man at all and not simply a rock formation or even a mirage -- Snakeskin was unable to gauge with any certainty.

Abruptly, the figure vanished from sight.

"I suppose that it could have been a mirage," the Frenchman offered. "The heat plays tricks with the eyes, *mes amis*. Just as my years as a prisoner played tricks with the mind."

"Not likely," Snakeskin replied, shaking his head.

Now that he thought about it, Snakeskin was certain that he had been looking at a human figure mounted on the back of a camel or horse and not merely a natural feature of the terrain or an optical illusion created by heat and light.

Nevertheless, regardless of whether the figure that had just been sighted had been a mirage or a man, there was nothing left to do but to remain alert and push on across the desert. And again, the appearance of a lone rider on the horizon line did not in and of itself signify any danger to the travelers.

But as Snakeskin rode the swaying hump of his camel mount, he began to feel otherwise. A gnawing sense of foreboding gripped him.

He felt as if the Mahdi were watching, toying with them like a cat with a ball of twine, waiting to unsheathe its claws and -- smiling, always smiling -- tear its captives to shreds.

FIVE DEAD MEN

32. The Beggar

Aday came and a day went.

An hour before sunrise, the heat was already building steadily as Snakeskin's raiders made their way across the flat, monotonous sand wastes of the eastern Sudan, searching for a wadi in which to pass the daylight hours in concealment before setting out again under cover of night.

Only a few miles inland from the coast, a vast expanse of desert wastes had abruptly begun as they had entered the Sudan.

No matter what direction they might look, the flat desert stretched away to a distant horizon. Overhead, the sky was a continuous, unvarying expanse of limpid blue, with the white-hot disk of the sun glaring mercilessly down on them like a hole drilled in the sphere of heaven to expose the infernal flames of hell encircled within its circumferential wall. Below, on the far horizon, sky and sands blended together, forming a shimmering, wavering line of heat distortion that was painful to stare at too long in the full force of day.

A sense of foreboding now fell across the small band of men like a pall of smoke. Already, and all too quickly, their supply of drinkable water had begun to run low.

The group had hoped to replenish their stocks of potable water from the oasis which their map showed lay at Tel Amadir and whose actual existence there was confirmed by Jahno. But upon reaching the oasis, they discovered to their chagrin that the wadi, long used as a caravanserai, was bone-dry. It was lack of water, Snakeskin recalled, that had doomed Hicks and his four thousand British and Egyptian soldiers the year before in these same parched lands, when cut off from the Nile by the Mahdists they ceased to be an army and became lambs for slaughter.

Still, the Brothers camped there at Tel Amadir by night, squeezing the sap from desert plants as a source of fluids. Snakes too were caught and killed, and their meat and blood proved to have some revitalizing properties, though not very much.

It was Jahno who found a small depression in the sand near the wadi containing a few precious ounces of brackish water that, after an hour of digging produced a miniature well fed by the same aquifer that nourished the oasis. The seasonal rains had not yet come, and the wadi itself was dry, but water still seeped along channels in the bedrock and could be found near the surface of the desert crust. Treatment with sulfide powder rid it of any parasites it might harbor, and it sustained the party throughout the burning heat of the daylight hours.

At night they waited in the wadi before striking camp and moving off across the desert wilderness once again. The thin air of the Sudanese desert made the transition from daylight to night time fast and severe. During the day, the heat of the sun was intense. Blazing relentlessly down, it

267

made the mind wander and caused the body to sweat profusely.

With the coming of the darkness, however, the reverse conditions very quickly took effect. A bone-chilling coldness spread over the desert like a freezing shroud. The teeth of a man chattered and the muscles of the mortal frame shook with a sometimes uncontrollable ague.

Before the coming of dawn on their third day of entry into the Sudan, the group was facing a severe problem that tested its members' wills, and their ability to survive. They needed to find a lasting supply of potable water soon or be forced to immediately turn back. It was impossible to go on through the desert without water. Food might be forfeited, but not water, and so far they had found too little enough of it to sustain life.

They moved from their hiding place in the wadi just before the break of dawn. The air still retained the chill of the night, but all of the travelers could feel it fading fast as the heat of the day began to creep up with its high temperatures climbing quickly to reach the burning highs of mid-day.

Proceeding on to the next wadi along their line of march, the group finally spotted it in the distance. They hastened toward the expected water hole as quickly as possible, eager to find shade and desperately needed water.

Soon the Brothers found tracks leading from the hole. The tracks, on inspection, were seen to have been made by men and beasts of burden. With Snakeskin in the lead, the group followed the tracks, their guns cradled or slung at shoulders but always ready, their eyes wary. They found the oasis deserted. But this wadi was not dry like the one they had come to before. Here there was a pool of water, cool and clear, and it filled the natural cistern up to its full height, staining the sands dark around its curving edges.

Now the Brothers drank greedily, and cupping water in their palms, splashed it against their parched faces and scooped it up in the brims of their hats to pour down on their heads, though not daring to bathe in the oasis for fear that Dervishes or Fuzzy Wuzzies might be watching and would use the opportunity to pounce on them while they were vulnerable to attack.

Suddenly they saw a human shape that had up until then gone completely unnoticed. The man had been sitting completely still, almost blending into the surroundings, which explained why they had not seen him as they drew up to the wadi. They approached him cautiously, their weapons drawn.

As it turned out he was an old nomadic tribesman, of a clan closely allied to the Kababish, wearing soiled rags that had once been a white burnoose and a turban that was not in much better shape.

The old nomad laughed at them.

"Why are you laughing at us, old man?" the Gurkha asked him.

"You have come to find the Mahdi," he answered them matter-of-factly.

"How do you know this?" Jahno retorted, alarmed that the ragged Bedouin had even the faintest inkling as to the nature of their mission.

"One who lives long sees much," the old man declared. "I see far. My name is Hassan, and I am a prophet."

He went on, "The sands of the desert are as innumerable mouths. They speak in tongues that tell of the future to those who have learned the trick of how to decipher their words."

FIVE DEAD MEN

"You speak in riddles, old man," the Frenchman said to this wizened anchorite of the desert. "Perhaps we may have to loosen your tongue to make your words come out clearer."

Lacrosse pulled his French legionnaire's field dagger and held the long-bladed knife menacingly in front of the old beduoin's grizzled brown face.

"You think of torturing Hassan, perhaps?" the old man asked, his dark eyes not blinking as he regarded the man scowling down at him, clutching a long knife in his bunched-up fist. "Yes, of killing Hassan, do you?"

Then Hassan began to cackle. His old body, little more than a bag of skin as dry as parchment that was stretched across bones that grew so close to the flesh that they could be seen moving beneath Hassan's flesh, began to convulse as his laughter grew and grew.

"You might as well try to torture the desert, oh travelers on the winds, oh brothers of the gun. Yes, I know of you. Yes, for I have learned to hear the sands when they speak and to understand the strange meaning of their whispered words."

"He is an old fool. He is, as the Arabs say, *majnoon*," Jahno uttered in exasperation, putting away the curved *janbiya* he had drawn while La Crosse still brandished the French legionnaire's knife. "He can do us no harm."

"Go on, old man," Snakeskin said, offering him some food from his rations.

The aged beggar accepted the offerings with a small bow and began to bolt the food ravenously. Despite his seeming madness, there did not appear to be anything wrong with his appetite.

"Thank you for your gift," he told Snakeskin after swallowing some dried dates and oiled pita bread to complete his hastily downed meal.

270

"Hassan sees that you possess wisdom beyond your years. I will repay your kindness with a warning: If perchance, you find the sword and take it, then with a feather shall you best replace it, else the friend of thy friend may wound you deep and break it."

"Forget this old madman," the Chinaman said to Snakeskin.

"Let us restock our supplies and move away from here. The heat is building steadily and we can't remain here much longer in safety."

Suddenly remembering the figure on horseback that had been spotted the previous day and which had seemed to be following them, Snakeskin asked the old man if he knew of or had come across any wanderers in the area, perhaps another Bedouin like himself.

"Warriors of a bygone age who walk a path yet leave no tracks behind," the wizened anchorite answered him. "Their ways are recondite, yet their fierceness can sometimes be a blessing to those they may chance to befriend."

He added, "If he has permitted you to glimpse him, then count yourselves blessed, for to those who are accursed, he shows himself not."

Snakeskin gave the old hermit some more of his rations, and in return he blessed Snakeskin with many salaams.

Then the party remounted their camels which, now watered and fed, did not complain at being ridden over the sun-baked desert crust of the sub-Saharan Sudan.

Blake thought about the possible meaning behind the old man's words as they rode away from the water hole. He wondered what exactly Hassan had meant by his arcane incantation and if there might not be more to the hermit and his words than had first met the eye. When he turned to take one last glance of the oasis, the old beggar was gone.

33. The *Khamaseen*

Continuing to travel by night, they covered more territory as the days passed in a slow, monotonous progression, each resembling the one preceding it and the ones that followed in train. Now, according to Snakeskin's map, his party of raiders was close to the Mahdi's main zone of activity and his domain of greatest strength.

In this region of the desert, the warrior chieftain's forces of savage and bloodthirsty *Ansari* ranged freely and without fear of reprisals, for their power was great, the forts of the Egyptian Khedive's soldiers were few and far between, and the might of the British empire had yet to send another armed force to try to take back the Sudan for England and avenge the massacre of the thousands led by Hicks.

The danger of discovery was great as well, as foraging parties of these Dervishes could be counted on to appear without warning around the next line of dunes or suddenly charge across the desert, mounted on horses and firing rifles, from an encampment at a distant caravanserai or oasis.

As flat as the desert terrain was, the stony, arid wasteland could also easily hide even large numbers of men and animals, especially if they were experienced at exploiting the terrain features for concealment within its vast expanse.

Drumlins -- mounds of sand and stony debris, many thousands of them -- marched away on every side, stretching away to the far horizons, some topped with dry treelike shrubs. The landscape of this virtual sea of sand was constantly changing its appearance. The shifting winds of the desert scoured and reformed the arid landscape hour by hour and day by day.

It was possible that while cresting any of the dune lines that marched ahead of them the small band of brothers might abruptly come face to face with an encampment of Mahdists. Such a contact would be sudden and -- through the sheer force of numbers of the opposition -- potentially catastrophic in its consequences.

Consequently, Blake's raiders moved cautiously, warily. They proceeded with painstaking slowness now. Snakeskin deployed his men in a diamond pattern in order to reconnoiter the terrain to best advantage and with the least chance of discovery by the Mahdists known to control the region.

At the front point of the diamond, one member of the team would act as a scout. Two others would form the lateral projections of the formation, with a fourth guarding the squadron's rear flank. In this way, they could quickly spot oncoming danger and, if necessary, regroup to form a fighting cell.

During one of these marches, Snakeskin, who was then on the leftmost point of the diamond, suddenly saw Jahno, who was in the lead of the formation, silently hold up his hand. This was a signal for the rest of the group to come to an immediate halt. Snakeskin relayed the Gurkha's command to the man behind him, raising his hand high to insure its visibility across the dips and rises of the uneven terrain. Soon Jahno motioned for them to join him at the crest of a sand dune.

"Beyond there, I think there is a group of men," he informed his compatriots as they drew together again and their beasts of burden got a brief rest.

"The tracks of a large number of camels have been blown away by the wind. While these are now faint, they are still visible. We must be extra cautious now."

Yet before they had gone much further, they were forced to reckon with a danger that they had not counted on before. This danger was the might and fury of nature herself, who in the desert, ruled her arid domain with a violence seldom witnessed in few other places anywhere else on earth.

Out toward the east, as the skies above them darkened, Snakeskin looked and saw what appeared to be a black wall of cloud, something resembling a moving palisade of billowing smoke, churning and reforming as it raced across the flat, sandy landscape.

So thick was the cloud that it completely blotted out the sun that had only minutes before beaten fiercely down on the surface of the stony desert. In its place a dense black shadow now scudded over the land, engulfing the desert in a surreal imposture of actual night.

"What the hell is it?" Snakeskin asked.

"It is a the *khamaseen,* the sandstorm," the Gurkha replied, his eyes fixed on a tall pillar of darkness rising to the west and the hard features grave on his broad, flat face.

"We must protect ourselves. Do as I do. Quickly! Or you die!"

Now they saw the Sultan's janissary wrap the cowl of his *jibba* over his face, leaving only a narrow slit for his dark eyes to peer through. So protected, the Gurkha moved frantically as the pace of the wind's intensity picked up, lashing down the beasts of burden and securing their precious stockpiles of food, medicine, weapons and ammunition.

With incredible speed, the sandstorm bore down on them. Now not only did the darkness engulf them, but the spreading blackness was accompanied by a sound that seemed to have come straight out of the very bowels of hell itself. It was something like the sound made by an onrushing locomotive, bearing down on them as if the concrete embodiment of nature's destructive forces.

The scalding hot wind was now whipping around them at incredible velocities, carrying particles of desert sands that struck with a punishing force far in excess of their size. In truth it was a wind no longer, but a talon armed with a million claws that sank into human flesh and gouged for the eyes.

Above the abominable keening of the wind, Snakeskin heard the terrified neighing of the party's pack mules, and the frightened braying of their camels. Like the others, there was nothing he could do, except desperately hang on against the savage brunt of the storm as it struck in its full fury.

The winds were now so fierce that Snakeskin was afraid he might at any moment be plucked up and whirled away into the howling blackness as unceremoniously as a dry leaf picked up by the blast from a chimney pot and blown, tossing and turning, across the rooftops.

Then, almost as suddenly as it had first come upon them, the *khamaseen* passed, its roar subsiding in the distance before fading away entirely. But in the wake of the sandstorm their badly frightened beasts of burden had broken loose from where they had been tied against the fury of the storm and were now running about haphazardly, fleeing across the desert in panic and trampling the contents of spilled saddlebags underfoot as they fled.

The party of mercenaries worked hard to recapture their spooked animals, running after the camels and mules in an attempt to salvage what gear they could save. In the course of these activities, while fighting the shifting sands of a high dune in pursuit of a braying donkey spilling ammunition belts as it bolted up ahead of him, and then cresting the top of the drumlin to grab for the reins, Blake again saw a familiar figure in the distance. Mounted on a horse, as immobile in the heat shimmer as a statue on a plinth, and still miles away across the open country, was the mystery rider they had caught watching them before.

Seen through the shimmer of rising solar heat, the faraway rider took on the semblance of an almost spectral apparition. And now once again, just as had happened on the first sighting of the spectral rider on the fringes of the Sudanese desert, he turned and was gone, disappearing into the dazzling solar haze as though he had never existed in the first place.

34. The Hidden Encampment

Fortunately the sandstorm, while giving them a bad turn or two, had done no long-lasting damage.

Their vital supplies were protected in oilskins and, after being largely retrieved, and then cleaned of sand and where necessary lubricated, their weapons turned out to function as well as before the storm had struck.

The repeating handguns of advanced design, contrived and built in Zanzibar by La Crosse needed more extensive cleaning, though, but the Frenchman had every confidence that the fine particles of Sudanese desert grit would not damage their finely balanced internal mechanisms.

The puzzling figure apparently following them notwithstanding, Snakeskin's raiders moved on, following the red line marked on Snakeskin's terrain map that guided them towards their destination. Having already traversed several hundred miles, their trek across the desert had brought them to the edge of the Mahdists' territory in the windswept fastness of inhospitable Kordofan.

They could not be sure that they had not yet been observed, despite their every precaution. While it still seemed possible that they had escaped the notice of Dervish patrols, it was also equally possible that they were being kept under watch, as Hicks had been, until the Mahdi deemed it the proper time to pounce.

Snakeskin now conjectured that the spectral figure which had been shadowing the Brothers from a distance was a Mahdist spotter, watching them and reporting back to his encampment after making and confirming each successive sighting.

But if that were the case, why hadn't the Dervishes attacked them already? Leaving the group of armed intruders to roam the desert at will would serve no purpose, nor was this in keeping with the usual modus operandi of the *Ansari* whose fighting style was to always attack in great strength and overwhelm the enemy by sheer force of numbers, sustaining as many casualties as it took to win the fight.

What was it that the old beggar at the oasis had told them? Snakeskin recollected that he'd said that the ghostly figure could in the end turn out to be a friend and ally. The words of the Bedouin had gone something like that, at any rate.

Be that as it may, it was decided that the small band of mercenaries continue their march in a zigzag fashion. Just in case they were in fact being spied upon in advance of a crushing Mahdist assault, such an unpredictably circuitous pattern of movement would have the effect of discouraging surveillance.

Complicated maneuvers such as those might or might not prove able to thwart the attempts of Mahdists to track their advance, but it was virtually certain that they would add at least another day to their already slow progress. Nevertheless, Snakeskin's raiders received an unexpected bonus shortly after commencing their evasive land navigation tactics.

Across the hump-backed landscape of desert dunes, on a broad, flat plain that lay beyond the marching line of drumlins, they spotted a large Mahdist encampment shortly before noon on their next mission day out of Zanzibar. Through his cavalry binoculars, Snakeskin saw that it was made up of hundreds of Dervishes; the *Ansari* themselves, their women, their children and their flocks of livestock.

Tents within the ubiquitous thorn *zariba* were scattered haphazardly across the encampment. The place he studied through the enlarged view given by his field glasses was really a moveable village. It bore all the signs of having been erected by nomadic Bedouins, nor would it likely remain in any single place on the desert for very long.

Taking council, the members of the raiding party decided that they would stage a surprise strike on the settlement. If they succeeded in clandestinely entering the place, then they might be able to gather important intelligence on the Mahdi. Such might come either in the form of maps, or perhaps they might even manage to capture one of the Dervishes alive and interrogate him.

This plan was unanimously decided upon, and Snakeskin and Chow Bang Chow together stole their way into the camp. The American freebooter and the Chinese Wu-Shu master both used their silencer-equipped La Crosse guns to deal with the sentries they spotted walking the perimeter. Their *Ansari* targets fell as if by magic as the Repeaters coughed in the night, and both infiltrators were awed by the efficiency and noiselessness of the Frenchman's weaponry in the guns' first true fielding in close-quarter operations.

FIVE DEAD MEN

Once inside the Dervish encampment, they crept up on a group of *Ansari* in the Mahdist garb of flowing patched *jibbas* and white turbans. Snakeskin and Chow Bang Chow crouched in the shadows, listening. In the stillness of the desert, they overheard one member of the group talking boisterously with his compeers, boasting of prowess both in battle and in the seduction of a *mahmoon* by himself and another Dervish.

Porting their guns, the two interlopers waited until the other Dervishes in the group had moved on, leaving their boastful companion alone in the darkness near the edge of the camp. Handing Snakeskin his weapon, Chow Bang Chow pounced on his target.

In a matter of moments, he administered a sleeper hold to his victim. Then Chow Bang Chow slung the unconscious *Ansari* up over his shoulder and carried him off. While Snakeskin flanked him -- eyes alert and both his and Chow Bang Chow's La Crosse guns fanning back and forth to get the drop on any Dervish who might happen by and cut them down with soundless bullet salvos -- they slipped out of the encampment.

Soon the two mercenaries were again safely back at their wadi base. Chow Bang Chow woke up the unconscious Dervish. His eyes widened in fear as his wits came back to him. When their captive tried to scream, Jahno's large hand clamped down over the mouth of the Dervish and stifled his screams before they had left his throat.

Now a prisoner, the Gurkha interrogated the captive Mahdist in his native language, a local dialect of Sfinaria. The Dervish, however, seemed to have no intention of uttering a syllable in reply. No matter what was said, he stared at them defiantly, his lips clamped shut. When words failed, Jahno decided that he had to resort to more forceful methods of extracting the information which the group badly needed.

For this he used a scorpion, plucking it from the sands as it crawled nearby. He dangled the scorpion over the frightened captive's head. Its poison stinger dripped its venom onto his face. The first drop stained the patched cloth of his *jibba*. It was followed by a second drop ... then a third.

"I will talk," the *Ansari* said ultimately as Jahno brought the tip of the stinger up to the man's right eye.

He stared at it as it whipped to and fro in a maddened frenzy and saw the drop of poison glittering darkly at the end of the pointed spike and his courage fled from him.

"May Allah forgive my tongue for its sinful wagging and replenish my faint heart with new courage so that I may die with honor in spite of my shameful cowardice."

Broken by the Gurkha's tactics, and determined to live despite his rhetoric, the Dervish began to tell his captors about the Mahdi. Once he began to talk there was no stopping him, and before long he had painted a detailed picture of the Mahdist base.

Suddenly, perhaps stung by the shame of betrayal, he jumped up and grabbed the legionnaire's knife from the Frenchman's hand as La Crosse sat cross-legged before him, cleaning the blade with sand. Now armed, the Dervish swung the knife viciously at La Crosse who somehow managed to leap back with only a hairsbreadth of clearance between his belly and the deadly tip of the knife as it sliced the air in front of him.

To end the matter Snakeskin shot the Dervish with a silenced burst of automatic fire from the submachinegun he held trained on the prisoner. This was just as well: had he not invited retribution they would have had to kill him anyway in cold blood. And, besides, thought Snakeskin -- he had simply answered the Dervish's prayer on Allah's behalf.

35. The Vengeance of the *Ansari*

"Hamid has vanished," reported the Dervish with the long black beard. "We have searched everywhere. It is as if the desert itself has gaped open and swallowed him up into its belly."

The chieftain of the band of *Ansari*, stroked his own beard, which was as red as the desert sunset. His name was Yusef and he was not a believer in supernatural explanations of events which could be far better and more easily explained by the treachery and deceitfulness of mortal men.

"Hamid would not have wandered off," Yusef thought aloud at the other Dervish. "He was a capable man, one who feared Allah. Some mortal harm must have befallen him in the night."

"Surely it is the work of the Infidels and unbelievers," offered the Dervish, who then kissed the amulet around his neck -- a leather pouch containing the written words of the Mahdi.

"Yes, without a doubt," Yusef agreed, nodding his head and again running his long, bony fingers through his beard. "The enemies of our Mahdi, blessed be his name, must be close. We have been warned of their presence. As I breathe, it is surely those self-same jackals who have taken poor Hamid."

"If they are near I will ride at the forefront of those who will hunt them down, by Allah, blessed be his name, even if it be to the ends of the far horizons," vowed the Dervish, raising his curved scimitar and shaking it menacingly, his dark eyes wide with menace. "It is I who shall delight in severing a head in retribution for every single hair of Hamid's beard."

"Yes, no doubt you shall," replied Yusef. "Allah in his mercy and all-knowing wisdom shall guide your hand when it delivers the righteous stroke of final vengeance to the neck of the hated Infidel!"

Despite the older Dervish's encouraging words, he had no use for the histrionics of this man, who was a fool as well as an incompetent and unable to best even a woman in battle.

But undoubtedly the Infidels would have to be hunted down. This was as certain to him as that the time to pursue them was right now. If they had taken Hamid in the night, they could not be very far off, thought Yusef.

Just then, another group of *Ansari* entered the tent of the chieftain. They were in a state of high agitation.

"What is it that besets you so?" Yusef asked with annoyance.

He supposed correctly that they were the harbingers of even worse tidings than already filled his bowl of sorrows.

"It would be better if you ventured outside, my sheikh," the first man of the group told Yusef, "to see for yourself."

"Very well," Yusef replied and went outside the tent following the man who had just spoken.

When he emerged, accompanied by the Dervish who had promised to cut the heads off the Infidels, he saw the slain men draped over the backs of donkeys. They too had gone missing overnight.

"Find them!" Yusef shouted, the cords on his neck standing out. "And do not come back without their heads, or by the sacred blood of the holy Prophet, your own shall be forfeit!"

By now the news of the slayings had spread throughout the entire Dervish encampment. Angry Dervishes crowded around the chieftain's tent, spears, rifles and long, upcurved swords brandished in outrage and indignation as vows of holy retribution flew through the air.

The chieftain of the Mahdist band looked into the hate-filled eyes of his *Ansari*, searching each face for signs of cowardice and fear. The fever of the blood, he could see, was upon them. None would falter. Each lusted to seek out the Infidels and tear them limb from limb to avenge the deaths of his brothers in jihad.

"Fetch my mount," Yusef commanded his servants, girding himself for battle. "You, Jameel, you will ride at my strong right hand."

Yusef was eager to give the fool a chance to prove himself, and Allah help him if he quavered in the face of trouble, for then Yusef himself would strike down the simpleton with his strong right hand.

"It is my honor to do so, my sheikh," the Dervish replied angrily, fire kindled in his words.

"Insallah, we will find the Infidels and wreak such holy vengeance upon their accursed heads that songs will be sung in its praise for ages to come. Yea, even live coals and plagues of insects might devour them, and it would be as nothing compared to the terrible slaughter the unbelievers shall suffer at our hands."

FIVE DEAD MEN

The chieftain did not reply to this flight of fancy, as was his custom concerning virtually anything that emerged from the mouth of the fool Jameel. He merely mounted his horse and raised his spear in silent determination. Moments afterward, the ground thundered as the hoof beats of many Arabian stallions shook the sandy plains of Kordofan, the sharp cracks of snapping rifle bolts and the war cries of the *Ansari* rising above the din.

By this time, however, Snakeskin Blake's raiders had already struck camp and begun another march across the desert, intent on leaving the area before search parties could be sent out to look for them. They were already many miles from the scene of their last encampment at the moment that Yusef mounted his Arabian stallion and rode out at the head of the *Ansari*, with the fool Jameel close behind the billowing caftan of his sheikh.

36. A Mark Made in the Sand

"It looks like they're still onto us."

In the redoubled circle of the cavalry binoculars raised to Snakeskin Blake's eyes, the band of Mahdists mounted on their steeds was magnified many times. The armed band of riders had halted. Blake now watched as the lead tracker held his face close to the ground while he clutched the reins of his beast in one hand, examining tracks too faint for anyone not born in the Sudanese desert to follow, scant traces of spoor lost amid the vast rolling ocean of sand and stones.

These artifacts of passage had been deliberately placed by the raiders with the intention of luring the *Ansari* in a direction different from the one in which they were headed. At first, at least, the tactic seemed to have produced the desired effect of throwing the hunters off the track.

But the native Sudanese were not to be put off for long. They had detected the blind trails leading eastward, had surmised their true purpose, and had veered the search party to the west. They were now following a much fainter trail left by Snakeskin and his men. This time it was their real trail and not the diversionary one which they had manufactured to send the Mahdists elsewhere.

Snakeskin snapped the field glasses shut and slipped the binoculars into the leather case at his belt. He slid down from the crest of the shallow rise at the base of which he, Jahno, Chow Bang Chow and La Crosse had stopped to rest and reconnoiter.

"What now?" asked Jahno, the slab-like simian features of the giant from Zanzibar impassive as a stone mask.

"Well, we don't have a chance in hell of taking on a Dervish raiding party head-on," offered Snakeskin, squinting in the hot sunlight. "There's only one thing to do."

"Really," the Frenchman put in, "and what might that be, Snakeskin, *mon ami*?"

"Convince the opposition that there are more of us than them, that's what," replied Snakeskin.

"Capital idea," Jahno asserted with a nod. "But I wonder how, unless you are in possession of the fabled trumpet of Jebediah, you propose to work a miracle of such magnitude in these accursed desert wastes."

"In exactly the same way as Jebediah did," Snakeskin responded, nonplussed.

Then he found a stick and began drawing a diagram in the loose sand at their feet. A broad circle represented the area of the northern Sudan in which they were located.

A large "X" at one end of the circle represented the sizable force of Dervishes hunting for them across the sun-blazed, sandy wastes. A cross near the center of the circle represented their present position. Snakeskin drew three smaller circles, each fanning out from the central one.

"Each of these circles stands for you, myself and Chow Bang Chow," Snakeskin said. "Jebediah worked his trick by convincing the raiding army of Antaxerxes that the Hebrews were attacking from three directions at once, and that there were many more of them then the small group which they actually were."

"I still don't see how, we're to pull this stunt off," the Frenchman put in.

"Here's how," Snakeskin clarified, going to one of their pack mules and producing a specimen of the Cosgrove Rockets they had brought along with them. "The Dervishes know about guns but they don't have any experience with these rockets," he said. "The superstitious bastards will think the devils of hell themselves are hot on their tails."

The Gurkha regarded one of the Cosgrove Rockets. It resembled something that was sent into the skies during celebrations during the holy month of Ramadan when fireworks were traditional. The chief difference lay in the size of the warhead charge. It was immense by comparison to those mere festival toys. Inside was a full pound of dynamite nestled in a metal cone that would splinter apart on detonation.

"They're heading into the setting sun," Snakeskin went on, further outlining his plan of attack. "That's to our advantage. We can fan out and at a pre-arranged time; hit those damn Dervishes with the rockets."

"But surely those alone won't do the job," Chow Bang Chow put in.

"No, they won't. But in the center, here," -- Snakeskin drew a straight line between the three circles -- "we plant a charge of dynamite."

He swept the stick toward the spot represented in the diagram where the dynamite would be emplaced.

"The Dervishes are herded to the center where La Crosse waits, ready to blow the main TNT charge with a detonator."

FIVE DEAD MEN

"Yes, that will make for a sweet coup de main, Snakeskin," the Frenchman said, grinning toothily, "you could have taught those old Hebrews a thing or two back then."

"Yeah, I suppose I maybe could have," Snakeskin retorted.

And now the mercenary group got moving again. Progressing stealthily, keeping low to the ground, Snakeskin and Chow Bang Chow and the Frenchman La Crosse crept across the desert wastes to positions aslope to the Dervish raiding party. Jahno, for his part, circled around in a flanking maneuver, his mission to deploy to the enemy's rear.

By the time that all four men were finally in position, the sun was already riding low on the horizon, a glowing copper disk that still cast a blinding glare across the treacherous scree of sand and broken rock that entirely covered the arid landscape.

Snakeskin had already set up the first of his clutch of Cosgrove Rockets. He positioned the launching rods of all the projectile munitions in the soft, crumbly-dry soil, with the nosecones of the rockets angled toward the oncoming force of Dervishes.

Sighting to compass points, Snakeskin saw the first signal flash appear across the dune line. This was from Chow Bang Chow, who had set up two Cosgroves and used a mirror to blink out the ready signal to Snakeskin. The Gurkha's signal came next. Snakeskin's final flash indicated, in response, that they were to fire a massed rocket salvo in thirty seconds.

Snakeskin could see the Dervishes coming up faster now. They had drawn near and they were close enough to be seen without the aid of his telescope. There were at least a hundred of them, Snakeskin broadly reckoned. Most of the

Ansari were mounted, and only their retainers -- unarmed spear-carriers -- were on foot and these latter trailed far behind the main group of horsemen.

Lighting the fuse of the first rocket, Snakeskin watched it burn down and down until its black powder charge ignited. Then the Cosgrove Rocket hurtled into the air and arced back down again into the bunched up contingent of mounted Dervishes. It exploded with a thunderous boom practically dead center amid the massed horsemen.

"What power makes this fearsome din?" shouted Jameel at the chieftain in a terrified tone of voice.

The sky had just seemed to explode. The warriors of his sheikh, Yusef, were falling from their horses.

"Has hell gaped open and loosed its very demons at the bidding of foul unbelievers?"

Just then, the second and third rockets launched by Chow Bang Chow and Jahno arced overhead. Jahno's rocket smashed into the flanks of the Dervish cavalry. Two horsemen and their mounts were instantly dismembered, their limbs flying out in all directions, spraying blood and hitting the dirt with audible smacks. Those Dervishes nearby were hurled to the ground, severely injured as the steeds of other Dervish warriors took fright and galloped off, while other equestrian fighters, spurring their stallions' flanks, turned and ran.

Jameel searched everywhere for signs of the hidden enemy. Yet he could detect nothing. And now the bold men who had set out from the tent of his sheikh were turning from soldiers to dogs before his eyes as the second volley of Cosgrove missiles impacted with a shrieking wail. Now panic spread through the ranks of the superstitious *Ansari* who had no familiarity with these weapons and who believed devils to be upon them.

FIVE DEAD MEN

As Snakeskin had intended, they turned toward the east from which direction no rockets had come, just as the third and final volley of Cosgroves exploded in the center of the reformed mass of Mahdist horsemen. Those members of the group that had not been killed outright raced in the direction of the Frenchman, driven there by the timing and position of the rocket hits.

In his place of concealment just below the embankment, La Crosse could now see the mass of Dervishes come riding his way, kicking up clouds of dust beneath their horses' hooves.

"It's a bloody rout!" he said to himself, as he pulled up the handles of the iron T-bar that he would plunge down into the detonator box to set off the charge of TNT strung out in a two-pronged ambush topology.

La Crosse saw the cloud of dust roll across the landscape and heard the ear-splitting cacophony raised by the thundering hoofs of the scores of stampeding Arabian stallions. He plunged the T-bar down hard into the detonator just as the center of the mass raced over the dynamite hidden a little ways beneath the sandy desert crust.

The ensuing explosions caused the desert to burst into a pattern of eruptions where individual toadstools of flame sprang up and grew together into a shuttling web of fire. Broiling geysers shot into the air to rain down chunks of charred flesh that lay smoldering where they hit. A pall of billowing black smoke and airborne dust particles obscured the center of the mass of destruction.

When the clouds raised by dynamite had finally cleared, La Crosse beheld a scene of almost unimaginable carnage. The main body of the Dervish force had been decimated. Those *Ansari* that had survived the ambush now stumbled about in a state of complete shock. The Frenchman picked up his automatic rifle and charged out, just as the Gurkha, Snakeskin and Chow Bang Chow did the same, killing the Dervish stragglers like mad dogs.

"Easy as shooting fish in a barrel!" the Gurkha cried with delight, sighting a La Crosse gun in each hand from his high perch atop the back of a camel and dropping his man, then training the weapons on his next target with the same effect.

Snakeskin was less sanguine as he fired at other Dervish stragglers, although no less willing to kill them where they stood. The safety, indeed the very lives of Snakeskin's raiders, and the ultimate success or failure of their mission in the Sudan, depended on their being able to move with speed and stealth across the desert.

Without this critical edge, they would be no match for the great numbers of *Ansari* that the Mahdists could march against them. Therefore, any Dervish left alive represented one more adversary who could potentially report their last known position, providing the enemy with a fix on the Brothers that might well prove fatal.

In the end, Snakeskin Blake's desert raiders grabbed what supplies and horses they could and rode away from the scene of battle as night fell, leaving the buzzards to deal with the corpses of the dead.

FIVE DEAD MEN

37. Volleys from the Gatlings

Snakeskin and his men struck on through the night. They had killed the *Ansari* that had been sent to hunt them down, but Snakeskin held few if any illusions regarding their chances of prevailing against an enemy intent on finding them.

The Mahdi's hordes knew that they were in the Sudan, and it was a point of religious honor that they capture and kill the Infidels who had dared venture into their midst. More of the Dervishes would be on their trail and soon. This much alone was a certainty.

Sunrise found the group of mercenaries making their way slowly across rough terrain. As they proceeded north into the heart of the Mahdi's territory, the character of the landscape began changing from flat desert country to a desolate expanse of low-lying, craggy hills broken by steep ravines that had been gouged out of the wastes of Kordofan by the violence of flash floods caused by violent if irregular seasonal rains.

Although Snakeskin and his company did not yet realize it, they were closer to engaging their enemy than they could have foreseen. For the Mahdists had already learned of the destruction of Kalifa Sheikh Yusef's gathering of Dervishes, and the Mahdi himself had mobilized his forces to search out and expunge the detested *kuffar* -- the Infidels and disbelievers in Islam -- from the length and breadth of the desert domain in which he reigned supreme.

As the Brothers crested a rock-bound slope, slipping on the treacherous scree of rubble that slid down and raised telltale clouds of gray-brown dust, another attack force made up of rifle-toting Mahdists mounted on horseback suddenly confronted them. Having first spotted the Infidels, the Dervishes seized the initiative and rode hell-bent toward the hated Franks, their swords and captured Enfield rifles raised defiantly aloft. Their war cries dinned above the thunder of their horses' hoofs as they shouted praise to Allah for delivering the unbelievers into their hands for capture and punishment.

The Brothers spurred their own mounts and raced at a gallop toward a maze of devil's draws -- shallow gullies and defiles -- that lay up ahead, desperate to elude the superior numbers of their attackers and to buy themselves some time in order to regroup. Their driven animals kicked up pebbles and small stones as they rode hard across a dry streambed that filled annually with the summer's rains.

Then it was into the crack in the rock wall that gave onto the twisting maze of sandstone galleries through which they were forced to progress at a snail's pace. Fortunately the Dervishes were equally encumbered. Forced to regroup and proceed single file, the *Ansari* wasted precious time in bickering among themselves in order to decide who had precedence to go in first.

Since this was a matter which tested the standing of individual Mahdists in the Dervish pecking order -- one which might inevitably lead to fights -- the stubborn jockeying for position among the pursuing *Ansari* bought the Brothers desperately needed time, and they used it to move as quickly as possible toward the way out of the maze whose existence was proven by animal tracks and spoor that Chow Bang Chow had detected.

In a short while, as the Chinaman had promised, they saw the second fissure in the rock wall -- somewhat narrower than the first, but still passable by men and beasts of burden -- and pushed toward it.

The first one out was Snakeskin, blinking his eyes against the bright desert sunlight that dazzled them as he emerged and shouted the single word, "Damn."

A word justified by the fact that directly ahead of them, as they emerged from the ravine, was yet another contingent of mounted, sword-brandishing, oath-shouting Dervishes. Only now, with the belated benefit of hindsight, did Snakeskin realize that they had been maneuvered into a trap, and rather expertly at that. They were now caught between two droves of well-armed, blood-thirsty fanatics, with no place to run or hide.

"It's back into the ravine, my brothers, if you want to live!" Jahno shouted, reining in his mount and pulling on the harness straps to turn the snorting and protesting beast back in the direction from which he had first ridden in.

"Hold off -- all of you!" Snakeskin countered at the top of his lungs, and gestured with an outstretched hand. "Look to your right!"

This they all did, and now each member of the group saw the ruins of what appeared to be an old desert fortress in the distance, one of several established by the Egyptians under the Khedive, Mehemed Tewfik Pasha, newly reinstated by the British army after the rebellion that had deposed the usurper Arabi Pasha the year before.

DAVID ALEXANDER

Following in the dust of Snakeskin's lead, the Brothers hastened for the ruins, reaching their sheltering cover as the Dervishes began firing at them pell-mell. The walls, they saw, had been constructed of blocks of stone held together by crude, and probably locally made, mortar, easily able to stand up to bullets and, to some degree, also to shell fragments.

As quickly as possible, the four riders dismounted and took up defensive positions behind rock outcroppings, their weapons drawn. Rifle barrels were propped atop boulders, and some of the Brothers sighted through them, working out aim points, while Snakeskin sought the best position from which the Gatling could fire atop its tripod mount.

"La Crosse," commanded Snakeskin, "set up the Gatling. Jahno and Chow Bang Chow, you each take one side. I'll cover you from the rooftop.

While the Brothers deployed to their positions, the Mahdi's *Ansari* crested the rise and then proceeded to descend down the opposite slope at a gallop, their rifles firing bullets and belching smoke as they shot on the move, shooting horizontally with the underbarrels of the rifles propped recklessly across the horns of their saddles.

La Crosse waited until the Dervishes drew up as close as possible to the gun emplacement so that they would be brought into optimum killing range. At that moment he depresesed the trigger on the water-cooled machinegun and opened up with the first volley of repeating fire. It was a Model 1881, newly manufactured with the new Bruce feed system that could fire an average 600 .45 caliber rounds per minute in combat operation.

The salvo of bullets struck into the onrushing mass of horses and riders, and the first of the Dervishes in the charging line of cavalry toppled off their mounts, their *jibbas* now pockmarked with holes and stained black with shed blood. Those behind the first wave to fall under the fusillade were cut down by the bursts that followed as Snakeskin and the rest of the company opened up with their repeating shooters to accompany the fixed automatic weapon.

After the initial volley from the combined fire of the Gatling heavy gun, their La Crosse Repeaters and Blake's matched LeMats, the Dervishes retreated back over the dunes. Within a matter of minutes, however, they had regrouped under the exhortations of their chieftain and had come back in a second rush as though eager for continued self-slaughter.

Now once again, the big Gatling machinegun stuttered out its death knell and the carnage of the first attack on the charging Mahdists was reprised with equally catastrophic results for the enemy. Enacted was a scene witnessed countless times since the Gatling's invention and its use as a tool in opening up India and North Africa to the onrush of European colonialism.

As had happened before in India, Algeria, Egypt, East Africa, and many other places that had already felt the lash of the Gatling's bullets since the invention of the fearsome weapon, scores of the Mahdist dead littered the barren, dusty battlefield and the Dervishes retreated again as the guns of the defenders mercifully fell silent.

"We've done it," shouted an exultant Fallicon La Crosse. "Look at all those fucking Dervish corpses. What a beautiful sight, *mes amis*! There must be hundreds out there."

"They'll be back, don't fool yourself," Snakeskin answered the Frenchman dourly. "Death means less than nothing to their likes."

Snakeskin then turned to his men adding, "There are many more of them than there are of us, and we can't hold off the Mahdi's desert rats forever."

FIVE DEAD MEN

38. A Strange Encounter at an Abandoned Fort

By nightfall yet another attack had been put down with no injuries to the men sheltering in the abandoned Egyptian fort. Nevertheless, their ammunition had already begun to run dangerously low while the supply of live human bodies on the Dervish side seemed to be inexhaustible. The Mahdi, through his *kalifas* and the tribal sheikhs who served as their generals, had time and again demonstrated the ability to quickly muster thousands upon thousands of Dervishes for battle.

Those immense numbers had proven the undoing of more than one British army that had stormed the Sudan and had either been driven back or, like Hicks's, utterly decimated. Attack followed attack, with the successive waves of caftaned, turbaned men with rifles charging pell-mell at the pith-helmeted, tan-clad soldiery, then pushed back bloodied by superior weapons and tactics, only to regroup and attack once again.

The only certainty about the Brothers' desperate situation was the fact that the *Ansari* hordes would be back. This and little else.

"If anyone has an idea of what in the fuck to do now, I am listening, *mes frères,*" said the Frenchman as he broke down and cleaned the now silent Gatling gun, a lit hand-rolled cigarette jutting from the corner of his wide, thin-lipped mouth.

"I fear I must announce to you all, *mes frères*, that I am already down to our last few hundred rounds of ammunition. After this, we must throw our shit at them like gorillas."

Snakeskin had already been thinking over their options. The supply of Cosgrove Rockets had earlier been used up in their first confrontation with the *Ansari* scout party, and besides that, the same trick would not work twice, despite the superstition of the Mahdists which -- like their almost infantile contentiousness over trifles of group status -- had so far helped to save their necks.

Some sort of diversion would have to be staged; Snakeskin had been pondering the Draconian alternatives since practically the moment they'd taken cover in the fort and had decided on risking everything on an escape bid. Their predicament was as easy to grasp as it was desperate: the longer they remained at the abandoned Egyptian fort, the closer they came to suffering the inevitable consequences of being on the wrong end of an unwinnable siege situation.

If it came down to that grim dénouement, there would be no alternative to surrender other than fighting to the death -- and of course, also dying, to the last man.

Snakeskin had no doubt that all his comrades would harbor few qualms about making a last stand, especially Jahno, for whom dying gloriously in the service of his Sultan and master would no doubt be almost a dream come true. Nevertheless, they had not ventured this far merely to empty their lifeblood onto the thirsty sands of the Kordofan desert. The Brothers of the Gun had an objective to secure, and if it was at all humanly possible to indeed secure it, then Snakeskin would see to it that they accomplished their mission to the letter.

"How much dynamite have we got left?" Snakeskin asked his companions. "Frenchman, you first."

"I have half my store, *Monsieur Peau de Serpent*," replied La Crosse.

"A little less than half for me," answered Chow Bang Chow.

"The same, as far as my own supplies go," the Gurkha, Jahno, responded.

"Fine, I make that approximately fifteen packing cases of TNT in all," Snakeskin calculated. "That's about enough to accomplish the outcome that I have in mind."

"And just what might that be, *mon ami Serpent*?" the Frenchman wanted to know, stroking his tanned, beard-stippled chin and grinning like the hobgoblin he resembled.

Snakeskin quickly outlined his plan.

It called for an application of high explosive similar to its use earlier on, except that now, instead of deploying individual sticks of dynamite as antipersonnel charges, the TNT would be set off in bundles in order to form a protective cordon sanitaire through which the Brothers might, with some luck, manage to elude and escape the Mahdists.

They got immediately down to cases once Snakeskin had outlined his intentions. Working under conditions that exploited natural tactical cover and terrain nap, Snakeskin and Jahno fell to the preparation of the TNT charges that they hoped would halt the suicidal charge and human wave attack of the *Ansari* that would surely come with morning.

It would be an all-out charge, they knew, one whose intention would be to end the contest with bloody finality, and there would be little margin for error on their parts. The quantity of blasting ordnance brought to bear against the Mahdists would need careful measuring out and effective deployment.

Hours passed, as they glanced toward the eastern horizon, out of which they knew the enemy would certainly come, for signs that the darkness that now protected them would begin to change to blue-black with the coming dawn.

But night still lay heavy upon the Sudanese desert as they completed crimping the last blasting caps to the bundles of TNT they had prepared, and darkness held steady as they ran the wires to the detonation boxes from the broad semicircle of high explosive that they had planted out there and covered over with the still cold sands, a semicircle that flanked the single corridor of escape through a ravine that led off, straight as an arrow, from the rear of the ruined Egyptian fort.

■

"Look alive, my dauntless but foul-smelling brothers in arms -- rise and shine. The damned bloody Mahdists are coming back for another charge at us," the Gurkha shouted suddenly in his mock Englishman's voice as men roused themselves from fitful sleep, seeing more turbaned Dervishes begin an advance.

Again it was morning, and out of the eastern horizon, like insects dark and small, seeming to wriggle like black grubs against the rising disk of the too-large sun at their backs, there came riding a multitude on horseback which grew in size steadily in the distance until the tiny black things resolved into recognizable figures of men and horses, still small, but growing bigger against the sky as they hurtled relentlessly forward.

FIVE DEAD MEN

Within moments the rest of the men inside the crumbling fort heard the now familiar war cries of the Dervish droves and the first faint pops of the rifles at their saddles' sides as the *Ansari* began to pile over the ridge toward their target, the long, curved scimitars they wielded catching the first rays of the sun and glinting dangerously as they pressed on toward their cornered quarry.

Snakeskin and the Frenchman kept firing the water-cooled Gatling as Jahno and Chow Bang Chow got on their camels. And, as the Mahdists rallied and returned in greater numbers than before just before the break of dawn, they rode their mounts from the shelter of the fort on the side still in the shadow of the sun.

"Get ready!" Snakeskin said to his sole companion still remaining within the confines of the ruined building when the others had gotten a head start.

Now, he kept up steady rifle fire as the Frenchman struggled to pack up the Gatling and place it, broken down separately from its ammo feed and gun mount, in the saddlebags of the pack mule.

Snakeskin went to the detonator and pulled its plunger from the wooden box, noting that the wires were firmly wound and screwed down into the two round-headed brass lugs that would take the electric spark from the armature within the box through the wires that led to the charges they had previously hidden in the sands. As he looked out through the windowless rectangle in the wall and saw the horsemen almost upon them, he turned to La Crosse.

"Get out."

The Frenchman shook his head, lifted his rifle and laid its barrel across the broken mortar and began firing at the Mahdist hordes, and Snakeskin turned back to the window, and without hesitation, he shoved the plunger hard and straight down into the box.

Almost immediately, the charges began to blow in such rapid succession that the blast was almost one huge, simultaneous explosion of tremendous force, and then they were on their mounts making for the back way and their escape route from the fortress.

Suddenly Snakeskin heard the Frenchman grunt in agony. As he clutched at his side, the American could see a bright spurt of blood stain the pelt of his mount. A Madhist bullet had hit La Crosse.

Snakeskin reached out for his stricken friend and tried to pull him onto his own animal, but the Frenchman slipped from his grasp and tumbled heavily to the ground.

"Go!" La Crosse cried out, floundering. "I am all right! Save yourself, *mon frère de l'arme*."

The Mahdists were charging now in great number, firing their rifles with such frequency that the air was as thick with bullets as the Sudan was generally with flies.

On top of that, the dynamite bundles that formed the *cordon sanitaire* were still going off, filling the air with dense clouds of black smoke. Snakeskin could no longer see La Crosse amid the mad confusion of the Dervish onslaught as his mount reared in fright and both rider and beast found themselves blinded by the dust of battle.

About to give up, Snakeskin caught a glimpse of the Frenchman through a rift that had opened temporarily in the dark mantel of acrid, billowing smoke. Reining in and calming his mount, he galloped toward where he remembered the Frenchman to have fallen.

And then he beheld a sight that, despite the indisputable evidence before his own two eyes, Snakeskin still refused to believe.

FIVE DEAD MEN

From out of the smoke an apparition had risen up. The gigantic figure was garbed from head to foot in the armor of a knight of the Medieval Crusades; his legs, from ankle to kneecap, sheathed in plated iron greaves, his huge head covered by a metal helmet, his broad chest mailed with chains. The broadsword in his hands seemed correspondingly immense as he hewed down charging Mahdists to the left and to the right with the ease of a harvester reaping a crop of ripened wheat.

Snakeskin could not be sure, but the Crusader -- if that's what he was -- seemed to also be making for the fallen Frenchman, although what his intentions were Snakeskin could not even hope to guess.

Not knowing quite what was happening, Snakeskin fought his way with LeMat pistols, bared knife and gloved fists toward La Crosse. As he came abreast of the Crusader, he saw that the figure who wore the knight's armor was a black Sudanese, his skin as dark and glistening as ebony smoothed by the carpenter's adze and polished with oil.

But smoke, dust and Dervishes had again closed in around the Frenchman, and amid the turmoil of the fight, Snakeskin had lost sight of him again.

"I fear that your comrade has gone the way of the fallen in battle," said the Sudanese, turning to Snakeskin. "But we two still live, and we must leave here quickly if we are to expect to continue living and to fight again."

"And just who the hell are you?" Snakeskin asked the giant.

"Know that I am your friend," replied the Sudanese, sheathing the immense broadsword in the ornately embroidered scabbard that hung at his belt. "The rest I will explain later, once we have found a place of safety."

Then he mounted his horse and rode off with Snakeskin spurring his own mount close behind, as he now realized he had no other choice except to do.

BOOK SIX

BROTHERS OF THE GUN

DAVID ALEXANDER

39. The Bashi-Bazouk

His name, he told Snakeskin, was Divi Divi Davi, and his fierce trade was that of the *Bashi-Bazouk*, a name synonymous with bandit, brigand, mercenary and -- more often than not -- plunder and rapine.

Like his fellows, this particular *Bashi*-Bazouk was outfitted in the armor and livery of a Crusader of the Knights Templar of some hundreds of years before, complete with sword, shield and visored helmet, gilt spurs over seven-league boots, leather baldric, and triangular black velvet apron emblazoned with the true cross in red, still colored brightly after centuries of exposure to the heat and light of the Sudanese deserts.

Though a walking anachronism, there was sound reason for this outfitting -- ready availability. Stockpiles of armament and armor dating back to this bygone era could still be found in relative abundance in the Sudan at that time, being the surplus legacy of thousands of Christian soldiers captured, then beheaded or burned at the stake, by the Turks, during the long decades of the Crusades. In the Sudan, time moves slowly, and the gaudy livery of knights was still in suitable condition for battle long after the last Knight Templar departed from the old Kingdom of Jerusalem, the short-lived domain of French nobility in an ancient land.

Now, all sides used this Crusader-era surplus equipment in the absence of more modern armament which was at first impossible to come by and later judged as a poor substitute by many Sudanese. The *Bashi-Bazouks* had made the ancient weapons of a long departed age their own, and in so doing had made the Crusaders live again -- in every respect.

Not only were they as able fighters as the knights of old, they were as dedicated to plunder, wenching, brawling and wanton acts of pillage and destruction as their long-defunct forebears, so much so that more often than not they were hated and feared by the very captains of mercenaries who had paid them handsomely in Spanish gold doubloons (their preferred form of remittance) to serve with their troops.

"I have been sent by Pasha Gordon to watch out for you," Divi Divi Davi revealed as the remaining Brothers made camp for the night, far from the scene of the carnage at the fort.

"So it was you who was following us through the desert, was it?" asked the Gurkha Jahno.

"It was I, yes," Divi Divi Davi answered the Sultan's man.

He added, "I have a letter from Pasha Gordon for the Sidi Snakeskin."

With that the Bashi-Bazouk produced a slip of foolscap paper that had been much folded and was stained with sweat.

Snakeskin held the letter up to the light of the campfire and read with interest.

My Dear Snakeskin,

DAVID ALEXANDER

*It is a pity that I cannot personally be with you in this undertaking, however I have been asked by Emir Abdel Kadir to head his troops in a bit of bloody awful, though undoubtedly quite necessary, business in Algeria (*sub rosa, *of course, though everyone knows what's really going on, as usual, make no mistake).*

In any event, my dear fellow, I have taken the precaution of sending you a "guardian angel" to protect and guide you in your endeavours. You may rest assured that Divi Divi Davi is both an able fighter and a native Sudanese who knows the entire territory clear across from the lower Sudan to the Belgian Congo pretty much as well as the back of his own hand.

If further credentials are in order, I refer you to the damnable business of '79 when I was last in the Sudan. It was then that Divi Divi Davi nearly got himself killed pulling my chestnuts out of one particularly hot fire. In a pinch, he won't hesitate to do the same for you and your colleagues.

I close with my heartfelt best wishes. May the Lord bless your endeavor.
Your faithful....
Charles Gordon.

Snakeskin folded Divi Divi Davi's letter of introduction from Chinese Charlie and stuffed it into the dusty pocket of his dusty sand-colored shirt. He carefully regarded the Sudanese, deciding that if looks meant anything there was no doubt that the Bashi-Bazouk was everything that Gordon had claimed him to be.

Having witnessed Divi Divi Davi wading into the thick of mounted Mahdists wielding modern repeating magazine-fed Enfield rifles, and having at the bastards with only his flat bladed Crusader's sword, Snakeskin had seen the Bashi-

FIVE DEAD MEN

Bazouk's prowess in battle with his own eyes, and knew him to be a man of great courage and formidable fighting skill.

However the Frenchman had been captured by the Mahdists, and his fate, if he still remained alive at all, was highly uncertain. Snakeskin did not want to leave La Crosse behind. He was determined to at least contemplate a rescue attempt.

In any event, there was a great deal of planning now to be done. Chief among the questions facing Snakeskin as leader of the group, was whether or not to attempt to establish the Frenchman's whereabouts as a prelude to saving him from his captors' tender mercies which included decapitation, burning at the stake, heavy shackling of limbs, and pulling out the guts with red-hot pincers.

The Bashi-Bazouk advised the Brothers to take heart and not to despair. La Crosse might yet be alive, and they might still find a way to rescue him.

"I have contacts among the people of this land," Divi Divi Davi advised the company of men. "If your friend still lives, I will find out about it. Then we can do what must be done."

"But what about you?" asked Snakeskin. "I have Gordon's letter, but I'm still unclear about your motive for being with us. Is it money? A personal dislike for the Mahdist cause? What's in it exactly for the likes of a Bashi-Bazouk?"

"Truly I have no love for the Mahdi," Divi Divi Davi explained. "He has stolen many of my wives and the sheep from my flocks. Nor does he leave behind what he does not steal, but destroys it by fire and sword. This man, Muhammed Ahmed, who calls himself Mahdi, is a wicked, wicked man. He must pay and his false Mahdiyyah must be crushed. I, Divi Divi Davi, will make him pay."

Snakeskin was satisfied with this explanation and was sure that the Sudanese would prove a valuable asset to the team because of his inside intelligence on the Mahdi's activities, in addition to his superb combative skills.

"To find the answers concerning your friend's condition, I must leave you for awhile," Divi Divi Davi told them. "But I will be back. Do not concern yourselves with waiting for me. Divi Divi Davi will find you, though you roam to the farthest corner of Africa."

Saying that, the Bashi-Bazouk mounted his horse and disappeared across the dunes almost as suddenly as he had first appeared.

■

Divi Divi Davi returned after two days absence. By then, the Brothers had already traveled miles from the first encampment, yet the Bashi-Bazouk had materialized one night as abruptly as if he had risen from some secret hiding place that lurked beneath the sands.

True to his word, he had discovered some important information regarding both the Frenchman's present whereabouts and the Mahdi's strategic position. The Bashi-Bazouk told the Brothers how he had stolen upon the encampment of the *Ansari* and seen La Crosse.

According to Divi Divi Davi the Frenchman was still alive, though malnourished and living under daily threat of execution by his captors. His weakened condition was the main reason why the Sudanese had not tried to attempt a rescue on the spot, he added. The Bashi-Bazouk feared that La Crosse might not stand up to it.

Another important piece of intelligence brought to Snakeskin by the Sudanese involved the fact that a fixture of the retinue of the Sultan of Zanzibar was in fact a spy in the

Mahdi's pay. More than this the Sudanese did not know, except that the spy was rumored to be a foreigner.

Beyond this, the Bashi-Bazouk reported that the Brothers' mission in the Sudan, as well as their general whereabouts, were matters well known to the Mahdiyyah.

"The Mahdi has taken precautions. He is moving his position from day to day in expectation of an attack," Divi Divi Davi told the Brothers.

And his legions of Dervishes had received orders to kill the interlopers and torture them by means of the dreaded *shebba* as an object lesson to anyone entertaining similar ideas.

As to the Frenchman, the Sudanese held it as an article of faith that, if he still lived, the Mahdists would have taken him with them as they moved to their new encampments at Tel Amar, an oasis located some three score miles distant from their present position.

"There we must hasten if we are to rescue your friend the Frank," Divi Divi Davi concluded, and wrenched the smoking leg off the spitted carcass of a wild Barbary ewe that had been roasting above the pit of the band's cooking fire.

Tucking into it hungrily, he tore off a strip of hot meat with his front teeth, and chewed lustily on the roasted mutton. Smiling at his comrades as he wolfed his meal down, Divi Divi Davi stretched out his hand and plucked the eyes from the sockets of the sheep's skull.

"It is by far the tastiest part, you see," he said and began to laugh as he popped the eyeballs into his mouth, chewed, and swallowed them with relish.

40. A Prisoner of the *Ansari*

Fallicon La Crosse was blindfolded and his arms were tied behind his back so tightly with coarse rope that his wrists, which had at first ached maddeningly, had gone numb. So had his emotions; he no longer feared that his hands, once so skillful with the knife of the assassin, might never again send a blade hurtling unerringly through space to find its mark low on the throat of an enemy and stop him in his tracks with the tip of the knife wedged deep in the collarbone.

Both mental and physical suffering had succumbed to the grinding monotony of captivity -- broken only by the constant prodding of a rifle barrel in the small of his back and the derision of the Mahdists whose words were spoken in a language the meaning of which he could not even begin to fathom -- and been replaced by a creeping apathy that fogged the senses and caused the Frenchman to lose all track of time.

The Mahdists had been moving him from place to place for what seemed like weeks. From time to time his blindfolds had been briefly removed, but the reprieve from darkness was by no means a reprieve from pain. La Crosse was severely beaten by his captors, spat upon and kicked repeatedly until his persecutors -- their anger sated for the moment -- left him lying bloodied and semiconscious in a dark corner of a foul-smelling tent.

That the Frenchman had survived such beatings as these was owed to the fact that he was by now used to such treatment and had learned long ago how to cope with it. He had received worse at Devil's Island from supposedly "civilized" Frenchmen whose own forms of gentle persuasion easily rivaled anything with which these heathen Dervishes had afflicted him so far.

However, the leg wound that La Crosse had received, aggravated by his subsequent capture and maltreatment by the Mahdists, had begun to fester. The bullet that had caused the wound had passed clean through without breaking bone, but putrefaction had set in, and with it an almost unbearable stabbing pain that traveled all the way up his right side. Gangrene might have already paid him a first visit, La Crosse feared, as in the uncertain light of captivity the wound appeared to have darkened.

The upshot of all this was that La Crosse had resigned himself to death. He entertained no illusions that the Mahdists would permit him to live, no matter what information he gave up to them. After milking him dry they would probably hack him to pieces, then toss what was left in the sun for the vultures to batten themselves on.

The Frenchman's main question was why the accurst Fuzzy-Wuzzies had not yet killed him outright. He was amazed that he had been spared from death for even this long, surmising that they knew how much agony his wound continuously caused him and had decided to torture him as long as possible before administering the coup de grace.

DAVID ALEXANDER

La Crosse's musings on the hopelessness of his lot were shattered by the sudden interruption of a Dervish who entered the prison tent, hauled him roughly to his feet, tied a black cloth blindfold around his head, and shouted loudly in his ear as he pushed and kicked the Frenchman toward the slit in the canvas.

As La Crosse stumbled toward the light on shaky legs, which threatened to give out at any moment, he smelled the odors of horses. Through the dirty rag that served as a blindfold he faintly saw the blazing sun turn into shadow and the heat abate somewhat. He suspected he was being moved to yet another encampment. Well, what was the difference. He reckoned that he was a goner anyway.

After more curses, shouts and blows with the knurled wooden cudgel the Dervishes called the curbash, the Frenchman felt hands beginning to work at the fastenings of the knot that secured the sweat-soaked and begrimed rag across his eyes. As his blindfold was removed, La Crosse tightly shut his eyes against the blinding glare of the sun. Only after the several minutes had painfully passed was he able to open them again to narrow slits.

As his vision cleared, La Crosse saw he was now inside a walled structure and that there were many Dervishes surrounding him.

Dusty light filtered through the small, irregular cracks made by stones, sticks and other bits of debris which had been jammed into triangular spaces cut in the crude cemented walls that served as makeshift windows. A bit more light shone dimly through cracks in the clumsily fashioned wooden ceiling overhead. The floor of the building was made of tamped earth which had been inlaid with flat slabs of what had once apparently been paving stones

317

purloined from who knew where and haphazardly laid to keep down the dust.

Then, without preamble or warning, one of the Dervishes raised his rifle and jammed its business-end into the Frenchman's belly. Barking out something at the top of his lungs, the Fuzzy-Wuzzy then spat a putrid wad of spittle -- laced copiously with the drug called *khatt* which he'd been chewing -- into La Crosse's face.

His anger kindled by *khatt*, the Dervish lifted his rifle and made to bring its butt smashing down on the side of the Frenchman's skull, and La Crosse feared that his earthly existence would come to an abrupt and painful end. But a moment before the first Dervish struck him, another of the fierce Mahdists pulled the one with the rifle away and hustled La Crosse into a corner where he sat guarded by shifting groups of Fuzzy-Wuzzies.

Soon he was brought something that was supposed to pass for food; a pasty mixture of stale, moldy bread and a piece of something putrid that might have been meat or fish or maybe dog or jackal, since the *Ansari* were fond of raising dogs for the purpose of roasting them for their meals. Used to eating fits and slops, and knowing he needed all the nourishment he could obtain, La Crosse stuffed the foul repast into his mouth, grateful that for the present, at least, his captors had not killed him outright and wondering what made him more valuable to the Dervishes alive than dead.

With that thought in mind, he turned the events of his capture over in his memory as he continued to bring oily and foul-tasting pieces of indescribable filth from the crudely fashioned wooden bowl to his mouth at the ends of his dirty fingers.

These musings soon began turning to thoughts of flight. With his bad leg, and the miles of desert wastes that he would need to traverse, escape seemed impossible. Still, he might make a stab at it, provided a credible opportunity presented itself.

Although La Crosse had been blindfolded again, his senses had not been totally cut off from the surrounding environment. He could still hear and smell and touch, and his mental faculties were still with him as well.

Though it was a rough guess, the Frenchman had managed to form a general idea of the approximate direction in which the Dervish band had been heading and also some approximation concerning the distance they had traveled since his capture at the ruined Khedivate fort. He was sure that he was much deeper into the Sudan than when he had first been taken prisoner.

Since, despite the reprieve he now enjoyed, he suspected he'd ultimately be killed by the Dervishes, La Crosse stood to lose nothing by making an escape attempt. Perhaps there were some kaffir tribes hostile to the Mahdists about, though it was doubtful that he would find any this close to the Mahdi's center of power who would not turn him over no matter what their feelings for the *Ansari*. Such was the fear that the local tribesmen held for the Mahdiyyah and those who served its ends.

Nevertheless, even death by exposure to sun and dehydration suffered in the course of an escape attempt would be far preferable to the fate that the Dervishes had in store, for with them death would be preceded by torture on the *shebba* at the very least, and at the worst, bodily mutilation prolonged as far as possible by savages who had made it into a kind of art.

Having finished eating his atrocity of a meal, La Crosse turned his attention back to his wounded leg. The rifle bullet that had caused the wound had passed through, only glancing off bone, if having struck it at all. While the wound had become badly infected La Crosse suddenly had an inspiration as he stared numbly into the fetid leftovers at the bottom of the bowl he'd set beside him on the tamped earth floor.

Numerous large blue bottle flies were buzzing around La Crosse's untidy leavings and -- as the few newcomers attracted more blowflies, and built to a small, buzzing swarm of noxious flying insects -- some of the flies began crawling over his face and sucking at the perspiration of his forehead. Soon more flies were gravitating toward his leg, attracted by the scent of rotting flesh.

Within a matter of minutes there were hundreds of them descending on their fetid banquet. La Crosse made no attempt to swat away the buzzing swarm.

On the contrary, he held his leg outstretched and kept it as still as was possible as the flies buzzed around their new-found treasure, alighting on the suppurating wound in a droning, seething, buzzing horde.

And now what La Crosse had expected began to occur, and despite the shudder of revulsion he experienced as he watched them plunge their posteriors into the rotting flesh and lay countless white eggs inside the festering lesion, a smile crossed the Frenchman's parched lips for the first time since his capture. It grew larger as his Dervish guardians drew close to watch what was happening, but did nothing to stop it.

When La Crosse judged that he had allowed the flies enough time to seed his wound with their eggs, the Frenchman swatted the crawling iridescent blue mass away and gathered up the rags of his trousers to cover the festering injury. Soon, the Frenchman hoped, the maggots would hatch and begin to feast themselves on the rotting tissue until they were gorged to bursting.

FIVE DEAD MEN

41. A Stubborn One

Meanwhile, as the Brothers of the Gun made distressingly slow progress across the sun-baked wastes of the Sudan -- trekking by night and using natural places of concealment, such as shaded wadis, in which to hide by day -- they had begun to formulate a plan to free La Crosse from captivity.

The plan grew from more intelligence that Divi Divi Davi, the Bashi-Bazouk, had brought back from another of his departures from the group. He had traveled far, he'd told them (returning in the hours before dawn to find their new hiding place by some unerring, unexplainable knack) and had learned that the Mahdi himself had set down a *fatwa* concerning Snakeskin Blake and his small mercenary group.

A fatwa, Divi Divi Davi explained, was an official edict carrying the force of religious law which could only be revoked by the Mahdi himself. The Mahdi's fatwa declared that the Infidels must be found out and captured by the *Ansari*, but that no immediate harm should befall them.

They were then to be brought to Mahdi Muhammed Ahmed directly, whereupon the Infidels were then to be given the choice of renouncing their plans and pledging instead to serve both the Mahdi and Allah, or to be beheaded on the spot.

The reason for this show of mercy on the Mahdi's part, Divi Divi Davi explained, was that Ahmed had learned of the unique new repeating weapons that the mercenaries carried. He coveted these weapons for his own, and beyond this he wanted to learn how best to operate and duplicate them.

As the Mahdi himself had given the order to his *Ansari* that none of the Infidels captured were to be harmed this new turn suggested a positive outcome to Divi Divi Davi.

"And so, you see, the Mahdist's interest in these new weapons of yours is in itself a good thing. It may mean that your friend still lives."

"Nevertheless, it is of little benefit if we cannot free him," Chow Bang Chow replied. "La Crosse is a stubborn man. He will not serve the Mahdi. Not under any circumstances I can imagine."

"How can you be so certain of this, thou Chinese?" asked the Bashi-Bazouk. "When men are held captive and subjected to the torments of the shebba, they usually agree to anything at all."

"You don't know La Crosse," Snakeskin put in, shaking his head in agreement with Chow Bang Chow as he cleaned the fine-grained sand -- sand finer than the dust of baker's flour -- from his rifle, a ritual they had all learned to perform as often as possible. "He's as stubborn as they come and then some besides."

A smile crossed his hard, lean face as he applied a rag to the trigger housing and thought back on experiences that he and La Crosse had shared.

Snakeskin's memories took him back to an incident at Peking. It was during the turmoil of the closing days of the

Taipei uprising when the chaos of rebellion and violence had reached its terrible peak of burning and slaughter.

At that point the entire city, he clearly recalled, had become engulfed in flames, which did little or nothing to quell continued attempts by rebels to gain control of many quarters of the town, or root out those who had already taken charge.

Snakeskin and the unit of mercenaries he commanded had been ordered into a particularly nasty section of the old city under the control of die-hard rebels with the mission of removing them. The fight was one-sided from the first, with Snakeskin's men getting the worst of it.

Still, they pressed on, their numbers dwindling from the attrition of gunfire from concealed rebel positions, until only a handful remained. Led by Snakeskin, the group attempted a last-ditch maneuver of scaling a low brick wall, only to be beaten back, as Highbinders and the rebels they led came spilling over it, brandishing long knives and shouting war cries.

At the last moment, the Frenchman had come bounding over the top of the wall and had snatched up the rebel battle flag. He held the flag aloft and used it as a spear to impale the Highbinders who were attempting to scale the wall in droves.

The holdouts were crushed, almost to a man. The Frenchman's stone balls became one of the many legends of the fierce campaign.

Snakeskin's thoughts returned to the present, and he began to clean the rifle's barrel, tamping the rag down with a ramrod.

"You wear a smile," observed Divi Divi Davi, interrupting Snakeskin's reverie. "Why is this, Sidi?"

"I was thinking of something that happened a long time ago," Snakeskin told the Bashi-Bazouk. "It concerned the Frenchman. And I can only repeat to you that La Crosse is a man unlike many another whom you might have run across. There is no way that he will cooperate with the Mahdists -- not while breath remains in his lungs."

"Then we had better do our best to rescue him," said the Bashi-Bazouk, sliding his newly polished broadsword into its leather scabbard. "Because if we do not then the Mahdi will put his head on a spike and feed his dripping entrails to his starved mongrel dogs."

FIVE DEAD MEN

42. A Plan of Action

Despite his great physical size and the heavy medieval armor that he wore, the Bashi-Bazouk moved with catlike stealth and graceful speed across the wind-swept desert sand dunes. With apparent effortlessness, Divi Divi Davi could track the Dervishes all over the landscape without their ever being aware they were being watched and followed.

In time all the Brothers had learned the trick of following the Mahdists with surprising ease across the desert. For all their fierceness in battle and their fanatical devotion to their leader's cause, the Mahdists were lacking in every respect when it came to field- and war craft. And while some of them might have been expert trackers, there were apparently none with skills in evading pursuit.

Because the mounted *Ansari* traveled in large numbers through the burning wastes of the Sudan, the Mahdists left spoor which could easily be followed by determined trackers.

The Brothers had little difficulty in keeping a close eye on the Mahdists as they ranged across the wind-scoured wastes of the Sudanese desert.

DAVID ALEXANDER

By night, the Brothers had reached the outer perimeter of the Mahdist encampments, watching and gathering intelligence on the security measures put in place by the Dervishes and noting also their patterns of activity within the confines of the *zariba*.

Not surprisingly, their search revealed little in the way of defensive measures. While sentries were posted to walk the perimeter, both by day and by night, the coverage of the enclave was spotty and the vigilance of those who were charged with keeping watch was prone to lapses for any reason at all. It was as if the Mahdists trusted in providence alone to protect them and did not seem to feel that they needed to take much responsibility on their own for their protection against earthly dangers.

Diligent spying on the encampment soon paid off with occasional glimpses of the captive Frenchman. Because of the thermal distortion and the distance at which his subject was viewed through military binoculars from his vantage point atop a high drumlin of windblown sand, Snakeskin could only establish the singular fact that the Frenchman was alive, but nothing more besides this.

Nevertheless, even this new development was enough to steel the determination of the raiders to rescue their captive comrade from the Mahdi's imprisonment. They waited an additional day until the moon -- then a fine sliver in the skies -- had waned to complete invisibility.

Now, the night turned wholly moonless, and with only the stars to provide their faint astral light, Snakeskin, Chow Bang Chow and Divi Divi Davi began to move on the encampment with Jahno staying behind in the concealment of the dunes manning the Gatling gun in case protection was necessary.

FIVE DEAD MEN

The buildings of the *Ansari* encampment were fashioned of mud, brick and stone; probably the place was a kaffir village which had long ago been abandoned, possibly due to the drying up of a reliable wadi during an especially dry spell or an assault by the hairy-chested locust -- a short-horned grasshopper that was native to both Kordofan and the Sahel and which devoured crops with unparalleled ravenousness when it flew across the land in great, hungry swarms.

The rescue plan called for Snakeskin and Chow Bang Chow to infiltrate the hostile encampment and reach the building where the Frenchman was being held. Once they had La Crosse in tow, they were to signal Divi Divi Davi. The Bashi-Bazouk was to wait in hiding just beyond the confines of the encampment, ready to stage a diversion to cover the rescue.

While Snakeskin and Chow Bang Chow invaded the Mahdist camp and freed La Crosse, Divi Divi Davi would prepare a gigantic palanquin, a drag constructed of flammable materials gathered expressly for this purpose from the ruins of a long-disused caravanserai they had crossed along their path. Divi Divi Davi also carried sticks of dynamite lashed together into bundles and ready to be hurled as makeshift bombs.

Divi Divi Davi would drag the palanquin around the compound attached to his horse, Saladin. The light of its flames, the dense smoke it gave off, and the reports of exploding dynamite, would make the Mahdists believe they were being attacked from the south.

While this diversion was taking place, Snakeskin and Chow Bang Chow would be bringing the Frenchman out via the northern side of the encampment. Once free, they would rendezvous with the Bashi-Bazouk and ride hard to put as much distance between themselves and the Mahdists as possible.

43. The Flash of a Knife Blade

In the darkened confines of the moonlit prison tent, the captive lay awake. Fast asleep, his guards were snoring loudly, but La Crosse was open-eyed, and vigilant.

He had seen the brief flash of sunlight that had glanced off the flat of the curved blade of a janbiya knife the previous day from the high ground that rose a little beyond the verges of the encampment. He knew that this was a good, if not an almost certain sign, that his comrades were nearby.

Snakeskin, he thought. *Mon frère Peau de Serpent.*

It had to be Blake and the rest of them. He might have known that his old comrade in arms would go through thick and thin to try and pull his chestnuts out of the fire. He might have known that Snakeskin wouldn't simply leave him to rot in this Sudanese hell, a prisoner in the house of suffering the Fuzzy Wuzzies called the Umm Hagar where prisoners of the Mahdi, bound with the iron fetters of the *tlal fatma*, were left to die.

La Crosse steeled himself to be ready for when the rescue attempt was made, as he was certain would be the case. When it came, he knew he would have to play his own part in it as well. La Crosse judged that Snakeskin would wait until the moon had waned completely and the nights were at their darkest. When that happened (he estimated another three nights were left before the moon again began to wax) they would certainly make their move.

La Crosse had not been idle. He had managed to secrete a piece of metal in the tattered remains of one of his boots. He had painstakingly sharpened this scrap until he had whetted it to a keen cutting edge. Despite the searches to which the Dervishes regularly subjected him, the Frenchman had managed to hold onto the makeshift blade. Soon his diligence might pay off.

His infected leg was much improved by now as well. The maggots that had hatched from the multitudinous eggs laid by the swarming Sudanese botflies had munched their way into the diseased tissue of the festering laceration from the bullet he'd caught at the abandoned stone fort.

Once they had eaten away the putrefying pus, the Frenchman had then killed the maggots by urinating on the writhing yellow-white mass -- not an easy thing to do, he'd learned, when one was a prisoner with a parched throat.

While the Frenchman was making his plans, Snakeskin and Chow Bang Chow had already passed the first perimeter beyond the *zariba* set up by La Crosse's *Ansari* guardians.

Now Snakeskin slit the throat of one of these sentries and hid the Dervish's limp corpse, while Chow Bang Chow entered the compound silently to do his own night's work. An open-handed blow delivered to the side of another guard's head quickly put the second Dervish sentinel out of commission.

But then, upon suddenly hearing footsteps that sounded without warning around the side of one of the ruined village buildings, the pair came to an abrupt halt.

FIVE DEAD MEN

Flattening their bodies against the adobe wall, Snakeskin and Chow Bang Chow saw two Dervishes walk past with their Enfield rifles slung across their shoulders, and their eyes riveted straight ahead. The Dervishes did not even notice the presence of the Infidels concealed only a few inches away.

When the Dervishes had passed completely by and were finally gone from sight, Snakeskin and Chow Bang Chow again progressed in broken movements, crouch-walking, taking cover, then crouch-walking again to keep their silhouettes down below the level of windows and hugging walls close to minimize the chances of being seen by lookouts posted on rooftops.

In the course of these maneuvers, they passed weapons storage areas, ruins occupied by sleeping Dervishes, and a corral containing the *Ansari*'s prized Arabian horses.

The guardhouse could easily be identified by the Dervish sentries posted outside it. In an encampment that was otherwise asleep and off its guard, here were to be found the few Dervishes that were wide awake and fully alert.

What was more, these guards, unlike most of their fellow *Ansari*, had the unmistakable look of hard and capable men about them -- men who counted on their own resources rather than merely trusting to providence or fate.

Snakeskin used hand signals to communicate to Chow Bang Chow that he would deal with the Dervish on the right while Chow Bang Chow took care of the Dervish who was posted on the left.

Chow Bang Chow took two *shuriken* from the cloth pouch at his belt. A moment later the many-pointed throwing stars of black metal were fitted between his clenched fingers, ready for throwing.

DAVID ALEXANDER

Flicking out his hand, Chow Bang Chow sent the martial arts throwing stars whirling through space like the blades of miniature buzz saws.

In a single instant, their needlelike cutting ends sliced into the neck of the guard that Chow Bang Chow had targeted for silent assassination, severing the windpipe and cutting off a startled cry for help before it could even form in the throat.

Already dying on his feet, the guard sagged to the dusty plain where Chow Bang Chow finished him off by stabbing him through the heart with a long knife drawn silently from his belt scabbard.

Snakeskin was finishing off his own designated target with a nearly silent burst of bullets to the Dervish's midsection. The noiseless machine pistol devised by the weapons genius of Fallicon La Crosse produced only a series of three rapid clicks as its hammering bolt serially impacted the cartridge ends, but little in the way of explosive report.

Pushing the slumped Dervish away from where he had collapsed, Snakeskin staved in the wooden door of the prison building. As the door burst open and flew back on its broken hinges, the Frenchman moved from his position against the wall where he had pretended to be fast asleep.

The makeshift knife went to the throat of one of his Dervish sentinels, slitting it quickly as his hand clamped tightly over the mouth of the jerking, thrashing Mahdist.

When twitching had completely stopped and the Dervish had gone limp, the Frenchman let him sag to the dirt floor of the ruined building. Wiping the blood off the makeshift blade by stropping it against the filthy, lice-ridden rags that were all that remained of his trousers, he shoved it into the rope that served as a belt.

FIVE DEAD MEN

"What has taken you so long, *mes frères*?" asked the Frenchman, but there was no time to waste in conversation. "I was beginning to grow a little bored."

After the passage of only a few minutes, the diversion staged by Divi Divi Davi was scheduled to begin. Snakeskin, Chow Bang Chow and the Frenchman would need to be very close to the previously determined escape corridor before then or they still ran a substantial risk of capture.

Now the three men moved hastily through the darkened encampment, abandoning the stealth and caution that had marked Snakeskin's and Chow Bang Chow's entrances and breaking into a run as suddenly the night erupted toward the east in a fantastic pyrotechnic display.

Flares and loud explosions roused the sleeping Dervishes of the encampment from their slumbers. Some of the now confused Mahdists saddled their horses and rode pell-mell toward the site of the explosions, while others spilled out of their quarters in a shouting, brawling and bewildered mass. Mounted or dismounted, the *Ansari* had been taken by complete surprise, and at the moment none of them fully realized what had actually happened.

While this confused stampede toward the diversion was taking place just as they had planned it to go down, Snakeskin, Chow Bang Chow and La Crosse used the chaos generated by the actions of the Bashi-Bazouk to escape from the tumultuous confines of the breached encampment.

44. The Well at Abbas Shabir

By the appearance of daybreak, the Brothers of the Gun had once again rendezvoused with the Bashi-Bazouk and the five companions in arms were again reformed as a unit.

By pushing their mounts to the limits of their endurance, the raiders had successfully eluded the questing Dervishes, who as a result of the diversion that Divi Divi Davi had staged, had fallen to futilely chasing their own tails.

As the sun rose, they made camp in the shade of trees encircling a desert well at Abbas Shabir where some caught up on much needed sleep while others stood lookout. Among these latter was Divi Divi Davi, who none of the Brothers had ever seen to sleep in the manner of other men. The Bashi-Bazouk took his rest in a seated position, his eyes narrowing, but never closing, his hand never far from the broad Crusader sword that lay scabbarded on the earth by his side.

They rode out again after resting, when the sun had passed its zenith in late afternoon. They had traveled only a few miles when, in the near distance directly ahead of their line of travel, and visible through the heat shimmer from the blazing sun reflecting off the burning sands, they saw what appeared to be the figure of a lone man stretched out on the desert and apparently dead.

Riding closer, they saw that it was in fact a human body whom they had spied from afar and not an optical illusion produced by heat and reflected light. Reigning in his mount, Snakeskin unsaddled, crouched on the sand, and turned the man over. He appeared quite dead; however as Snakeskin put his ear against his chest, he detected the faint albeit unquestionable presence of a heartbeat.

Snakeskin called to Chow Bang Chow, who possessed the skills necessary to revive the stranger and followed the Chinaman's instructions while Chow Bang Chow administered artificial resuscitation by means of flexing of limbs and breathing into the nostrils of the apparent victim of severe heat stroke and dehydration.

Now, as the stranger came around, they splashed water from their goatskin bags and canteens on his face and gave him little dabs of it on the lips in place of a long draft that might in all probability kill a man in the advanced stages of dehydration such as he apparently was. The transformation from apparent death to life was as amazing as it was speedy, and before long, the man they had found was fully revived and was well enough to sit up.

He identified himself as Sir Montague Strawplait. He informed the Brothers that he was a British subject who had been sent as a missionary to the Sudanese.

During one of the Mahdi's raids, sometime earlier on his march to conquer the region, Strawplait had been captured by the Dervishes of the Mahdiyyah led by one of the Mahdi's ablest *kalifa*s. Brought directly to the Mahdi himself, the captured Infidel was forced by the Dervish chieftain to become his personal servant.

Treated like little more than a dog by the Dervishes, who held themselves superior to all Franks as they styled Europeans and Englishmen, no matter what their actual nationalities might have been, Strawplait bided his time until a chance to escape from the Mahdists presented itself.

Strawplait said that he preferred the prospect of death from exposure in the desert to the promise of further humiliations at the hands of his heathen captors whose greatest pleasure was apparently to make every moment of their unfortunate captives' lives a time of hellish torment.

But Strawplait also claimed to have learned the exact whereabouts of the Mahdi's main encampment -- the Expected One's *mukhayyam*. By his reckoning, he had made good his escape only three days before, which meant that it was better than likely that Strawplait's directions to the power base of Mohammed Ahmed were correct.

Strawplait had fled the *Ansari*'s terrible grasp while gathering water at a nearby desert well. His captors had begun smoking hashish and chewing *khatt* all morning, with the result that after the initial elation produced by the drugs, they had begun to become drowsy and listless. Before long the *Ansari* had lain down besides their rifles and begun to doze, while the single guard they had posted also soon fell asleep with the rest.

It was then that Strawplait seized the opportunity to make his escape and ran off, carrying the slops they had thrown him in his pockets and the goatskin of water he had drawn at the well. By Strawplait's estimate, he had been lost for days in the desert when his meager supply of food and water had finally given out, and the sun had begun to addle his brains. He could not recall having collapsed, but it was obvious that a few more hours stretched in the hot desert sun might have seen him completely gone.

FIVE DEAD MEN

The escapee's story seemed plausible, at least on the surface, but Snakeskin didn't entirely buy it. Neither was there any way of checking the facts that Strawplait had presented for accuracy. Still, the events as the Englishman had described them could have actually happened much as he'd presented them.

In the end, the Brothers fed the newcomer, replaced his captive's rags with new tan fatigues like the ones they themselves wore and, though remaining wary of the possibility of a trap, followed his directions to the Mahdi's obscure laager of sequestration.

45. The Khamsa

Before setting out towards their objective on the final leg of their journey, Snakeskin's raiders bedded down for the night. But when morning ultimately broke upon the land, they realized that the Sudanese had left the overnight encampment.

Once again the Bashi-Bazouk had disappeared completely. Furthermore, Divi Divi Davi had taken absence of the company without leaving so much as a word or a sign of either his intended destination or his reason for leaving the group at a critical moment.

Snakeskin and his compatriots were bewildered.

"Don't trust those damned Sudanese," Strawplait advised them. "They're no bloody good. Wouldn't be a bit surprised if the bugger was in league with the Mahdi all the time."

"Still, Divi Divi Davi has left before," Chow Bang Chow put in. "He was never bound by oath to remain."

"Yes, but never without informing us of his intentions first," Snakeskin mused. "This is unusual."

Though they didn't agree with Strawplait, the rest of the team recalled how the Bashi-Bazouk had mysteriously appeared during their initial entry into the Sudan.

FIVE DEAD MEN

The rest were surprised when Strawplait unexpectedly presented them with some tangible proof to back up his claim.

"Here's a Mahdist icon," he told them. "I found it quite by accident in the blackamoor's bed roll."

He turned to the former prisoner of the Umm Hagar.

"Indeed he did," La Crosse affirmed. "The blackamoor Bashi-Bazouk is no good, *mes amis,* I say. Just another *foutu* kaffir who can't be trusted."

By way of emphasis the Frenchman spat on the sand.

Strawplait held out a small palm-shaped amulet depicting an open right hand bearing an open eye in its center. The charm was common to those parts. It was called a *khamsa,* and showed the crescent and star symbols emblazed on the five fingers that all the Arab tribes held to be a token of good luck.

"That doesn't prove much," Snakeskin commented. "I've seen these in bazaars all the way from Zanzibar to Cairo. Practically all the natives carry them as good luck charms regardless of whether they're black Sudanese or desert Arabs, or for that matter even you Englishmen and Frenchmen. The blacks call it the Hand of Fatima and the whites the Hand of Mary. What's the bloody difference?"

"Yes, but look closely on the back," Strawplait advised, turning the charm over in the palm of his hand. "Note the inscription in Arabic which reads 'Blessed be the Mahdi and his holy war.' Surely this is no ordinary bazaar trinket."

"Maybe," Snakeskin replied, still skeptical. "But so far our Sudanese friend has proven himself trustworthy time and again."

Snakeskin Blake was a man who set great store by his impressions of people. The Sudanese was a man who did not strike Snakeskin as a traitor. And intuition to the contrary,

Divi Divi Davi had appeared bearing the letter from Chinese Gordon, which Snakeskin still carried. The letter was entirely genuine.

Snakeskin had recognized not only Gordon's unique handwriting, but his epistolary style as well. He saw no reason to remove his trust from the Bashi-Bazouk, but on the contrary his mistrust of the newcomer, Strawplait, was raised to a new level by the escapee's seeming discovery of the khamsa. It could have merely been a crude plant, after all.

Nevertheless, treachery was as commonplace as desert flies in this part of the world. Strawplait's charges, though superficially implausible, demanded the vigilance that was their due here in the parched reaches of the lower Sudan.

Despite their continuing refusal to lend credence to Strawplait's claims, the party decided to break camp and leave the area immediately.

Just in case there was any truth in the assertions that Divi Divi Davi was a Mahdist spy, the mercenary band wanted to be as far away from its last known encampment as possible. It would not take long for a Dervish band to find them with good directions supplied by a traitor -- if there was indeed a traitor at all.

"Anyway, it doesn't matter now about the bloody Sudanese," Strawplait put in. "I'm pretty sure I recognize the landmarks hereabouts. I reckon I'll be able to lead us to the Mahdi's encampment from here."

Snakeskin and his company broke camp just after sundown and the group proceeded across the now darkening desert. The trip was conducted with utmost caution because they had by now ventured deep into the heart of the Mahdi's territory which swarmed with his Dervishes.

FIVE DEAD MEN

Chow Bang Chow and Strawplait scouted ahead with Snakeskin and the Sultan's janissary Jahno proceeding a few hundred yards behind them.

After several hours of steady march across the sands, Chow Bang Chow held out his hand in a signal for Strawplait, directly behind him, and the others in the group, to come to a sudden stop. His sharp ears had picked up faint sounds in the night, and because of the tricky acoustics of the desert they might have been made by something just as possibly very near as possibly very far away.

Hunched low across the ground, their repeating weapons held at the ready, the two men in the lead moved stealthily toward the sound with Chow Bang Chow in front of the Englishman. After a few minutes the Chinaman motioned for Strawplait to crawl toward his position and look down at what he saw below across the bend of a winding canyon which etched the undulating, sandy landscape.

"Damn, we've had it! They're coming right for us!" shouted the Englishman as he saw the mounted patrol of Dervishes. "The bloody Dervishes must outnumber us ten to a man!"

All of them were alert and the group seemed clearly to be searching for something of importance as indicated by their slow and deliberate movements. It was not a wild guess to surmise that it was the Infidels in their midst for which they searched.

Chow Bang Chow sent the Englishman back to warn the rest of the company. Soon the Brothers at the rear had crept up to the vantage point. Strawplait, Jahno, Chow Bang Chow and La Crosse looked on impassively as Blake sized up the situation.

It did not look good to say the least. The contact with the enemy had been completely unexpected.

342

Then, without warning, a rifle shot rang out, cleaving the silence of the desert. From above the defile, Dervishes had crept up unobserved and were now in an advantageous tactical position. Bullets were *spang*ing down and ricocheting off the rocks and boulders below.

Snakeskin and his men had no cover to protect them and only a footbridge of rope and planks of lumber strung across the chasm as their single corridor of escape. Snakeskin held up his hand and gestured for them to make for the bridge as he dismounted and led his camel forward.

The rest of the Brothers did the same, following Snakeskin's lead as the footbridge loomed in the distance. It was a rickety affair, spanning a deep defile over a rocky gorge that plunged at least seventy feet straight down to the bed of a river that very briefly overflowed with the summer rains but was now reduced to little more than a trickle.

The group reached the bridge under a fusillade of bullets fired by the Dervishes. Their beasts of burden would need to be left behind now. What equipment they needed to take with them would have to be carried on their backs from here on in.

Snakeskin detailed Jahno and Chow Bang Chow to set up the Gatling gun and hold off the attacking swarm of Dervishes while he, along with the Englishman and La Crosse struggled to unload the pack animals.

Jahno forsook the tripod of the big gun to hold it in his massive hands, cranking out withering automatic fire at the angry and excited Dervishes. The *Ansari* fell by the dozens, tumbling off the sides of the steep ravine. But with every man that came a cropper, another two Fuzzy-Wuzzies seemed to rise up from the stony desert scree to replace them.

FIVE DEAD MEN

By now Snakeskin and Strawplait had completed unloading all the supplies from their pack animals that they could carry on their backs. They had also hefted the leather saddle bags across their shoulders.

More bundles lay on the ground for carrying by Jahno and Chow Bang Chow who Snakeskin now hailed to withdraw toward the relative safety of the rickety bridge. Any gear that could not be carried was thrown straight down into the ravine to deprive the Mahdists of its use.

With the few seconds in which to make his choices, Snakeskin knew that valuable war matériel, which included military kit and explosive ordnance that might be needed later on would have to be discarded.

With little choice except to challenge the foot bridge as a route to safety, the pack animals and mounts were driven off and the unit staged a fighting retreat in two-man pairs, alternately firing at the Dervishes to force them to tuck down their heads and negotiating the swaying bridge as fast as they were able to under the precarious conditions of the crossing under fire.

They were nearing the other end when the Dervishes spilled toward the bridge in a teeming, shouting and wildly firing mass driven by holy rage at the escaping disbelievers. In the middle of the bridge, Jahno and Chow Bang Chow were still firing, shooting at the Dervishes who were hacking away at the ropes securing the bridge to its moorings on the other side of the defile.

"Come on!" Snakeskin yelled at them, nearing the opposite end of the gorge.

Within a matter of minutes he knew the bridge would fall to the bottom of the gorge, taking them down to their deaths along with it.

And then suddenly the bridge did fall, just as Chow Bang Chow was crossing to its other side. As the flimsy contrivance finally broke apart and tumbled straight to the bottom, the Chinaman executed a daredevil leap toward safety across the yawning abyss below and grasped the edge of the cliff with fingers and boot toes jammed into small crevices in the rock face. As ricocheting bullets bounced off the sides of the stony palisade, he'd climbed nearly to the crest of the bluff, where the rest of them were able to roughly haul him over the top and onto the summit of the plateau.

Now rejoined, Snakeskin's company had succeeded in escaping the Dervishes, so far. But by this point they were bereft of their pack animals and had forfeited valuable supplies in the course of their abrupt and headlong break for safety. Their situation was growing more desperate with each mile they covered.

FIVE DEAD MEN

46. Within the *Zariba*

Finally, after many days' hard travel, the Brothers had advanced to within direct visual range of the Mahdi's main laager, the *mukhayyam* or encampment where he had set up his private residence, deemed holy by the faithful *Ansari* and even allied nonbelievers, such as the Hadendoa tribesmen who fought as Dervishes in the Mahdiyyah.

After having staged their fighting retreat from the *Ansari* at the ravine bridge, and by dint of stealth and with luck on their side, the mercenaries of the Sultan of Zanzibar had succeeded in crossing the remaining miles without making contact with a Dervish patrol.

Now, having neared their objective, Snakeskin took stock of the group's position from a concealed vantage point, making notes regarding his observations in the small journal he kept tucked in a shirt pocket and marking their precise location on a well-worn map kept folded behind it.

The *mukhayyam* of the Expected One, Mohammed Ahmed, was concealed in the natural depression of a large, shallow wadi encircled by rocky rises on the mainly flat desert lands covering the interior reaches of the Sudan. The

346

circle formed by the low-lying, stony hillocks was a bulwark broken at many points, but it sufficed to screen the *mukhayyam* from view until one was almost hard upon its shielding verges.

As with all fortified encampments constructed by the *Ansari*, the Mahdist stronghold was surrounded by a *zariba* of densely planted acacia bushes, whose branches entwined to create an almost impenetrable rampart as formidable as that of barbed steel wire. This particular stockade fence was both higher and considerably more densely constituted than any of the others which Snakeskin had encountered so far.

Within the encircling confines of the *zariba* there stood a scattering of dwellings of various kinds, from tents, which the Arabs called by the word *khiba*, to one or two large domiciles built of broken stones that were held solidly together by mortar made from calcimined limestone and clay mixed with sand and desert gravel.

Now, looking down upon the small village, as the light of midmorning bathed the brown peaked tents, watching the smoke of cooking fires within curl lazily upward from the circular openings atop their peaked roofs, hearing snatches of distant voices drifting on the hot wind, and watching the green pennants emblazoned with the ancient eye symbol that was the icon of the Mahdiyyah fluttering in the hot desert thermals, Snakeskin appreciated the wisdom and cunning of the Mahdi in all things he undertook. This hidden village seemed to melt into the parched brown landscape, and so well camouflaged was it within the bowl of an ancient wadi encircled by high dunes, that in the vastness of the great Sahel it was virtually impossible to find deliberately or accidentally without a map.

Snakeskin could well understand how the encampment would have proven extremely difficult to locate if a search party did not expressly know where to look, and to this end the Englishman's assistance had proven an invaluable aid.

Snakeskin drew a diagram of the encampment for future reference and returned to the Brothers' own well-camouflaged hiding place beyond the bowl of the village. There he quizzed Strawplait on the layout and daily activities that took place within the stronghold.

The Englishman pointed out that the largest and most imposing of the various structures in the entirety of the *mukhayyam* -- a sprawling brown tent at almost the exact center of the village -- was the Mahdi's headquarters. Other *khibas*, somewhat smaller and showing less artfully peaked roofs, belonged to the Mahdi's chieftains or *kalifas* and his main commanders of the *Ansari*.

While tents made of a coarsely woven brown cloth predominated, a few, squared-sided *khibas* were fashioned from woven branches of local acacia, boxthorn and other thorn-bearing shrubs and trees. Snakeskin had noticed them on his *shufti* of a few minutes before. These, explained Strawplait, belonged to the unbeliever Hadendoa nomads, which the British (often in common as a term denoting Mahdists) called Fuzzy-Wuzzies.

Still other buildings were constructed of blocks of broken stone partially plastered over with a kind of stucco or cement. Strawplait indicated that one of these was a guardhouse, while another large structure located at a relatively empty end of the *zariba* enclosure was used by the Mahdists as a storehouse for arms, ammunition and explosives. Yet another of the stone-walled buildings, this one positioned somewhat closer to the Mahdi's own tent, served as a treasure house which was kept guarded day and night and was the sole property of the holy one, Muhammed Ahmed.

Finally, there was the *haram* of the Mahdi. This structure was a brown *khiba* with another peaked roof resembling a top stood on its flat end. The seraglio of Muhammed Ahmed was almost contiguous with the palatial tent in which the Mahdi himself dwelled. A covered walkway between the two palatial tents enabled discreet passage from one *khiba* to the other. The *haram* of the Expected One also was kept under continuous heavy guard by hand-picked *Ansari*.

Having heard what the Englishman had to say, Snakeskin made a few more notations in his pocket journal and rubbed his eyes, now gritty with sand and hot from having pressed against the eyepieces of the binoculars through which he'd *shuftied* the encampment.

Snakeskin said little as he rejoined the other men, but his mind was turning and turning like a hunting falcon in a widening gyre -- for there, within the confines of the brown *khiba* of the Mahdi's royal *haram*, was where Angelica Fairchild was almost sure to be found.

FIVE DEAD MEN

47. By the River

Strawplait now claimed that Snakeskin's band of desert mercenaries might be able to enter the Mahdi's encampment via a secret underground passageway that he knew about, or about which he had at least heard reliable reports and thought he had good reason to believe actually existed. He had, so he also claimed, at one point drawn a map based on information gleaned while in captivity.

The Britisher asserted that the tunnels of the passageway collectively made up an underground system of ancient catacombs used by prehistoric inhabitants of the region as a vast burial chamber. While being held in captivity within the *mukhayyam*, the Englishman had been given to understand that the village occupied a site considered holy by the *Ansari* and that the remains in the ossuaries below ground were still objects of reverence by the Hadendoa -- who were animists and not Muslims -- at least. What's more, the encampment rested upon ground laced with *ganats*, or weathered holes in the landscape with steep drops into natural caverns beneath the rocky crust -- caverns which, like this one, often contained streams or even minor rivers of fresh running water.

"The Sudan was not always desert, parts of it were in fact quite lush," Strawplait explained. "The underground river was discovered only quite recently, and quite by accident, by the Khedive's men when conducting a mapping survey."

"Why didn't you use it yourself?" Snakeskin asked the Englishman, feeling a renewed skepticism. "You could have escaped with ease."

"Because, my dear Snakeskin," Strawplait replied with a sardonic smile that Snakeskin had grown to dislike intensely, "it was not at all possible at the moment. My situation was such that I was far too well guarded at all times to even consider attempting an escape by those means."

But Strawplait explained that the same situation would not apply to men attempting to break their way into -- instead of out of -- the Mahdi's desert stronghold.

■

"There it is!" cried Strawplait, stumbling across the rock-strewn rubble of surface scree as he rose from where he had been digging. "I'd marked the entrance with stones. They've not been touched since then, thank goodness."

The entry point to the caverns was indeed to be found where Strawplait had promised that it was located.

Snakeskin and Chow Bang Chow accompanied Strawplait into the mouth of the cavern which was concealed behind a jumbled pile of boulders. If one did not know where to look, Snakeskin saw, it would be as impossible to discover as the well-hidden Mahdist encampment itself.

Lighting makeshift torches they proceeded to venture inside the mouth of the cavern complex. Stalactites grew down from the ceiling and merged in the middle with

351

stalagmites that had grown up from the cavern floor. Mineral veins in the gray-black rock bulged with crystals of white and yellow that flashed in the torch light. Overhead, droves of small black bats nested by the thousands on the ceiling, while some flew silently through the humid air that, while still hot, was considerably cooler than the dryer air at the surface.

As they probed further, the flickering light of their torches revealed dank walls oozing water from more of the often large, mineralized veins that had crystallized over incalculable periods of time. Snakeskin paused at one of these, ran his fingers along the shining crystalline scar in the black rock wall, and tasted the water on his tongue.

The water was pure and could be collected to fill canteens and goatskin bags for drinking if necessary, although it tasted of saltpeter, which Snakeskin supposed was among the main minerals that bulged from the gaps in the stone gallery walls.

The tunnel seemed to extend scores of feet ahead, narrowing into a gloomy vanishing point in the distance far beyond the glow of their torches.

"It makes a bend to the left then extends directly beneath the central courtyard of the Mahdist encampment," Strawplait told them as he took the lead, motioning for the others to follow him. "Be careful of your footing and follow in my footsteps as closely as you can. There are pits down here that drop for hundreds of feet straight down and are hard to spot in the dark."

The invaders pushed on, treading carefully in a line as their enormous shadows cast by the torchlight seemed to stalk them along the subterranean walls past which they carefully followed Strawplait who seemed to know exactly where he was going.

This was a perception that had been slow in dawning on Snakeskin, but which struck like a kick in the pit of his stomach as its implications suddenly registered on his mind. Strawplait *did* in fact seem to have a great deal of familiarity with this treacherous place, Snakeskin admitted silently to himself. A great deal ... and perhaps far too much familiarity for a mere captive of the Mahdists to have gained during the relatively brief time of his imprisonment.

"You seem to be fairly conversant with the lay of these tunnels," Snakeskin said to Strawplait as he drew abreast of the band's leader.

"Not really, old man," he answered with complete sangfroid. "In addition to the map I drew while a prisoner, I'd studied the entire topography of the area carefully prior to my departure from London. Bit of a hobby, you might say. During my sojourn as an unwilling guest of the Mahdi, I at one point gave a great deal of thought to the prospect of using the caverns to stage my escape, though I found I couldn't in the end. I've simply burned the layout of the catacombs into my mind, you see."

Strawplait flashed Snakeskin a broad, gap-toothed smile, one that looked to Snakeskin more like a rictus grinning in a death's head than ever.

"Well, since you're obviously the expert, were are we now?" asked Snakeskin. "And how much further do you think we need to travel in order to get out of this underground hell?"

The group had navigated the straightway and had turned the right-angled bend in the cavern just ahead of them. The flickering torchlight that illuminated their path showed that they had emerged from the tunnel into what appeared to be a large cavern with a high ceiling that formed a natural cathedral vault.

FIVE DEAD MEN

"Patience, old man. We've almost reached our destination," Strawplait offered without a moment's pause.

"Indeed I dare say that just beyond this gallery we shall soon find an entrance to the subterranean dungeons beneath the encampment. Do be a good chap and inform the others of this, as I would advise us all to be on our guard and remain as silent as possible from this point onward."

Inside this section of the catacombs, there were rows of small, dank cells. The barred cages were set on various levels within the tunnel system.

Snakeskin looked into one of these. It contained the ossified remains of one of the Mahdi's unfortunate victims, with rags still clinging to the heavy shackles of the *tlal fatma* that had bound its legs, possibly for the space of many years.

He passed the Englishman's instructions to Chow Bang Chow, behind him, who passed it to Jahno, and then to La Crosse.

Suddenly Dervishes came swarming upon them in dark and motley droves, seemingly emerging from everywhere at once.

"*Ihtijaz al kafiri!*" Strawplait shouted at the Dervishes. "I have brought the Infidels to you, my *Ansari*! Take them, oh brothers! Bring these Frank devils before the holy one, our Mahdi, whose feet I kiss, the sublime light of whose eyes I long to bask within!"

A fanatical light now glowed in Strawplait's gray eyes as well, as he pointed a skeletal finger at the Brothers.

Shouting in response to the traitor's instructions, the *Ansari* surged forward and Snakeskin, Chow Bang Chow and the Frenchman were overwhelmed by sheer force of numbers despite their weapons. As tall as was the bearded giant Jahno, the Gurkha too found himself overwhelmed by sheer numbers, a goliath surrounded by a swarm of pygmies, who seized his firearms and the curved sword that they had forcibly drawn from his scabbard and then pushed him forward at the bayonet points of their rifles.

Strawplait smiled with undisguised glee as the raiders were unceremoniously led away by their Dervish captors.

"Yes my brothers!" he shouted, his cadaverous, torch-lit face bobbing in the yellow flames as he hopped with unconcealed maniacal glee at having delivered the Brothers into the Mahdi's hands.

"You have them now! To the Mahdi with the captives. Then to the *shebba* with them all!"

"*Alam! Alam!*" Snakeskin heard them shout as he and the others were pressed forward at gunpoint, their hands now bound tightly behind them and their weapons in the custody of the *Ansari.*

"*Alam! Alam!* Glory to Allah who has delivered the unbelievers into our hands!"

Amid the crushing sway of the mob that punched and kicked the Infidel captives along through the tunnel, Strawplait ran a little of the way beside Snakeskin.

His face was transfigured with a madman's look of intense pleasure. The glee he obviously felt so strongly was sickening to behold.

"Do you know what they're shouting, Snakeskin?" he asked. "No, you don't, after all. I can see that you don't, dear fellow."

Then he stopped in front of Snakeskin. Placing his palms flat on the bound American's shoulders, he shoved his cadaver's face into Blake's and explained what he'd meant.

"*Alam! Alam!*" he screamed maniacally.

"It means '*torture*! *Torture*! Torture upon the rack. Slow death upon the shebba!"

FIVE DEAD MEN

It was now apparent that like fools they had been duped by the man they had found in the desert. Equally obvious was that Strawplait had been a spy in the Mahdi's pay all along. And now he had delivered Snakeskin and his Brothers of the Gun into the chief Dervish's hands.

"The sight of your bones popping from their very sockets, my dear fellow, will be like sipping ambrosia itself."

Strawplait's words were now faint, as the mob of *Ansari* pressed them hurriedly forward, striking them with rifle butts and curbashes.

Snakeskin did not hear the rest.

"And ambrosia, Yank, in case you didn't know it, is the very nectar of the gods."

48. In the Presence of the Mahdi

Upon a throne set majestically atop a dais in his palatial tent, surrounded by rifle-cradling *Ansari* whose faces were hidden behind the scarves of their turbans, sat the Mahdi. His large, dark kohl-rimmed eyes brooded as he stroked his thick black beard.

To either side of Muhammed Ahmed's sacred presence stood his counselors and viziers, their features twisted with scowls of contempt at the interlopers now led chained into the magisterial presence of the ordained one.

"I would deign to meet the Infidels who have so tenaciously pursued me," the Mahdi told Snakeskin.

With that, the American was chevvied forward with the butt of a rifle rammed into the small of his back toward the gaudily clad figure seated on the throne. No sooner had the prisoners reached the foot of the dais, than the *Ansari* flung them onto the embroidered rugs that covered the dirt floor -- a position within kissing distance of the Mahdi's washed and fragrantly perfumed feet.

"Kiss! Kiss! It is good!" shouted the guards, and pushed their prisoners' faces toward the extended toes, but to a man the captives preferred even death to such an act of abasement, and not even the kicks and blows of the *Ansari* could force them to plant their lips on the ordained one's pleasantly scented and perfectly manicured toenails.

Seeing that the expected kisses were not to be bestowed upon his offered feet, the Mahdi magnanimously bade his prisoners to rise with a flick of his be-ringed fingers.

As they rose, and standing close to the dais, Snakeskin could now see that the Mahdi was hardly a figure to inspire awe.

In fact, he had a clownish appearance. His face was fattish, and his mouth a small bud pursed in a petulant pout. The Mahdi's eyes were edged with black rings of kohl, which heightened the effeminacy in his face.

Despite his elaborately patched *jibba*, the stamp of physical cowardice was imprinted on the Mahdi, befitting a man who would sooner have others do his fighting and dying for him rather than take the risks himself.

Snakeskin could not help noticing that Strawplait – now resplendent in Arab dress -- was also sitting near the Mahdi's seated position upon a heap of damask cushions. Strawplait wore a characteristic smirk on his face and inclined his head by way of greeting.

"Poor fellow, poor Snakeskin," he announced with a shake of his elongated and almost bean-shaped pate. "You should be a trifle more discriminating in your choice of friends, one might suppose."

The Mahdi again gestured with an effeminate upward flick of the fingers of the hand he had brought from stroking his neatly trimmed black beard.

"You are but Infidels, this is understood," began the Mahdi in his thickly accented English. "I pardon you from your transgressions."

Snakeskin judged that by this he meant the failure of the Mahdi's captives to bestow their kisses upon his hallowed toes.

"Further, I shall spare your lives," the Mahdi went on. "No harm shall come to you while you sojourn among us."

The Mahdi gestured again and plates of food were brought out. The food was and still is a Sudanese delicacy -- raw camel's liver dashed liberally with salt and pepper.

Once this was done, the guards sliced the ropes binding their wrists and the choicest of the Mahdi's many wives brought cushions for the Infidels to seat themselves on, and finally, a hookah for each to match the far more elegant hubble-bubble pipe that was brought forth for the Mahdi's own personal pleasure.

Thus ensconced, the Mahdi began a new tack. He had some things to discuss with the captives.

Strawplait translated the Mahdi's questions where the Ordained One's English faltered, and did the same to clarify Snakeskin's replies.

Over the course of the council with the Mahdi, it became apparent that the Mahdi wished to use the newcomers in a bid to score a propaganda victory over the British and Egyptians.

He had already tried out the new repeating weapons of advanced design that had been captured with the disbelievers and was now eager to have more of their like with which to arm his *Ansari* for war against the English.

The Mahdi also wanted Snakeskin, Chow Bang Chow and the Frenchman to join with those who waged jihad with the Mahdiyyah and who extolled the blessings of the Mahdi's quest. With his characteristic smile, he pointed out that Strawplait had only profited by his conversion to the Dervish cause, and that they would as well.

FIVE DEAD MEN

If the unbelievers consented to conversion to the true faith and embracement of the lofty aims of the sacred Mahdiyyah by swearing *bayat,* or the unbreakable oath of allegiance to his holy person, he, Muhammed Ahmed, was prepared to permanently spare their lives and treat them as brothers in holy war and not sworn enemies.

Snakeskin refused these blandishments unequivocally. Through the interpretation of Strawplait, the Mahdi informed them that Snakeskin and his company were to be thrown into the prison beneath the encampment for an indefinite period. The Expected One smiled as he spoke, as he always did when pronouncing the severest of punishments.

After they had had time to think the proposition over -- while wearing the heavy chains of their bondage, the *tlal fatma* -- the Mahdi's sworn pronunciamento would be put to them again.

49. The Shebba

The Mahdi's chief jailer, torturer and executioner was a man of many talents named Pierre Soucy, an expatriate Frenchman who, originally taken prisoner after a previous effort to oust the Dervish presence from the Sudan, swore *bayat* to the Mahdi and became an ardent believer in Mahdiyyah. Above all, Soucy had also in time become a master of the dreaded shebba, reputed to be able to play the infamous Arabian torture rack with the dexterity and bravura of a virtuoso musician.

Soucy's personality matched his calling in life. The torturer was fat and greedy, addicted to hashish which he loved to mix with the scented tobacco called *Mu'assel* by natives of the Sahel, and inhale amid the humid vapor of his hubble-bubble pipe.

When not plying his disreputable trade, Soucy smoked his favorite Egyptian *sheesha* (as the Sudanese called the hookah) while sitting upon his well-larded haunches on tasseled cushions of embroidered damask silk throughout the relentless heat of the day.

But Soucy's most cherished pleasures lay in tormenting the prisoners entrusted to his custody. To this end he made certain that any breach of the rules, however minor, resulted in severe punishment by lashes inflicted with the cat-o'-nine-tails as his victims hung from the strappado or lay racked upon the infamous shebba.

In the case of the latter machinery of torture, Soucy enjoyed awakening a prisoner in the small hours of the morning and taking the miserable wretch to the place of torture to administer punishment, listening to the jingling of the chains of the *tlal fatma* as the unfortunate shuffled along.

"Come, Hakeem," he said as he now prepared to engage in this pastime early one morning. "It is again time."

"I have done nothing!" the prisoner protested, cowering in a corner of the dank and fetid cell. "By the gray hairs upon the beard of the Prophet, I am without blame! Show mercy, bold one, I beg of thee!"

The hapless Hakeem made a feeble gesture of pathetic supplication of his gnarled brown hands which only elicited a laugh from deep within Soucy's ponderous belly.

The chief jailor's men, however, already held the hapless Hakeem firmly by the arms and were dragging him to the torture chamber that Soucy had outfitted with the latest implements of pain.

Not even if the angels of paradise appeared and interceded on the prisoner's behalf would he stand a chance of escaping the torments awaiting him from Soucy's tender mercies.

Still, as Soucy's assistants strapped the man condemned to the Shebba onto the rack, none of them noticed the figure of a man moving stealthily through the shadows.

The man had entered the *zariba* only a few minutes before, killing a sentry in the process of silently and stealthily penetrating the defensive perimeter manned by Dervish watchers. He had moved with the litheness of a cat toward the torture chamber, where he went inside completely undetected.

One of Soucy's two assistants suddenly felt a hand clamped across his mouth. The apprentice torturer struggled, but already the man behind him was pulling him back, rendering his stomach muscles incapable of helping him to right himself again. Another moment, and his neck snapped with a carrot-like crunch and he slumped lifelessly to the dirt floor.

The second apprentice torturer had turned and clawed at his belt for the long knife he kept in a scabbard, but was stopped cold by a single thrust of a broad-bladed sword that ripped his stomach open in a single stroke and passed through his innards to thrust out bloodied from the small of his back.

Soucy was too frozen to speak and he sank down to his knees begging for mercy.

"By Allah's name, I am a worthless mongrel!" he whined. "Spare me, bold one, and I promise that you shall not regret it!"

The dark, hooded eyes of the tall black man held nothing but contempt for the master torturer. He would have as soon killed him then and there, but he still had use for Soucy.

The hangman was a useful instrument with which to wipe the blood and gore from his sword, an action he calmly performed on the crouching and terrified Soucy. Then the giant Sudanese reached down and with one hand easily hauled up the cowering chief jailer's entire overweight body, pulling Soucy roughly to his feet by the topknot that graced the crown of his skull.

"Take me to the Franks," growled Divi Divi Davi, "or I will cut your pig's throat right now."

FIVE DEAD MEN

"Yes, yes," pleaded Soucy, "whatever you wish I will do. Only stay your hand and spare my life, bold one."

"No more talk," said Divi Divi Davi, pushing the worthless cur forward with a stout finger in the small of his back. "Take me where I wish to go. And remember that any treachery will mean your worthless life is forfeit to my thirsty sword."

"Yes, bold one. As you command, bold one."

The Bashi-Bazouk was too disgusted with this craven coward to strike him for speaking when he had expressly warned him against opening his mouth again. So the Bashi-Bazouk merely kicked the Mahdi's torturer in the lard of his huge ass to hasten him along.

In a matter of moments, Divi Divi Davi was being led by the frightened master torturer to the cell where members of the mercenary company were being held prisoner.

"Release them," the Bashi-Bazouk next told Soucy, emphasizing the command with the point of a sword in the hangman's back.

Soucy did as ordered, using his keys to unshackle Jahno and Chow Bang Chow from their iron constraints. They stood up, rubbing the sore places where the chains of the *tlal fatma* had bitten deep into their flesh.

"Where are the Frenchman and the American?" asked Chow Bang Chow.

Soucy knew, and although he was mortally afraid of the Mahdi's retribution for his treacherous turnabout, he led them without protest first to the Frenchman's place of imprisonment. They found La Crosse alone in a single cell. The Frenchman was lying on a dirt floor with a black stone for a pillow.

"Again you are late, *mes frères*. What kept you?" he asked them, rising to his feet while two of the Brothers set to work with Soucy's keys to unlock his fetters.

"What shall I do with this worthless one?" asked the Sudanese when Soucy had freed Snakeskin, the last mercenary to be found, and the master torturer was no longer needed for anything. "It is best that this son of a pig be killed."

"I agree," Snakeskin stated.

He pulled back his hand and let fly a punch that landed on Soucy's face with the force of a hammer blow. Soucy let out a pig's grunt and crumpled to the floor unconscious.

"Except that I don't want his stinking blood on my hands. Tie him and leave him."

"What happened to you?" Snakeskin asked the Bashi-Bazouk when they had left the prison house behind. "We thought we would never see you again."

"There was difficulty in my village," explained Divi Divi Davi telling about how he had seen the fires on the horizon and knew that he had to leave the encampment immediately.

"I was forced by custom of my tribe to leave without hesitation. I told the English one Strawplait to inform you of this. Did he not do so?"

"That bastard was in the Mahdi's pay all along," Snakeskin replied, thinking of how Strawplait had led them down the primrose path with consummate skill. "He was a clever one, though. Had us all completely gulled. I've got to give him credit for that much."

"My apologies," the Sudanese told them. "I should not have left you all in such great haste, my good friends."

"Apologies accepted," said Snakeskin. "Now let's do what we came here to do."

FIVE DEAD MEN

Moving hastily from the catacombs the regrouped force soon came upon the weapons storage rooms of the Dervishes. There, they succeeded in rearming themselves with the weapons that the Mahdi had taken from them upon their capture.

All their formerly appropriated guns seemed to be in working condition, including the big Gatling machinegun. As an added bonus they also found numerous crates containing thousands of rounds of ammunition. These had apparently been captured in the course of the numerous raids and military engagements undertaken by the Dervishes since the beginnings of the Mahdiya.

With these weapons now in hand, Snakeskin's raiders moved to accomplish their primary objective. This was to liberate the Sultan's British wife, the favorite of the royal seraglio of Zanzibar, whom the Mahdi had taken hostage, and whom the Brothers of the Gun had been well paid to return to her rightful place.

DAVID ALEXANDER

50. The Favorite Bride is Rescued

Within the confines of the *haram*, Angelica Fairchild, now the unwilling bride of her captor, faced her imminent punishment with noble bravery.

The Mahdi had grown weary of her recalcitrance. The Frank woman, as he styled her, was sharp-tongued and disobedient. Though the tresses of her hair shone with the brilliance of spun gold, and though her features were more fair than those of the *zaniya* -- heavenly prostitutes -- promised to the faithful in *Behest Zahra*, the paradise of blessed rewards that awaited stalwart believers, her mouth spat an invective that was oftentimes fouler than the venom of a serpent found under a rock.

For some time, then, the Mahdi had seen to it that this Frank woman was taught obedience by the ancient customs. In a special chamber of sequestration, she would be forced to obey the whims and serve the pleasures, not of the Mahdi, but of his basest and lowliest of servants.

As a result, Angelica was now styled a mere whore by the inner circle of *Ansari* who served the Mahdi, as well as by the other women of the royal seraglio, who mocked her disheveled hair and bruised breasts and buttocks as she returned to their fold following a session in the room of harsh instruction.

Today, again, Angelica had been seized by the Mahdi's retainers and hauled rudely into the chamber. As they removed themselves to stand guard outside the entrance, Angelica had seen the flaps at the other end of the chamber part and a black Sudanese enter the room. Without uttering a word, his retainers removed his robes and he stood naked before her. As the blackamoor grinned toothily, Angelica gasped -- his member already stood erect, and it was as huge as that of a horse.

By this stage of things, there was no point in trying to flee. She would merely be tossed in again by the Mahdi's guardsmen.

Instead, she daringly exposed her breasts and held them impudently out to the Sudanese, who wasted no time in squeezing them like the ripe white honeydews which they so closely resembled.

Then she took his hand in an attempt to lead him to the bed, but he shook his head and roughly turned her about, then pushed her down upon her knees. She knew well what was about to happen next. She tried to break free of the giant's grasp, but it was impossible.

"No, you bloody bastard. It's too big for that!" she screamed, but the blackamoor wasn't paying attention, as he stretched out his fingers across her plump, soft roundness, and then plunged into the moist divot that gleamed invitingly between.

It hardly all went inside, and it hurt with enough of a shock to bring tears of pain to her eyes, but the giant held her tightly by her trim waist as he began to thrust.

Mercifully, for all his size and girth, he had no staying power, and blundered out rather quickly.

"Bastard, stinking bastard," Angelica could only curse as she felt the dense milt spurting on the deep end, and then spattering the creamy white hillocks as the elephant's trunk was plucked from the water hole.

She at least was comforted that the torture of the pleasure chamber would end at this point, but to no avail, as the two guards posted outside burst without warning into the Mahdi's ordained place of harsh instruction. They too were fully turgid, and as she was rudely hauled atop the cushions, the two of them knelt at her head to prod at her lips while the Sudanese knelt likewise to have at her again, this time in the puckering star that shone darkly between two plump and gleaming white moons.

Angelica nursed at one member, then then other, then took each swollen appendage in hand and stroked them until the milt again flung itself onto the ends of her breasts. The Sudanese groaned, and thrust forward into her again, and again there was a spurt of sticky milt upon her nipples.

Suddenly the flap that divided the chamber from the corridor outside connecting with other parts of the sprawling *haram* tent burst open and another man entered. Angelica caught only a glimpse of him through eyes fogged with sweat and pungent, sticky salve, but she could tell that his skin was white.

The next thing she knew she was being spattered by hot new fluids that were crimson in hue as the men who had been with her upon the bed grunted in pain and fell aside, thudding heavily -- and she quickly realized -- *lifelessly* to the floor of the tent.

"As the poet said, ''tis a pity she's a trollop."

FIVE DEAD MEN

A strong pair of hands pulled on Angelica's arms to lift her up as Snakeskin stepped over the three corpses and came to her side.

"I suppose you never bothered to mention your -- shall we say, calling -- to the Sultan upon your betrothal and engagement to his Excellency's *haram*? Or had you intended to go straight, my love?"

Blake's smile was broken -- along with part of a tooth and lip -- by a punch thrown at his face by Angelica.

"Same old girl," Snakeskin said with a somewhat bloody grin. "But we've got to leave. And don't bother trying to find anything to cover those smashing tits of yours, my darling. We'll find something later."

Before Angelica could protest, he'd shoved her out through the entranceway of the pleasure chamber helped, in part, by a boot placed solidly on her bare rump.

Having her gather up her things and don fresh apparel in the royal *haram*, while the Mahdi's other wives were now silent and wide-eyed as they stood by and gaped, the raiders made ready to leave the Mahdist stronghold. But Snakeskin had one more item to liberate from the Mahdi's hoard of booty before they would leave.

The sword. The precious, irreplaceable, bejeweled sword of the Mahdiyyah that at once comprised the prime token of the Mahdi's power and right to lead, and was also worth a king's ransom on the antiquities markets of London and New York, where Snakeskin would have little trouble in exchanging it for dollars or pounds. The sword that Gordon had secretly asked for, describing it in minute detail so that there could be no mistaking it for another like it.

Snakeskin Blake had wondered at the reason for Gordon's insistence on having the sword brought to him, but he had pledged to himself that if he did in fact acquire it, he would deliver it to Gordon only at the price of a king's ransom.

Locating the Mahdi's treasure room became a simple matter at the appearance of Jahno, holding a captive firmly in an arm lock.

"Look who I've found ... actually *what*, since one can hardly consider the miscreant as a fellow human being."

Sir Montague Strawplait frowned as he was forcibly marched toward the waiting Brothers in the Gurkha's strong grip.

"As Allah has willed it, blessed be the Mahdi," Strawplait cried out as he continued to struggle in the bearded giant's iron grip. "I fear nothing you can do to me. I accept death with calmness, for I am companion of the Prophet and warrior..."

Before Strawplait could finish his speech, Jahno threw him to the floor and planted his large booted foot in the small of his back.

"I want to know something, Strawplait," Snakeskin said, crouching at his head. "If you tell me, Jahno won't grind his heel into your sacrum and crack your back in two."

"I fear nothing you can do to me..." Strawplait began again, but in the end he told Snakeskin Blake what he'd wanted to know. Unfortunately for Strawplait, Jahno made a rather clumsy job of it as they left the turncoat on the floor and went to find the sword.

"Jahno, what was that snap I just heard?" asked Blake.

"My foot must have slipped, my brother," replied the Gurkha.

Strawplait was lying on the carpeted floor of the tent, howling in agony.

"I shoot him, *mes frères,* yes?" asked La Crosse.

FIVE DEAD MEN

"I'm afraid you'll have to now," Blake said, adding, "Jahno, that was just a bit careless of you. Don't do it again."

The Gurkha grunted in assent as three rapid but muffled reports from the silenced La Crosse repeater into Strawplait's head put the turncoat permanently out of his misery.

Having located the Expected One's treasure room, Snakeskin in the lead at once saw the sword of the Mahdi. He recognized this weapon right away. It was prominently displayed on a plinth of carven ebony, flanked with two burning censors of filigreed bronze. Blake took the sword in his hands and inspected it. The sword's cutting edge bore the inscription of the Templars etched into it, while its hilt was encrusted with precious gems in a variety of colors, all twelve of them cut in rectangular baguettes.

The inscription was just as Chinese Charlie had given it -- given it with a gleam in those diabolical gray-blue eyes of his that always masked a host of deeper sinister secrets -- *Viou Re Aut Vio Gungard. Vicere Ant Mo Glori Igarni.*

Gordon had not revealed to Snakeskin Blake that the sword had once belonged to a Grand Master of the Knights Templar, and while he had made sure to describe in detail both inscription and appearance of the gems inset upon its hilt, he had given him no reason as to why its recovery should have been so hotly desired. This alone had immediately convinced the American privateer that, if ever found, he would keep the relic until he learned the answer.

Snakeskin now took the sword of the Mahdi as all of the other members of the team grabbed up as much gold and jewels from the Mahdi's hoard of plunder as they were able to carry -- all except for the Gurkha. Jahno foreswore the taking of any booty, having pledged himself to the service of the Sultan, settling for a fine *haram* concubine whose firmly jutting brown nipples he pinched in wolfish anticipation. As an afterthought while leaving the treasure room, Chow Bang Chow decided to overturn the two censors that flanked the now bare ebony plinth.

Snakeskin turned to see the Chinaman holding one censer in each hand and understood the intention of his brother in arms.

"Good idea. Wish I'd thought of it," said Snakeskin, and Chow Bang Chow flung the censers into the corners of the tent where things immediately began catching fire. The Brothers were pleased to see the drapery and sumptuously embroidered wall hangings beginning to burn as they left.

Now, however, the Gurkha viewed Angelica as ritually unclean, and would undoubtedly so inform his master the Sultan. All to the better, thought Snakeskin. As was the case with the Mahdi's sword, the American had all along never entertained any intentions of returning Angelica to the palace of the Sultan of Zanzibar.

Angelica might have been a trollop, but Snakeskin liked trollops, and Angelica -- say what one might -- was no mere trollop by any standard of measurement.

The Sultan of Zanzibar had made him a solemn promise -- a promise that had been witnessed by the assemblage of the royal court and set down in a royal decree. Snakeskin could ask for one boon and the Sultan had sworn to grant it.

The thing that Snakeskin would ask for would be Angelica.

She was a prize for the taking and a trophy for a strong man to possess, and Snakeskin was that man. She was his, not the Sultan's, not the Mahdi's and not any other's. Trollop or not, Angelica Fairchild was his and his alone.

Dispatching other Dervish guards, Snakeskin's raiders and their comely charge found their way to the Mahdi's stables. There they seized some of Muhammad Ahmed's prize Arabian stallions and rode the swift horses out of the stronghold.

Dervish sentries spotted them as they made their getaway, though, and one, riding faster than the rest, with *khatt* lending power and trueness to his throw, hurled a Dervish *azzagâyah* with deadly accuracy from a full gallop.

As the hunting spear of the *Ansari* cut through space, Chow Bang Chow turned and saw that it would strike his brother between the shoulder blades. In that split instant, he placed his own body between the onrushing spear point and its intended target, Snakeskin Blake, and took the full brunt of it through the center of his own chest.

"Go, my brothers!" he shouted, as the Dervishes caught up with him and began to encircle the mortally wounded mercenary.

"No, I won't leave without the damned Chinaman!" Snakeskin cried amid the sudden din of the fighting.

"You must, Snakeskin!" shouted the Bashi-Bazouk.

"Chow Bang Chow is finished. He has forfeited his life for the rest of us. We would dishonor him to refuse his gift of sacrifice."

Snakeskin knew this to be true. His last sight of the Chinaman was Chow Bang Chow fighting off the horde of Dervishes, two La Crosse repeaters chattering in his fists.

Chow Bang Chow had fallen in the final attempt to leave the Mahdi's stronghold behind.

As death closed over him with a wave of total blackness, the brave Chinese had finally learned the true significance of the pool that he had jumped into at the Shaolin monastery back in China: it was indeed the pool of death.

But he had bought the others precious time by his valorous act, and the raiders left the Mahdist encampment behind them, riding their mounts across the Sudanese desert as quickly as the beasts could speed their way over the parched and broken landscape of the Dervishes' dusty realm.

FIVE DEAD MEN

51. The Locusts Gather

Dawn was breaking and their getaway attempt had not gone unnoticed. From far and wide, Dervishes soon heeded the call to arms.

Gathering into swarms as was their habit, they mounted their horses in great numbers in order to recapture and kill the Infidels.

On the backs of their hastily stolen mounts, Snakeskin and his company of freebooters made good their escape from the Mahdist encampment. Hundreds of the Mahdi's horsemen still pursued them now -- hundreds that were only a fraction of the numbers that the *Ansari* were known to field when necessary.

Exhorted to capture the Infidels at all costs, the tribesmen had been promised lives of eternal pleasure in the Blessed Paradise called *Behesht Zahra* if they died as warriors of Allah in the pursuit of this goal.

The sound of the thousands of beating hooves thundered across the desert landscape of the Sahel as the pursuing Dervishes gathered together and charged after their fleet quarry.

DAVID ALEXANDER

A cloud of fine ochre dust raised by the charging mounted legions of *Ansari* rose toward the sky, so thick that it almost obscured the glaring light of the sun. The terrifying war cries that issued from the throats of hundreds of desert warriors split the air with its raucous din.

At the lead, Snakeskin Blake searched the parched flat landscape that lay ahead for the terrain feature that he had marked before their entrance to the humid caverns beneath the Mahdi's *mukhayyam*. Then he spotted the three flat rocks propped between two medium-sized boulders lying some quarter of a mile ahead of them and indicating that he was heading in the right direction.

Turning to look behind him, Snakeskin saw to his dismay that the Dervishes were catching up to the Brothers. In response, he spurred on his stallion, desperate to make for the marker rocks while shouting at the others to spur their horses for maximum speed.

There, beginning at the line of specially yet discreetly marked stones, he and his men had labored to set up an array of antipersonnel traps for the pursuing horsemen in case the eventuality arose.

They had used the last of the high explosive salvaged from their pack mules before crossing the rope bridge after the surprise meeting with the Dervish patrols days before.

Now that he was almost abreast of the first marker stones, Snakeskin unshipped one of his matched LeMat pistols. With one hand he pointed the dual-chambered weapon at the marker and flicked the stud above the trigger spur to switch the action of the gun. Then he thumbed back on the spur to cock the single action revolver and pulled the trigger to cook off the buckshot shell nestled in the revolver's smoothbore underbarrel.

FIVE DEAD MEN

The burst of iron shot struck the marker rock with perfect accuracy, most of the spreading fan hitting home and throwing up a shower of thick dust, rock chips and hot white sparks. Beneath the red circle drawn on the stone there was a bundled dynamite charge that exploded as the hot buckshot struck it dead on, in turn igniting a fuse to begin what Snakeskin hoped would result in a chain reaction of multiple detonations.

The exploding sticks of TNT hurled boulders from the top of the cliffs, causing a landslide. The avalanche of enormous rocks tumbling down the slope of the narrow defile took its toll in Dervishes who were killed by the falling boulders which crashed down on the mounted desert warriors. *Ansari* and their war horses alike fell and died beneath the avalanche.

Only a small percentage of the Dervishes were killed by this stratagem, though. The deadly surprise maneuver slowed down the Mahdists' attack somewhat, but did not bring it entirely to a halt. Now having come out of the defile, the enraged survivors were thundering their steeds across the sandy plain that lay beyond, more determined than ever to win glory by slaughtering the Infidels, the detested *kuffar,* the enemies of Mahdiyyah who had ventured into their midst to cast their dirt upon the Expected One's holy jihad against the Franks and their Egyptian puppets.

Rifles cracked, punctuating the fearsome war cries uttered by the pursuing Dervishes. A hail of bullets whined past their ears as Snakeskin's surviving raiders and their rescued charge made tracks across the desert. Snakeskin now looked out for the second trap that he and his men had prepared to aid their getaway.

This was in the form of a huge pit that they had excavated beneath the sands. The sides of the pit were lined with explosives. To maximize the effect of this second booby trap, Snakeskin and his company had laced the explosives with crude shrapnel made from scraps of found metal that the charges would propel at the oncoming Dervishes from the left and the right.

A tripwire lay across the path, stretched tautly just an inch above the surface of the desert and virtually invisible. Snakeskin's steed tripped the mechanism that armed the timer device by breaking a thin wire with its hoofs as it ran at full gallop. Seconds after the hard-riding raiders had cleared the trap, the charges went off just as planned, and thousands of splinters of shrapnel were hurled at the main mass of the Dervishes.

Again, the slaughter among the ranks of the *Ansari* was extensive. Men and their steeds died by the hundreds, falling to the sands in bloody masses amid spinning, tumbling clouds of high explosive debris and pillars of dust and flame that the explosions sent spouting high into the air.

Despite the extent of the carnage, there were nevertheless still enough Mahdists surviving to overwhelm them by sheer force of numbers. The five riders could not beat such odds.

It looked, in the end, like they might be stopped and taken back to the Mahdi in chains after all.

■

Suddenly, though, the sky darkened.

It seemed for a moment as though an eclipse of the sun was taking place, or another great *khamaseen* had blown up to blind the eyes and choke the lungs with a yellow fog of dust.

"Blimey, what on earth is happening?" asked Angelica in panic as she clutched Snakeskin on the saddle behind his seat.

FIVE DEAD MEN

"I don't know," he replied, perplexed.

This was no sandstorm, nor for that matter was it an eclipse. But in a matter of seconds Snakeskin could make out the source of the darkness that obscured the sun. It was a great spreading cloud, one that was accompanied by an ever-loudening buzzing sound, and was not in the least formed by windblown sand.

After a few more moments Snakeskin and his comrades realized what was actually taking place. A swarm of hairy-chested locusts had come up over the mountains surrounding the plain.

It was a swarm that contained millions of insects, a swarm so thick and so enormously dense that it entirely blotted out the light of the sun while its buzzing had grown so deafeningly loud that the noise it made drowned out even the sound of one's own breathing.

The swarm of locusts descended upon the scene of the chase, covering the pursued and their pursuers alike with millions of biting, creeping, crawling insects.

The locusts returned again and again to cover the human frame with a living mass that writhed and squirmed and wriggled and gnawed no matter how many of them were brushed off and stomped to gooey muck beneath the feet. The Mahdists, superstitious and fearing the locusts with a special apprehension, were suddenly seized with a wild and unmanning horror that struck them to the depths of their souls.

The locusts had been feared by the desert people for as long as they could remember as omens of ill fortune. As the descending cloud of hairy-chested locusts swarmed all over the Mahdists, they lost their minds. Jumping from their steeds they began rolling around on the ground where their maddened horses trampled them beneath their stamping, kicking hooves.

52. The *Ansari* Defeated

The locusts took no sides, however.

The buzzing hordes of millions of ravenous insects had alike descended on both the host of Dervishes and Snakeskin's far smaller group.

Human eyes, ears and nostrils all became targets of the sudden insect onslaught. The bodies of pursuer and pursued were quickly covered over by the swarming short-horned grasshoppers which clung to their clothes by the thousands, crawling all over them, crawling into their nostrils and ears and -- when they cried out in terror -- into their mouths and down their throats to cut off their cries and stop up their breath.

Eyeballs too were no match for the insects' spine-covered forelimbs and rows of saw-like cutting teeth. Felled by the swarm, the *Ansari*'s eye sockets were picked clean of the jelly inside, while other locusts got inside their skulls to eat up their brains and crawled up their anuses to devour their intestines and stomachs.

Mad with fright, horses reared and threw their riders to the ground, whinnying in primeval terror as the living cloud descended on them and the insidious mass of biting, sucking, cutting, piercing insects enveloped the once proud desert warriors from head to foot.

In the midst of this utter carnage, and as the Brothers saw the black cloud racing across the skies to overwhelm them too, Snakeskin reached into the saddlebag that he had hastily draped across the back of the stallion pirated from the Mahdi's stable. He had two sticks of dynamite left -- all the rest of the explosives had been exhausted.

But before he lit the fuse he yelled for the others to fire their weapons.

"The noise of gunfire can disperse even large swarms of these things," Snakeskin shouted at them to explain his actions. "Give it all you've got."

Then he lit off the dynamite and flung it high in the air.

Nobel's high explosive blasting compound -- the same that had recently blasted out the tunnels of the new London underground commuter railways -- went off seconds later with an enormous bang that dispelled the noxious buzzing of the locust's wings as it detonated within the midst of the low-flying swarm.

At the same time, the Gurkha and La Crosse each raised their repeating arms skyward and triggered long bursts into the air.

"*Merde*, Snakeskin, you were right. It's working!" the Frenchman cried out exultantly. "The damned swarm is letting up somewhat."

Indeed, the strategy seemed to be doing the trick. The sharp reports of the exploding dynamite combined with the chatter of the rapid-firing automatic weapons had caused the locusts to begin to disperse. The swarm was still thick, but already hundreds of the insects had fled the vicinity, now in flight to their next landing spot where the scattered patches of the once great gathering would recombine and fly off again like an airborne armada to infest some other corner of the Sudan.

The main body of the locust swarm had already passed them by, surrounding the Dervishes in its midst who had not fared as well as Snakeskin and his band of brothers in arms.

As they whipped their steeds forward, and galloped across the level plain, they could see the frenzy of men and horses as the locusts spread panic into the ranks of the *Ansari.*

As the locusts departed, Snakeskin struggled to calm his terrified horse and finally managed to get the beast reigned in. At last they were able to regain control of the horses and ride on through the far less dense vestiges of the departing swarm, trampling over the twitching corpses of thousands of dead locusts that littered the ground beneath them.

■

Snakeskin's company of raiders rode on throughout the day as hard as they could. By nightfall, they and their steeds were completely exhausted and unable to take another step farther. An encampment was made at a dry wadi that provided shelter from any form of discovery other than mere chance detection by Dervishes.

"I know of a shortcut to the coast," the Bashi-Bazouk told Snakeskin as they ate wild Sudanese pig and desert hare that had been caught while foraging for food.

The Sudanese went on to explain that the path he knew should bring them to their destination quickly and with only minimal risk of being intercepted by Mahdists.

Still, a new set of questions had begun to concern Snakeskin Blake.

This involved the Sultan.

How would he respond to his desert mercenary's new plans?

Would the Sultan honor his word to allow Snakeskin to have anything he wanted -- including the Sultan's own wife?

53. Plundered Treasure

With the help of the Sudanese, the surviving members of the mercenary band reached the coast of East Africa, the long coast that the Sudan shared with Egypt and Ethiopia, whose jutting horn marked the demarcation point between the Red Sea and the Arabian Sea below it, which in turn trended into the Indian Ocean lying far to the southern reaches of the vast watery spaces.

Once on the African coast, Blake and his company were far enough from the Mahdi's center of power to secure passage across the straits by boat. It was here too that the Bashi-Bazouk took leave of Blake, La Crosse, Jahno and the Englishwoman for the final time.

For Divi Divi Davi, the Sudan, for all its perils, was home. Yet, as the giant warrior in Crusader dress turned, mounted his stallion and rode away, neither of the four he left behind had the slightest inkling that his first destination would be the dusty ground where the Chinaman had fallen amidst the Dervishes, and his mission to find his body and bury it in a hero's grave.

Ferrying across the narrow twenty mile-wide headwaters, the survivors of the mission to the Sudan reached Zanzibar within a matter of hours, debarking on the quayside where all but one had set off several weeks before.

Once Snakeskin and his party had set foot on the island, the word spread far and wide that the Sultan's raiders had returned once again.

A contingent of the Sultan's personal honor guard rushed to the wharf to greet the returnees as they reached the sanctuary of the island after their extended absence without word of their progress.

Having been received into the Sultan's presence, the newly returned adventurers were accorded a welcome befitting heroes, while Angelica was received as a returning queen.

Snakeskin had omitted much of the treasure that he had taken and all mention of the Sword of the Mahdi which he had stolen and planned on keeping for himself.

Nevertheless, the Sultan soon found out about both matters. He too, had his sources of information.

The entire Sudan was abuzz with the news that the Mahdi's hidden and impregnable camp had been invaded, a captive rescued from the Expected One's harem, and hundreds, perhaps even thousands of Dervish warriors trampled into the dust of the Sudan during a fruitless chase to overtake and wipe out the fleeing mercenary band sent by the Sultan of Zanzibar.

But the most incredible news of all concerned the Mahdi's fabled sword. To the Sultan's utter shock, he learned that it too had been stolen from the Sudan -- by Snakeskin Blake himself.

This act, the Sultan feared, and rightly so, would only inflame the supporters of the Mahdi even more, and result in the commission of still greater acts of barbarism in the Sudan than those which had already been carried out, for the Sword of the Mahdi was by far the most sacred of all relics in the Expected One's possession and because it ranked high among the signs of his imminent victory over the English, their Egyptian puppets, and all disbelievers everywhere.

There was even talk now that to avenge this outrage, the Mahdi had sworn to attack Fort Omdurman -- the final major defensive position of the British-backed Khedive of Egypt still remaining intact in the wastes of the Sudan -- and to slaughter every man, woman and child found within its walls in order to avenge himself of the intolerable slight that the American and his band of thieves had dealt to his towering ego.

And so the Sultan became suddenly afraid. There had been no provision made for Snakeskin's stealing the Sword of the Mahdi in their original agreement, only the rescue of his favorite wife and harem concubine from the Mahdi's stable of palace odalisques. The American's transgression might have cost the Sultan his crown and even, if worse came to worse, his very head.

Gripped by a mounting terror, the Sultan panicked and ordered his retainers to arrest Snakeskin and his entire group at once.

But tipped off by the Gurkha, Snakeskin, the Frenchman and Angelica fled the palace before they could be apprehended. They took the Sword of the Mahdi and the plundered treasures with them.

DAVID ALEXANDER

54. A Hasty Departure from Zanzibar

With the assistance of the Gurkha, Snakeskin and the last of the Brothers, La Crosse, made their way through the winding streets of old Stone Town with Angelica in tow.

Zanzibar was not large, and the docks were not far from the palace, but the streets were narrow and could easily be blocked by the Sultan's constabulary, boxing them in. Yet they managed to reach the docks without interference, where their plan was to get hold of a boat and sail as far and as fast from Zanzibar as possible.

The Sultan's arm was not very long, nor was his reach very strong. His was a vest-pocket kingdom, and despite the considerable wealth of his royal house, he was nonetheless a small frog lording it over a small pond compared to the greater powers that surrounded, and which in large part controlled, him.

With Angelica freed from the Mahdi's captivity, the reaction of the Sultan's European protectors would not be any more dangerously hostile than that of the Sultan himself if Blake and his comrades in arms chanced to be apprehended by the British or the French.

FIVE DEAD MEN

Still, on reaching the harbor the luck that had hidden them from the Sultan's police patrols had finally run its course. Retainers from the royal court had been dispatched there to cover the most likely avenue of escape from the island kingdom.

A chase developed through the length and breadth of Stone Town, with Snakeskin, Angelica and the Frenchman fleeing through the streets under cover of repeating gunfire with the Gurkha running interference for them in defiance of his royal master as he brought up the rear to guard their retreat toward the waterfront.

Upon reaching the Zanzibar docks they formed a circle and decided to make a last stand with their backs to the ocean and their guns aimed toward the Sultan's advancing gendarmerie.

55. A Courageous Rescue

T hen, without warning, the thudding of cannon fire split and hammered the air. Snakeskin instantly recognized the reports of the armaments that had fired the incoming ordnance -- they were unique, and belonged to only one source in the world that he could name.

That source was the 254 millimeter Armstrong guns mounted in the twin pillbox turrets amidships of the Courageous.

Snakeskin's heart leaped up as he realized that it was his own ship, the Courageous, that was shelling the quayside from the harbor of Zanzibar, its colors flying atop its main sail.

The Sultan's men were unhorsed as the salvo struck its target and blew the island constabulary and its mounts apart with ease. Then Blake heard another report, the throatier roar of the ship's single 40 pound Armstrong gun mounted aft of the turrets, firing a salvo of 120 millimeter rounds at the Zanzibar gendarmerie. It was aided by the smaller, but still formidable 12 pound cannons mounted on the second turret at the Courageous' stern.

FIVE DEAD MEN

In its devastating consequences, this next result was similar to the first, except that the Sultan's guardians of the realm had already begun to scatter in fright and prudently run for cover anywhere they could find it as the shattering fire came pouring down on their heads.

Turning toward the quay, Blake saw Jopling waving from the starboard side of the Courageous as the pilot easily maneuvered the low-draft converted gunrunner toward the Stone Town dockside and began to draw abeam of the quay.

"Come on, Cap'n! Hop to it!" the first mate cried out, now within earshot as a boat was lowered.

"Make for the skiff before the damned wog bastards return for a second helping."

They climbed onto the boat and set off from the quay. The Sultan's men were firing on them from the shelter of the square near the quay but they were neatly cut off from all possibility of pursuit thanks to the continued shelling and enfilade fire from the pirate ship that poured additional machinegun rounds from the two Gatlings -- one mounted on the ship's aft brigantine mast and the other fitted to moveable mountings amidships.

Reunited with the pirate crew, the captain of the Courageous, Snakeskin Blake, now took command.

"Your orders skipper?" asked Jopling, as bullets from the quay whizzed overhead.

"Obviously -- haul fucking hell out of here fast as possible."

"Aye, skipper," replied Jopling with a smile. "I'd expected you might have that particular order in mind."

Jopling made circular motions of his own hand to the helmsman who immediately issued the order to apply main power to the ship's engines. Snakeskin felt the Courageous lurch as her twin screws churned under the combined force of half of her four boilers and she swung out into the chop and swell of the sea.

Within a matter of minutes, the pirate vessel had slid past the small, rocky islands off the coast of Zanzibar, her stacks blowing dense plumes of black-brown smoke as all four 1500 horsepower boilers turned the ship's screws to bring the Courageous to her top speed of 15 knots.

Minutes after that the Brothers of the Gun were completely beyond both the range of the Sultan's weapons and the length of the Sultan's reach.

56. Epilog: Chinese Charlie

It has often been said by the Arabs of North Africa that when Allah in his wisdom originally made the Sudan, he suddenly began to laugh.

Remembering this adage, the Sultan of Zanzibar finally made his peace with Snakeskin Blake and then turned his attention to a new favorite of his royal harem, knowing also that by conquering the Sudan, the Mahdi might have sought to establish an empire lasting a thousand years, but had only succeeded in sowing the bitter seeds of his ultimate undoing.

In London, Chinese Charlie Gordon was approached by members of the Queen's War Cabinet. Told of what had happened by men with stern faces in the frock coats of diplomats and the uniforms of soldiers, Gordon -- like his counterpart of Arab fable -- laughed aloud. The uniformed, medal-bedecked stalwarts to whom a sense of humor was a thing as alien as a flying horse, glared at Gordon in stark bewilderment.

"Exactly what are you laughing at, man?" he was asked by Major-General Godfrey, who led the party. "Perhaps you find something funny in the bloody Mahdi lopping off

British heads left and right and throwing the best of Her Majesty's forces from the Sudan with careless ease?"

Gordon fought to control himself. There was much funny, much indeed laughable, in the entire affair. But these pompous asses, he knew full well, could never even begin to understand the dark humor that so tugged at the soul of the soldier-adventurer that he was and had always been.

Barely managing to suppress another gale of laughter, Gordon succeeded in making a suitably sober reply.

"Nothing, funny. Nothing at all. I quite agree. You were saying?"

"What we have come here today to inform you of is that there is obviously only one thing for it -- one course and one alone."

Godfrey's stern demeanor beneath the cockaded bicorn hat was so ridiculous that Gordon, who had in the course of his lifetime seen ten times the amount of war and killing that Godfrey and his ilk had ever witnessed, feared he'd burst out again.

"Pray, sirs," he began, surprised at the seriousness of his voice despite everything. "Share your plans with me."

"Omdurman," put in Admiral Prime, who stood beside Godfrey, another cabinet war hawk with close ties to war factions in Parliament.

"The fortress there must be held at all costs."

"And you want me to do it?" Gordon asked. "You want me to go to the Sudan?"

"Yes," they replied, "you're the only man for the job. After this impossibly bloody botch, the PM asked for a magician, and of course your name popped right up."

"Wouldn't Merlin have been a more appropriate name with which to conjure?" he muttered. "He could at least lift stones with a mere wave of his wand."

FIVE DEAD MEN

"What's that, Gordon?" asked Godfrey.

"Sorry, my lord. I was saying that I'll think this proposition over," Gordon replied, not telling them that he had already made up his mind to indeed go to the Sudan and take over command of the fort at Omdurman, and also knowing that the Mahdi would not permit him to ever leave the Sudan alive.

When they'd left, Gordon lit another of the Moroccan cheroots from the butt of the one he had been smoking previously. He'd developed a taste for them during his sojourn in the holy land in 1882, during his year's leave of absence, about half of which was spent in Jerusalem and the better part of the other in that lovely house he'd taken in Jaffa.

Yes, he thought, he would inform the PM straightaway that he would take on the ... well, the bloody suicide mission. They hadn't called it that, of course -- those pompous asses -- but that is exactly what it was. Plain suicide, no two ways about that.

Yet in a way Chinese Charlie felt that he owed Snakeskin Blake a vote of profound thanks.

If not for the Cain which the American had raised recently in the Sudan, the cabinet hawks would have never flocked to him as they had just done.

Looking out over London as the sun set, Gordon smoked his slim cigar and inhaled the fumes of the Napoleon brandy in the snifter whose stem he gingerly fingered, so as not to bring the heat of his hand up to the bulb of the glass. He drank in the scene as if it were the last time he would ever witness it. Then he did the same with the brandy.

Soon he would be back in the Sudan, facing an enraged Mahdi, but also being in the place he most loved on the entire face of planet earth. He might not live to see London again, but his end would be a glorious one, and the fools who had sent him to do their dirty work for them would lionize his name forever.

No man need ask for more than that, Gordon thought, as he stubbed the cheroot in a cut glass ashtray, set down the brandy glass upon the gleaming top of the carefully waxed Empire escritoire -- an heirloom from his mother -- and put on his checked woolen topcoat.

Nothing was finer than a stroll about London on an evening with good, clear skies overhead, and walking amidst its ancient Roman circles beneath the oddly flickering glare of the new electric lights was a pleasurable experience that sharpened his appetite for a good supper. And after that, perhaps another peek behind the door in the secret room in Whitehall beneath the statue of Clive at the steps leading up to King Charles Street.

And, of course, further pondering of the possibilities of that which occupied a portion of that room -- to which Gordon alone possessed the key -- one of Babbage's Difference Engines, a special model of the incredible calculating machine that he had commissioned upon returning from that pleasant house in Jaffa where he had completed a year of immersion in the study of some of the more interesting arcana of both the Bible and of the history of the Knights Templar. It was then that Gordon had first heard of the Phalanx, and had joined them in their quest, and had been introduced to Strawplait, tool of the Mahdi and cat's paw of the Héiron du Val d'Or.

Strawplait had failed, but the more capable Blake had not. The telegram from Blake had thrilled Gordon to the very quick -- Blake had telegraphed four words: Sword on its way. It was expected that same evening.

FIVE DEAD MEN

Before the Moroccan cheroot -- a blend that some claimed was laced with the resin they called kief – had burned out there was a knock at the door.

"Pardon, sir. A package has arrived."

Gordon thanked his servant and placed the long box atop his cherished Empire writing desk. If the sword were indeed inside, then the jewels inlaid on its hilt -- those lozenge-shaped gems taken by the Templars from the breastplate of the old priests of the Temple Mount -- might yield an intelligible pattern that could point the way toward the still unknown place in the Sudan where the Templars had hidden the Ark of the Covenant and perhaps even the Grail itself.

Babbage had assured him that this was possible, and Babbage, on instructions of the Phalanx, stood by at any moment's notice to come to the room beneath Clive's unmoving brass feet to set his diabolically clever creation to work to decipher the age-old secret.

The box felt heavy, as though the Sword of the Mahdi were indeed within. Gordon's hands trembled slightly as he unwrapped it, and as he raised its cover, the burnt end of the cheroot stung the corner of his mouth. Then, raising the cover, his eyes widened and he cursed softly in the silence of the room.

The box contained crudely fashioned ingots of iron. Nothing else.

Except for one thing.

A mottled gray feather.

Gordon made it out to be an ostrich feather. The same type, he recalled, with which the effeminate Mahdi loved to bedeck himself.

As Gordon closed the door to his study, a thought idly struck him. Snakeskin Blake. Chinese Charlie wondered what he was doing at just that particular moment.

A wry grin broke unbidden across Gordon's face as the answer came to him. Of course. Bloody Yank probably had one hand on some slattern's rump and a glass of dark pirate's rum in the other.

"Hmm. Not such a wretched idea for all that," thought Gordon, as he left his sanctum sanctorum, to which the adventurer would soon never return alive, closing the French doors against the bustle and hum of the street outside and becoming part of the London night himself. The night was indeed fine, and Gordon enjoyed the sublime flavor of yet another cheroot as he strolled along, finally reaching the foot of old Westminster Bridge.

As he mounted its north side, and leaned over the dull green balustrade to watch the clock atop Big Ben strike the hour, he finished his smoke and tossed the spent butt into the waters of the Thames below. He followed this with the key that had long nestled in his trouser pocket.

Also by David Alexander:

Snake Handlers
Habu Patch
Under Attack
Under Attack II: Kill Chain
Chain Reaction
Co-Co-Caleevio
Threatcon Delta: Assault on the Pentagon
Trainjack
War Pigs
Death Pulse
Brooklynese
The King of West Brooklyn
Bloodbath
Stealth Warfare (nonfiction)
Puzzle Palace (nonfiction)
Military-Industrial　　　　Complex　　　(nonfiction)

DAVID ALEXANDER

Bonus Preview Excerpt

Brooklynese

From the mean streets of New York City's prime Mafia boro, comes a chase after savvy and streetwise bank robbers and jewel thieves that crosses international boundaries and time zones with the speed of a jet plane. Alexander weaves everything together with the skill of a true master of the action thriller category in an unforgettable extravaganza of capers, mayhem, hot gems, hot dames, and accomplished criminals who will stop at nothing to gain possession of a treasure whose value is almost beyond calculation. When a billion dollar diamond deal cut by one of New York's heaviest crime families goes sour, and the consignment of rare gems is lost overseas, a crew of wise guys straight out of Brooklyn is ordered to get it back -- any way they can. This is an international caper novel to end all caper novels, a nonstop page-turner jam-packed with action from start to finish and one of Alexander's boldest books ever.

FIVE DEAD MEN

Brooklynese
Reviews

"Brooklynese is an accomplishment by an author whose narrative skills are clearly at their peak and can sustain an ambitious plot, like the daring young man on the trapeze who flies through the air with the greatest of ease." -- Desert Sun

"If every crook could pull off a caper with the ease and skill Alexander ably demonstrates in Brooklynese, we'd all be broke." -- Globe Literary Supplement

"From the mean streets of New York City's toughest borough, comes a chase after savvy and streetwise bank robbers and jewel thieves crossing international boundaries and time zones with the speed of a rocket plane. Alexander weaves everything together with the skill of a true master of the action thriller category in an unforgettable extravaganza of capers, mayhem, hot gems, hot dames, and accomplished criminals who will stop at nothing to gain possession of a treasure whose value is beyond calculation. As crime thrillers go, Brooklynese is the boss of bosses." -- Brookline Beacon

DAVID ALEXANDER

Brooklynese

An excerpt

A briny grey fog swirled across the collection of low-rise cinderblock warehouse buildings that made up the South Brooklyn Industrial Park. Out on the dark waters of the Buttermilk Channel, a tugboat honked a loud Bee-ohh!

Whitey MacDonald took a last drag on the foul-tasting plain-end Lucky and flicked it like a piece of snot across the rain-glazed tarmac where it hit and quickly sizzled out.

The Irishman climbed into the high cab of the truck parked outside the warehouse. The computer printout cargo manifest he'd just glanced through stated the truck carried a sealed and bonded load of consumer electronics items. Televisions, stereos, fax machines, home computers, CD players. The grinding of the truck's engine echoed through the rainswept night in the deserted lot of the industrial park as Whitey put the truck in gear and lumbered toward the lighted guard station directly ahead.

■

By midnight the rain had tapered off to a slow, easy drizzle, but a heavy pea soup fog had rolled in off the Hudson and blanketed the streets with a cottony mist, whose rotten-egg stink of sulfurous gases, courtesy of the Bayonne,

FIVE DEAD MEN

New Jersey sewage-treatment plant directly across the river, made it smell like a pay toilet in purgatory.

The side street in Sunset Park sloped down toward the gunmetal superstructure of the Gowanus Expressway extension overpass. The canal of the same name, known variously to local residents as "The Vile Nile," and "The Odor River" due to its own unforgettable fragrance, lay just beyond. The neighborhood took its name from Sunset Park, from which spectacular sunsets over the Hudson could be visible, but it might just as aptly refer to the fact that the sun had long since set over this urban wasteland from which Walt Whitman had once seen visions of "magnetic lands."

Squat red-brick industrial buildings, chiefly warehouses, flanked the deserted street on both sides. Spaced between them at odd intervals were vacant, weed-choked lots full of garbage that had somehow made it over the high chain-link fences, churches bearing huge neon-crosses and Spanish names, and two-story saltboxes with shingle siding rented by absentee landlords to a succession of Latino immigrants who rarely stayed longer than a few months.

With headlights doused, Wheats parked the car in front of a closed-down chicken slaughterhouse. The stench of enough chicken blood to fill the Gulf of Mexico from the barnyard fowl butchered since the shop first opened up in 1908 permeated the building and added its stench to the infernal-smelling fog as they waited for the truck to make its appearance. If chickens ever ruled the world, they would make this their Auschwitz. A fine film of blood had permanently stained the sidewalks brown.

Joey and Frankie-Boy checked their pieces. The Glock semiautomatics were cleaned and oiled and there was a round chambered just in case they were needed, although shooting never had been necessary before. The black nylon stocking masks, the same tactical face masks used by police SWAT teams, remained for the moment out of sight. They would come on just before the score went down. And come off again for the getaway.

The cops from the Seven-Eight who patrolled this stretch of Brooklyn South were like a classic Zen koan -- both a problem and not a problem. The boys in blue in this precinct did not get any more corrupt this side of the Bronx or Abu Dhabi. If they were not on the take, then they didn't last long. In the Seven-Eight an honest cop quickly became a dead cop.

Frankie-Boy had assured them that his father, and Joey's godfather, Don Antonio Casabianca, had seen to it that the right people had been paid off to do the right thing. But you never could be totally certain about the cops. In many ways New York's Finest were, de facto, the major crime cartel in the city. In some respects they put the Mafia to shame. They were great blue sharks that often swam past without giving a shit, but who could turn on you in a second and rip you to shreds in a mindless feeding frenzy if you didn't watch your shit.

Suddenly the Motorola handset squawked in the back seat.

"Melon to Prosciutto. You hear me, Prosciutto?"

"Yeah, yeah. I hear ya. I hear ya," Frankie-Boy said into the commo unit he'd pulled from the pocket of his brown leather jacket. "What ya got?"

"The truck's on its way. It just turned off Fourth Avenue to come down your street."

"Where are you?"

"We're right behind it."

"You see any security around?"

The freight dispatcher had checked and made sure that there would be no backup security tailing the truck, but plans could be changed at the last minute and you could never be absolutely sure anyway.

"We're the only other car in the area. And we cruised the streets a couple of minutes ago to make sure."

"You sure it's the right truck?"

"Hey, I can read a fuckin' license plate!"

The dispatcher had given them the plate numbers and truck number of the rig, but Frankie-Boy knew better than to count too much on the intelligence of the people who worked for him, especially freelance stick-up artists like Nicky and Paulie, two yo-yos from Baldwin, Long Island, a town where they grew yo-yos like other places grew squash.

"You know what you gotta do?" Frankie-Boy asked finally.

"Yeah, we know it. Don't worry. We're on the case."

Frankie-Boy squelched the radio and tapped Eddie Wheats on the shoulder. "Get ready, the truck's gonna be here any minute."

■

The telltale grinding of gears boomed and echoed through the dense, swirling fog. The spreading cones of two headlight beams shone on the rain-slicked street. The heavy truck lumbered around the corner from beneath the BQE overpass. One of the dispatchers at the freight transport company who had tipped them to the cargo load of high-tech consumer electronics knew his shit and knew that if he was wrong, he'd take his lumps. He didn't turn out to be wrong tonight.

"Go," Frankie-Boy said.

Wheats threw on the brights and stepped on the gas. The car bolted from the curb, tires spinning and screeching on the slippery tarmac. The truck's cab was bathed in an unearthly white light that seemed to freeze the raindrops in place, making them look like penny nails spilling from heaven as God built a better world someplace else. Joey could see the driver's big, white, meat-slab shanty Irish face contort in shock as he reflexively stomped the brake pedal.

As the truck came to a hard, screeching halt, Wheats fishtailed the Pontiac sideways. Frankie-Boy was already out the door; wired on coke he was faster than a speeding bullet. Two long strides brought him to the running board of the truck where he jammed the nine-millimeter automatic into the side of the driver's head through the cracked-open window.

"Stop the truck," the ice-cold doer in the black face mask said to the scared-shitless doee.

Whitey MacDonald threw the rig in park and killed the ignition. Frankie-Boy waved to Joey who bounded out of the car, his face now also masked. Joey's role was critical. The trucks were heavily alarmed. To foil hijacking attempts, the freight companies were engaged in an ongoing effort to improve security using a variety of high-tech gizmos and gadgets that would make James Bond throw up his hands in despair. It was a Cold War in the streets, with a fortune in hot merchandise at stake.

Joey jumped on the rig's opposite running board. He took a Maglite from his pocket and shone its sixteen thousand candle power beam inside the truck's cab. Beneath the dashboard he glimpsed a corner of a small computer keyboard.

"Here's how it works, okay," he said to the frightened driver. "You tell me the truth, nothing happens. You bullshit me, we fuck you up. You got that?"

"Yeah, I got it," Whitey replied.

"'Kay," Joey went on. "I want you to punch in the passcode that opens the doors without tripping any alarms.

Then you get out and you give it to me so I can check it out myself."

Whitey glanced at the masked gunman and had no second thoughts about cooperating. He reached under the dash and keyed in a seven-digit access code. The locks popped and the door buttons jumped like obedient elves. Frankie-Boy pulled open the door and yanked Whitey out of the cab, nodding at Nicky and Paulie in the second car behind the truck.

Joey quickly climbed into the driver's seat and slid down under the dash, playing the high-intensity Maglite beam across every concealed nook and cranny. He snapped off the torch and nodded to Frankie-Boy who held the muzzle of the gun pressed to the driver's head.

"What's the code?" asked Joey.

"Four-two-five-oh-oh-four-four."

Joey keyed the seven digits. The locks popped. He tried the ignition. The engine started right up. There were no audible sirens, no alarms. The driver had been too scared to lie. Joey flashed Frankie-Boy the thumb's-up then slid over into the passenger seat. Frankie-Boy handed MacDonald over to Nicky and Paulie, holstered his piece and slid behind the wheel.

The truck groaned as Frankie-Boy shifted gears and pulled down the deserted, fogswept street. Eddie damped the brights on the Pontiac and followed in the first rental. As Joey and Frankie-Boy pulled off their face masks, Whitey found himself staring at the freshly vacuumed carpet between the front and rear seats of the second car.

"You stay like that till we tell you it's okay," Nicky said as he leaned over the front seat and got out a Camel. "You fuckin' move and I'll make you fart your brains out your asshole."

DAVID ALEXANDER

■

Ten minutes later, the truck trundled up the darkened ramp of a warehouse a couple of blocks away, just off Fourth Avenue. A crew of unloaders was waiting to take off the hot cargo load.

Frankie-Boy brought the truck to a stop and the drone of the hydraulics shutting the two-inch thick, three-ton steel entrance door echoed through the interior that stank of gasoline, moldering tires and rusting sheet metal. Joey hopped out and lit a cigaret as he pulled a VHS cassette-sized Hewlett-Packard palmtop computer from his pocket.

The first part of the score was the easy part. Getting the access code. The second part was the hard part. Defeating the silent satellite-uplinked alarm that would instantly flash the truck's location on a grid position map of the city to a private security firm based in the World Trade Center in Manhattan if the doors were incorrectly opened. The code that opened the doors was known only to the supervisor at the warehouse to which the goods were being shipped. The driver didn't have it.

Joey slid under the truck and found the controller box he was searching for. Using a ratchet driver with a torx bit, he unscrewed four Allen lugs and removed the galvanized steel plate that protected the box. You'd think they would alarm the controllers but they never did. In an unpredictable world the security companies' Achilles Heel was that they were always predictable.

A printed circuit board containing a group of microprocessor chips was inside the metal receptacle. Lying on his back beneath the undercarriage of the truck, with the HP palmtop sitting on his stomach, Joey attached a custom-made cable to the computer's serial port. On the other end of the cable, where a standard twenty-five pin connector would normally be found, Joey had crimped on six color-coded mini-alligator clips.

Joey carefully attached four of the mini-alligator clips to the exposed pins of the large IC on the board, which bore the ID number 4803W on its surface. The IC was a 4803-series microprocessor chip, one of two types manufactured by either Westinghouse or Hitachi -- in this case the W suffix identified it as Westinghouse silicon -- but in both cases virtually identical. These chips were EPROMs -- erasable programmable read-only memory chips -- whose pins three, nine and fourteen on one side and five, eight and eleven on the other, were linked to memory registers containing alarm instruction sets. Once Joey accessed these, he could reprogram the EPROM so that the alarm would be neutralized and the truck doors would open.

Numbers flashed on the palmtop's backlit screen as Joey tapped out commands on the small keyboard.

The software loaded into the HP's three megabyte RAM memory interrogated the IC chip and would quickly extract the instruction sets. The HP was lousy for showing baby pictures but the old contender was perfect for this type of job. Joey had paid a hacker he'd found on the Internet to disassemble and rewrite a commercial data acquisition program from its source code. Nobody knew each other, nothing was traceable. Joey sent cash to a mail drop and downloaded the hacked program from a bulletin board mailbox.

Originally intended to monitor the performance of industrial machinery, the revamped software was now deactivating the alarm and locking mechanism. In under three minutes the palmtop emitted a low electronic warble as the DEFEAT SUCCESSFUL message flashed onscreen.

Joey detached the cable, slid the palmtop back into his inner jacket pocket and crawled out from beneath the truck.

Nodding at Frankie-Boy, Joey walked around to the back and pulled open the truck's rear doors which were now unlocked. Like a well-oiled machine, the unloading crew -- four guys splitting four of the five thousand dollar payoff between them -- got immediately to work.

Unloading the truck completely would take most of the next hour, after which the crew would drive it a couple of blocks and abandon it under the Gowanus Expressway overpass, or some other convenient spot, such as the swamps around Marine Park near Plum Beach. If ever questioned, the night foreman of the warehouse, who was in on the score and got the last grand of the five thou, would say that he had no idea that any wrongdoing took place on his watch, well aware that nobody could ever prove otherwise.

Joey and Frankie-Boy walked out through a steel door set in the red brick wall next to the big corrugated metal partition covering the access ramp through which they had initially driven the truck. Eddie Wheats was sitting behind the wheel of the rental, whose motor was turned off. Joey and Frankie-Boy climbed into the car, which Wheats soon rolled into the rainy night, still thinking about eagles over the Marine Park Bridge.

■

Frankie-Boy took Whitey's commercial driver's license. "Just walk back to the warehouse and report a hijacking," he told him, stuffing a hundred dollar bill into his wallet and handing it back. "Tomorrow you report the license missing to the DMV."

"I'm gonna need proof," MacDonald said, his eyes wide.

Frankie-Boy nodded. He balled his fist and hit the driver square in the face. Blood spurted from his busted nose.

411

FIVE DEAD MEN

"There's your proof," he told him. "And don't forget we know were you live. You fuck with us, we kill you and your family. Your wife is dead. Your kids are dead. Your dog is dead. And you're dead too."

"The cops are gonna ask me questions."

"Just make sure you give 'em the wrong answers," Frankie-Boy advised, then turned and walked away.

Whitey MacDonald stood shivering in the rain with blood pouring from his shattered nose and running down the front of his jacket and watched the two cars drive down the street, turn the corner, and vanish into the night.

DAVID ALEXANDER

Bonus Preview Excerpt
Trainjack

One

Van Keel had wasted his time in Paris, as he'd wasted it in London in April and in Barcelona through the summer months, and Pamplona's bull running of that August had seemed an empty farce, a rite of some lost spring of youth that had once made him feel alive, but whose meaning was now as indecipherable as hieroglyphics on the wall of a Pharaoh's tomb.

It hadn't helped that he'd taken along a woman he'd met on the Internet, although the verb wasn't entirely appropriate. He hadn't actually met anyone. Keel and Lisa had struck up a cold-blooded and pragmatic arrangement based on mutual needs for money, companionship and sex through a travel dating site. It had turned her on to know that she'd be making the trip in the company of a man who habitually carried a loaded, if holstered, Glock semiautomatic. The novelty of it was what stimulated Keel. That and several of the photographs that Lisa had emailed him, each showing her in an increasingly more interesting array of poses and costumes.

The relationship, for what it was, had had its moments. The first night in London had been spent in blowing to smithereens the forced, businesslike air that had prevailed on the cross-Atlantic plane trip. Softened up like a hard military target by proximity close enough to feel each others' body heat and liberal helpings of airline alcohol, their walls of propriety and sobriety were more ready to crumble than fabled Jericho's as they negotiated the rubbery floor of the Heathrow jetway.

In the spacious back seat of a black London taxi, the final battlements of besieged decorum had all come tumbling down, and the cabby had discreetly turned up the volume on the radio to mute the barnyard sounds from the passenger compartment when Keel's hand, clutching a fifty euro note, came through the Plexiglas divider.

The Roman Bacchanal for two continued, warming the cold London spring for most of the remaining two weeks in the city, but for Keel, at least, it had began to flicker and die well before he and Lisa had boarded a southbound express to Spain.

In Barcelona, Keel had come to accept that they were now merely going through the motions, performing physical acts from which the tart sap of pleasure had been crushed out in the wine-press of reality. He had left her in Pamplona, by mutual consent. One by one, the grapes of passion had been plucked from their stems, and those still left had shriveled with the noble rot of bedroom fatigue.

And now it was already deep September, and the cold north winds blowing along the Rue Mouffetard in the Latin Quarter had warned Van Keel that the cold European autumn was coming fast, and that he had no plans -- other than to ride out the deepening depression that had seized hold of him since the first boisterous, drunken week in Spain, when the alcohol and the excitement of a hypodermic needle of false freedom had filled his veins with zombie life.

Why exactly he'd returned to Paris, Keel didn't know. When you first came to her she was as demure as a princess, but then, suddenly, she'd lift up her skirts and pass foul wind in your face. That was Paris. But Keel understood that to see Paris beneath her upraised skirts, pimpled ass and all, was to know her truly.

Keel understood Paris. If returning to her was like returning to a sailors' brothel, then so be it. At least Paris, unlike other places, was home to Keel, at least of a sort. There had been the call from O'Goldberg in New York too, but Keel could have dodged it, he could have made an excuse and avoided it. The fact that he'd accepted had told Keel that he'd accepted the inevitable. He'd decided to go to ground in Paris.

As he dodged morning rush hour traffic roaring out of the Place de la Concorde roundabout at a fast jog, and then took the steps leading toward the Seine embankment at a lope, Keel reflected on the evening's presentation. As the N.Y.P.D. liaison to Interpol, Keel was, as O'Goldberg had put it months ago in Brooklyn, "the embodiment of everything New York's Finest stand for."

O'Goldberg's remark had elicited more than one snicker and comment out of the corner of the mouths of the other department members at the brief ceremony in which Keel was presented with his tokens of ambassadorship, including letters of recommendation from the mayor and police commissioner, and tokens of friendship between the N.Y.P.D. and its brethren across the bounding main, which included ceremonial shields, commemorative plaques and other regalia. It was all a sham, and everyone, including Keel himself, well knew it.

After the speechifying and hoopla had died away, the truth was that Keel was being shipped off into limbo to save a lot of people in the present city administration a lot of tzuris, and, last but not least, to save the life of Inspector Van Keel. What Keel had done in the line of duty should normally have gotten him either killed or, if in the absence of death's absence, kicked off the force. Keel had been lucky. He'd done the killing, not his intended murderers. Yet in that transformative moment, his life had been altered irrevocably, and in a way he had died just as surely as if the bullets and shrapnel intended to rip his body to pieces had done their bloody work.

All in all, Keel was glad of having gotten O'Goldberg's call a few days before. While Keel's putative role as NYPD liaison to Interpol was largely a sham, his appointment as guest lecturer at the international conference on organized crime sponsored by Interpol in Paris that fall was one that he was more than competent to handle. The subject of Keel's presentation was to be the hidden connections between crime and terrorism, a nexus he called the Medusa.

Like the mythical chimera it was named after, the Medusa was a head from which sprouted a plethora of venomous snakes. Each of those tendrils was a criminal or terrorist organization. Overtly separate at their heads, they were linked at their hidden roots deep within the nourishing violence inside the Medusa's head.

Keel saw the Medusa as representing more than any criminal undertaking in history. It was a new threat. A powerful new convergence of crime, terrorism and rogue governments that might in time destroy the last vestiges of two thousand years of civilization and replace it with unimaginable chaos.

In preparing his series of lectures to Interpol, Keel had plumbed his reserves of knowledge. His first lecture had gripped the attention of the usually complacent cops hailing from Tokyo to Canberra that ranged the large auditorium in the Palais de Justice, the palatial former palace on the right back of the Seine in the Île de la Cité now housing the Paris high courts and various French government offices.

It had also made Keel a new friend. Paris Police judiciare Special Investigator Fabian Mechanique had been impressed. Mechanique had invited Keel to discuss his thesis at a good restaurant in the vicinity.

He had been impressed, as a Frenchmen and fan of old American and French movies, when Keel -- a few vodka martinis under his belt, and tickled by a sudden whimsy -- had rocked back the cover of the Steinway grand piano in the lounge and proceeded -- drink on a coaster in front of him -- to launch into a rendition of Gershwin's "Rhapsody in Blue" which, commended by unexpected applause, soon became Jelly Roll Morton's "I Can't He'p It."

The American cop had then segued into a totally impromptu medley of jazz, classical and show tunes fired by multiple, on the house, refills of his drink and the fulsome applause of his now hopelessly enthralled listeners.

Mechanique had invited him to his Thirteenth Arrondissement apartment for late brandies and cigars. The French cop's flat was one of those immense, pre-war Parisian juggernauts that ran around the top floor of a seventeenth century building on three sides, an apartment that would have dwarfed the most posh suites in Manhattan's Dakota. It commanded an incredible view of the Eiffel Tower, which, lit up at night by multicolored spotlights, with a cluster of brilliant white lights ringing its tip, was in darkness probably the most unabashedly phallic structure on the face of the earth.

Keel had liked Mechanique from the first. It was that way with him; some he loathed at first glance, and others not. Mechanique had been one of the latter. The Frenchman was honest, and told him his story. They found that they shared a great deal in common. It was close to three in the morning when Keel had cabbed to his own hotel in the Eleventh Arrondissement with the strong beginnings of a hangover, but Keel had parted from a man who would always be more than a friend. Mechanique was a brother. A brother cop and a kindred spirit.

The morning run along the Seine embankment would help, as it always did, and Keel, a creature of habit, would never let the sun rise without being out and running. The precious few hours of near-sleep had helped, like the Motrins he'd gulped, and as he ran along the Left Bank of the Seine, watching a Batobus race past bearing a crowd of passengers beneath the steel span of the Liberty Bridge, the brain chemicals released by the vigorous aerobic exercise were bringing the added relief of a runner's high.

The slanted scar on the side of Keel's face, a souvenir of a knife a rapist had pulled on a long-ago night patrol through the streets of Brooklyn's Brownsville district, began to throb, a sign of the blood now coursing through his veins.

Keel's brain began to float as his lungs, heart and muscles labored to propel his body forward across the hard cobblestones that paved the bank of the river, and he began to mentally plan the night's lecture. It would -- as the synopsis he'd presented to the Interpol steering committee had indicated -- concern the threat to the world order posed by maverick criminal-terrorist hybrids using high-technology weapons and global communications to either destroy high-priority targets or seize and hold them for payment of super-ransoms.

The last thing on earth that Van Keel suspected, as he ran beneath the single Seine bridge of steel construction -- the

Liberty Bridge, commemorating the liberation of the city by American tankers in World War Two -- was that at almost that precise moment a ship had departed the Istrian coast at Pula, Yugoslavia.

It was a ship bearing death that was to be the manifestation of everything that Van Keel would warn of later that night in his symposium address, and before the week was out, would catch him up in its dangerous whirlwind's gyre.

Milton Keynes UK
Ingram Content Group UK Ltd.
UKHW022026301123
433552UK00015B/758